The Waiting [Room]

F. G. Cottam is also the author of *The House of Lost Souls*, *Dark Echo* and *The Magdalena Curse*.

'Beautifully written and highly engaging.' *Daily Mirror*

'F. G. Cottam has crafted a superb and tautly told tale of manifest evil. A perfect ghost story for this or any other season.' *The Times*

'A well-paced horror thriller.' *Canberra Times*

'F. G. Cottam's complex, tautly atmospheric thriller delivers plenty of chills.' *Daily Mail*

'A terrifying encounter with manifest evil . . . His adrenaline-charged prose is drawn tight with suspense.' *Financial Times*

'A riveting supernatural thriller. Rich in atmosphere, the book builds to a shattering finale.' *Publishers Weekly*

'Old-fashioned suspense combined with modern horror imagery to produce a fine example of the genre.' *The Times*

'Thrilling, addictive, dangerous, hypnotic and deadly . . . The book is a cross-genre treat. Beautifully written, with frighteningly invasive descriptions, literate, complex, conspiratorial and threatening . . . pervasively believable.' *The Times*, Johannesburg

Also by F. G. Cottam

The House of Lost Souls
Dark Echo
The Magdalena Curse

About the author

F. G. Cottam lives in Kingston-upon-Thames.
After a career in men's magazines, he is now a
full-time novelist. He has two children.

*F. G. Cottam*

# The Waiting Room

**HODDER**

First published in Great Britain in 2010 by Hodder & Stoughton
An Hachette UK company

First published in paperback in 2011

1

Copyright © F. G. Cottam 2010

A CIP catalogue record for this title is available from the British Library

ISBN 978 1 444 70423 5

Typeset in Sabon by Palimpsest Book Production Ltd,
Falkirk, Stirlingshire

Printed and bound in the UK by
CPI Mackays, Chatham ME5 8TD

Hodder & Stoughton policy is to use papers that are natural,
renewable and recyclable products and made from wood grown
in sustainable forests. The logging and manufacturing processes
are expected to conform to the environmental regulations of the
country of origin.

Hodder & Stoughton Ltd
338 Euston Road
London NW1 3BH

www.hodder.co.uk

For Avalon May, for your gift of joy, with love always.

I would like to thank Caroline Michel and Tim Binding for their belief and their encouragement, without which I can honestly say this novel would not have been written. Their support has been inspirational and I am deeply grateful for it.

# *Strange Meeting*

It seemed that out of battle I escaped
Down some profound dull tunnel, long since scooped
Through granites which titanic wars had groined.
Yet also there encumbered sleepers groaned,
Too fast in thought or death to be bestirred.
Then, as I probed them, one sprang up, and stared
With piteous recognition in fixed eyes,
Lifting distressful hands, as if to bless.
And by his smile, I knew that sullen hall
By his dead smile I knew we stood in Hell.
With a thousand pains that vision's face was grained;
Yet no blood reached there from the upper ground,
And no guns thumped, or down the flues made moan.
'Strange friend,' I said, 'here is no cause to mourn.'
'None,' said that other, 'save the undone years,
The hopelessness. Whatever hope is yours,
Was my life also; I went hunting wild
After the wildest beauty in the world,
Which lies not calm in eyes, or braided hair,
But mocks the steady running of the hour,
And if it grieves, grieves richlier than here.
For by my glee might many men have laughed,
And of my weeping something had been left,
Which must die now. I mean the truth untold,
The pity of war, the pity war distilled.
Now men will go content with what we spoiled,
Or, discontent, boil bloody, and be spilled.
They will be swift with the swiftness of the tigress.

None will break ranks, though nations trek from progress.
Courage was mine, and I had mystery,
Wisdom was mine, and I had mastery:
To miss the march of this retreating world
Into vain citadels that are not walled.
Then, when much blood had clogged their chariot-wheels,
I would go up and wash them from sweet wells,
Even with truths that lie too deep for taint.
I would have poured my spirit without stint
But not through wounds; not on the cess of war.
Foreheads of men have bled where no wounds were.
I am the enemy you killed, my friend.
I knew you in this dark; for so you frowned
Yesterday through me as you jabbed and killed.
I parried; but my hands were loath and cold.
Let us sleep now . . .'

Wilfred Owen, 1918

# Chapter One

Through the wide two-way mirror on the wall of his office, Julian Creed observed his visitor and tried to imagine the impression being imposed by the artefacts surrounding him. The man sat patiently in one of the low-slung leather chairs facing Creed's hardwood desk. He was dressed in a sober suit and wore a tie. Against the wall to his left, there was a cabinet housing the trophies garnered by a successful media career and he glanced at this with narrowed eyes. Above it, there was a shelf of Creed's bestselling books and his eyes rose to read the titles on their spines. To the right of where he sat, pride of place on the far wall was occupied by an old news picture Creed had had blown up and enhanced to increase the contrast and detail it showed. He grunted with satisfaction now as his visitor got to his feet to examine closely this framed image. It had been taken almost thirty years earlier on a choppy sea in the South Atlantic by a foolhardy Fleet Street veteran of conflict, leaning out of a helicopter and using a telephoto lens. It showed the upturned faces of three young soldiers clad in combat fatigues and webbing and smeared with camouflage cream. They were each carrying a semi-automatic assault rifle and were aboard a rigid inflatable boat.

The picture had been taken during the Falklands War and Creed had been nineteen years old and had passed SAS selection only a tender fortnight earlier. Behind the mirror, he sipped at potent coffee in the paper cup he held. His features looked no different now, he thought, from how they had then. The skin was still taut over strong facial bones. He had allowed himself to gain no weight. Regular exercise had kept the muscles toned. A few grey hairs were the only real difference. He had come through a dozen subsequent conflicts unscathed before leaving the service. And then the real adventure had begun, in his civilian life.

He considered that his visitor would by now be sufficiently intimidated and impressed. Creed had observed his hauteur on a security screen as he stood waiting in the building's foyer on arrival. He had emerged, tall and oddly familiar and impeccable, from the rear seat of a white Bentley when the big car braked smoothly at the kerb. He would be humbler, fifteen patient minutes on. It was time to enter the room and meet the man and discover what someone so wealthy and private could possibly want with the nation's most celebrated ghost hunter. Creed tossed his empty cup into a bin in the corridor and strolled towards his office.

The man turned from the picture. It occurred to Creed that he too had aged well. This was not common in his profession. Drugs were not kind to the metabolism. Usually, they grew bloated and dishevelled and their flamboyant clothes sadly anachronistic, though there were austere exceptions to this general rule.

'Martin Stride.'

He held out a hand and Creed shook it. 'I know. I bought the first and second albums. I've got all the stuff that charted on my iPod.' He grinned. 'I'm standing in front of a legend.'

Stride gestured back towards the picture on the wall. 'That war seems so long ago. At least, it does to me.'

'It's ancient history,' Creed said, 'and it was fittingly barbaric. The parachute regiment fought with their bayonets fixed. And they used them, too.' He gestured for Stride to sit. He sat in the opposing armchair. He did not want the imposition of his desk between them. He thought it interesting but not surprising that Stride had deflected mention of his own hugely successful career.

There was a moment's silence between them. Creed had

granted the appointment without his PA having discovered whatever the matter was that Stride had come here to discuss. He had been unwilling to explain it over the phone. He had simply said that it was both important and urgent. Creed had cancelled a scheduled meeting to see him today. It was up to him to open the conversation proper, to reveal whatever it was that was troubling him. But he seemed to be struggling both to overcome a natural reserve and to find language appropriate to what he wanted to say.

'I am a huge fan of your series.'

'Thanks.'

'It's required viewing in our household.'

'I'm flattered.'

'It must be quite something, to possess a psychic gift.'

Creed hoped the small smile he indulged at this compliment a sufficiently modest expression. 'It can be a curse as well as a blessing, Mr Stride.'

'Martin, please.'

'And please call me Julian. Why have you come to see me today?'

Stride got out of his chair. He went across and looked at the Falklands photograph again. In his own chair, Creed shivered. But this was nothing to do with his psychic gift. The photograph was black and white. It had been a cold and monochromatic war. That said, the dead had worn their fatal wounds in colours vivid enough.

Stride spoke, still facing the picture. 'I'm not delusional,' he said. 'Back in the day, we once headlined in front of three-quarters of a million people in Rio de Janeiro. We sold out the Hollywood Bowl for ten consecutive nights. For a couple of years it was as though we owned the world. It's a strange existence, Julian. It can mark and ruin you. But I never really bought into it on a personal level. No groupies. No entourage. And I never got into the narcotic side, beyond a bit of dabbling very early on.'

3

Stride paused. Creed remained silent. He judged silence the best means of coaxing his visitor out of his reticence.

'I have a young family now. My son is eleven and my daughter just eight. I am very happily married. We live on the Kent–Sussex border. Because I value my privacy, I've purchased any land I've been able to around the house I bought a decade ago. It now stands at more or less the centre of a fairly substantial estate.'

Creed considered. He thought that 'fairly' in Stride-speak probably meant 'very'. 'I take it this is an old house?'

Stride turned from the photograph and nodded. 'Parts of it are very old. It was originally built in Norman times as a manor house. There's a chapel that might be even older. It looks Saxon to me. But the house is not the source of my concern, Julian.'

Creed got up. He went to his desk and pressed a button on his phone. 'Let me organise some tea or coffee and then let's sit down properly and talk. Try to relax a little. You came here because you are troubled. I am sure that I can help. Merely talking about it will help.'

'I'll just have water, thank you.'

'Still or sparkling?'

'Still,' Stride said. He smiled, but without humour this time. 'There's enough sparkle in the tale I have to tell.'

He did not know much about the abandoned railway line. The piece of his estate across which it had run was land he had owned for about ten years. The rails themselves had long been torn up for scrap. The sleepers had been dug out of the earth and taken away. The gravel bedding under them had been overgrown and obliterated by thorns and weeds and wild grass. All that remained amid this verdant eruption was a crumbling island platform and on that, a derelict waiting room.

The waiting room was Edwardian. With its roof of russet tiles and mock Gothic arched windows, it looked incongruous, there in the wilderness of bushes and trees where it now found itself. But its explanation was mundane enough. The line had been closed in the early 1960s as part of the infamous Beeching cuts, when the motorways had started to be built and the car and lorry had started to supersede the railways as the nation's staple means of transportation of people and of freight. Beeching had seen the future. And the future ran on rubber tyres on ribbons of straight road and was fuelled by petrol engines.

The waiting room was not a listed building. Stride could have had it demolished. But he had not seen the point of that. He had no urgent need to domesticate his land, to press it into profitable service. Its purpose was seclusion. It was there to put him at a remote distance from people he did not know and had no wish to meet. He did not need to farm. He had earned his livelihood and fortune in the days of his celebrity and commercial success. The royalties still rolled generously in. The waiting room did not obstruct ambitions for the ground on which it stood. And when he had it surveyed, the structure itself was sound. It posed no hazard to his children should they choose in the course of their roaming adventures to play in it. Its walls and roof were not just intact, but sturdy. It was a charming oddity. And his children naturally liked it, inventing a purpose and history for it, as children are apt to do. It was sited half a mile from the house, a distance that made it properly exotic in their young minds.

The waiting room lay to the east of the house, to its rear. One evening about a fortnight prior to seeking his meeting with Creed, Stride had been gathering windfalls in the orchard, which was situated a few hundred yards on from the kitchen garden. The orchard was small and ancient and the apples of a unique variety. They were good to the taste, but tart enough for baking too. They ripened in early September. A brisk easterly breeze was persuading them from the trees and Stride had gathered half a large basket full. It was dusk.

And he felt the easy contentment of being engaged in a pleasant task. There was the sound of ripe fruit falling to the earth in dull staccato thumps. There was the rustle of the branches and the whisper of the breeze and the harsh cry of a rook. And borne on the wind, there was suddenly the faint, insinuating rumble of a long train pulled by a steam locomotive.

'It was a sound I recognised from films I've seen,' Stride told Julian Creed. 'I may have heard it in life as an infant child and carried the audible memory. But I knew unmistakeably what it was I was hearing, just as I knew it was impossible.'

Full darkness was approaching. The sound began to fade. It was not as though the train was receding in distance, though, so much as fading altogether, as though being forgotten, falling away through time. That was fanciful thinking, of course. Stride had generally confined the fanciful inclination of his mind to the creation of melodies and song lyrics. Walking across the ground towards the source of the sound, over ever wilder terrain beyond the old fence that bordered his orchard, he wondered if stalled creativity wasn't the cause now of this aural hallucination.

The sound had faded completely. There was not silence, because there was never silence in the country early on an autumn night. But so familiar were the sounds on his domain to Stride's ears that they might have well as been silence. The strangeness had gone. It had left no trace. He stopped. He had almost tripped on the sinuous root of something breaking the surface in the gloom. By starlight, he was close enough to see the black bulk of the waiting room on its island platform, still and silent and serving its forgotten line. He began to debate with himself the point of continuing on. He was more intrigued, truly, than afraid. But the ground under his feet was hostile in the gathering night. So he paused and considered and stared at the motionless shape, blacker than the darkness, ahead of him. And the breeze soughed, easterly, into his face. And he sniffed boiler coal and steam and engine oil burdening the air. This spectral cocktail of odours provoked a shudder in him. Then the air was clean again. He turned back towards his orchard and home, fighting the instinct simply to flee.

He groped amid the orchard trees for his basket of windfalls only because Monica would ask after them, intent on baking pies for their son's school fête. His instinct was to hurry home and lock the door securely behind him and shut the windows and build the fires and turn on every light. He considered himself a restrained man generally and did most things not before a degree of calculation. What imagination he possessed had been profitably channelled into his music. He was given neither to daydreams nor nightmares. He thought that he was probably too happy and secure for either affliction. But regaining his home, he was sure he had just endured the sounds and scents of something otherworldly. He hefted the apple basket at his kitchen door and mouthed a silent prayer to a God he didn't believe in that there would be no repetition. If there was, he would be obliged to tell his wife.

Two weeks passed before anything else that could be described as strange occurred in the Stride domain. When it did, it happened in the music room. Autumn was coming reluctantly to the south-east of England. Most days it was still as warm as it had been in the middle of August. It was a Sunday. Eight-year-old Millie Stride had enjoyed a picnic lunch with three of her schoolfriends at a grassy spot by the stream that ran through the estate in the shade of a weeping willow a few hundred metres from the house. Her friends had been ferried aboard their Range Rover back to their various homes by Monica at around five in the afternoon. And Millie had watched a bit of television and then gone to the music room to practise piano.

She had inherited her father's talent for music. And as is

so often the case, she had inherited it in a much more concentrated form than he had ever enjoyed. She was gifted both at performing and composing. He did not know how far she would progress with either. Neither he nor Monica was the sort of parent who would push their child, or worse, put her on show. She would go with it only as far as she wished to. But at the age of eight, she was enjoying piano very much and Stride liked to watch her play, thrilled by her accomplishment, gratified by the obvious pleasure it brought her.

The music room was very grand. It was part of the early eighteenth-century, rococo additions to the house and was large with four narrow, rectangular windows that reached from low sills almost to the high and ornately plastered ceiling. The floor was of polished oak boards and the acoustics of the space superb, if unforgiving. Stride recognised the tune even before opening the door. His daughter was playing a sentimental favourite from the trenches of the First World War. She was playing 'Roses of Picardy'. He knew that a British Army officer had penned the song in 1916. He knew that the great Irish tenor John McCormack had recorded it after the armistice. He did not know where on earth his daughter could have come across it. She read music. But they did not have this score, he knew, in the house. He did not think it was something she could have become familiar with on the radio. And she was surely too young to be studying such an awful period of history at her tender age at school.

The windows of the music room faced east. It was late September now and seven o'clock, and night was encroaching on the day. Millie had switched on no lights. When he entered the room, he saw that she was playing in near darkness. The sun was setting on the other side of the house. He went to the window. Beyond the dark shadow of the house, the dusk flushed the land he owned in a gentle amber hue. Notes decayed and he heard his daughter gently close the piano lid. It was a Steinway Grand. It had cost him the better part of a hundred thousand pounds. Usually, he got a *frisson* of pride and amusement at seeing Millie's little figure manipulating such an imposing instrument so ably. Not tonight. She stood beside him. He smoothed her hair with an absent gesture of affection. He was not a demonstrative man, but he loved his children very deeply.

'Where did you learn that tune, Millie?'

'I haven't learnt it,' she said. 'I was playing it by ear. I heard it this afternoon, at our picnic. It was sort of drifting, Daddy. It was drifting on the breeze.'

'On what was it played?'

She shook her head. 'It wasn't. It was just men singing,' she said.

'From which direction was it drifting?' he asked her. But he knew the answer to the question.

'From over there,' she said, pointing eastward, towards where the dipping sun deepened the land to umber and beyond the colour of blood and the waiting room on the abandoned railway line prepared for the coming of night.

'You played it beautifully, Millie. You should go and get some supper now.'

After she had left the room, he stared out of the window. His breath smeared a patch of one of the panes in a cloudy oval of condensation as the glass cooled with the onset of evening. He thought of the ghosts of soldiers crammed into wagons built for cattle on their way to fight a war. Infantrymen, cannon fodder for the Western Front. But why was this happening? Why here? Why now? He stood there staring outward for a long time. But no answers came to him.

The third and most recent incident involved Martin Stride's son, Peter. He had been mountain biking around the estate with two friends from school. They had strict instructions to return to the house before dark. Stride thought mountain biking about as wholesome an activity in which a healthy eleven-year-old could indulge. But in darkness over rough terrain it wasn't only no fun to do, it was genuinely dangerous. When the boys had not returned by dusk, he was irritated, but not really alarmed. They had mobile phones with them. Nothing catastrophic had occurred. But fifteen minutes later, when the light had pretty much gone, he started to feel concerned. He phoned his son.

'Sorry, Dad,' Peter said. 'Joe punctured his front tyre.'

'Where?'

'Doing a jump off the island platform.'

Stride swallowed. 'You're there now? You're in the dark, near the waiting room?'

'No,' Peter said. 'We're two minutes from the house, wheeling the bikes.' He sounded different, subdued. He was normally a buoyant sort of character. 'I'm sorry, Dad.'

'No need to be, son. See you in a bit.' This time it was Stride's turn to ferry the visitors back to their homes in the neighbouring village. Neither seemed any the worse for the puncture incident. They had successfully repaired it with the stuff from an emergency kit and seemed pretty proud of the fact. The bikes were in the back of the Range Rover and on the journey, in the pauses in the boys' conversation, he listened for the tell-tale hiss from the patched tube of escaping air. But he did not hear it.

Monica was waiting for him at the door when he returned. She had her hair tied back, which always gave an alert look to her lovely, high-boned features. But Stride saw something more than alertness in her expression tonight.

'What's wrong?'

'Peter's wrong. Something has happened, Martin. He's acting guiltily, like he's done something he shouldn't have. Will you go and have a word with him?'

It was the way of their family. They believed in their hearts they loved their children equally. But when Peter needed to confide, he did so in his father, just as Millie did in her mother. There was no jealousy over this. It seemed natural. It seemed to work to everyone's advantage. It might have caused problems were Martin Stride still obliged to tour an album every eighteen months and spend prolonged periods away. But his touring days were thankfully behind him. He had deliberately waited for retirement from the industry before taking on the responsibility of parenthood.

He found Peter in the games room, desultory over the snooker table. 'What's up, son?'

'Nothing's up.' Peter clicked balls, bouncing them by hand off the shoulder of the table. He averted his gaze, would not look directly at his dad. He was a very good-looking boy. He had inherited his mother's wavy, corn-coloured hair and pale blue eyes. The eyes were transparent. He was adept at most things, but much to his father's secret amusement, had proven to be a terrible liar. Martin Stride was not amused now, though. He was concerned.

'Something near the waiting room frightened you, didn't it?'

And Peter did look at him. 'It was not near the waiting room, Dad. It was inside. I saw it.'

'But Joe and Ethan didn't, did they?'

'They were busy with the burst tube. It doesn't take three people to mend a puncture. They didn't see it and I didn't point it out. It was there and gone. But I saw it, all right.'

Stride walked to Peter's side of the baize and put his arms around his son. He held him and Peter returned the embrace.

'Do you think you could bear to describe what you saw?'

Peter sniffed. He was close to tears, a tremor his father could feel running through his slender physique. 'I'll draw it,' he said. 'I'll sketch the thing I saw.'

As Millie could play, so Peter could draw and paint, his draughtsmanship ill named, since it was his mother's gift. It was how Stride had met Monica. Just out of art school, she had designed the cover for what became his band's most successful album. 'I'll fetch my pad and pencils and do it in here, Dad. I don't want Millie or Mum to see it. I don't want to frighten them.'

'Aren't you worried about frightening me?'

Peter looked at him and the look was very frank. 'You already know there's something wrong with the waiting room. You wouldn't have asked me the question you did, otherwise.'

Peter went and presently returned and started to sketch. Stride practised with his hand-built, monogrammed cue at the table. He was good at snooker and the table was true. And tonight he could not pot a ball. Eventually, he heard Peter tear a sheet of cartridge paper from the pad. 'Here, it's done.'

It was a portrait of a young soldier. He was framed by one of the waiting room windows, so his lower half was concealed. He was bareheaded and wore a Sam Browne belt over his pressed tunic. There was a revolver in a leather holster closed with a press stud on the belt. He was fine-featured, with a thin moustache, and his hair was centre-parted after the fashion of the time. He would have known 'Roses of Picardy', Stride thought. He might have hummed it at the head of an infantry platoon as his men marched three abreast behind him, singing it through the fields of Flanders, or France.

'Did this apparition's eyes really have that expression?'

Peter nodded. He looked very pale. 'It is an accurate drawing of the thing I saw, Dad.'

Stride held the sketch between his fingers and blew out a breath. He thought he knew the word for the blank cunning in the expression of the face his son had rendered there. He did not know if Peter would be familiar with the word, which was feral.

'Why do you call it a thing, Peter? Why do you not refer to it as a man?'

'You need a soul to be human, don't you, Dad?'

Stride examined the sketch. 'Yes, I suppose you do.'

'Well. When that thing grinned out at me from the waiting room today, I knew it did not have one.'

Creed listened to the last of Stride's account over the steeple of his fingers. His palms felt moist. But he needed the reproach of his fingertips against his lips. He thought that without their restraining touch, he might grin and whoop at what the reclusive rock god had divulged. But he gave in to neither temptation. Instead, in a measured voice, he filled the silence that followed his visitor's story. 'You told Monica, of course?'

'First, we burned the sketch. Peter was insistent on that. He seemed to think it had been more drawn out of him than drawn by him and might possess some talismanic power of its own. He said it could only be a bad thing. He wanted it destroyed and I acceded to his wish.'

Creed nodded sagely. 'In the circumstances, that was the wisest course. You did the right thing.'

'Thank you. Then, after Peter went to bed and with his knowledge and consent, I told his mother. And I told Monica about the other previous phenomena too.'

'Her reaction?'

'Fear and trepidation.'

'She wasn't incredulous?'

Stride spread his hands. 'She knows me. I'm not the type of man to make this stuff up or even to embellish what I've actually experienced.'

'Yet you believe in psychic phenomena. You believe in my gift. You've admitted you are a fan of my show.'

'I am, which I wouldn't be if you were a crude show-business charlatan, Mr Creed.'

Creed cocked his head to one side. He allowed himself to look amused. He was a man who in his life since leaving the army had learned the value of the double-bluff. 'For all you really know, I might be the most successful fraud since that monster lurking in the peaty waters of Loch Ness.'

'You can assume me gullible if you wish,' Stride said. 'But I know of your other accomplishments. You don't parade them here, do you? Where is the triumphant Himalayan picture? Where is the photographic proof of that Antarctic endurance record you set? Decades of achievement and yet, here, none of it is anywhere to be seen. You've confined yourself to a few media baubles in a cabinet with tinted glass and that archive shot on the wall from the Falklands War. I've met plenty of people driven by ego. If this office is anything to go by, I don't think you are one of them.'

Quietly, Creed said, 'There were fundraising aspects to some of the more celebrated things I did earlier in my life. There was a charitable element. I don't believe in profiting from good causes. Perhaps it is a karmic thing. What I need to establish is what it is you want from me.'

'Simply, your gift,' Stride said. 'I need your gift. And I will pay very handsomely for the use of it.'

After Stride's departure from his office, Creed cancelled his appointments for the rest of the afternoon and asked for Elena Coyle to be summoned to him. To his intense irritation, he was informed by his PA that she was working from home while some domestic plumbing issue was addressed. He emailed Elena. Then, in the absence from her place of work of his full-time researcher, he did a bit of preliminary digging himself. He spent two absorbed hours on that. With the implications of what he had discovered reverberating through his mind, he decided to take himself off to the one dark and ramshackle Soho pub where he knew he was unlikely to be bothered by any of the seven million viewers who regularly tuned into his show. He did not drink during the day. It was a rule he strictly observed. But today had been exceptional in every way and he knew that he needed a drink more badly now than, in civilian life, he ever had before.

The challenge was to rid Stride's domain of its waiting

room ghosts. Before his departure, Stride had described his family life as nothing short of idyllic. Now that idyll was threatened by something spectral and fearful, auguring chaos and worse. Creed was to use his proven talent for confronting spiritual malevolence. He was to discover what had summoned the waiting room back into baleful life and return it to rest. He was to do it now, immediately, before things progressed to the point where Stride's family began to associate their home with terror. They had experienced joy and contentment there. They loved their home and did not wish to be driven from it.

The complication, Creed thought, looking around the pub, at its dusty, contented squalor, was Stride's insistence on confidentiality. He sipped his whisky, the hand that held the drink as steady as his hands had been aiming a sniper's rifle in Belfast a quarter of a century ago. Stride wasn't just publicity-shy. He was damn near reclusive. The waiting room was a two-part cliff-hanger guaranteed to send Creed's series ratings through the roof. Stride's celebrity status would make a premise that was already good, utterly compulsive viewing. How many records had his band sold, seventy or eighty million? There was wealth, cute kids, a glamorous wife and the supernatural present on the most atmospheric of stages. What could be more haunted than an abandoned waiting room? In television terms, the scenario was nothing short of irresistible. But Stride wasn't interested in ratings. He was only interested in exploiting Creed's psychic gift to free his family from a threat from beyond the grave. He was prepared to pay very lavishly for this. But he was only prepared to do so if the task was carried out in total privacy. Any hint of exposure and Creed felt certain he would never hear from the man again.

Then there was the secret. Stride believed in him. And Creed knew that he had enormous belief in himself. What he didn't believe in, not remotely, was his own psychic gift. It was a marketing myth that had become a necessity when they got the ratings for the pilot show at the outset of his ghost hunting career. As the genial television adventurer, he had not needed a psychic gift. Survival skills and a capacity for endurance and wit and a ready grin had been enough. And his looks, he supposed. He'd had the kind of all-round on-camera charisma that could provide an ex-soldier with a good if precarious living.

The psychic sensitivity changed everything. It was only after the first series that the penny dropped with him about this. It gave him a spiritual dimension. Elements of the show might be scary and sensational. And he was of course its star. But to his growing audience, he was a man conversant with the mysteries of what lay beyond. He understood the resonances of grief. He was sensitive to the yawning chasm of sudden death. He was asked to sit on a committee examining the rise in suicides among the young. He was commissioned to pen philosophical pieces for the heavyweight newspapers about the real meaning of dying. A more interesting class of women courted and sometimes propositioned him.

Very soon, it reached the point at which he knew the gift he faked essential to his success. And yet he was convinced by nothing he could not see and smell and touch. Having killed upwards of a dozen men in the past life he did not really talk about, it was his experience that they never came back. He had a quasi-religious status, he thought, groping for his wallet on the way to the bar. He answered a craving in people to believe. More, he validated what they wanted to believe in. In this, he was more of a prophet to them than a priest. He was a fraud, but he was a necessary fraud. He had invented himself, but a needy world had colluded in his creation. And now Martin Stride had beaten a credulous path to his door. You couldn't make it up. Except that you could and he had and had made a very lucrative career from doing so.

The pub door opened on the wan Soho daylight outside and Elena Coyle slipped into the gloom within. She looked around disdainfully, and Creed saw the full mouth and arresting grey eyes in a face framed by her glossily bobbed black hair and was reminded afresh of just how much he desired and quite how badly he had blown it with her. Who dares wins had been his regimental motto. Oh well. You couldn't realistically expect to win them all. He got her a white wine and soda, which was what she drank when she drank. She shed her coat and hung it on a hook by the door and spotted the table on which he had left his BlackBerry and notebook and sat down there.

He told her about his encounter with Martin Stride. He stuck to the salient points. Then he told her what he had discovered in his brief study of the railway line that ran through Stride's domain and the derelict station sited on it. During the Great War, the station had been the hub of troop movement. Tens of thousands of men had passed through there in transportation headed for the Channel ports of Dover and Folkestone on their way to the conflict on the Western Front. After the war, it had principally featured as the stopping-off point for a local lunatic asylum until the asylum had been shut down in the late 1920s.

'Then came thirty years of slow decline until inevitable closure and abandonment,' Creed said.

Elena sipped her drink. She straightened her back on her stool and stretched out long legs.

'Plumbing sorted, I assume?'

But she ignored this remark. She said, 'That waiting room must chiefly have functioned as a repository of fear and despair both during and after the war.'

'Certainly in psychic terms,' Creed said. 'And there's insanity as well. It's one of those "if these walls could speak" scenarios.'

'It sounds as though they are doing just that,' Elena said. 'But Stride will not allow anyone to hear them.'

'I'll deal with that little problem,' Creed said. 'Consider it a technical challenge. What I want from you is chapter and verse on the history of that station and its locality. I want to know everything about the loony bin. I want to know, is there any acrimony between Stride and whoever it was sold him that land five years ago. I want to know about his enemies. Music is a business where the knives are always out and you don't get to be as successful as him without seriously fucking someone over on the way. I want to know if Stride has or has ever had a drug habit. I need whatever you can discover on the state of his mental health and his religious beliefs. Is his marriage as happy as he claims? I need to know what sort of internet activity the kids have been up to. Is his little girl a Goth? Is his son a cyberspace warlock? I want to know. What do you know about Stride anyway?'

Elena sipped her drink. 'From what I've heard, he does a great deal of good work very discreetly. He doesn't want to shake the hand of world leaders or share a podium with the Pope. He's not the type at all for a photo-call on the White House lawn. But rumour has it he gives an awful lot of his money away.'

Creed grunted and drank. 'So he's some sort of secular saint.'

'Rock culture has changed since the days of the Doors and Led Zeppelin, Julian. The fascination with the occult that prompted Jimmy Page to buy Aleister Crowley's house is pretty much the province these days only of death metal bands from Scandinavia. I'm not saying he's a saint. But Satanism would be a stretch for him.'

'When you were a little girl, Elena, did you ever lift a stone to see the pale things writhing in the dank patch exposed there?'

'What's that got to do with anything?'

'Don't anticipate what's under the stone. Just lift it for me. That's what I pay you for. And I pay you well. Work on this. Drop everything else. This is your sole priority.'

'When do you want the information?'
Creed drained his glass. 'Yesterday,' he said.

After he had gone, she reflected on that last question and the answer she had known before asking he would give to it. It was a matter of pandering to his ego. Sometimes it had to be done. He had been pissed off about her plumbing drama and the absence it had necessitated. So she had fed him a compensatory morsel and he had snapped it up. The trouble was, it was like feeding a shark. The titbits could never satisfy its hunger. It swam in diminishing circles. And the thing it really wanted to devour was the person feeding it.

She shivered, walking the short distance from the pub to the office, thinking that there were many media sharks swimming the streets of Soho and that hers was probably not the most vicious or greedy of these predators. He had squirmed off to his private members' club now. She by timid contrast would be working very late. That was the thing about sharks, though. They were constantly moving. If they ever stopped swimming, they just sank to the seabed and drowned.

She discovered very quickly that ecstasy had been Martin Stride's drug of choice. He was fairly open about it. Not to the point where it could have been construed as laddish bragging, though. He admitted to having taken it when everyone else did, in the loved-up summer of '89. He had taken speed at university and done the odd line of cocaine at parties. But by the age of twenty-five, he had apparently decided that drugs were counter-productive creatively and people on drugs were boring. Elena agreed with this latter conclusion, but she thought it a very mature one for someone to reach at such a young age, enjoying his degree of success in such a hedonistic industry.

Then she uncovered what she thought probably the real reason for his abstemiousness. There had been a girlfriend, a girl from Düsseldorf, the singer with a support band he'd been rumoured to have started dating on tour. In the spring of 1990 she had died of an overdose in a Paris hotel room. Stride was not there. He was in Italy with his band. The news reached him in Rome. There was a picture showing him at the funeral, flanked by a band mate and the brother of the dead girl. His eyes were raw with grief in the picture but there was strength and resolution in the set of his jaw. His hair had been shorter then. He wore it down to his shoulders now. She studied him. He was a gifted musician, of course. But she did not think being such a handsome man could have done anything to very seriously hurt Martin Stride's career.

He brought down the curtain on that career in 1997. The last, reluctant interview recorded had been granted in the September of that year. He was all talked out by then, barely quotable, exhausted of things to say and clearly very bored and disillusioned with who he had become. Sometimes people in his position affected disillusionment, she knew, as a way of offsetting the resentment provoked by their success. But his seemed genuine. The one memorable remark he made in that final interview was to say that autumn was a good time to quit. 'Things perish,' he said. 'Everything perishes. It's in the nature of things.'

As a career suicide note, she thought those three sentences eloquent despite their brevity.

There had been the inevitable speculation recently about a band reunion. Stride had been emphatic in dismissing it. The break-up of the band had not been acrimonious. He had written all the songs but there had been enough shared credits on their hits for the subsequent royalties to make all of them comfortably off. He had apparently planned it that way. And it meant that there was no one living in bedsit squalor and nursing murderous resentment against him now. His band mates had moved on. The drummer still drummed on occasional sessions but his real passion seemed to be the organic farm he owned. The lead guitarist owned and ran a country house hotel on the

Isle of Wight. The bassist had become a sought-after record producer. If any of them hankered after the spotlight, they weren't saying so in public. It sounded like a happy ending. What it actually seemed, to Elena, was gracious acceptance in a generally graceless industry. She was beginning to think grace a defining feature of her subject's character.

There were ways of gaining access to and tracking the internet use of the Stride children but Elena would not do it. It was unethical and illegal. Creed's instructions to her on that score in the pub had just been bluster. But he would get the information, she knew. He would just use someone with fewer scruples than she had to hack into their hard drives. He'd have what he wanted in hours and would pay for this clandestine information in cash. She thought the idea of an eight-year-old goth somewhat far-fetched, personally. Stride seemed the sort of thorough, scrupulous man who would monitor his children's internet use simply out of parental duty. She doubted the kids had anything to do with the strange emanations from the waiting room. They seemed potentially more likely to be victims than unwitting perpetrators of whatever it was that was going on. She was personally sceptical about psychic phenomena. But she was not agnostic, like her boss. She kept what she considered an open mind.

She turned her attention to the asylum. Falcon Lodge was opened in 1916, the gift of a wealthy philanthropist who had fought in the Boer War at the start of the new century and, reading between the lines, knew first-hand of the toll that battle trauma could exact on a young mind. It wasn't called that then, of course. It was referred to, when it was referred to at all, as neurasthenia or shell-shock. Elena thought it significant that Paley, the philanthropist, engaged the services of Professor Edward Brody as his asylum's chief psychiatrist. Brody had brilliant academic credentials. But he came from a military family. He had lost a brother at Mons in the first months of the war. Near to its conclusion, he was to see another badly wounded at Paschendaele. He would almost certainly have followed them into uniform, she thought, if it was not for the fact that he suffered from tuberculosis.

Instead, he came to Falcon Lodge, young, gifted and profoundly sympathetic to the suffering of the men the same age as himself who comprised most of his patients up to and even beyond the armistice. She found a letter from Paley, congratulating him on the effectiveness of the rehabilitation work he was achieving. She found two letters from the War Office on a similar theme. And it went beyond empathy with the young. One letter referred to a very senior officer who had suffered a breakdown after a failed assault. He had not believed the casualty figures. He had been sceptical, confronted with their enormity. He had gone to see for himself. He had believed the corpses and the sight of them had robbed him of his capacity to command. The breakdown was severe. But after six weeks under Brody, he was seen to be fit to return to his staff position, his recovery complete.

Brody had died prematurely, in 1934, killed by the disease afflicting his lungs. But Elena learned that his papers from the asylum period had been saved. They were at the Imperial War Museum in Lambeth. She did not know whether what she was discovering would ever form part of Julian Creed's next television series. But she had his firmly imparted instructions to unearth anything she could about two specific locations. The asylum was one of them. And she had her instinct. This told her very strongly that if whatever was happening in and around the derelict waiting room on Martin Stride's estate was genuinely paranormal, it was more likely to do with past events at the asylum than anything else.

She did not think she would see a Tudor figure clanking through the halls with his head under his arm should she spend the night alone at Hampton Court Palace. She did not believe in comic book spooks. But equally she did not find it difficult to believe that certain events reverberated through time. They had repercussions. Those likely to find an echo, to make the most resonant noise, were surely those involving the most intense pitches of emotion. Men had lost their capacity to govern their minds ninety-odd years ago in the clamour and savagery of battle. And they had brought back their pain and assaulted senses and disembarked and waited in that room on the platform on Stride's estate for the car that would deliver them to a home for lunatics.

That was how those wounded young men would see it, in their wounded minds. 'If those walls could talk,' she said to herself, shaking her head, switching off her computer, 'they would not talk at all. They would scream.' She gathered her things. She looked at her watch. It was a quarter to ten. Creed would be in full flow at his club. It was Friday night. He was always entertaining company. He was always good value. He was generous and attractive and filled with a happy, contagious vitality. And she thought she probably hated him as she had never hated any man. She had no plans herself for the weekend. She would not be able to access any of the information she wanted from the War Museum until Monday morning. The place would be open and packed with visitors over the weekend of course, but none of the library or archive staff would be in until the start of the working week proper.

Elena put her things in her bag and took her coat from its hook. She decided she might walk the route along the river to her flat in Bermondsey. Julian Creed had a flat five minutes away in Fitzrovia. But then he had a large house in Surrey and a villa in Portugal, too. At least her flat was watertight now, thanks to the recent expensive ministrations of the plumber. At least if she got wet over the weekend, she would be doing so by choice. She might go to Borough Market tomorrow morning. She might go along to the War Museum, just to look at the exhibits from the Great War, just to get a feel for the period and that mammoth, tragic conflict. She was alone now. Freedom of choice was one of the compensations of being single. She had not dated anyone since the sordid catastrophe of her last date with her boss.

In the lobby outside their office suite, waiting for the lift, she examined her reflection in one of the narrow mirrors that decorated the walls and enhanced the light from their fashionable low-energy bulbs. Objectively, she thought she looked pretty good. But she could take no pleasure, really, in her appearance. It was as though the incident with Creed had deprived her of something, had taken something permanently away from her. It wasn't sexual innocence; it had been much too late for that. Was it pride?

Her mobile rang. And it was him. She had been wrong. He was not at his club. There was no background noise. There was no traffic noise either. It occurred to her, incredulously, that he must already be at home. She looked at her watch again but it was not yet ten o'clock. Was his latest conquest so irresistible he hadn't been able to wait?

'Brief me,' he said.

'Can't your curiosity wait to be satisfied until Monday, Julian?'

'No,' he said. 'It can't.'

He sounded completely sober, on a Friday night. She thought this, in her experience of him, unprecedented.

'You have uncovered stuff?'

'Of course I have.'

'Excellent. You're hard work sometimes, darling, but no one can say you're not bloody good at your job.'

Neither the insult nor the compliment really registered. What did was the fact that he sounded both nervous and relieved. 'You really want the briefing now?'

'Everything you have, love. Fire away. Martin Stride has agreed to my spending tomorrow evening in the waiting room. I want to go to bed early tonight and sleep soundly on everything you've learned.'

# Chapter Two

Engaging the help of Julian Creed had been Monica Stride's idea. Her reasoning had been very simple. She listened carefully, later on the evening of Peter's apparition, after the children had gone to bed and as they slept soundly in their rooms above. She took in everything her husband told her. She did not comment or question until he had finished his account of the strange and gathering events impinging upon their home and lives. Even then, when he had completed his story, she did not say anything for a few moments. He had chosen to tell her in his study. It was a room built on an intimate scale, wood panelled and with a fire of pine logs burning in its grate. They sat on the plump of comfy chairs to either side of the fire whilst he spoke. His study was a cosy refuge. That was one reason why he had chosen it. But he had chosen it also because he had not wanted her, after his revelations, to associate any of her own familiar and more fondly loved parts of the house with the delivery of such disturbing news.

Stride sat, aware of the sound of the flames flickering in the little grate and the rhythmic pendulum swing from the walnut case of the old clock on the wall. He waited. And then Monica spoke.

'The things you and Millie experienced could have been benign. They were creepy and therefore they were unwelcome, but they were essentially harmless, were they not?'

Stride thought about this and then nodded. His wife's words had been delivered in a calm and fluent voice. But her accent had strengthened. Usually her pronunciation was no different from that spoken by a native Englishwoman. Her accent had diminished to almost nothing over the time they had been together. In moments of stress, though, she sounded more again the child of her Danish father.

'The thing Peter saw, by contrast, sounds as though it was malevolent.'

'I don't think a ghost can cause physical harm,' he said.

'But you don't know. Neither of us does. It frightened him.' She raised her eyes to the direction of the room in which he slept above them. 'And neither of us is an expert on this sort of thing.'

'No,' he said. It would be a lie he would not indulge to offer her reassurance he did not feel. He felt that if his wife had seen the thing that Peter had drawn, she might lose this present struggle for composure altogether.

'That is what we need, Julian. We need an expert in these matters. And we are fortunate in that we can afford to engage the best qualified we can find.'

'I could just have that building demolished. I'm in the fortunate position of being able to arrange that too. I could have a demolition team here by dawn. They would bring bulldozers, a wrecking ball and a fleet of lorries to carry the rubble away. They would remove all trace of our derelict railway station. Every brick, every tile, every fragment of plaster could be off our land by nightfall.'

'That might be a mistake,' Monica said. Carefully, she reached forward from where she sat and picked the brass poker from its stand and stirred with the iron tip of it at the burning logs in the fire. Flames erupted, sending a faint flare of warmth into the room. 'What if something, the thing that Peter saw, has left the waiting room? What if you destroy the waiting room and it cannot return from where it came? And what if it blames us for that? We should do nothing so radical or dramatic.'

'Or so irrevocable,' Stride said. Monica was right.

'For now, we keep the children away from that part of the

grounds. We stay away from it ourselves. We can do nothing more, really, until we know what it is we are confronted by.'

He said nothing.

'And why it is confronting us. And why it is doing so now.'

Stride stared into the flames of his fire and thought about this. 'Is anyone qualified to tell us those things?'

'I would say so,' she said. She held her husband's eyes with hers. 'I would have belief and confidence that one man could reveal the mystery and defuse the threat and restore normality to us.'

Stride nodded. 'You're talking about Julian Creed,' he said.

'He will come at a pretty price.'

'I will pay it, regardless,' Stride said. He was remembering Peter's face after the ordeal of rendering in pencil the thing that had leered out at him from the window of the waiting room. 'I would pay any price to have normality restored to us.'

Two floors above them, their children slept. But the interference of the day had not yet ended. Millie dreamed. And her dream was one beyond the powers of an eight-year-old to understand or interpret. She dreamt of a man and a woman in a room with windows of opaque glass where everything except the two people it contained seemed to be coloured brown. The woman wore a white blouse with puffed sleeves and a rope of black beads and had her hair pulled back in the style Mummy sometimes wore. To Millie, she was more of a lady than a woman. She seemed very grand. And she was crying, which was shocking in someone so grand-seeming, to Millie.

The man wore a suit like the one Philip who came sometimes to help Mummy plant in the kitchen garden always wore. It was bristly with leather patches on the elbows. The man held a handkerchief. But it was not for the lady's tears. He coughed softly into it between the quiet words he spoke, and then he folded it. He did this to hide the stains that came out of his mouth when he coughed. The stains were not brown, like everything else in the room. They were tiny, bright speckles of red.

The morning after her late departure from the office, Elena took the short walk from her flat to the Monmouth Coffee House to wait for the neighbouring Borough Market to open up for trade. But before more than half a dozen stalls had started to prepare their day's displays, she had decided she would after all take the opportunity to travel back the better part of a century to examine those relics of conflict and loss gathered together at the War Museum. The sky was grey and a light and melancholy London rain was falling and she thought she was probably better in than out on such a day. But she still walked to Lambeth and the museum, along the river as far as Blackfriars Bridge, buying an apple from the fruit vendor on its south side to eat on the last part of the route.

The cast figure of a soldier stood at the basement entrance to the rooms containing the displays concerned with the Great War. He held a Lee Enfield rifle between sturdy hands and the expression on his young face was stoical and the arms emerging from his rolled sleeves brawny with bronze muscle. This sentinel was the work of Charles Sargeant Jagger and it set a sombre tone. Elena knew that Jagger had served as a rifleman at Gallipoli and on the Western Front. He had been severely wounded. And he had been awarded the Military Cross for some probably typical act of gallantry. It was worth studying his sculpture. He had tried very hard to be true in his art to what he had witnessed in his life.

It was still not long after the museum had opened. It would get very crowded later in the day with tourists, she knew. But now it was quiet. Because it was a Saturday, it was free of school parties of excited children ticking off the exhibits they were supposed to see in chattering, gleeful files. This early, she could stand in front of the dimly lit displays for as long as she wanted to, with an unobstructed view and able to contemplate their contents, their physical character and implications, in silence and relative seclusion.

Up to a point, weapons were weapons; a rifle looked like a rifle out of mechanical function and ergonomic necessity and the same was even truer of a sword. But some of the improvised trench weapons displayed in their cases seemed so savage and primitive to Elena that they might have been fashioned in medieval times. Even the Maxim gun looked primitive, squat on its tripod, clumsy and simplistic in character rather than flaunting the lethal intricacy it had certainly possessed.

What really shocked her were the defensive exhibits: the flimsy periscope sight for firing from the shelter of a trench and the chainmail waistcoat worn in the hope of repelling high-velocity bullets. And the iron, no-man's-land observation post disguised as the trunk of a shell-shattered tree. Masks constructed from rubber and canvas and glass were designed to protect the wearer from gas that burned the skin at the touch and turned the lungs to liquid on the intake of a single breath. Medical kits were little more than pins and patches of lint and rolls of hopeful bandage.

When she had studied it all, she sat at a far table in the museum café and looked out at the grass and high trees of the parkland to the rear of the building. The exposed trees, still in leaf, shivered wetly in gusts of wind. She thought about the patriotic optimism of the men embarking for France on those trains that must have rolled through the station on Martin Stride's estate. There would have been a protocol. The waiting room would surely have been only for the officers. And she thought of the return of those damaged ones passed after their ordeal into Edward Brody's compassionate charge. Had they felt defeated? Disgraced? Betrayed?

Without learning more than she had, it was impossible to know. Brody himself might tell her in his notes in the archive here on Monday. She could not guess at what had gone through the minds of those returning casualties of war. Poetry and propaganda and revisionism had made the necessary objectivity impossible. It was impossible to span almost a century of legend and disinformation with clarity, let alone empathy. But she thought her visit had been worthwhile despite this. And she had had, if she was honest, no other pressing impositions on her time.

She thought about Julian Creed. She did not think she would comfortably spend a night alone in the station waiting room on the Stride estate. She considered old waiting rooms to be almost intrinsically sinister locations because of all their blind walls had been witness to over the years. They endured about their visitors what was transient and shifting and incomplete, without the settled routine brought by the permanence of solid occupation. Such places just saw too much that was fretful and unresolved and it left a residue of remembered melancholy that was sometimes almost palpable. These days, on branch lines, most of the old waiting rooms seemed to have a seized-up padlock securing their locked doors. They required costly maintenance, as did the public lavatories fast disappearing from the platforms of branch-line stations. They were obvious locations for robbery and assault and it was simple pragmatism to close them against the possibility, particularly on stations that were undermanned.

But a waiting room on a forgotten platform, there in isolation, unused by any traveller for better than forty years, would be a testing place, she thought, for a night vigil on your own, particularly when it had the history that this one did. Creed did not believe in ghosts. He had proven himself a man of very considerable physical courage during his eventful life. But she thought it might be a challenge, even for him. He would not think so. He would be thinking only about the ratings potential and no doubt looking forward to it.

She wondered how Creed and his host would get on. They

seemed to have got by so far on mutual admiration and modesty, but on Creed's part at least, that was bogus, she knew. He had the easy affability that came from rock-solid public school self-assurance. His father had been a wealthy stockbroker and he had thrived on the regimentation of the army and ridden on his breezy, laidback confidence ever since. He was posh, almost a toff in the old sense of the word, because his family had been prosperous for generations. His father had been master of the local hunt. But his blokey persona worked on most people. He would flirt with Monica Stride, charm the daughter and have the boy spellbound with authentic war stories embellished by his raconteur's gift.

She could see tension arising though, at some point, between him and Martin Stride. Stride had been the son of a Lancashire colliery worker who had died of lung disease in the immediate, bitter aftermath of the miners' strike in the mid-1980s. The family had known poverty before the strike. Stride's father had been ill on and off for a decade. There was a sister somewhere, but his mother had committed suicide shortly after his father's death and the children had been obliged as teenagers to fend for themselves. Stride had been bright and talented enough to overcome his circumstances. He had not been embittered by the bleakness and deprivation of his upbringing. Not if the way he gave money away was any indication. He gave exclusively to domestic charities and generally they were those that helped disadvantaged children. His son's village school had benefited recently from a new library, privately endowed. It had not been that difficult for Elena to discover the real source of the money.

Creed the media cavalier would be on his best behaviour, careful around this host, with his sober ways and fastidious values. Nevertheless, he would certainly be looking forward to his visit to the waiting room tonight. But she thought that he might be in for a shock. She did not know why, it was just a suspicion, a sort of hunch. It was strong and persistent, though, the way she imagined a premonition might be. She finished her coffee and buttoned her raincoat with a sigh, thinking about the weekend opening up emptily before her.

Creed arrived at the Stride estate at the wheel of the Morgan with the hood down in the late September sunshine. He had calculated the Jag would be probably a bit on the flash London media side and might create a negative impression. Martin Stride was seriously rich, but unostentatious about it, relatively at least. The Morgan might charm various Strides with its idiosyncratic looks and cute size. The canvas roof and split windscreen and wire wheel spokes were picturesque features hard to resist. He felt that key to his overall objective was to get on the right side of Monica Stride and the kids. He had worn for his arrival what he privately called his Van Helsing ensemble. It was a thorn-proof three-piece country suit from Cordings of Piccadilly. Over the top in town, it was perfect for the field and if the Strides really were fans of his series, it would make him all the more familiar and reassuring. He had worn it famously for the outing off the Orkneys when he identified the phantom on the Black Bay lightship.

A savvy freelance stylist hired by the first series producer had come up with the idea of his dressing to suit the mood and atmosphere of the specific location under investigation. So for the haunted hospital he had worn a clinical white coat. For the garage plagued by a poltergeist, he had worn blue mechanic's overalls. He had worn a boilersuit for the disused power station and had dressed as a gloomy sartorial cross between a detective and an undertaker investigating the alleged torture chamber in Edinburgh haunted by the victims of an equally alleged serial killer. Originally, he had been going to wear a yellow oilskin and sou'wester for the Black Bay lightship investigation. But drama could easily stray into farce where the occult and television were concerned. It was a very fine line indeed.

'I'm not dressing like Captain fucking Birdseye,' he had said, seeing himself on a monitor in the original costume. He did not think of himself as a style guru, but his instincts had been right. A ghost hunter without dignity offended the dignity of those who chose to believe in the supernatural. They faced enough ridicule without someone apparently on their side provoking more.

On the ninety-minute drive to his destination, he listened to the CD of Stride's band's greatest hits. He had lied about having them on his MP3 player. He was not particularly fond of pop or rock. His preference was for jazz vocalists and vintage blues. But these songs were very evocative of their time. They had aired then in every restaurant and bar. And listening to them now brought back memories of a grimly uncertain period in his life. Anyone over thirty and not of very senior rank was superfluous to requirements in the combat units of the British Army. Training and action were very wearing. The body could only take so much. Even if you stayed mentally and physically fit, and he had, the mindset was that after thirty, you were past your sell-by date. He had opted out at thirty-two, no longer wanted and with no real plan for the balance of his professional life.

He became a personal trainer. He built a client list purely by word of mouth. Some of his clients were in the media and show business fields. One of them was a film director shooting a picture centred on a criminal gang of ex-special forces men. He found himself hired as a weapons expert with the job of training the actors to look familiar with the hardware they used. He co-ordinated action shots and battle scenes for other movies. Some of these were big budget epics and he enjoyed the lavish locations and real-life drama of working with stars and the brief illusion of stardom by association. But the work was unreliable and irregular by its nature and there wasn't really enough of it.

He got his television break because he trained, without

charge, a fat disc jockey called Paul Baines for a Polar trek being done for charity. It was discovered during his mandatory medical that Baines had high blood pressure. Creed gave him an exercise regime and diet plan that was effective in reducing it. But he could not reduce it sufficiently to satisfy the charity's insurers. In the end, the premium they would have had to pay would have put too great a dent in the total they hoped to raise and Baines reluctantly pulled out. By that point, Creed was training everyone else on the team of C-list celebrities and, of course, doing it for free. The satellite channel covering the trek suggested he go along to motivate the motley group he had tried to ready for the challenge. He agreed. And his optimism and resilience and facility for a wisecrack won him more camera time than anyone when the trek had been completed and the series came to be aired.

That was his break. But even then, he did a lot of things for joke networks that embarrassed him even at the time with their crassness and lack of dignity. Until the ghost hunt pilot came along. He had been third choice for the anchor role. That wasn't common knowledge, but he had known it. He had come under consideration because it was felt his combination of physicality and wit would prevent the series from becoming too scary. The psychic sensitivity had been his own idea, his unique contribution. The anchor role had evolved into something much more substantial, even defining. And it was coming up for five years now and he was broadcast in forty-odd foreign territories and bought a villa in Portugal just on DVD royalties and he had never really looked back.

He was looking back now. Stride's melodies were forcing him to examine the period of uncertainty when the spectre of failure at civilian life had truly haunted him for a time. Stride was taking him back. But, he thought with a grin at the wheel of his spiffy little roadster, these songs were at the same time reminding him of just how far since those days he had come.

He switched off the music and, aware that he was only a few miles from his destination, had a look around. The land was hedgerows, undulant fields, occasional mature trees of majestic size and the odd whitewashed cottage and coach house, all of these under a soft wash of autumn sunlight. The south-east of England was supposedly overcrowded. But the gentle rural landscape close to where the Strides had chosen to live would have been an England familiar to Chesterton and Belloc and Virginia Woolf and Brooke. And to M. R. James, he thought to himself, since his subject matter here was spooks.

He had resisted the temptation to bring the concealed camera along. They had one, but he did not honestly think there would be anything for him to film. He'd hosted a very brief conference call that morning with Tony Pullen and Mickey Joyce, his regular cameraman and lighting technician, and with Alison Slaney, who did the digital trickery that had his audience on the edges of their seats and sometimes behind their sofas with their hands over their eyes. He had brought them up to speed with what Elena had discovered. They all agreed the story potential was massive. But Tony and Mickey in particular said there wasn't much point in prolonging the discussion until Creed returned with something for them to work with. They needed the physical character and dimensions of the building. They needed something on the architectural style. He could provide all that, once he'd seen it himself, with sketches and verbal description.

He'd thought Mickey a little grumpy. Tony had been too, if he was honest. They were both fathers and did things with their kids at the weekend. They resented the imposition on their time of a call from the boss on Saturday morning. By contrast, family stuff had rather passed him by. He blamed the army when anyone from the press asked in interviews and said he was married to his work. Pressed, he said he did not think psychic sensitivity of his sort compatible with nappies and nursery rhymes. The truth was a bit more complicated. But when did celebrity profiles ever have anything to do with the truth? Alison Slaney had sounded excited. The asylum might give her a screaming madwoman to work on. Creed grinned. Alison was Irish and liked to get creative on the banshee theme. Then he stopped grinning, because he was through an open gate between tall, carved gate posts and was there.

The family were out in their entirety, playing croquet on a pitch on a sweep of lawn to the left of the long drive, a couple of hundred metres from the house. They were all wearing T-shirts and baggy shorts except for Monica Stride, who wore denim cut-offs. Martin Stride walked over smiling, with his mallet swinging from one hand. He was fit-looking out of his formal clothes, hard and sinewy. Creed climbed out of the car.

'My God,' Stride said. 'It's Gabriel Van Helsing.'

A lean, good-looking blond boy Creed knew must be Peter appeared beside his dad. 'Killer wheels,' he said, gazing at the Morgan. Then he pointed. 'You wore that outfit when you rid the Scottish lightship of the spirit of its dead captain.'

His show had done this, made arcane words like 'rid' and 'expunge' and 'vanquish' the lexicon of the pub and play-ground.

'Guilty as charged,' Creed said.

'I told my dad he ought to buy a suit just like it. He said with no vampires to hunt, it wouldn't get the necessary use.'

Creed shot a cuff. 'I find it equally suitable attire for dealing with phantoms.'

That remark cast a shadow across the faces of the man and boy in front of him. 'I'm sorry,' he said. 'Tactless.'

'Not at all,' Stride said, surprising him with a hand on the shoulder and a friendly squeeze. 'We know exactly why you're here and we're all truly grateful.' He called his wife and daughter over from the clutter of white hoops on the lawn to be introduced. Monica Stride was cool and beautiful and appraising. Millie had her father's grey eyes. Creed invited Peter to ride shotgun on the short drive to the house and then delighted him with a sly skid when they reached the garages, over on the gravel to the right, behind a high hedge and out of sight of those following on foot.

'Cool.'

'Who won the croquet?'

'We hadn't finished. My dad was winning.'

'I've heard it described as a ruthless pursuit.'

'He always wins,' Peter said, grinning. 'He must be a ruthless man.'

It was four o'clock. They would eat at six. It went dark at around seven forty-five. Creed would settle for the night in the waiting room at seven thirty. Before dinner, Stride suggested that the two of them should tour the grounds. He said that the best way to do it was on quad bikes.

'They the only clothes you've got?'

Creed smiled. The Strides were much less formal than he had expected them to be. He did not know what had made him think they'd behave grandly and stand on ceremony. And then he thought he did. What he had taken for formality in Stride's bearing and demeanour in their one previous meeting had actually been nervousness, he realised. He might have performed in front of three-quarters of a million people in Rio, but Martin Stride was quite a shy man. His family emboldened him. Surrounded by them, the nervousness was gone. Already, he thought he might have wasted Elena's time with the direction of some of the research he had told her to carry out. The Strides were obviously happy. You could not fake the ease and intimacy evident among the four of them.

'I've got a pair of jeans and a leather jacket in a travel bag in the boot of the car,' he said. 'Is there somewhere I can change?'

'I'll show you to your room.'

'I'm using the waiting room.'

37

'Not to change in, you're not. And assuming you survive the night, you'll want a shower in the morning. Every guest gets a room. And we're honoured to have you as our guest, Julian. The kids are thrilled.'

'You let Millie watch the show?'

'Selected episodes and with some judicious editing, but yes, we do. She doesn't really differentiate between your show and *Scooby-Doo*. She thinks you're Fred, by the way, not Scooby.'

'So I'm Van Helsing or I'm Fred from *Scooby-Doo*. These are comparisons that could go to a man's head. I can't recall having ever been so flattered,' Creed said.

'Come on,' Stride said. 'Let's get you changed.'

He wanted to see the apple orchard and Millie's picnic spot, of course. His mind was on the drift of acoustics caused by atmospheric pressure in certain wind conditions. The terrain was flat, so sound would travel without distortion over it for miles in the right circumstances. The source of the sound, of course, was another matter. Where in this region would a male choir sing 'Roses of Picardy' without accompaniment? Millie was a gifted musician and she was adamant that she had heard no instrumentation.

Creed had listened to the John McCormack version of the song himself in his hours in front of his computer prior to his meeting with Elena in the pub. It was a soupy old shellac recording from the days of 78s and the orchestration had been pushed right back to allow McCormack's superb light tenor its rightful dominance over proceedings. But the orchestration had been there: brass and woodwind and lachrymose strings. There was no question really of Millie having heard that, or any of the other recordings of the time because the arrangements were all of a type. She had heard lots of men, not a soloist. It really had to have been a choir. He would have to get Elena to investigate the churches in realistic proximity.

Then, of course, there was the train to account for. That was much more simple a sound to replicate. All you required was a decent 5.1 surround home entertainment system powered by a really muscular voltage. Creed hadn't toured the house, but he was fairly sure Stride would have one of them himself. He wasn't monkish where telly was concerned; why should his attitude be any different towards film? A well-heeled neighbour had been viewing *Brief Encounter* or *Von Ryan's Express* or some other train related classic too loud after too much to drink and the sound had simply travelled to the orchard on a gust of night wind.

Which did not, did it, explain that cocktail of railway smells Stride had described. That was a puzzle. Elena had said ecstasy had been his drug of choice. But that had been twenty years ago. In the short term, heavy use of the stuff could provoke depression and anxiety. In the long term, it was said to lead to memory loss. But the research findings were inconclusive and he'd never heard even anecdotal stories claiming happy pills created imaginary odours. Maybe Stride had simply smelled the drift of something burned on a neighbouring barbeque and after thinking he'd heard a train, his fraught imagination had done the rest.

It would have to be some barbeque and some drift, he conceded to himself, riding his quad bike in his host's wake. The Stride estate was vast. And it was a wilderness, totally overgrown and uncultivated in all directions beyond the immediate area of the house. There were two distinct areas of woodland almost big enough to be called forests, full of ancient deciduous trees. There were ash, elm, beech, willow, oak and alder. He thought that you would have to travel to Hampton Court or Kew to see so many yew trees, except that these were growing in the wild.

They threaded through the wood to the north-east of the house and then were through the trees and at the top of a long, gentle slope of grassland descending to a shallow vale.

Stride braked and switched his engine off. Creed did the same. Stride pointed. 'There it is,' he said. 'When it was still a station, this was called Shale Point.'

The other side of the vale rose to a horizon topped by a single, isolated building more or less centred on the rise from where they looked. It was entirely still, of course, and quiet and rather dusty-looking with its patches of exposed stonework under fading paint and umber roof tiles. The windows from this distance were black, sightless. Creed shivered. He did not know why. It was not cold. The work of steering the heavy bike through the trees had warmed him and he wore his leather jacket and the late afternoon was mild. He smiled secretly to himself. Perhaps he was psychically sensitive after all. Wouldn't that be too ironic?

Stride turned back to him. 'What?'

'Terrible pun,' Creed said. 'But it looks like it's waiting for something.'

'Come on,' Stride said.

The platform was skirted by wild blackberry bushes heavy with ripe fruit and the smell of these was strong and slightly cloying in the air. They climbed onto it through the one area where these bushes had been trampled down and Creed thought it obviously the spot where Peter and his school friends had done the bike jumps that caused the puncture. The platform itself was impressively intact, only the odd weathered scuff at the edges of some of the slabs that paved it signalled its age and the absence of regular maintenance.

The single building on it looked utterly surreal to Creed, this close to. It was a functional construction deprived by fate and time entirely of its function. It was rectangular and had a gabled roof and the quite large mock Gothic windows Stride had spoken of. The panes were clear up to where they narrowed to accommodate the arch. There, they each had a leaded section depicting railway engines trailing steam. The eye recognised this building and then searched in vain for all the missing accoutrements: the signal and the rails and the platform numbers and the news kiosk and rolling stock and most of all the passengers. Everything that defined it was absent, Creed realised, walking slowly around its perimeter. There was one wooden door facing the western side of the platform. It was a sturdy slab of varnished oak, with a brass bulb-shaped door handle burnished by the friction of countless hands and then allowed to weather and dull.

Creed put his hand on the door handle. He tested it back and forth and it moved freely. Of course, the door was not locked. He looked at Stride, who merely shrugged. He was aware that there were no birds singing now. It had become very quiet. He opened the door and walked inside and gasped.

He had expected dereliction. But it looked within as though someone might have waited for a train there only yesterday. A blued iron stove stood at the centre of the room. Bench seating skirted its walls. There were recruitment posters above the benching, between the windows. There was a brass framed railway timetable. Chains trailed from a gas lamp suspended from the ceiling. Creed fingered these, knowing that their job was to adjust the level of the wick and thereby the brightness of the light.

'This is interesting,' Stride said. He had gone over to a tall, narrow cupboard set into a section of wall. The key was in the lock. He turned it and opened the cupboard and pulled out something long and cylindrical. When he had put it on the floor and unfurled it, Creed saw that it was a canvas stretcher, the cloth stitched between wooden poles. There were pairs of restraining cuffs of stiff leather screwed halfway along the poles and again at one end of the stretcher. These were for the wrists and ankles, Creed supposed.

'Grim old relic,' Stride said. He had stood after squatting to display the stretcher on the floor. He touched one of the cuffs with the toe of his boot. 'Can't imagine why you'd have to strap down the victim of a railway accident.' He looked at Creed. 'To combat shock, maybe.' He looked back at the grotesque assemblage and shook his head.

And Creed saw that he really didn't know about the history of the place, about the asylum and the madness that had passed through here. He had heard his sounds and scented his smells without knowing. The grinning apparition drawn by Peter had spooked him. It had not been the knowledge of what had gone on here in the past. He looked around. He could barely suppress his glee. It was better than good. He'd been on film sets far less convincing on movies with massive budgets. It was perfect, he thought, looking at Kitchener's mad eyes above that bristling moustache in the famous poster on the wall opposite the door. It was better than the light-ship, better even than the de-commissioned power station with the turbine rotor that kept churning inexplicably back into life. It was, as they were apt to say in the language of the football pundit, different class.

'Don't know about you, Julian, but I'm hungry,' Stride said, rolling the stretcher back up.

'Famished,' Creed said.

'I trust you're a carnivore?'

'I'll eat anything.'

'Good. We're having lamb.'

'As long as it's not of the sacrificial variety,' Creed said.

But Stride did not laugh at that. Either he did not hear it, or he did not think the joke funny.

Creed thought that their early dinner had the atmosphere almost of a wake. He realised that the Strides were genuinely afraid for him. It was there in the awkward, subdued conversation and the way they kept averting their eyes. It was touching in a way and even flattering, but it did not make for a very comfortable meal. It was a shame, because the food was delicious: loin of lamb perfectly roasted, vegetables the family had grown in their own kitchen garden. And then Peter Stride rescued the situation. He cleared his throat and coloured slightly in the cheeks and asked when had Creed first become aware that he was in touch with the phantom world.

'We're all in touch with the phantom world,' he said, a statement delivered deadpan to guarantee he had their every ounce of attention. 'You saw what you saw, Peter. Millie heard what she heard. And before that, there were your dad's experiences to consider. All of you displayed a strong degree of psychic sensitivity.'

'But not like you,' Monica Stride said. And Creed detected an accent, subtle and charming.

'What you have experienced is a sort of symbolic or coded communication,' he said. 'For reasons I still don't understand, people from the spirit world choose to communicate with me more directly. They tell me things. They confide their secrets. They are not as coy as they are for the most part in their contact with the physical world.'

They were all staring at him openly now. You could only wonder, he thought, at the power of television. Television had done this. 'So I will answer Peter's question. I was still in the army, then.'

'The SAS,' Peter said.

His mother shushed him.

Creed did his modest smile. 'We were on a training exercise, climbing in the high Alps. We were a party of three. We were somewhere above the Swiss-French border when the weather closed in.'

The regiment did most of their winter training in Norway. But the level of technical expertise required of Alpine climbing was considered worth acquiring among some units. The Hereford men were supposed to be the best fighters in the world. It didn't hurt to have a dash of virtuosity in every area of physical endeavour.

They were almost at the peak when the weather changed, tantalisingly close, but it might as well have been the moon they were reaching for, as the gale grew rapidly to ferocious strength. They were very fortunate to find the hut to which they descended. The descent was desperate, a ragged retreat handicapped by the fumbling near panic of men who knew they were now entirely at the mercy of the elements in an environment that could hardly have been more hostile to the possibility of human survival.

It took them four hours to reach the hut. Creed calculated the distance actually travelled over that time from their position below the summit at perhaps three hundred metres. They reached the hut exhausted and suffering the first serious symptoms of hypothermia. Jackson and Clegg, the non-coms in Creed's nominal command, sought sleep. They fumbled their sleeping bags with frozen fingers from their packs and snuggled into them, groaning and foetal. But Creed somehow discovered the mental discipline and organisation to light a lamp and get his field stove going under a pan of snow-melt. He ripped open packs of dehydrated soup with his teeth and stirred, and in the pan the stuff eventually warmed and grew hot. He kicked and cajoled the soldiers under his command into a sort of numbed wakefulness and made sure they drank down everything in the enamel mugs he filled for them. Then he gave them a ration of chocolate. And then he let them sleep. Outside, the storm was a shrieking wall of ferocious noise. But even after consuming his own rations, Creed felt more dead than alive. He started to unbuckle his rucksack, unconsciousness till this tempest blew over the only imperative in his dull, half-frozen mind.

When the door opened on the wind's roar and a climber came in amid snow flurries, he thought that he was simply hallucinating. Then he saw the snow in the man's beard and the creases of his climbing clothing and realised it was another storm refugee, this one come from a snow-hole he must have dug when the blizzard first descended. Creed, incredulous, asked the man had he been climbing solo.

'No,' he said sadly, shaking his head. 'My comrades all fell.

We were at the summit when the storm hit. We were a party of five. I dug myself in but the weight of snow . . .' He shook his head. 'The face is becoming unstable. Avalanche is inevitable.'

Creed pondered the implications of what he had just been told. They had scant rations and almost no fuel left. They had been travelling very light. The forecast had been good. They had planned logistically for a rapid climb and lightning descent of the mountain. It was how they operated. Everything the regiment did, they did at pace. It was the culture. It meant they were ill-equipped for an elemental siege. But that was what he thought confronted them now. Nobody would be able to climb on the unstable snow to reach and rescue them. The rotors of a helicopter, even the engine noise, would trigger avalanche if what the stranger said was true.

Towards dawn, the storm began to blow itself out. The stranger announced his intention to begin his own attempted descent at first light.

'Will you join me?' he asked Creed, with a grim smile.

Creed looked at his sleeping men and glanced at his watch and made the decision. 'No,' he said. 'They need more rest, at least a couple of hours. Fatigue provokes mistakes and if we make one, we are dead men. We will have to attempt our descent before the afternoon, before the sun hits the face and softens it even further, but my comrades are too exhausted for it yet.'

'They are not as strong as you,' the stranger said.

Creed smiled tiredly at that. 'No,' he conceded, 'they are not. It is why I lead and they follow.'

The stranger took a piece of paper and a stub of pencil from the rucksack he had placed on the table between them. He drew a partial sketch of what lay beyond the door.

'You will follow a funnel down from the hut,' he said. 'It runs for about two hundred metres. When it peters out, you will be tempted to take the snowfield to the left. It is steep, but looks possible. It is not possible. The crevasses make it suicide. Instead, traverse right. The overhang will protect you from snowfalls. It is a difficult traverse, hellish, to be frank. But you will find our ropes secure in the face there to help you. That is the way down.'

Creed studied the sketch, folded it into a pocket and thanked the man, embarrassed that he could not even offer him a brew. He had used the last of their fuel making the soup. They played a couple of hands of cards together. Outside, the wind withered and died against the wooden walls of the hut. Shortly before dawn, on a handshake, the man shouldered open the door and, under a cold sky of crystal clarity, began his precarious, downward trudge.

'And you did get down safely, the three of you?' Monica Stride said.

'We did.'

'And he was dead, wasn't he, the man who helped you?'

'He was, Millie,' Creed said. 'The party of five mountaineers above us all perished. They were still roped together when they were found.'

'How real was he?' Peter said.

Creed sipped water. He had taken no wine with his meal. He would be vigilant tonight.

'He was as real as you are, my lad. I could smell pipe tobacco on his breath. When I shook hands with him, I felt the calluses on his palm caused by handling rope. His name was Hans Pedersen. He came from what your accent suggests is your part of the world, Monica. I identified him from a newspaper photograph. He was a distinguished climber. He was forty-three when he died. And after he lost his life, he saved mine. And I learned from him about my psychic gift.'

There was silence around the table. Dinner was over. It was time. 'I'll escort you to the waiting room,' Stride said.

'It lies half a mile east of here, right?'

'It is, unless you take the scenic route we followed earlier.'

'Enjoy the rest of your evening with your family, Martin. I'll find it OK.'

Aboard the quad bike, in the gloaming, he thought about the story he had just told and its effect. There was certainly no one left alive to contradict it. Pedersen and his party had indeed perished on the peak. Jackson and Clegg had both been killed when the Chinook they were aboard took a direct hit from a surface-to-air rocket in Bosnia in '93. They had found the ropes secured to the face under the overhang and left there by Pedersen's group. They had gambled on the traverse. Most importantly, no one had returned from the dead to quibble with his own somewhat elaborated version of events.

The thing was that he was not going back. In the days of his most desperate media whoring, he had done a pilot for a prospective series called *Soap Shy*. It was the idea of a producer with a coke-addled brain who had read that special-forces soldiers neither washed nor brushed their teeth when they conducted jungle operations. This was because things like talc and deodorant left a strong, tell-tale scent. He thought it would be a hoot to have someone do this selling mobile phones or working as a traffic warden or a bank cashier, just getting filthier and smellier by the day. Creed had been that person. The series, thankfully in retrospect, had never been made. All he had got out of it were a few blackheads and a nasty infestation of lice.

Worse still was *The Poacher*. With the same producer and the same addled thinking, that had been made into a series. He was supposed to use his survival skills to sustain himself without money. The idea was that he would live off the land, avoiding gamekeeper surveillance on country estates to feast on pheasant; that kind of thing. He supposed it might have worked in rural Kent in the summer, living off apples and tomatoes and raiding poly-tunnels for berries. But the filming was done in East Anglia during a bitterly cold January. He ended up shoplifting at four in the morning from the aisles of an out-of-town Tesco superstore. Once, he was so desperate he stole a child's satchel in the hope that it would contain a packed lunch. It hadn't.

The waiting room had come into sight. It was sunset and its roof was the colour of dried blood and its windows were black sockets and Creed shivered. The thing was, he was never going back to being *The Poacher*. It had been made for a junk channel, thank God, and the ratings had been dismal. He had seen the rapt faces of the Stride family around the dinner table as he related his supernatural tale tonight. He was Julian Creed, distinguished ghost hunter, fearless possessor of a proven psychic sensitivity. His name could secure a table at the Ivy even if the booking was made on the day he wanted to eat there. He always polled high in magazine lists of eligible men. He was paid a hundred grand a year just to stay loyal to one brand of wristwatch. He was Julian Creed and for him, there was absolutely no going back.

He looked at the waiting room, climbing off the bike, switching off the ignition. It was curious. His instinct was to take cover, as though vulnerable out here, exposed. It was a feeling he had not felt in civilian life before. He associated it with the obvious risks of being close to the enemy in the field. He looked around, to the tops of the slopes of the shallow glade the railway remnants sat in, at the grass slopes themselves and the blackberry bushes skirting the platform. Everything was still and silent under the vacant sky. And the sense that he was being observed and that the observation was hostile grew stronger in him. And there was no getting away from it. He felt that he was being watched not from out here, but from within the waiting room itself. Maybe a tramp had taken refuge for the night there. Maybe a poacher, he thought. And wouldn't that be ironic? With a grim smile and with darkness gathering, he walked towards his destination.

# Chapter Three

As dusk crept over the Stride domain, Elena Coyle sat at her desk in her flat in Bermondsey, discovering what she could about the life of Professor Edward Brody and his enlightened, even pioneering work at Falcon Lodge. It was a Saturday evening. Outside on Borough High Street, she could hear the throngs of early evening drinkers, gathered outside the pubs, where they could still smoke with impunity. The area was attracting tourists now in numbers, becoming more and more like Covent Garden, which was a shame. When she had moved there at the start of the new century, it had still been something of a secret, which was now sadly no longer the case.

It was not professionalism that made Elena work in her leisure time. It was not dedication or even curiosity. The truth was that she was bored and lonely. The temptation was to open a bottle of wine and switch on the television or slip on a DVD. Or it was to go and sit outside a bar on the river in the mild approaching night with the novel she was halfway through reading. Either scenario involved drink, which was the trouble with both. Drinking alone was not a very clever way of dealing with boredom and loneliness. It would merely exacerbate those feelings. Not immediately, of course, but inevitably and viciously afterwards, when the hangover struck. So she occupied herself with work and Edward Brody, not really expecting to discover anything significant or surprising until the moment that she realised she had.

She naturally assumed ill-health to be the cause of Brody's resignation from his job at Falcon Lodge. He had left in 1924.

He had died ten years later and she had just assumed he had been an invalid for the last decade of his life, perhaps travelling for rest cures to places with clean air or more forgiving climates. Switzerland was a popular choice in the period among consumptives. Robert Louis Stevenson, a famous sufferer, had made the South Seas another fashionable destination for those hoping to ease the burden on their corroding lungs and perhaps prolong the time left to them. But this had not been the case with Brody at all.

She found a letter from Brody to Paley on a website dedicated to debunking psychiatry. The style of the writing seemed to express his authentic voice, but the letter had been written with such bleak and bitter passion that she suspected it might be a forgery. Against this was the fact that Brody's achievements had been obscured or forgotten almost entirely. He was no longer a distinguished name in the history of his discipline. What would be the point of forging a letter in his name? Then she discovered specific references to the same letter in an essay about the significance of Paley's philanthropy. So apparently the letter was genuine. It was dated 6th October 1924. She printed it off and read it again.

Dear Sir Robert,

With a heavy heart but with no real alternative, I feel compelled to offer my resignation with immediate effect. I believe my current state of disillusionment leaves me unable to practise effectively or with the required integrity. Psychiatry requires belief in one's methodology and mine has quite vanished in the circumstances pertaining to my treatment of the patient I shall refer to only as Lady R, but of whose background and character I know you are personally aware.

She is an out-patient now, of course. And I saw her for what has inevitably become the very last of our consultations yesterday evening. I had been treating her for delusions you and I both assumed her to have been labouring under for the past two years. But last night, to my horror, she brought with her the triumphant proof that her claims have all along been true. I say triumphant, but that is wrong. She was triumphant; the proof she exhibited was ghastly and grotesque.

More than most men, I understand the fragility of the human mind. We need our moorings, our foundations, our educations and most profoundly our faith, to enable sanity and rationality to prevail over chaos. Last night, Lady R produced the evidence of her claims about P. And it was irrefutable. And it cost me my faith that I am fit to help anyone achieve recovery from the difficulties afflicting them.

The beliefs that underpinned my world are shattered and unstable now. I cannot continue with my work, much as I have loved it. The ordeal of last night has made it meaningless. I must get away. I do not know to where or for how long I will need to be gone but it is beyond my strength to stay and struggle against this. I thank you from the bottom of my heart for your loyalty and generosity over the past eight years. I hope that you will not think of me that I have betrayed either.

Yours humbly,
Edward Brody

So Brody had treated a woman Paley had known, presumably through their shared social circle. Lady R would have been a woman of prosperity and breeding. Perhaps Paley had even recommended the treatment of whatever they supposed had ailed her mind. But who was this P to whom Brody referred? It was very strange. The tone of the letter was almost hysterical; perhaps Brody himself had been on the brink of breakdown when he wrote it. Mental illness was not contagious like disease, but treating its severe victims for eight years would test a young man struggling with his physical health.

She would have to see if Brody's papers revealed the mystery on Monday. She had that date at the top of the letter to guide her. Would his case notes be so punctiliously compiled as to contain an account of that final session with Lady R? Elena doubted it. But she thought that she probably still had sufficient clues to identify the patient accurately. She looked at her watch. It was a quarter to ten. She had been hard at work for almost three hours. She wondered how Creed would be getting on in his night vigil in the waiting room. He was brave. But it was a crude, unbelieving bravery he possessed where this sort of thing was concerned. It was more smug and ignorant scepticism than authentic courage.

She had her window open a chink. It was a mild evening. She could hear the revelry of Saturday night outside. She thought she might nip out to her local, the Market Porter, for a drink. She would just have the one small glass of white wine. What the hell. Maybe she would go totally to the dogs and have a vodka and tonic. The barman had a friendly face and in her isolation, just seeing his smile and swapping mindless pleasantries would be a comfort to her, she knew. Sometimes life was difficult. You had to take what consolation you could find.

In his regimental days, Creed could recall having slept in far less salubrious conditions than those offered by the waiting room. But he did not intend to sleep for a while yet. In the bag he had brought was a flask of fresh coffee brewed by Monica Stride's own fair hands and he sipped from its screw-on cup, thinking about what an attractive woman she was and how very fortunate his host had been so far in his life generally. He had wealth, contentment and a beautiful family who were devoted to him. He had a very sexy Scandinavian wife. Did he deserve all of this? Not really, he didn't. Nobody deserved such a surfeit of happiness. Despite this conclusion, he thought there was little point in any serious flirtation on his own count with the lovely Monica. It might alienate her, would definitely alienate Martin and could jeopardise the entire enterprise. He was on probation, despite the apparent warmth of the welcome. It would take them a little time to come to trust him fully. And he needed their trust. He needed that to persuade Martin to allow the waiting room to feature as the subject of his show.

Sitting in its still darkness, he thought about the nature of the haunting. He had already decided that the establishing shots should be done during the day and the interiors shot exclusively at night. Just doing that would shift the character of the building abruptly from picturesque curiosity to place of potential menace. The identity of their ghost would depend on what Elena dug up. But it was incredibly promising ground to dig, with the tragedy of the war and the lunatic asylum. They could go for anything from heartfelt loss to gross mutilation to raving insanity. He had an open mind at the moment. But he was leaning towards a post-watershed level of scariness for this one. *The Waiting Room* would be a classic, maybe even an awards candidate.

He sipped coffee and then almost spilled it as that pale flicker occurred in the window for the third or fourth time since he had sat down and unpacked his bag and made himself at home. It was startling. If it caught your peripheral vision, it looked like the looming face of someone watching you. But look back at it and it seemed to dip out of sight. He had decided it must be an oval patch of light-coloured fur, the coat of some nocturnal creature, perhaps a wild cat or hare or even a badger, curious at his unfamiliar scent, drawn by that inquisitiveness to investigate. Stride had told him there were deer on his land. But he had said they did not stray in this direction. It was disconcerting, whatever it was. It spoiled his concentration when it seemed to loom there and this time seeing it had raised the hairs on the back of the hand that held his coffee cup. The curious thing was that it made no sound. It did not scrabble as a badger would. A cat, he decided. They were silent creatures. If he saw it again, the gleam of its eye would probably give it away.

In what scant light there was from the moonless night outside, he could see the gleam of Kitchener's eyes unblinking in their poster on the wall. And it occurred to him for the first time that the furnishings and décor of the waiting room were actually somewhat anachronistic and even odd. The station had been used until the 1960s. But time seemed to have stopped in the building he was in at some point during the Great War. The posters were from that period. The gas light, with its hanging chains, was surely Edwardian. That grim stretcher in the narrow cupboard in the wall had served the asylum, which had closed down and then been demolished in the 1920s. It was as though the waiting room had returned, retreated, to the time of its real validity. It was as though it had stolen or crept through time and slyly restored itself.

He distinctly heard then something approaching from along the platform with a wet and slithery sound. He waited and heard it again, closer, and decided it sounded like something being dragged. Maybe it was the poacher he had earlier suspected, hauling a deer carcase into the waiting room and out of sight of prying eyes for the night. But why would any poacher do that? You would want to be away with your prize under cover of darkness. He heard it again, outside the door now, no more than a few feet away. And he pictured in his mind a young infantryman, left limbless by artillery fire, the bleeding stumps of his legs trailing blood-soaked bandages, being hauled in there by orderlies to await his gibbering ride to the madhouse.

This was bollocks, Creed thought, slamming his cup on the bench with a snort of contempt for himself. And it would not do. He got to his feet and walked outside onto the platform. And all was silence and calm. He walked the perimeter of the platform, smelling the succulent fruit of the thorny bushes that surrounded it, enjoying the sweetness of the berries. He bent down and plucked one and put it into his mouth. It tasted cool and delicious. To the west, he could see the glow of light above where the house would be. Perhaps Monica Stride had crumbled cannabis resin into his coffee. Old rockers thought nothing of getting casually stoned. Maybe they were just obliging a guest. But he knew that wasn't the case as soon as the suspicion occurred to him. Martin Stride was clean and his wife the last woman you would ever describe as a rock chick.

He turned back towards the waiting room. He endured a

shiver that was nothing to do with the cold. It wasn't cold. The place was atmospheric and creepy, was all. It had succeeded in spooking him and stoking his imagination as nowhere previously had. He hoped this sinister aspect to the place would translate to televised pictures. If it did, they had a certain ratings hit on their hands. Word of mouth would compel a weekend repeat. The ad guys could name their own rates. Shale Point station was the creepiest place he had ever visited in his entire life. It was perfect. He collected a handful of blackberries and sauntered back inside.

In the house half a mile away to the west, the children slept. Martin and Monica Stride sat at their kitchen table sipping wine from a shared bottle. They drank sparingly, aware of the strange circumstances of the night, of their illustrious guest and the sober vigil he was enduring on their property.

'I wouldn't be doing it,' Monica said. 'Not for a king's ransom, I wouldn't.'

'He doesn't fear the supernatural as most of us do,' Stride said.

'Nevertheless.'

'And I think he might have a motive other than the fee we're paying him.'

Monica thought about this. She sipped from her glass. 'He must know that he could never persuade you.'

'It's what he does, darling. It's who he is. The penny dropped with his mountain anecdote this evening. He lives for an audience. He needs a crowd.'

'Or a congregation?'

'There might be a bit of that in it, yes. He craves attention. He requires belief. And he probably enjoys a degree of adulation.'

'Did we make an awful mistake, do you think, bringing him here? It was my idea to approach him in the first place, remember.'

Stride reached for her hand across the table. 'We didn't have a choice. What alternative was there?'

'There was the priest,' Monica said.

Stride had omitted to tell Creed about the priest. But Stride had been raised a Lancashire Catholic and a priest had been the first authority he had considered when the waiting room had ceased to be benign. The priest had been summoned after consultation with a Catholic bishop Stride had become acquainted with through his charitable work. He was a Belgian who had spent a lot of his ministry in Africa and he was a veteran and reputedly very powerful exorcist. He came and he looked around the waiting room on a cloudless afternoon a full week before Stride requested and got his audience with the ghost hunter. Afterwards, he took tea in their conservatory. He sipped it from bone china and ate his cucumber sandwiches with his little finger raised. Stride observed that his fingers were deeply nicotine stained. He sat in his black cassock with his biretta on the side table next to his chair. The shoes were heavily polished on his splayed feet.

'I will perform your exorcism,' he said.

'The waiting room is possessed?'

The priest merely stared, coldly. 'You will burn and raze that abominable building afterwards and you will sow the bare ground beneath with salt. Only then will you have rid yourself for ever of the demon.'

But Stride had baulked at this advice. Something about the priest had made him uneasy. He had been an altar-boy as a child and had seen lots of priests, from the heretical old men who still mumbled the Latin liturgy to the whisky-soaked variety, too pissed to separate with their fumbling fingers a single host for consecration when the moment came on the altar for that routine miracle to be performed. His caution arose from a suspicion that the exorcist was unbearably vain. This was borne out when he researched him and discovered the acres of newsprint his adventures in vanquishing evil spirits had generated down the decades. Stride wanted no part of any lurid demonic cabaret on his land. Instead he took Monica's advice, and plumped for Julian Creed.

'Out of the frying pan,' Monica said, reading his thoughts. Except that she said it 'fryink pan'.

Stride laughed and stood and walked around the table and put his arms around her. 'I think Creed has a good heart, under the bluster,' he said. 'I also believe, as you do, that he has the necessary credentials. I just wish he wasn't so gleeful about being famous.'

'There is something childlike about him,' Monica said. 'Maybe that's why the ghosts are attracted to him. Maybe there are fewer barriers between him and them because like a child, he lacks the pervading adult cynicism about the supernatural.'

'A survey done a couple of years ago found that a third of the British population believes in ghosts,' Stride said. 'That's a third of the stodgy, phlegmatic old British. Recent events here have certainly cured any cynicism I might have had.'

Monica turned her head to where the waiting room lay in its vale half a mile to the east of where she sat. 'I wonder if he has experienced anything yet?'

But Stride did not answer her. He was thinking about fame and how much he had come to loathe it. Sometimes he would catch a glimpse of one of the band's old promos on MTV as Peter or Millie channel surfed in the television room and the sight of it would make him almost physically sick. It wasn't that the songs had been bad or the performances embarrassing. Both had dated mercifully well. It was remembering how it had been then, living in the glass bubble of relentless exposure, reading about his fictional antics in the red-tops, coming across his own face on magazine covers on the hoardings outside street kiosks, deflecting invasive questions, dealing with intrusive fans who thought the fact that they had paid for a CD or a concert ticket meant that they owned a piece of his body and an exclusive insight into his soul. God, he had detested it in the end.

He still had his arms around his wife. He bent and kissed her neck. 'Do you know the real reason why I didn't permit the exorcism?'

'Tell me.'

'I don't think what's out there has anything to do with the Devil. If there is anything malevolent out there, and I think there is, it's the work of men, human mischief that caused it. That's what I think. And I don't really think it has anything to do with us.'

'But it can hurt us.'

'Yes,' Stride said. 'I believe it can. But we did not cause or provoke it, I don't think. What I mean is, it's not our fault.'

'Just our bad luck,' said his wife.


Creed dozed. The pale face outside the window was very still now. It could not have been taken any longer for a patch of light fur on the flank of some nocturnal creature. It watched the visitor within and the eyes above its leer of a mouth did not blink. Its features showed no curiosity or surprise. It just watched without any expression at all. Within, under the clear sky in starlight, the shadows deepened and crept.

He was dreaming and the dream was troubled. It was night time and he recognised the terrain. He was at the summit of Mount Tumbledown. All around him, the dead lay shattered and prone in the aftermath of battle. And then they began to move, to twitch and stir and rise, wrestling themselves to their feet. Their wounds gaped and their mouths stretched in silent screams of horror at themselves. And their hands flapped coldly for him as they gathered and encircled and approached. Bone scraped on the ground among those from whom the minefield protecting the peak had taken the legs. They tottered and lunged and he knew that he could not escape their cold embrace of comradeship.

He woke. He remembered where he was. He saw the white blur of that thing outside the window and then it was gone again. He no longer thought it was a cat. It moved too quickly. He stood and stretched out the stiffness inflicted by sleeping on wooden bench slats and then poured the last of Monica Stride's coffee from the flask, gratefully blessing her for it. He looked at the luminous dial of the watch he was paid to wear. The watch was big and robust like he was supposed to be. It was close to four in the morning and the dream was fading. Such nightmares were the price he paid for his past and he did not know any of his old regimental mates who did not sometimes endure them. But that had been a bad one, he thought, as its detail disappeared from his conscious mind.

He noticed then that the windows were black, as though shuttered or painted over. It was odd, because there was sufficient light to see by inside but he could not see out at all. It was impossible, of course, in practical terms. It defied the laws of physics. But he realised he was becoming more accepting of the way the waiting room behaved. It did not submit to practicality. It was not a normal place. He knew that now. He might feel differently about it on a bland afternoon in jocular company. But alone there in the depths of the night, he did not any longer believe the building in which he endured his vigil innocent or benign.

He heard the train, then. He heard its distant approach and the rattle of its weight vibrating the rails that no longer existed outside. The sound of it grew louder and he jumped when its whistle tore the air with a shriek. He could smell hot engine oil and steam and burning coke. Men were being marched on the platform outside. He could hear the thrum of leather-booted feet and the scream of a drill sergeant. A newsboy hawked papers in a piping, unbroken voice. There was a chaos of noise out there. He could see nothing of its cause through the blind window glass.

He approached the door. A clock on the wall that had not

been there before began to toll the hour. The train braked on the platform with a screech and then a whoosh. He heard its heavy doors opening and slamming shut again. There was the shrill of a porter's whistle, harsh laughter, luggage being manhandled, disembodied sobbing. The brass doorknob was in his hand. He turned it.

And dread engulfed him. All the instincts that had kept him alive in conflict seemed to arrive at once in his heart and mind with the urgent command to stray no further from the spot on which he stood. He actually heard the voice in his head, compelling and flat and speaking with utter conviction. *Go out there and there is no coming back*, it said. *Go out there now and you are lost*. He stopped. He grinned; it was ridiculous. Something battered at the door then and he snatched his hand from the knob and recoiled. Outside, something flapped and skittered and he became aware that the railway noises had gone now and silence pervaded generally again.

Creed walked back to the spot next to his bag on the bench with his head bowed. He sat down with his fingers linked between his knees. He closed his eyes and for the first time since childhood, muttered a prayer. He prayed that the thing outside would not get in. The pale-faced thing he had seen when the windows had still allowed him to see outside meant him harm. He knew that now. So he prayed, imploring God to keep him safe until the light came. Please, just until the light came. He thought that he would be all right once light returned to the world. He did not think about the implications of what had happened. He was too stunned and they were too profound for his numbed senses to contemplate yet. That would come. But it would be like being born again and he could not endure just now the necessary trauma of becoming someone new. Now, all he hoped and prayed for were sanity and survival until the morning brought daybreak.

He woke at seven from a dreamless sleep, astonished that he had slept at all. But sometimes sleep was a refuge in itself and there had been no further events after the attempt to get in of the capering thing outside the door. Perhaps his prayer had been answered, he thought grimly to himself. He put his things in his bag and looked out of each window but they all showed the same bland verdant vista to him. So he opened the door and walked out into the warmth and light of the early autumn morning. His stomach grumbled. Strong coffee and wild berries had not been an ideal supper. Once, the combination would not have challenged his digestive system. Perhaps he was getting old.

Something odd had happened to the quad bike. It wore a thick patina of coal-coloured dust and the headlamp was smeared with some sort of grease. There was a tired, industrial smell to the grime layered over the vehicle. Creed cleaned it as best he could with a handful of dewy ferns. Then he started it up and rode it back to the house, wondering what on earth he would tell the Strides about his night ordeal.

He would lie, he decided. The events had bewildered him and his bewilderment in the face of them, if he related them truthfully, would be evident to the Strides. He was here only because of his supposed expertise and in offering a true account of what had happened, he would expose himself as someone as clueless as anyone else in matters supernatural. He would lose his credibility, their respect and any future access to the place in which he had just endured the worst night of his life. There was an authentic mystery here and he wanted to solve it. The first thing he had to do was to rationalise in his own mind what had really happened to him. That would take time and calm reflection. Then he would decide what to do next. But if it was to be his decision, he had to lie in the meantime to Martin Stride.

He wondered if the night's pyrotechnics had impinged upon the Strides themselves, whether they had heard what he had from their home. Even if they had, he could still stick plausibly to a story that nothing had manifested itself within the waiting room. Strictly speaking, that claim was actually substantially true. He decided that he would extemporise, based on what they said to him. He would probably be wise to give them some taste of something otherworldly. Maybe he would tell them about the spectral figure whose pale face he had glimpsed through the window. They could link that to what Peter had seen and drawn and it would make them eager for him to discover more.

Now he was drawing away aboard the bike from the physical reality of that baleful building behind him, he found that his nerve and composure were returning to him. He had undergone a revelation in there. It had terrified him and had he not listened to his instinct and opened the door on the frenetic lost world of that railway platform, it might even have claimed him. But what he actually felt now, overwhelmingly, was a sense of relief. He no longer needed to sustain the fraudulent myth of himself. He had undergone a real psychic experience. It meant he had become at last the man he had for so long claimed to be. That was what he had meant just after waking in his muddled mind about being born. It was like the Van Morrison song, the one on the one Van Morrison album he really liked, the song in which Morrison sang that repeated refrain about being born again. The album was *Astral Weeks* and the song he was thinking of was the title track. Its vibrant, chugging chords and chorus echoed through his mind in the clear bright morning and he realised he was starting to feel happier and more excited than he could ever remember he had in the past.

The revelation he had undergone had another, very significant implication. It changed the role of Elena Coyle in his life quite profoundly. Her job was no longer to provide colour and atmosphere and a sense of factual conviction for essentially fraudulent stories. Her job now was to discover and reveal the events crucial in creating whatever it was he had just authentically experienced. He did not think that she would ever forgive him in her heart for the way he had treated her during their brief romantic liaison. He did not think that he would ever forgive himself. But he thought she might find validation in a job related to truth rather than the propagation of myth.

The Stride family were eating breakfast in the conservatory when he parked up the bike. Monica beckoned for him to join them. They had heard the train the night before. It had woken the parents, though the children had slept through, oblivious. It did not seem to have troubled them unduly. All of them looked far better rested than he felt. Creed said his night had been uneventful, except for the presence of the pale spectre, which apparently wanted to communicate but could not.

Then he surprised himself by saying, 'I'd like to stay there again tonight, if I may. I sense the barrier between me and a psychic breakthrough is gossamer-thin. By tomorrow morning, I might have something of substance for you.'

'It's fine by me,' Stride said. 'Monica?'

Monica shrugged. She blew a strand of hair off her face. In the airy light of the conservatory, to Creed, she looked beautiful. And the events of a few hours ago seemed outlandish and impossible.

'I need to go into town and sort a few things out,' he said. 'I'll return late this afternoon if that's OK.'

It was OK. He ate his breakfast hungrily and winked at Peter and blew a kiss to Millie and was gone.

He pulled into the first lay-by he came upon and called Elena. She answered on the second ring, sounding wakeful and alert. She had lost her past appetite for hard partying. He had cost her that. Good coming out of bad, but little consolation for either of them. 'Can you spare me an hour of your time this afternoon?'

'Sure. I've something interesting to tell you, actually.'

'Likewise. What's the weather like there?'

'It's bright and sunny.'

'I'll meet you outside the Market Porter at noon. We'll

walk and talk and if you're so inclined, I'll buy you some lunch.'

'Walk and talk sounds good.'

'Thanks, Elena. This is your time we're talking about and I appreciate the sacrifice.'

'It's fine,' she said, 'really.'

'It's above and beyond, strictly speaking.'

'Is there any such thing any more? I wouldn't particularly like to be out there just now, looking for another job.'

Resuming the drive back, he tried to think about what he had recently experienced from every possible angle. Perhaps because the act of driving was so practical and mundane or perhaps because the waking day was so open and innocent, he found himself becoming more incredulous at the night's occurrences with every mile he travelled. It had confounded a belief system based purely on what could be proven. It had even provoked him into prayer.

Was there any explanation that did not admit the existence of the supernatural?

There was one. And it needed to be considered. What if he had been the victim of an elaborate practical joke? He had been ruthless in his career in the pursuit of his success. He had made media enemies. Some of them were clever and potentially vindictive. What if he had been covertly filmed begging God to help him after not daring to step out onto the platform? Where would that footage, if broadcast, leave his reputation as the fearless ghost hunter? In ruins, was where.

But he could not really see it. It would require the complicity of the Stride family and Martin and Monica Stride had too much dignity and integrity to get involved in anything so spiteful and puerile. They were his admirers, not his enemies. The Strides and their basic decency was the reason it could not have been a joke played out at his expense. And if he felt reassured by this certainty, it also made Julian Creed feel guilty. This was because he was about to deceive the Strides still further. He was on his way back to London to pick up the miniature camera he would conceal from them and carry in case the vigil of his second night in the waiting room provided him with anything worth filming.

Elena knew straightaway that events had taken a significant turn when she met Creed at noon as arranged. She had in her pocket a print-out of the resignation letter sent to Sir Robert Paley by the Falcon Lodge psychiatrist Edward Brody. She had re-read it several times that morning. Its elliptical language had seemed stranger to her on each reading, begging more questions than answers. Patient confidentiality was a prerequisite of course of a profession Brody had, up to that point, followed with honour and distinction. But he seemed to have been hinting in the letter at something terrible that had shaken him to his core.

As Creed strode along the street towards her, she thought that he looked pretty shaken himself. She had not really wanted to meet him so close to home. The antipathy was natural after what had happened between them but, practically, she had to try to overcome it. It wasn't as though his presence polluted the area. Objectively, he was an attractive man, tall and athletic and with a mane of hair he had grown to give him a sense of theatricality on the screen. She saw people doing double-takes as he passed them on the pavement, approaching her. He seemed for once oblivious to his celebrity. He also seemed to have aged overnight, sullen lines under eyes raw with fatigue and a grim set to his usually smiling mouth.

They walked west, over the riverside cobbles past the Clink and the moored replica of Drake's *Golden Hind*. Creed recounted the events of the previous night, leaving nothing out. They had reached Gabriel's Wharf by the time he had finished, and found a bench on the edge of the river and sat.

The tide was out. Elena looked down at water-rotted pilings and slabs of stone from ancient moorings there. She produced Brody's letter and Creed took it from her and read it and then folded the paper and put it into his pocket.

'I'm going back tonight,' he said. 'The Strides are amenable. I'm taking the button-hole camera. It's what I came back for.'

'They're amenable to filming?'

'No. They're not.'

She said nothing for a moment. A tourist boat with a double hull passed, going eastward on the river, and people aboard waved at the bank pointlessly. 'This has gone way beyond the ethics of breaching the Strides' privacy, Julian. Everything is different now. I have a hunch Brody's letter is the clue to something really significant and also pretty ghastly.'

'I may discover whether it is tonight.'

'I'm amazed you're prepared to do it.'

He smiled at her. 'I'm the fearless ghost hunter, remember? I'm the intrepid and relentless character who solves these mysteries.'

'But this is different. We didn't create this. This is real. And I have the sense also that it is very dangerous.'

He looked at her directly and the look on his face was tired but open. 'I think it is dangerous too. I'm not stupid. But events are escalating on the Stride domain. After a very long and peaceful interlude, things are astir at Shale Point. Something with real momentum is happening around that abandoned building. People have waited a long time for conclusive proof of the paranormal. They want it. I'm the man who is going to give an impatient world something it craves. It won't just be vindication for me, Elena. It will change the world's perspective on reality.'

Elena was quiet. Then she said, 'Life was more comfortable twenty-four hours ago when all this stuff was yarns we concocted and clever Alison Slaney's digital effects.'

Creed nodded. 'It was more comfortable then. It is vastly more interesting now.'

This time he did not take the quad bike. He had the curious feeling it had caused offence. Not in the emotional, but in the physical sense of offending. It had been an affront to the world that had briefly re-established itself outside the waiting room. It had very definitely not belonged.

Stride walked with him on the half-mile journey. Once again, he carried the fortification of a flask of Monica's coffee in his bag. This time, he was wearing his Van Helsing suit. He felt that he needed his armour after the previous night. The miniature camera was concealed under his right coat lapel. He felt tired and excited but not really afraid. He felt there were rules or conventions surrounding what he could and could not do when the psychic phenomena occurred and that, last night, he had almost breached them. He needed to be extremely careful. He needed to keep his composure in the face of manifestations that felt quite terrifying. But if the force confronting him had wanted only his life, it could have taken it. It was certainly strong enough to have done that.

They stopped walking. They were there. Stride looked at him and the look was appraising. 'I think you are a very brave man, Mr Creed,' he said.

Creed hefted the bag in his hand, acutely aware of the camera concealed beneath his lapel.

'You haven't been at all truthful about what you experienced here last night, have you?'

Creed tried to smile but his mouth was dry and his lips felt glued to his teeth. 'Why do you think that?'

'You didn't see yourself this morning. We did. You looked a fright. I think you'd had one. Monica is of the same opinion and my wife is a very intuitive woman.'

'Your point being?'

'More than anything, Julian, I care for the wellbeing of my

family.' He nodded towards the waiting room. The light was going. Creed could see lines of concern etched in the skin around his eyes. 'If the thing here is malevolent, if it means my family harm, I need to get them away.'

'You engaged me because you love your home,' Creed said. 'I don't believe, in the confines of your home, you will come to any harm tonight. I think you will be safe and untroubled. In the morning, I think I will have a clearer picture of what it is we are dealing with. Then, I think, will be the time to make a decision. Trust me till morning.'

Stride did not answer. He merely reached out his hand and Creed shook it and then he turned and began the walk back to the house.

Nothing happened until almost one o'clock in the morning. The pale and sly apparition appeared a few times on the edge of his alert vision outside the windows, but Creed tried to ignore the troubling sensation seeing it brought to the skin on the back of his hands and his scalp. Then, just before one, he heard a train approaching. It sounded like a smaller engine this time, a local service that had once run on the scheduled timetable perhaps, rather than the coal-hungry beast of the previous night, with its monstrous tonnage of troop wagons. Its arrival at the platform outside was sedate. And the windows allowed a glimpse of it. He saw steam briefly engulf the platform and a trail of sparks from a puffing funnel against its roiling grey.

There was the sound of the shrill guard's whistle to signal the engine's departure. There was the sound of the train slipping away, the vibrant song it sang on the rails he knew weren't there silenced to an eventual hush. And then he heard footsteps, clipped and precise on the flags of the platform, approaching. There was a pause, a tiny hesitation in time itself, it seemed to the building's occupant. And then the door opened and a figure entered.

# Chapter Four

She was tall and strikingly attractive and was attired in period clothing. A blue wool coat reached down almost to the top of buttoned leather boots. A cloche hat covered her head. She carried a handbag and a furled umbrella. She was sobbing quietly and as she put down her things at a spot on a bench and took off her hat and shook out her heavy mane of auburn hair, Creed became conscious that she was quite unaware of his presence. She sat and he studied her. She was strong-featured, with sculpted lips and sharp cheekbones. Her eyes were the same cornflower blue as her coat. Her lips were red, he thought from being bitten rather than from anything applied to embellish them. She had bitten her lips in an attempt at restraining her emotions. But the effort had been unsuccessful. She slipped off a pair of pale leather gloves. She was not attired in mourning but brightly styled, the furled cloth of her umbrella a bold purple. But she seemed grief-stricken, nevertheless.

Creed realised with a start that the gas lamps above them had come on. Their fuel gave off a slight odour and brightened and gave colour to the waiting room. The room itself seemed to have gained a sudden lustre where before it had been faded and drab. Paint looked freshly applied. The windows had a polished sheen. He could smell disinfectant as though from a recent mopping of the floor. There was, too, a floral scent. He lifted his eyes and saw baskets of fresh blooms hanging from angle-iron frames in each corner. As though from a recent watering, they drip-dripped softly onto the floor, forming little puddles beneath each one. It was as though in experiencing a visit from the dead, the place had come to life. And the woman in front of him was dead, he was sure. The ensemble she wore put her at the latest in the 1920s. Alison Slaney's ghosts were not like this. They were grainy and groaning and always furtively glimpsed escaping the edge of the frame. He had the strong suspicion that if he rose and reached for the cheek of this woman, the flesh would be warm to his touch. He had the feeling, too, that if he did that, she would scream. This was because there was no question, he was invisible to her.

She unbuttoned her coat. Beneath it, he saw an ivory blouse buttoned to the throat and worn over that, a heavy double-rope of black beads. She wore a skirt with a hem almost the length of her coat and had a very slender waist. His military training had made him an expert judge of those he observed and he put her age at around thirty-eight. She took a silver case of cigarettes from her bag and screwed one into a tortoise-shell holder and lit it with a tiny petrol lighter. She drew deeply on the cigarette and when she exhaled, the sound of her breath emerged from her like despair and she started to cry again and held her free hand over her face in a gesture so broken Creed felt it committing a violation just to witness the woman's anguish.

He switched the camera on. It made no noise. The available light from the gas burning in the mantel above them was more than sufficient for so sensitive an instrument to record excellent pictures. There was no ambient sound, no background noise. The woman's every utterance would be picked up clearly by the microphone. All Creed had to do was to stay still and he did so, unblinking, his breath shallow and his heart steady as he fought the exultant thrill of the thought that he might be making history.

She stood and began to pace. He heard the swish of her skirt and felt the faint draught from her trailing coat as it fanned the air. He could smell too the strong, rich tobacco of the cigarette she had lit. She began to speak, to talk to herself in low, confidential utterances that seemed to make little sense. She was mad, after all, Creed thought. She was here because of the asylum. She was an inmate, or about to become one. But if that was the case, where were the restraints? Where were the warders with their straitjacket and manacles and rubber clamp to stop the woman biting off her tongue? Mysteries for later and for Elena, he thought. His job now was simply to film and to record. And he did, as the pacing and the moaning became more restless and frenetic and then abruptly, the woman paused. She grinned. And the grin appeared as painted on and lurid as the grin of a clown on a circus poster and her eyes glimmered and Creed felt a chill of foreboding.

'Is there somebody here?'

He said nothing. He sat, frozen.

'There's someone here, isn't there?'

He thought about trying to communicate. But the same instinct for survival that had told him the previous evening not to open the waiting room door was just as insistent now. He should stay still and silent. It was not what the Strides required of him, quite the opposite in fact. They wanted information and reassurance that their home was free of menace and they wanted beyond that, precise detail about what had caused the psychic activity here to suddenly erupt in the spectacular way that it had. All in good time, he thought. The febrile spirit in front of him, so corporeal he could smell the fresh sweat under her heavy perfume, was not a safe subject to contact, much less to interrogate. He had shamelessly faked his knowledge of and credentials over the spirit world. But he felt he was learning quickly about the caution necessary to handle it safely.

The woman tilted her head. She clasped her hands together and turned her shoulders back and forth in a gesture reminiscent of a little girl waiting in anticipation of a treat. She smiled and raised her eyes and was the little girl no longer but coquettish, spoiled. 'It's you, isn't it, Patrick, darling. It is, isn't it? It's you.'

No one replied to her. There was no one to reply. And then very slowly, Creed twisted his own head to face the window at his rear. He had become aware of being watched. It was the pale shape he had seen so furtively and that had made his scalp crawl and the hairs stiffen on the back of his hands. And it was furtive no longer. It was Peter's sketch come to pallid, leering life. It grinned emptily at him. The woman strode to the waiting room door and flung it wide. The air outside was grey, soot-spangled. It smelled of sulphur and cordite and under those strong odours, subtle and rank with decomposition. She had not seen the face at the window. He did not understand why, but it was apparently as invisible to her as he was.

'Patrick!' she said. 'My darling, please come to me.'

Creed closed his eyes and awaited the slither on the platform of the thing's boots as it came, summoned by this command. But he heard only silence.

'Patrick!' the woman said. And her voice was abject once more with loss. Creed opened his eyes. She reached for the handle and slowly pushed the door closed. He looked out of the window again but the apparition had gone. The woman gathered her things. She made ready to leave. Creed noticed that the lamplight was fading and that the petals of the flowers in their hanging baskets had started to curl. The puddled water under them smelled sharply stagnant now. The woman had a crushed, defeated posture as she buttoned her coat and put on her hat. She had been brought beyond hope, Creed thought, and also beyond the spilling of further tears. The light had diminished from the lamp almost completely and the approach of her train was a mournful rumble on the tracks when she slipped out of the door. She was not going to the home for lunatics after all. This had been her destination, the location for her failed assignation.

Creed waited for a while after the woman's departure for Peter's apparition to join him. He did not relish the idea of its company. In fact, he faced the prospect with a feeling of dread purer and stronger than anything he had felt so far in the strange place the Shale Point waiting room had become. But no one else came in. And he was fortified by careful rations of Monica Stride's coffee. And eventually the dawn arrived. He unclipped the camera from his lapel and put it into his breast pocket. He ventured outside. The sweet, cloying smell of the ripe berries was strong on the platform in a playful gust of wind. He could smell approaching autumn in the brackish odour of turning leaves on the branches of restless trees. And there was a freshness that almost bordered on a chill to the morning once he leapt down from the plat-form and began to walk through the vacant land. It was as though the further he got from the waiting room, the more alive he became. It was a place of contagion, he thought with a shudder, and a repository also of despair. Elena Coyle, who had never even seen it, had said that to him. And she had been dead right.

He told Martin Stride about the woman. He did so out of earshot of the children. He had shared a room with a ghost, it was unequivocally true. The children knew who he was, what he did. But it was different, hearing that a place familiar from play was haunted. It was not like visiting somewhere remote through the miniaturised distance of your television. He did not want to frighten Peter or Millie. And he did not think his ghost's distress an appropriate subject for them to hear about, either. It had been so deep and abject it had driven her mad. That was why she had been there. That was his supposition, anyway. She had come and departed again on a train serving a line that no longer existed. But the long-demolished madhouse had to be the reason her ghost had been familiar in the first place with the station.

'Did she communicate with you?'

'No. She sensed I was there. But she could not get beyond the barrier of her grief.'

They were walking amid the gnarled and twisted orchard boughs. Stride stopped. 'What do you think was the cause of this grief?'

'I'd guess she lost a husband or a son in the fighting at the Front. Grief had pretty much engulfed the nation by 1916 and it did not really lessen or recede until after the Spanish 'flu pandemic at the very end of the conflict.'

'Jesus,' Stride said. 'What an awful period to live through.'

'People were more stoical then, better disciplined emotionally.'

'Or simply more accepting,' Stride said. 'A grateful nation gave Field Marshal Haig five million pounds raised by public subscription. And Haig's bankrupt tactics had been largely responsible for the losses on the Somme.'

'So you know a bit about the history of the Great War.'

'I'm not completely ignorant.'

'Only about the part your waiting room played in it.'

Stride folded his arms across his chest. 'Bring me up to speed then,' he said.

'It was a hub of troop movement. It was the stopping off point for a local lunatic asylum.'

'I know about the asylum. It was demolished back in the 1920s. And the Great War was concluded more than ninety years ago. We have lived here for a decade in tranquillity. Why is all this happening now?'

Creed was very aware of the camera in his pocket. 'I don't know,' he said, looking east through the orchard trees. 'But I promise you I'll find out.'

'We're going away,' Stride said.

'You can't.'

'We can. And it's just for a week, from this afternoon. Peter's class are going to the Isle of Wight on a school trip. Monica and I are among the parent volunteers helping out.

74

We're taking Millie, of course. We'll do alternate days of helping with the class so Millie will always be with one of us. I like the Isle of Wight. Ventnor is one of my favourite places in the world.'

'You can do the Tennyson Trail,' Creed said.

'You know the Island?'

'I'm no longer as close to my father as I was,' Creed said. 'It's his choice and a long story. But when I was a child, we used to go to Freshwater Bay for holidays and I've some very fond memories of the place.' He realised that this was the first unequivocally truthful sentence he had yet spoken to Martin Stride and the knowledge made him feel suddenly ashamed in the gaze of the honest and dignified man in front of him. He remembered then that Stride had endowed the library at Peter's school. And that he had done so anonymously. 'I expect you'll be relieved to get away.'

'I'd rather you didn't prowl about the place in our absence, Julian. Can you bear to wait for our return?'

Creed nodded. He thought that he could. There was plenty of stuff to unravel about this mystery beyond the baleful reach of the waiting room itself. The last two nights, revelatory and terrifying, had taken their toll. He would be glad of the excuse for a rest from it, he realised. It would rejuvenate him and ready him for the remainder of the challenge. Today was Monday. He would view the film on the camera as soon as he got to his office. He might get Alison Slaney and Tony Pullen and Mickey Joyce in to view it too. First though, he would watch it with Elena. She was his confidante. She might resent and even hate him, but she was still the closest thing he had to an ally in this enterprise.

He remembered the reason for the estrangement from his father, then. And he was forced to admit to himself that this was not turning out to be the proudest morning of his life. Only twenty-four hours earlier, he had felt re-born, exultant. But he'd been enervated by that watching face, with its soulless stare and vacant grin outside the waiting room window. And he felt bruised by the exhibition of raw grief he had been subjected to in there for what had seemed like hours. And he felt ashamed of the betrayal the camera in his pocket represented.

Elena went straight to the War Museum. She was permitted to see the Edward Brody archive after filling in a few forms. It was intensely disappointing. There were no case notes. There was just a long and fusty paper on the treatment of neurasthenia generally. And there was an essay on the supposed effects of exposure to the noise of prolonged artillery bombardments on the central nervous system. It was dry, theoretical and totally impersonal stuff. She had been hoping for individual case studies and anecdotal colour, for a cache of psychiatric gossip. All she learned was that if you lived with the sound of Howitzer shells detonating close by for sixty hours, you could expect to get tremors in your hands. It seemed too obvious a point to be worth the writing up.

There were fifty or so letters from grateful soldier patients he had successfully treated. Elena thought it a distinctly mixed blessing, being made well enough to be sent back to the fighting conditions that had unmanned you in the first place. But she was a twenty-first-century cynic and these had been for the most part patriotic young men who believed in the nobility of their cause. Nevertheless, she could not help wondering how many of these men, expressing their effusive thanks, had survived till the armistice. The letter cache reminded her of how much social habits had changed over the years. People had written letters then. It was an obligation and sometimes an art. Almost nobody wrote them any more.

There was a studio portrait of Edward Brody. His lung disease had made a thin man of him by the time of its taking, but consumptives were usually thin. She thought he would have looked boyish, had he been healthier. He had a mop of unruly curls and smooth, unlined features. He looked a bit like someone you might expect to see in a church choir, except for his tweed suit and high starched collar. He was pictured too in a group shot in black-tie. The rear of this photo was helpfully captioned and dated in fading pencil, and the other people in it had a glamour and sense of importance the self-effacing Brody totally lacked.

The group he was among were his patron, Sir Robert Paley, Sir Samuel Ross and his wife, Lady Ross, and someone called Mr Bruno Absalom. They were pictured seated at a formal dinner and they looked imposing and prosperous and Brody looked more than ever a boy among them. Paley was clear-eyed and serene. Sir Samuel and Lady Ross made a very handsome couple indeed. Absalom, with his dark features and heavy moustache, looked of Mediterranean origin. 'Johnny Foreigner,' Elena said to herself, remembering the xenophobia of the period. The date on the picture was 1918. The time of the Great War had not been a comfortable one in England for men who looked like Bruno Absalom. There was presence and glamour and more than a touch of the exotic about him. She wrote down his name in her notebook. Though she did not really need to, as it was not the sort of name she thought she would easily forget. He intrigued her more than anyone in the picture, certainly more than the ailing psychiatrist. She sought permission to scan the photographs and it was given and she emailed both to her office address.

When she got to the office, she went in to see Creed, who looked as disappointed as she felt by her wasted morning's work. It was twelve thirty when she arrived, almost lunchtime. She had walked in the morning from her flat to the War Museum on a very light breakfast and felt hungry. But she knew he might have filmed something important and knew that she would be expected to watch it with him.

'How was the waiting room?'

He sat back in his chair and rubbed his eyes. 'It's thrown up a technical challenge.'

'Oh?'

'The War Museum?'

She briefed Creed on the little she had discovered. He just nodded his head distractedly. 'I think I'll take an early lunch,' she said.

'Meet me in the edit suite at two,' he said. She nodded. So there was something to see. He had been successful in breaching the trust of Martin Stride and filming something during his second night spent on the Stride estate.

The figure of the woman was a pale, insubstantial blur, her voice just a series of incomprehensible moans that seemed dragged through time and degraded. When she moved, the movement was spasmodic and unnatural, like a puppet moving unstrung through a mist. Of the waiting room itself, no background detail at all was apparent.

'It's terrifying,' Elena said.

'It's no bloody good at all,' Creed said. 'It's useless.'

'It looks real, Julian. It looks like a real spectre, the genuine article, with the ripples of movement, the way that awful voice ululates.'

Creed sighed. 'It looks like what Alison has conditioned you to think of as a spectre. It sounds like the programme we make has prepared you to expect a ghost to sound. I shared that room with the woman on that screen and she was as real and vital and vivid to me as you are now. There must be something wrong with the lens or the memory or the chip in that camera. What a wasted bloody opportunity. I'll have to give it to the tech boys, see if they can't do some digital enhancement. We must be able to salvage something out of this.'

But Elena did not think they would be able to. She did not think that the camera was at fault. She did not think the woman whose faded image occupied the screen had come to the Shale Point waiting room at all the previous night. She had never been in the present, had she? Creed had instead been shunted into the past. And the journey had done for the film in the camera because the camera was an affront to the world Creed had been transported to. The camera had endured something similar to the insult suffered by the quad bike. And if she was right, and Creed had been taken to some long-ago limbo of human despair, the danger to him was all the greater. He was of the present. And the present was an affront the past could not in nature tolerate.

It was just a theory. She would not share it yet with her boss. He had told her about the Isle of Wight trip before switching on the film. There was a week to wait before he risked another visit to the Stride domain. Perhaps she would have to tell him, but she wouldn't do so yet. She needed some substance, some reasoning before she could do that. He had recently come to believe in ghosts, but the notion of slipping through time he would dismiss as crude science fiction. His belief in ghosts was not a matter of faith or imagination, after all. It had been forced on him. He believed only because he had been obliged to.

'You got nothing at all at the museum, then?' He had frozen the image on the screen. It looked arrested there, like a thick rope of smoke coloured cornflower blue. There was a purplish smudge halfway up its length. You would not have called it human, let alone female.

'I'll show you what I got,' Elena said. She went over to the laptop in the corner of the edit suite and accessed her email and opened up the group shot of Brody and his table in their formal attire. She heard Creed rise up out of his seat behind her. He approached and she heard him gasp. She turned and he was as pale as she had ever seen him.

'That's her,' he said, pointing with a shaking finger at the picture retrieved from the War Museum. 'That's the woman I saw weeping in the waiting room last night.'

'Mary. Lady Ross,' Elena said.

'Who was she? What's her story?'

'I have not the faintest idea. At least, not yet, I don't.'

Creed was breathing heavily. He was sweating at the hairline. He looked to Elena like he'd seen a ghost and she almost made the joke out loud but thought that it might possibly cost her a job. He was not in the mood to appreciate humour, least of all at his own expense.

'You're sure it's her?'

'Print it off. Use the colour printer.'

'It's a black and white shot.'

'Yes. But full-colour black and white has more detail.'

She did as he had told her to and went to get the hard copy from the printer. When she came back, she looked at the frozen image on the big viewing screen against the far wall. She could have sworn the shape projected there had moved. *It has squirmed*, she thought. *It shouldn't be there. It is not of this world. The colour will fade from it. It will shrink and recede and bleach to nothing. It will escape.*

Creed snatched the print from her hands. He studied it. He switched on a lamp and they looked at it together.

'She's very poised and beautiful,' Elena said. 'That's her husband, to her right, Sir Samuel Ross. That's the psychiatrist, Brody, on her left.'

'And the picturesque fellow seated next to Sir Samuel?'

'Bruno Absalom. I know nothing about any of them. But I promise you, I will by tonight.'

'She was very beautiful,' Creed said. 'But she wasn't very poised, not when I saw her last night. She was disconsolate.'

'I'll get on it,' Elena said.

Creed grunted something unintelligible and ran his hand through his hair.

'Go back to your flat and sleep, Julian. You look tired out.'

'I'm going to go to the gym,' he said. 'I'll see you back here for a de-brief at five thirty?'

'Fine,' she said.

He had this saying from his regimental days, she remembered: 'There's plenty of time for sleep when you're dead.' She stole a glance at the fading apparition on the big screen over on the far wall, thinking that it might not after all be true. But he honestly looked like the gym was the last thing he needed. He looked exhausted.

He was a member of two gyms and both memberships, of course, were complimentary. He went to Gym-Box in Holborn to hit the bag and speedball and skip with the heavy leather rope that gave him the muscle definition in his upper arms and shoulders that helped make him what one tabloid rag had termed the Housewives' Choice. But his preferred gym most days was the Third Space in Soho. He liked the illusion that his time was so precious he could not afford to travel for exercise further afield from his place of work. He liked the beaming, obsequious smiles on the faces of the reception staff. He liked the way that the other recognisable faces in there, the celebrity chef and the breakfast show presenter and the quasi-famous actresses, acknowledged him. They were people from his world of restaurant reservation shortcuts and tacit London Marathon pre-inclusion and televised charity campaigns and he was happy among them and even grateful for their complicity in the whole wonderful business of being apart from the proles outside in the hopeful, desperate streets.

In the Third Space, he lifted heavy metal for an intense ninety minutes and thought about his relationship with his father. Stride's talk of Ventnor and the Isle of Wight in the morning had brought his father to the forefront of his mind. The old man was approaching eighty now and he was his only child. The feud between them had been going on for five years. His dad thought him thoroughly demeaned by his ghost hunting antics, by his persona as an investigator of the paranormal. Exploiting gullibility, he called it, when he wasn't calling it media prostitution. His dad had sustained and added to the family fortune the traditional way, wearing a pinstriped suit in the City. Five years ago, he had cut his son out of his will. The only positive was that he had not gone public on the breach between them. He was too disdainful of the press for that and it was a small mercy Creed was grateful for.

Perhaps, when he produced incontrovertible proof that ghosts existed, they would be reconciled. But he thought probably not. His appetite for fame was distasteful to his father. In temperament, his father was more similar to Martin Stride than to himself. That was kind of odd, because Stride's roots were solidly working class and his father's route to the Square Mile had been the traditional and privileged one of Eton and the Guards. But they shared the same fastidious, slightly snobby attitude to notoriety. It hurt Creed that he did not have a relationship any longer with his father. He remembered the occasion a decade and a half earlier when he had picked up his gallantry award in a private ceremony in honour of the covert job he had distinguished himself carrying out in Sarajevo. It had been the last time he had seen his father take any pleasure in his accomplishments. His father had been very proud that day, fingering the medal on its coloured ribbon, beaming at him. Now, by contrast, he was embarrassed and ashamed of his only son.

He took a sauna after his workout. He had not bathed in the morning, in the guest room Stride had given him. He had been too anxious to hurry back with his secret, damaged film. In the heat and steam of the sauna, he saw that an oily layer of grime was oozing out of his skin and sitting on its surface. It had a sheen to it, like coal tar or something. And it carried an industrial stink. He had smelled it before, he remembered, trying to clean the soiled quad bike with a handful of wet ferns. Fortunately he was alone in the sauna and so no one was there to see this strange stain emerging from him. He took a scalding shower until his skin glowed pink and the stuff was washed down the drain and away.

He went to his club. There was lots of other stuff he could have done. When he switched his BlackBerry back on after taking it from his locker and leaving the gym, it positively sang with neglected texts and email messages. There was plenty for him to do in the office. But he could concentrate on none of it. He needed Elena's information about Mary Ross. She was all he could think about, in her spectral distraction and ghostly misery of the early hours of the morning in the waiting room. He wanted her pain explained, her loss justified and her mystery solved. He had to think of a way to safely break the barrier between the living and the dead and communicate with her. He could not do that without knowing her secrets. He would talk to Tony Pullen and Mickey Joyce about why the attempted filming had produced such poor results. But he had a hunch that Lady Ross's story would, eventually, have his audience gripped as he had never gripped them before.

He nodded to the director with the heavy coke habit he had once tried to wean off drugs on the treadmill and the stationary bike. They still talked sometimes. But they didn't talk about the director's habit or his own past occupation. He waved at the weather girl who was an object of desire on every building site from Edinburgh to Torquay. He knew that she preferred women, had been in a steady relationship with her hairdresser for more than a decade. But the red-tops were happy to peddle her salacious myth in frequent, sexy photo-shoots. Good on her. You had to make a living. Her looks weren't going to last for ever. You made hay while the sun shone. She had a degree in meteorology so knew better than most that it wasn't going to go on shining on her indefinitely. He kept looking at his watch. He thumbed up his father's number on his BlackBerry screen. But he did not attempt to put through a call. He drank filter coffee and ate a tiny serving of Caesar salad and listened in the fashionable gloom to Norah Jones and Madeleine Peyroux until it was time to go back to his office and discover whatever Elena Coyle had learned.

Sir Samuel Ross had been a very wealthy man. The Great War had made him even wealthier. In the year the Germans widened the Kiel Canal, in the escalation that preceded the outbreak of actual conflict, he had invested heavily in the development and manufacture of high explosives. He held a number of important patents. By 1916, relentless massive bombardment and the laying of huge underground mines were seen as the only viable tactics in ending the stalemate of the Western Front. Hundreds of thousands of tons of artillery shells were being manufactured in factories commandeered for the purpose. There was no such thing as a licence to print money, Elena told Creed. But by then, Sir Samuel was as close to any man in England to having one.

He also had a conscience. It was how he came to be friendly with Sir Robert Paley. Paley was an expert at philanthropy and Ross sought him out to ask him how most effectively he could begin to give his money away. He built hospitals. He funded medical research. He paid for missionaries to take vaccines to far flung places afflicted by disease. He had lifeboats and rest homes and sanatoria built. He endowed scholarships.

'Did all that compensate for the slaughter he enabled?'

Elena shook her head. They were in Creed's office. Her notes were spread across his desk, at which she was seated. He was in the chair Stride had occupied on his visit. She looked at the picture taken in the Falklands on the wall. It was hard not to look at it. It was positioned cleverly to claim the eye, hung against white space.

'It wasn't seen that way at all,' she said. 'Sir Samuel was already a hero in the public mind. His scientific ingenuity was helping win the war. In beating the Hun, Britain was saving the world from the spread of barbarism and his was a crucial role in achieving the victory. No one back in those days ever accused Alfred Nobel or Hiram Maxim of mass murder. Attitudes to war were different. Anyway, how long have you been a pacifist?'

'It's the scale of the slaughter,' Creed said. 'It's just the war to end wars that did nothing of the sort, the old clichés, the futility.' He was thinking of his dream of two nights ago, of the cold reach of dead and mutilated comrades on his own battlefield. 'What happened to Mary Ross, Elena? She lost someone, didn't she? Who did she lose?'

Elena lifted a printed-off picture from the desk and Creed reached for it. It showed Sir Samuel and Lady Ross against a screen and flanked by ornate pillared plant pots. Between them was a boy posing proudly in a uniform.

'Patrick Ross,' Elena said. 'He was believed to have been killed in an assault on a German-held position in the last days of the war. It was the same action that claimed the life of the poet, Wilfred Owen.'

'The Sambre Canal, near Ors,' Creed said. 'Owen was leading units of the Second Battalion, Manchester Regiment when he was hit by machine gun fire. It was a week before the German surrender.'

'You sound as though you know a lot about him.'

'Show me an old soldier who doesn't know his Owen and I'll show you a liar. Or an illiterate,' Creed said. 'That man knew the truth about war.'

Elena looked at him, looking at the picture of the Ross family. It was funny, how little he spoke about his own military past. He traded heavily on a sort of machismo and bravura but she could not remember his ever once recalling verbally a single factual detail from his decade-plus of active service as a soldier. He'd make the odd cryptic remark about Chinooks or field rations. But he gave away nothing autobiographical. Perhaps there were secrets he harboured for a reason. Maybe there was just something of himself he needed to keep private for the sake of what little self-respect he still possessed.

He put the picture back on the desk. 'Believed to have been killed, you say. You mean he wasn't?'

Elena related what she had learned with certainty. Patrick was Lady Ross's only child. She had been eighteen when he was born in the spring of 1900. He enlisted at the age of eighteen in the last months of the war. He was reported killed in one of its last engagements. Unable to reconcile herself to the loss, driven mad by grief, she was admitted to the asylum run by Edward Brody in 1921. Sir Samuel's philanthropist friend, Sir Robert Paley, had no doubt recommended it as a place where humane and enlightened conditions and effective treatments were what patients could expect.

'Inmates,' Creed said. 'People housed in asylums were inmates, not patients. She wouldn't have been there by choice. Her husband must have had her committed.'

This was true. She had been committed at the age of thirty-nine in 1921. In 1924, she made the claim that Patrick had not been killed in the war but was still alive. She manifested no other sign of madness, but stubbornly persisted with this claim. Sir Samuel had divorced her by then. He died of a fatal stroke at the age of forty-eight in 1924. Grief for his lost son as well as his former wife's insanity was said to have compounded the problems afflicting his heart. And that was the extent of what factual information Elena had been able to discover over the course of the afternoon.

'So we have Brody's Lady R and we know the identity of P,' Creed said.

'Yes. I think we do.'

'No thanks to Brody himself. You've done really well, Elena.'

'Sir Samuel was an important man. It's all in the public

domain. It's my job to know where to look,' Elena said. But she was pleased at the compliment. Creed did not offer them without justification.

He got up and leaned over the desk and looked at what she had assembled there. He picked up the picture taken at the dinner in 1918 in which he had first identified Lady Ross as the woman in the waiting room. He studied it afresh. 'Happy days,' he said. 'This was taken before her son's death. She's serene as well as beautiful in this shot, poor thing.'

'Thank God they didn't have a crystal ball.'

'On the contrary,' Creed said. 'If they had, they wouldn't have let him go.'

Elena was silent.

Creed continued to study the picture. 'What about Bruno Absalom?'

'He might have a part to play in the story and he might not. All I know about him so far is that he and Sir Samuel were undergraduates together at Cambridge. They both studied chemistry. I think it's safe to assume they were friends. But Bruno Absalom and whatever mystery he represents is my project for tonight.'

'No hot date?'

'No. No hot date.'

'One could be arranged, you know.'

She smiled at him, but the smile was not one of amusement. 'Let's just carry on as though you never said that, Julian.'

'I'm sorry,' he said. 'Sorrier than I can say.'

'Yes,' she said. 'I'd imagine we both are.'

Sir Samuel had been plain Sam Ross at Cambridge, a bright scholarship boy from Manchester. Bruno Absalom had been born in Italy, at the family estate about thirty miles from Rome. He was very wealthy and the wealth was dynastic, princes and cardinals featuring in his illustrious family history. He had been a flamboyant presence at the university, collecting

Pre-Raphaelite art and founding a society in 1898 called the Night Brotherhood. The society had been secret, as these undergraduate cults had tended to be in Victorian times. There were rites of initiation, elaborate costumes and nocturnal rural gatherings.

But the Night Brotherhood never got into any trouble with the university authorities. Elena pictured sexually confused young men dressed in wizards' robes chartering a charabanc to take them to Tintagel or Stonehenge for a decadent picnic. A picture taken of Bruno at the time pretty much confirmed this. He had a Pre-Raphaelite head of dark curls and was dressed in what King Arthur and his Round Table knights probably wore when they weren't buckled into armour on their Grail Quest. The 1890s had been a florid time. Bruno Absalom had been very much a young man of it.

And the Brotherhood had not interfered with his academic work. He had been a brilliant chemist, achieving distinctions again and again in his course work. This seemed to be the one thing he had in common with Sam Ross. As far as Elena could discover, Ross had been a rather conservative character and certainly not a member of Absalom's Brotherhood. But the two had nevertheless become friends and for over a year had lodged together at a mill house Absalom had rented at a secluded spot on the banks of the Cam. They had collaborated on a couple of projects and sold a chemical formula to a stone quarrying company for quite a lot of money. This had earned them a rebuke from the university authorities but they had avoided any disciplinary action such as suspension or, obviously, expulsion. There was nothing in detail for Elena to discover about how things had been smoothed over, but she had the suspicion that some of the money might have found its way into college coffers. A young man brought up in Italy then would have been familiar with the institutionalised culture of bribery. Or perhaps it had, more innocently, been Ross's first real act of philanthropy.

Ross had gone on after graduation to establish his company and take out his patents. Absalom, having no real need to earn an income, had lived a more mysterious life. At least, it was mysterious for a researcher like Elena Coyle, because she could find no records or receipts or anything else to account for his time or actions or even his whereabouts. For almost twenty years, he just disappeared. When he did turn up again, it was in circumstances she thought most peculiar and completely out of character.

In 1918, he was prosecuted by the police for running a house of ill-repute. The case went to trial in Brighton, where he was apparently living. Elena could imagine no less likely brothel keeper than a wealthy and clever man from an aristocratic Italian family. Why on earth would he bother? But it had not been a brothel at all, she discovered when she read the trial account in the Brighton *Argus*. He had been holding not an orgy but a séance when the police raided the property after a tip-off from a suspicious neighbour. There was a picture of a dishevelled Absalom in handcuffs between two burly constables to accompany the court report. He had grown corpulent in the years since his undergraduate dressing up and that haircut from a Tennyson poem. Mature now, rumpled and shorn and manacled, he looked absolutely furious at the predicament he was in.

The jury did not convict him. He was Johnny Foreigner, as Elena had earlier observed, and they were times of great xenophobia in a Britain afraid of spies and sabotage and Zeppelin raids. But the evidence had been so flimsy and contrived that he was found not guilty and allowed to go free with his reputation unblemished. One interesting detail was that Lady Mary Ross had been cited as a character witness. She had not been called to the witness stand. Absalom's barrister had not been so desperate. But she had travelled down to the trial from London on the train. So presumably his friendship with Sir Samuel was still strong. It explained the dinner table picture taken with Paley and Brody. Elena did a calculation. Lady Ross had attended the trial at Brighton about four months prior to the death in France of her son.

It was almost midnight. Elena rubbed her eyes. Her failed efforts to track Bruno Absalom through the early part of the twentieth century had made her tired. It had been a long day and she had made progress. But people had paid in cash for things in those days: for theatre tickets and restaurant meals and hotel accommodation and in the case of a man with the wealth Bruno Absalom had enjoyed, maybe even for a Mayfair mansion. He'd had no bad debts. He had not reserved a first-class berth aboard the *Titanic*. He had never spent any time at His or Her Majesty's pleasure. He had published no books, at least in his own name. He had not registered a limited company. She could find no record of his marriage or the birth of any children or his death. Yawning, with her hand over her mouth and her eyes watering with the strain of sitting for so long at a computer screen, she read again the most compelling paragraphs in the trial account. They concerned part of the prosecution evidence presented by the Crown.

*The accused claimed to be a scientist and, indeed, to hold a degree in chemistry from the University of Cambridge. And these were claims the prosecution did not dispute. But they pointed out that when Police Sergeant Teague inventoried the contents of Mr Absalom's laboratory, he listed such items as mercury, powdered gold, lead, arsenic, sulphur, the preserved foetus of a human baby and an entire umbilical cord in formaldehyde. There was also what was later identified as several vials of human blood mixed with the blood of some still unidentified creature. There was, too, ground ivory and the ground hooves and horns of an ibex. Not least, there were several powdered human teeth.*

*This does not sound to the Crown like the laboratory*

*of a scientist, it was suggested to the gentlemen of the jury.*
*It sounds more like the workplace of a medieval alchemist.*

*'Did you find the philosopher's stone?' Sgt Teague was*
*asked by the prosecution barrister, under oath.*

*'We looked for it, My Lord, but it was nowhere to be*
*seen,' the officer replied, to guffaws of laughter from the*
*public gallery.*

Elena smiled. The witness had not just been led but coached.
Someone had had it in for Bruno Absalom. But alchemy was
not spiritualism and the charge had been concerned with the
holding of a séance and the legality of that gathering in what
presumably had been a private address. Much of old Brighton
remained intact. Perhaps it was still there. Perhaps Bruno
Absalom was still living in it, surrounded by vials of powdered
teeth and pickled foetuses, since she could find no record of
his death. It was time for bed. Elena saved her work and
switched off her computer.

She went to the window to close it. On the other side of
the street, in a pool of light from a streetlamp, a burly man
in an astrakhan coat stood smoking a cigar. She looked at
her watch, frowning. It was late, certainly late for loitering
in the street. It had been dark for hours. Smoke from the
cigar drifted in a pale, dissipating cloud and for a moment
Elena had the curious thought that the man was looking up
and studying her from where he stood there. It was a foolish
suspicion. But before she went to bed, as a precaution, she
made sure that she double-locked her door.

Elena dreamed that night of a thin man in a tweed suit in
a room in which the colour brown predominated in fabrics
and furnishings that had a drab and institutional character.
The intention had been neutrality, perhaps. The effect was
dispiriting. At first, she thought the man was in the room
alone. Then she realised he wasn't. He shared it with another
man who sat almost concealed by the wings of the armchair

he sat in and the sly self-effacement of his posture. Only a fraction of his face was visible and he concealed that with a hand. The thin man was asking him questions. He was writing down answers, or observations, in a pad on his lap. Elena could not hear in the dream. But the tweed-suited man, who she knew was Edward Brody, asked his questions and the pale visitor answered them and then shaped his mouth, all of his face she could see, in a vacuous leer.

She saw that Brody was trembling under the suit. His hand shook when he used his pen and the ink emerged from the nib in a spidery scrawl on the page. He shook his head slowly at some of the answers he was given and to one, raised the back of his free hand to his forehead in a gesture that seemed to the dreaming Elena like one of pure despair. She was afraid in the dream. She was frightened of what she would be obliged to see if the man dropped the hand concealing his face. The skin was very pale and the smile was cruel and she did not want to see the visitor's eyes.

When she got to work at nine thirty the following morning, she briefed her boss straightaway on what she had found out the previous night. She felt rumpled and vulnerable after her nightmare and had a bad feeling, like her War Museum premonition of the previous Saturday, about where all of this was taking them. She had begun to think that some things were best left unknown, that some secrets were kept for a very good reason. It was heresy in her profession, but she was beginning to think it nevertheless. Some mysteries were safer endured than uncovered.

'I want you to go home and pack a bag, Elena,' Creed said.

'You want me to go to Brighton?'

'Why would I want you to do that?'

'You want me to visit the Absalom address. I Google-Earthed it this morning, Julian. The whole street is intact.'

'It might very well be. But you won't find him there.'

'Where will I find him?'

Creed was staring at his wall, at his Falklands picture, at himself nearly thirty years ago. 'He was born in Italy. My hunch is he died there. The trail went cold because he went home, Elena.'

'Why would he do that?'

'He was a Catholic. He did things he should not have done. Alchemy, spiritualism, they would have been enough in the eyes of the Church in those days to merit excommunication.'

'You really think I'll find Bruno Absalom in Italy?'

'He sinned, Elena. And then he repented and went home to seek absolution.'

'What sin do you think he committed?'

'I'm hoping you will find out when you're there. And while you're there, I'll be here, looking for the answer to the same question. And the answers to one or two others concerning Lady Ross and her lost son and Edward Brody and the waiting room.'

'You won't go back, will you, in the absence of the Strides?'

Creed just grinned at her.

'He won't have left the place unsecured, you know. He's not an idiot. There'll be goons and guard dogs.'

'Goons and guard dogs don't frighten me.'

*No,* Elena thought, *they don't.* But she thought she knew what did.

# Chapter Five

The phone on Creed's desk rang from reception. He reached across and pressed the hands-free button. 'Yes?'

'A call from a Mr Martin Stride,' his receptionist said.

'Put it through.'

'Hello?'

'Good morning, Martin.'

'Julian. I want to ask you a question. Are you familiar with the poetry of Wilfred Owen?'

Creed looked at Elena and the look was uneasy. Elena felt the presentiment of fear grow stronger in her chest. 'Yes,' Creed said. 'Very much so. In fact, I was discussing him only yesterday with Elena Coyle, my principal researcher.'

'Oh? Why?'

'A link with your Shale Point waiting room, actually. It's a tenuous connection only, but nevertheless a link.'

Stride was silent for so long that Elena thought the line had gone dead. Then he said, 'So then, you will be familiar with the Owen poem, "Strange Meeting".'

Creed was still looking at Elena. 'Of course,' he said.

'What would you say that poem was about, Julian?'

'Hell,' Creed said, quietly. It was a tone of voice Elena had never heard him use before. 'It is a poem about hell.'

'I need to see you,' Stride said. 'Now, today, without delay, Julian. I cannot just abandon the voluntary work I've committed to this week, so you will have to come to the Island. But it needs to be now. Something has occurred. There's been an escalation.'

Creed cleared his throat with a cough. 'I'll be there this

afternoon,' he said. He thought for a moment. 'Do you know the Spyglass Inn at Ventnor?'

'Yes,' Stride said.

'Shall I meet you there at five?'

'Thank you,' Stride said. He broke the connection.

'I take it I'm not going to Rome after all,' Elena said.

'Why would you assume that?'

'Don't we need to know the nature of Stride's escalation?'

'That will be revealed to me at five o'clock. By then, you will be in Italy or at least in the sky above it, and significantly closer than you are now to unravelling the enigma of Bruno Absalom.'

'OK.'

It was so easy, she thought. And at the same time it was so sad. She had no partner to break the news of her sudden, unscheduled departure to. She had no personal engagements she would be obliged to cancel at short notice. Her work had become her life to the point where nothing outside it but a dull domestic routine existed for her. She was good at her job. But one day Creed could decide that their personal history and the friction it continued to cause was no longer tolerable on a day to day basis and simply let her go. If that happened, what would she have left in her life? She would have nothing that was worth anything to her at all. She would surrender her office keys and her company credit card and her computer access codes would be erased and her name would go from the list of contributors at the end of the successful show she helped create and she would cease in any meaningful way to exist.

The next series was not due to be aired for another four months. They already had a provisional schedule and five of six completed episodes to broadcast. They would need to have a firm schedule to enable press and preview publicity a minimum of six weeks before the first episode in the series was screened. Creed had not even approached Martin Stride about the possibility of making and airing a programme based around the waiting room. But in theory at least, there was time to prepare something if they could get to the bottom of the mystery over the next couple of weeks. Elena thought this was clearly Creed's intention. But he had failed to factor in something she thought really crucial. The waiting room and its ghosts would have to co-operate in what they had planned. She was not sure it was ghosts they were dealing with. And if they were, she did not think it was certain that they would co-operate at all.

'Off you trot, Elena,' Creed said. 'You'd best be off to Bermondsey to fetch your passport.'

'It's here,' Elena said. 'I keep it in my desk drawer.' And how tragic was that? Foreign travel had become a feature and function of work. She had no life at all, did she? She even kept a change of clothes in the office. And she could buy a pair of sunglasses at the airport. There was no need for her to go home at all.

She looked at her watch. She could be at her destination by late afternoon or early evening, by the time her boss sat down over a pint of beer in the atmospherically named Spyglass Inn. She would be on the cold trail of Bruno Absalom and if her private life was an empty sort of joke, that at least was a challenging prospect. She knew she was good at what she did. She was dogged and tenacious and gifted at exploring causal links. She had an excellent memory and an organised mind. She would go to her desk and arrange her flight and accommodation and car hire. But first, she would switch on her computer and read the poem about hell Wilfred Owen had written. She was unfamiliar with his verse and Stride's mention of it, and Creed's reaction to that mention, had made her very curious indeed to read the poem. She would print a copy off and analyse it during the flight. Maybe it was because the caffeine from her morning coffee had kicked in. Perhaps it was because the shock of the Edward Brody nightmare had now faded somewhat. But she had forgotten, for the moment, her earlier suspicion that some secrets are best allowed to remain as such.

Creed thought about chartering a helicopter to take him to the Island. But he decided against it. He did not think it would be a wise move emotionally. He would approach in a rush with a roar of engine noise and assaulting clatter of rotor blades and no time to prepare himself for the sadness he thought memories would impose on him somewhere once so fondly familiar. His had been a very happy childhood. He had been privileged and loved. His dad had been a wonderfully attentive father and most of their happiest times together had been spent on the stretch of island coastline between Ventnor and Freshwater. He needed time to prepare for the blow to his heart he knew seeing the place again would be bound to inflict. So he drove to Portsmouth at the wheel of the Morgan and took the ferry across the Solent to Fishbourne and drove south across the Island to his destination.

On the road high in the hills above the steep descent to Ventnor, just beyond Greatwood Copse, he stopped. The weather was innocent and the car roof was down and the sea glittered blue and green in the deeper patches of late sunshine to the distant horizon. His BlackBerry was on the seat next to him. He picked it up. In the trees in the copse to his right, the birds were singing loudly. *I could give it up*, he thought. *I probably have enough money to live comfortably on for the rest of my days. I could give up this ghoulish pantomime existence and be real instead of fraudulent and call my dad and tell him I'm sorry and if I'm really fortunate he might just find it in his heart to forgive me. Life is short. He is old. I am his only son.*

He switched the engine off and got out of the car. He walked to the side of the road, to where the forested land began to slope downwards to eventually meet the water. The

97

salt-smelling wind ruffled his clothing and blew his hair about. The problem was, he wasn't fraudulent any more. It was no longer a pantomime. He was involved in something real and compelling and he could not walk away from it now. He smiled. Had he come there intent only on further fabrication and fakery, this, now, would have been his moment of epiphany. He was sure of that. He knew it in his soul. Recent events had changed him and the change was permanent. But he had been summoned to help a man in fear to deal with the thing frightening him. He had other imperatives, other murkier, less noble motives, it was true. But that was the main one, he was sure. That was his priority. And he would have to call his dad another time.

Stride was seated alone at a table outside the Spyglass. The inn was the last building at the eastern end of the bay. It faced the sea and the hills rose behind it and beyond it ragged cliffs rose from the strewn boulders between the high groynes on the beach. Creed could hear the slap of waves on the rocks of the breakwater beneath them as he sat. He could smell salt and seafood and the gulls agitating for scraps low in the sky. They were sounds and scents from a cherished time and they filled him with melancholy for all the mistakes and miscalculations of his adulthood. And he thought suddenly, bitterly, of what he had done to Elena Coyle and was forced to blink back surprised tears of shame.

'Are you all right?'

'I'm fine,' Creed said. He sniffed. There was a child's exercise book with a pale grey cover on the table. The breeze fingered its pages but was too light to lift them. Their Indian summer was continuing. It was almost warm enough to enjoy a swim. Stride wore sunglasses and a summer shirt and Creed noticed again what good shape he was in, the veins vascular cords in his muscled arms, the cleft in his chest between sharply defined pectoral muscles. Either he worked out seriously or he was very seriously blessed by nature. The rock star regimes of choice were yoga and Pilates. They did not give you a physique like that Martin Stride possessed.

'What would you like to drink?'

'The Ventnor brewery does a bottled ale called Admiral's. I'll have one of those.' He was driving, but the one bottle wouldn't hurt.

Stride went inside to buy the drink. Creed read the upside-down name on the exercise book. It belonged to Peter Stride.

Stride emerged from the pub and returned to the table. Creed poured his drink and sipped.

'Thanks for coming.'

'You're paying me generously.'

'Just the same, it's a long way and short notice. I'm grateful.'

'You sound a bit more relaxed than you did this morning,' Creed said.

'Well,' Stride said. He smiled tightly. 'I'd had a shock.'

'Are you going to tell me what shocked you?'

Stride turned the exercise book around so that its cover faced Creed. Then he pushed it across the table. Creed opened it. It contained pages of spelling and grammar tests done in columns in a neat, sloping hand in blue ink and with far more ticks in red biro against them than crosses.

'Bright boy,' Creed said.

'Keep going.'

Creed sipped beer and turned pages. He stopped when he came to what Stride had brought him there to see. The centre-spread was occupied by a handwritten poem done in pencil. The poem was Wilfred Owen's 'Strange Meeting'. The writing was quite childlike, but it was not that of Peter Stride. Creed recognised it straightaway. It was Owen's.

'Peter was to have shared a double room with another boy,' Stride said. 'But his room-mate went down with 'flu over the weekend and couldn't make the trip. He's in the room on his own. When he went to sleep last night, that poem wasn't there. It was there when he looked after breakfast this morning. He was revising some spellings while we waited for the minibuses to arrive to take us on a tour of Carisbrook Castle. And he saw it and brought it and showed it to me. It was done during the night. Owen did it, or the ghost of Wilfred Owen. And as you rightly observed when I called you earlier, this is a poem about hell.'

Creed did not know what to say. He had never felt so profoundly out of his depth. The confidence he had felt on the route down to Ventnor, the smug assumption that he was here to help, had perished in him.

'I asked you here because I couldn't come to you and I wanted to do you the courtesy of telling you what I have to say in person,' Stride said. 'Your investigation is at an end. There will be no more visits to the waiting room.'

'You're firing me.'

'I'm a great admirer of your show on television. I've even been a bit envious of your psychic sensitivity. But this is a warning I can't ignore. I will pay you double what we originally agreed, Julian. But I'm going to do what I should have done in the first place and have the building exorcised by a priest familiar with the ritual and then torn down. I can't have the souls of my family put in jeopardy while you attempt to chat with manifestations of spiritual malevolence. As I say, this is a warning. It is one I fully intend to heed.'

'Give me one more night.'

'No. If it was just the paranormal we were dealing with here, I would say yes, of course. You have demonstrated again and again a rare and undeniable gift for communicating with confused and restless spirits. But this isn't your ground.' He gestured to the exercise book. 'Those verses make it plain my family is threatened by something diabolical.'

'Do you have a priest in mind?'

'I've consulted one already.'

'I can think of only three,' Creed said, after a moment's

thought. One of the three had attacked his series repeatedly in print. 'My money would be on Monsignor Degrelle.'

'Then you would not lose your money.'

'He's said to be very powerful,' Creed said, 'also a showman.'

'Well,' Stride said. 'You are the authority on that. These days, you would know far more about showmanship than me.'

Creed said nothing. There was nothing to say.

'I'm sorry, Julian,' Stride said again. 'Read the poem if you doubt the reason for my decision and the fear for my family that has obliged me to make it.'

Creed held Stride's eyes with his own. He did not need to look at the page. He knew the poem by heart. It was a favourite. And every time he read it, it delivered a chill to his soul. He spoke:

> *'I am the enemy you killed, my friend.*
> *I knew you in this dark: for so you frowned*
> *Yesterday through me as you jabbed and killed.*
> *I parried; but my hands were loath and cold.'*

Stride tried to smile but the smile came out a broken, twisted thing, a grimace of concern where he had aimed for good humour. He rose and held out his hand and Creed rose too and shook it firmly in the embrace of both of his. He liked Martin Stride. He both admired and envied him his unsullied integrity. He envied him the love and devotion of the family he had nurtured and, Creed now saw, fully deserved. He had adjusted to the shock of being fired. It had not been his first or most humiliating experience of rejection; Stride's dignity and tact had seen to that. He still thought he might be able to help with whatever threat was posed by the waiting room. Owen had set his poem in hell; hell was its location. He would not and could not argue with that. He believed, as Stride did, that it had been written out by the ghost of its author as a warning. A week earlier, the very thought would have seemed absurd to him. He believed it now. But that did not necessarily mean the threat posed by the waiting room was demonic.

Degrelle would kiss his stole and bark his liturgy and splash a lot of holy water. And to what avail? Whatever the waiting room harboured, whatever lurked outside it, would still be present when he closed his missal and uttered his last, sanctimonious Amen. Elena Coyle would be back before the priest's flamboyant little ceremony could be arranged. And Elena might have uncovered things Stride would want to hear about. And by then, Creed would have been back to the waiting room himself. He really did have very little regard for goons and attack dogs. He had dealt quite ruthlessly with both in the past he remembered vividly but chose never to talk about.

'You're a resilient man,' Stride said to him, apropos of nothing, showing his own sometimes shrewd judgement of character. Creed just nodded and turned and walked to the place on the seafront where he had parked his car. He walked with the sea boundless to his right, beyond the pretty, painted beach huts and past the chandlery and the low double-front of the Longshoreman's Museum and the Minghella ice-cream parlour and the gift shops and amusement arcades lining the promenade to his left with their bright displays of beach balls and buckets and spades and body boards and crab nets for the kids. And he was thinking that Owen had known and led Patrick Ross in the assault on the canal that had killed them both in the autumn of 1918. If it had killed them both, that was; if Ross had died at all. His insane mother had claimed otherwise. Brody, in his oddly couched letter of resignation, had seemed to come to believe this claim to be true. But he had seemed also to hint that Patrick Ross had suffered some terrible transformation. Was it some awful wound, or mutilation? Creed's only certainty on reaching his car was that the part he had to play in solving this deepening mystery was far from concluded.

She drove her hire car through the unremitting rain of southern Italy with a map on the seat next to hers and her mind on what had happened between herself and Julian Creed. The wipers squeaked shrilly on the windscreen. This was not a climate familiar with autumn rain and there was a residue of polish in the Fiat's toughened glass screen that the rubber of the wipers stalled and stuttered against. It was a raw, uncomfortable noise. It made the perfect soundtrack to her thoughts about her sexual misadventure with her boss. Perhaps it was what had provoked them.

Television had not been her first career destination of choice. Neither had full-time research been her first choice of job. She had taken a degree in journalism and graduated a decade earlier with an ambition for working on a monthly consumer glossy that had seemed realistic at the time, even if it had not remained so for very long. She had liked magazines. She liked the combination of glamour and stimulation and women's issue agenda-setting the very best of them sustained. She was taken on as assistant features editor of one of the most credible and aspirational titles on the market. It was her dream start. She did not know the effect the internet was going to have on printed media. But then at the time, in fairness to her, nobody else did either.

A monthly glossy averaging three hundred pages an issue satisfied her appetite for hard work and the journalistic vanity that insisted her stories have as long a shelf life as possible. She had been there a year when the weeklies started to eat into the circulations of even the best-established monthly titles. Frequency was becoming a crucial consideration in a world where the internet gave you entertainment and information instantly. Advertising started to dwindle and with it, pagination. Circulation started to decline. Frequency was cut from twelve to ten issues a year. Revenue fell. Redundancies were made. The features editor became one of the casualties and Elena was promoted into the job at just over half her predecessor's salary. She didn't think this a slight. She saw her opportunity. Everyone said she would do a brilliant job. A new editor supervised a costly redesign. It did nothing to arrest the decline in circulation. A new business plan only pointed out the obvious and after an enervating period of uncertainty and gloom, the magazine inevitably folded.

She freelanced for a while. It got tougher and tougher as more and more titles went to the wall and the number of freelancers seeking work saw the supply outstrip the dwindling demand for lifestyle features at a rate that was dismaying. She worked for a pittance on a promising start-up that never got past the dummy stage. She worked on an absurdly optimistic property-based fortnightly that limped along for three issues before the collapse in the housing market claimed it as a casualty.

She was living on the margin of her credit card limit when she saw the research vacancy advertised by Creed Productions. The paranormal had always intrigued her. She had watched the first series avidly. But then, everyone had. She counted herself a fan. It wasn't just the subject matter. Julian Creed's onscreen persona was and remained irresistible. She had interviewed for the job and at the second interview, met the man himself. She had been on form, confident and witty, and the rapport between them had been instant.

They had not begun to date then. She had worked for him for a full year, researched more than a full series, by the time he first asked her out. She wondered in retrospect whether this was a necessary qualification. It was conceivable he would not have seen her as date material if she had failed to make the grade as an employee. She wasn't sure. He was not sexist in the conventional sense. He objectified women, but subtly. He would never have fancied a page-three girl or a pole dancer.

He'd have considered even the prospect of a romantic evening alone with a WAG type intolerably tedious. He liked intelligent, opinionated, capable women. He liked brains along with refinement. Where women were concerned, Creed was a bit of a snob.

On her second date, over dinner, she had asked him a question. 'What's the characteristic you find least attractive in a woman?'

He held her eyes with his. 'Guess,' he said.

'Cellulite,' she said.

He shook his head slowly. His gaze did not waver. 'Vacuity,' he said.

Everything had gone very promisingly at first. He was funny and self-deprecating and stimulating company. His agnosticism where the supernatural was concerned had not yet then impinged upon her conscience. She thought it more an outrageous secret they colluded in than something that mugged the viewing public and ate away at her own integrity. And if she was really honest, she liked the luxury of sinking into the upholstery of the Jag when he put his foot down on the way to some surprise weekend destination. She liked the gifts in small, exquisite boxes from Cartier. Not least she liked him, naked from the shower, dripping and laughing and so tautly muscled he rippled beneath his towel.

It had all gone wrong four months ago on the night of a television awards ceremony the series had been expected, in its category, to dominate. They had drunk too much too early in premature celebration of a triumph that failed to materialise. Elena, her mind champagne-befuddled, remembered trying to process the disappointment looking at Creed, flushed and angry and shiny with pointless grooming, fighting for the dignity of restraint in his black tie at their expensive table. And then she had gone to the loo and been offered a line and accepted it, thinking it might bring much needed mental clarity. But she remembered nothing after that, except waking in her own bed, feeling bruised and violated with him already gone the following morning.

She should not have got so drunk. She should have said no to the coke. But he should not have indulged in such aggressive sex with someone as intoxicated as she had been on the night. Had it been date rape? She did not think so. He had probably been as out of it as she was. Probably they had cavorted, equally willing and senseless. She really could not remember. But it had been rough and he should have known better and it had made her ashamed and been the end of things between them and her mouth felt dry and bitter when she thought of it, like someone wanting to spit out something vile and unable to.

She slowed the car. She thought that she might be at her destination. There was a village, pale in the rain under its clustered roofs, in the valley to which the road descended in front of her. There was a church on a hill beside the village. There were white crosses and tombs of black and purple marble in a cemetery on the slope of the hill. It was a desolate sort of a place in the wet. And it was very small, a settlement that had endured but never flourished, she thought. It was not a pretty settlement, through the bleared windscreen of the car. It possessed only the dead virtue of quaintness.

It was odd, she thought, how completely Bruno Absalom had been erased from history. She suspected that he had done the erasing himself. It had been an easier thing to do in the days before data banks and computerised credit ratings; before the ubiquitous cameras of the surveillance society. There had still been parish registers of births and deaths and criminal records and travel visas and public declarations of bankruptcy. But for a man who came to maturity with such a taste for flamboyance, Absalom had steered well clear of the kindof publicity people deliberately courted. There was that one curious trial account in the Brighton *Argus* and afterwards, nothing.

Creed had opened her mind to the possibility of her subject's willing exile in the land of his birth. His reasoning had been records from the Second World War. Absalom would not have escaped internment for the duration. The authorities were very thorough and nobody did. Yet there was no record of his having been sent to a camp. It followed that he hadn't been in Britain any longer by 1939. He could have moved to New York or Paris or even Berlin. He had possessed the money to resettle anywhere. And of course, he could have done so under an assumed name. But home had been Julian's strong inkling. And it was Elena's job sometimes to follow such hunches to wherever it was they led.

Creed's hunches were more often right than outright guesses were. But there were two possible barriers to her progress in researching Bruno Absalom here. If Absalom had come home to seek absolution for some secret sin, a man of his status would surely have gone to the Vatican rather than to the priest at the church in the village neighbouring his family estate. And she would surely find no grave in the churchyard. He would be interred in the family mausoleum and that would be housed in a chapel on the land owned by his forbears. She had contacted both the Vatican and the family to make tactful enquiries. But neither had even responded yet. Her email was regularly monitored in her absence from the office and her phone calls there fielded. If there had been a response, someone from the office would have contacted her when she had touched down in Rome and got off her plane.

She did not in honesty expect a response. If Creed was right and Absalom had returned home seeking divine forgiveness, the family would hardly wish to talk publicly about the nature of their dead relative's crimes against God. And the Vatican did not disclose the secrets of the confessional. Priests did not do it, let alone princes of the Church. Confession was a Blessed Sacrament and they swore at ordination a solemn vow to observe its rule of total confidentiality. Your confessed sins went no further than your confessor and the Almighty. She knew this because, though she did not know much generally about Catholicism, it was the principle that had propelled the drama in a number of Hollywood films.

She went to find her accommodation. She wanted to visit the little graveyard before darkness fell and had about an hour and a half before then. She found the guesthouse she was staying at and was shown to a room under the eaves. It was of whitewashed stone and furnished with a single cot and had a black wooden crucifix on the wall. The rear window, above the porcelain sink at which she was expected to wash, looked up at the church on its hill. The church from here had a locked and shuttered look about it. Elena tested the springs on the bed. They were firm, excellent value at an off-season rate for the room of only twelve euros per night. It wasn't that Creed was parsimonious with expenses, quite the opposite. But this was the only place in the village a visitor could stay.

Elena took off her coat and unpacked her laptop and switched it on and discovered that there was no internet coverage there. There was no signal either displayed on her mobile. She took her change of clothes for the following day from her overnight bag and hung the items from the hangers in the single wardrobe. There was a knock at the door and the elderly woman who had shown her to her room came in with a tray bearing a small pot of coffee and a plate with a pastry on it. She drank the coffee and ate the pastry and put her coat back on and put her notebook into a pocket and went back out into the rain.

She picked her way methodically between graves. Most of the headstones were very old and there was not much variation in the names engraved into them. People died here. But it was plainly evident that people did not come here to die. The grass between the graves was recently cut and very green between neat borders of gravel on the slope. It trailed wetly, clinging to her shoes. She could feel the rain patter on the shoulders of her coat when she shifted the small umbrella she had brought the better to see some detail of an inscription. The surname Absalom featured nowhere in the cemetery, as she had expected. She kept an eye out but saw no movement from the church. She did not know what service might be performed at dusk on a Tuesday evening. She thought that on a weekday, unless there was a funeral service, there might be only an early morning mass.

The little graveyard had only one other visitor. He was an elderly man in a plastic raincoat that reached almost to his ankles. It was a garment of the pocket variety and the crease marks looked like a subtle over-check pattern until she got close to him, where their paths intersected on the gravel as he made to depart after leaving flowers at the base of a head-stone. The bouquet he had placed was a bright blur in the prevailing grey of the rain from where Elena looked.

'Good evening,' the man said, in English.

He wore spectacles. The lenses were frameless and wet with drops of rain. They magnified his eyes, giving him a frank look that was almost childlike.

'How—'

'How did I know you are English? I lived there for a time. Your clothes and hairstyle are suggestive to me of London. Anyway, I am right.'

'Yes. You are right.'

'Besides, you brought no flowers. You are not attending a grave.'

'No, sir, I am not. But I am looking for one.'

'Not your own, I hope,' he said.

Elena thought the joke lost in translation, even though he had made it in English. She opted to ignore it.

'Whom do you come here to remember?'

'I honour the memory of my wife.'

'I'm sorry.'

'There is no need to be. We were very happy for longer than anyone has a right to expect. And soon I shall rejoin her.'

Elena nodded. The man had silver hair. In the diminishing light, it had dulled to pewter. His skin was brown from the Italian sun and she could not have guessed at his age. He looked around at the rainy hillside, dotted with its collection of graves. 'She tells me she looks forward to the day. She says that it will not be long now.'

There was nothing to offer in reply to this. Evidently the man felt it was possible to communicate with the dead and for the dead to talk to the living. Love and grief were strong enough emotions to warp fact and she did not rule out the possibility herself. But it seemed a strange belief for a Catholic to hold.

'Who among the dead do you seek?'

'Bruno Absalom,' she said.

The man smiled. 'Then you look in the wrong place. Here, the ground is blessed, sanctified. The man whose grave you search for sought absolution. But it was denied him.'

'You know this for certain?'

'I'll show you the proof,' the man said. 'Come this way.'

The grave of Bruno Absalom was not very far from the church building itself. It was to the left of the church, high on the hill, a few feet from the dry stone wall that bordered the cemetery. It was marked by a large, black marble obelisk grander than almost anything commemorating the dead within the border described by the wall. But it was almost invisible until you came across it, obscured by the height of the wall at that point and to its right and left, by the thick trunks of overhanging cypress trees. The trees were ponderous with leaf, and rain gurgled from their abundant foliage onto the white stone chips of the Absalom grave. There were no flowers and there was no metal vase for them as she had seen on other graves within the sanctified perimeter. But the grave had a kept look, nevertheless. Someone maintained it.

'What offence against God did he commit to earn this exile of the soul?'

'That question is very elegantly put, madam. But I do not know the answer to it. He came here in the time of *Il Duce*. There were many secrets then. Most of them remain as such today. There is no willingness to uncover them. They stir our nation's conscience far too greatly.'

'Does anyone know the nature of his offence?'

'I would say no one living. His brother renounced their family's wealth and eventually became the priest here. It was to Father Absalom, Bruno confessed upon his return, so the story goes. To no avail, as you see. And Father Absalom would have told no one. Father Berra might know more of these circumstances. He will be here to serve mass in the morning.'

'He is old?'

'On the contrary, he is young. But he takes seriously the traditions and history of the faith. If he does not know, you may find yourself asking a ghost.'

Elena turned to ask her new companion a final question, but when she did so, he had gone. She could see him receding through the thickening murk of approaching night down the hill towards the village. She read again what had been carved into the black marble face of the obelisk and shivered damply and decided on retreat to warmth and light herself. The persistent stranger's talk of speaking with the dead had troubled and unsettled her.

The schoolchildren and the staff members on the trip were staying at the same hostel the school booked them into every year. Martin and Monica Stride were staying at the Hambrough Hotel in Ventnor with Millie. They had asked for the exorcist Degrelle to contact them at ten in the evening, after she had long gone to sleep in their room, the best at the hotel and somewhere all four of the family often stayed together. Peter's absence was very noticeable, Monica thought, sitting on their balcony, looking at the harbour lights bobbing in the darkness below, listening to her husband on his mobile placate and court the snubbed servant of God in low, insistent tones. Eventually he completed the call and joined her.

'I thought vanity was a sin,' she said.

He shrugged and sat heavily in the chair beside hers. There was usually a grace about his movement, but he was tired tonight. There had been Peter to try to counsel in the morning. There had been his bishop contact to consult. There had been Julian Creed to dispense with and finally the self-important priest to plead with now. And he had also had to take Peter's class to Osborne House and help monitor their visit there. Queen Victoria's old residence on the Island was a majestic and fascinating place. But going there in charge of a dozen excited eleven-year-olds was not a relaxing experience. Peter was the reason for his fatigue, she thought. The other stuff he could deal with. But Peter had been terrified when he discovered the exercise book poem. And when his children suffered, it took something physical out of Martin. He could not help but suffer on their behalf.

Monica reached across and stroked his head and, as he always did, he took her hand in his and kissed it.

It had taken him a long time to convince Peter that the poem was not the trick of the leering soldier ghost from the waiting room. 'He's followed me here, Dad,' Peter had said, sobbing. 'He's come to get me because I saw him and I shouldn't have.'

'If he was going to get you, he would have got you,' he said gently to his son. 'He can't get you because he only exists as a spirit. He can no more harm you physically than fog or your reflection can. And he isn't here, he's there, in a derelict building.'

'That we own,' Peter said. His eyes were raw. He smeared snot around his face with the back of his hand. They were in his room at the hostel. They had it to themselves but if his crying got any louder it would be heard beyond the door.

'Sit down,' Stride said. And they sat on the bed together and he put his arm around his son and told him that the man who had written the poem was a good and heroic soldier who had been a teacher himself before the war that claimed him and had been always kind to the children in his charge. He had even got into trouble because he would not use the cane at a time when corporal punishment was considered important in building the character of those it was used on. He was not the leering phantom of the waiting room. He had been a handsome man with kind brown eyes.

'Then why did he come and leave his poem?'

'I think it is a warning,' Stride said, truthfully. He did not see any point in lying about this to his son. 'We have not dealt with the problem of the waiting room in the right way. We need to do something else. I will organise it today.'

'Does that mean Julian won't be coming any more?'

'I'm afraid it does.'

And that had provoked more tears. Peter liked Julian Creed. Both the children did. They had grown fond of him in a very short time. Probably, because of his television show, they had assumed they knew him already. And in the flesh he was even better value, warm and funny and conspiratorial with them. And he had been reassuring too, Stride thought, because he had no fear of ghosts.

'Will we ever be able to go home, Dad?'

'We're going home as soon as this trip is over,' Stride said. 'We're not budging from home.' He hoped these words sounded bold and defiant to Peter. But his reasoning was practical. The placement of the poem proved they could neither hide nor escape. They had succeeded only in antagonising what they needed to confront and expunge. The waiting room needed its exorcism. 'You won't be sleeping alone here tonight,' he said to his son. 'Ethan is sharing with you. I've arranged it.'

'Thanks, Dad.'

'When will he come?' Monica asked, on their hotel balcony.

'We're scheduled to get back early on Monday morning. He promised to be there by two o'clock on Monday afternoon.'

'It gives him plenty of daylight.'

Stride smiled at his wife. 'Exorcists don't fear the dark,' he said.

'Or they don't admit to it if they do.'

'I meant that his ritual is ancient and indifferent to the hour.'

'What did we do to deserve this, Martin?'

Stride thought about this. It was a question he had pondered at some length. 'Nothing,' he said. 'Nothing specific, I mean. We did nothing to deserve this. Perhaps I was greedy in buying the land.'

'It is not a punishment for greed,' Monica said. 'You could have bought a kingdom with the money you've given away.'

Stride did not reply.

'The stuff you told Peter about Wilfred Owen,' Monica said. 'Is it true that he was kind and brave?'

'Certainly it is. He was a good and courageous man.'

'At least he is on our side,' she said. She shivered. It was quiet. Below them, they could hear the night waves break and hiss on the shingle of the beach.

Elena's interview with Father Berra took place at a table on the lawn of a rectangular cloister to the rear of the church on the hill. When she saw it, she realised that the church had once formed part of a small monastery. Bruno Absalom's brother, Roberto, had been a Franciscan monk before his ordination. After the dissolution of the monastery in the early years of Mussolini's rule, he had stayed on there to minister to the people of the village.

'Very close to what had once been his home,' Elena said.

'I think that was the point,' Father Berra said. 'Franciscans take and then observe a vow of poverty. I think being so close to the temptation of his family's wealth strengthened his resolve.'

'He sounds a very devout man.'

'From what I have heard, he was.'

'In contrast to his brother?'

Father Berra smiled. 'Would you like some more tea, Miss Coyle?'

The lawn was bathed in bright morning sunshine. The cloth on their table was a dazzle of white linen that fluttered and snapped in the breeze that had cleared the clouds during the night. Elena had slept soundly. Father Berra was a slim and handsome man with a strong, swarthy jaw and eyes almost as dark as the wood of the crucifix on the wall of her room. She had sat through his celebration of morning mass and then approached him. He had been courteous and charming. He had not been as surprised, she did not think, as he should have been by her request to talk to him about Bruno Absalom.

'I can tell you nothing about the character of the brother,' he said.

'Nor about the nature of his sin?'

'I know about that only what is commonly known. Roberto loved his brother as he loved all men. But he could not in conscience offer absolution. He sought Vatican advice. He was told that his conscience had guided him well. He was told to reject his brother's pleas. Bruno stayed here paying daily penance despite the judgement. Then he died. It was said he died a much diminished man and that he willed his own death despite the fear of damnation to follow. But this is only what I have heard. These events occurred fifty years before my own birth.'

'I thought if you were truly sorry, no sin was unforgivable in the eyes of God,' Elena said.

'There is the mercy of God,' Father Berra said, 'and there is the judgement of the Church.'

'They contradict one another?'

But he only smiled and shrugged.

'There must be papers in the Vatican pertaining to the absolution plea.'

'There very well might be,' Berra said. 'If it was a matter of theological debate, almost certainly there are.'

'Do you think I could get permission to see them?'

He chuckled at this. 'My dear woman,' he said. 'In pursuing that ambition, to use an English phrase, you haven't a prayer.'

'So my visit here has been a waste of time.'

'No,' Berra said. 'I do not think it has. If you will wait here a moment, please?' He rose and dabbed at his lips with a handkerchief and turned and went back through the door behind her from which they had entered the cloister garden. She looked away from the white dazzle of the tablecloth and the shining silver items assembled upon it: the teapot and milk jug and sugar bowl with its heaped crystalline cubes. The lawn was intensely green in the light and smelled of the rain of the day before which the heat of the sun was drying from it. Elena blinked. Her eyes focused on the far section of the cloister. And for a moment there, she thought she saw a sturdy figure in an astrakhan coat, smoking a cigar and watching her, very still and cloaked by deep shadow. She rubbed her eyes and looked again. And the figure was gone.

Berra returned and sat down. He held out an envelope. The paper was stiff with quality but faded and stained by time. 'This is not for you to read,' he said. 'It is for you to present to Coutts Bank on the Strand in London. It is the precise instructions of Bruno Absalom and concerns his deposition, stored in a strong-box there. It will grant you access to the contents of the strong-box.'

'Why?' Elena said. The question seemed inadequate, but it was the obvious thing to ask. Before Father Berra could answer it, she asked another. 'You were not surprised to see me here today, asking about Bruno Absalom, were you, Father?'

'The man whose mystery you wish to solve left a letter addressed to his brother. It was the last request of a dying man. It was not a further, hopeless plea to be absolved of his sins. It was a strange request. It was also a prophesy. One day someone will come asking questions about me, Bruno wrote in his letter. When they do, you are to give them my permission, which will enable their access to my deposition and the answers they seek concerning my life and my crimes against God.'

Elena reached out and took the envelope.

'How do you know about this?'

'Roberto told his successor here. And he told his and so on, all the way down the years to a new century and the priest who sits here before you.'

'How do you know I'm the person Bruno had in mind?'

Berra had linked his hands in his lap after parting with the document he'd fetched. He looked down at them and smiled. 'You are quite precisely described. Not just your gender, Miss Coyle, but your appearance, also. There is no doubt in my mind you are the person he had in his when he wrote the letter.'

She was silent. She had not anticipated a breakthrough of this magnitude. How could she have? Matters were accelerating with a momentum that was ominous and alarming. The young priest on the other side of the table raised his eyes to her and she thought the expression in them complex and even contradictory. There was warning and sympathy in his look but also, she thought, a hint of fear. And she had provoked this in him. Vaguely, she thought she smelled a drift of cigar smoke, at once pungent and faint in the bright air, as though more remembered than truly sensed.

'You will not require a translator for the deposition,' Berra said. 'I mention this in case the possibility of that complication had occurred to you. He knew you would be English, you see. It was among the details about you he specified. And of course he wrote his deposition in the language of the country in which his crimes against God were committed.'

Elena swallowed. She looked at the envelope in her grip. In faded black ink, in a florid hand, it was addressed 'To whom it may concern', at Coutts Bank. She put it into her bag. She thought that Julian Creed's hunch could have found no greater vindication than it just had. And she felt that she had just been given a very good reason to be concerned for her own wellbeing. Her eyes briefly roamed the empty cloister as she rose to go.

# Chapter Six

The momentum of events stalled for Elena Coyle later on that same Wednesday after she had driven to Rome's Ciampino airport. England lay indolent under the blameless skies of an Indian summer. But in Italy, the September weather was proving less predictable. When she reached the airport, it was fogbound and her flight delayed indefinitely. Her mobile reception was restored a few miles out of the village on the route to Rome. There were two text messages and they were both from Creed. The first had been sent late the previous evening and told her that Stride had called everything off. The second had been sent during her breakfast with the priest that morning and asked what progress had she made in resolving the Absalom enigma. The second message might have seemed contradictory, because surely the first made any information about Bruno Absalom of academic interest only? But Julian Creed had never given up anything without a fight. It was not in his nature to do so. Except that was, for her. He had given up Elena without a fight. She considered herself the exception that proved his general rule.

He called her half an hour after she had arrived at the airport and asked for an update. She was deliberately vague and evasive, telling him that she would brief him fully on her return.

'Well, have you found out anything or not?'

'Nothing I wish to discuss over an open line.'

'For fuck's sake, Elena, this isn't espionage we're involved in.'

'I don't know. Aren't spies sometimes called spooks?'

'Talk to me. Encourage me. After my trip to the Isle of Wight yesterday, I need cheering up.'

'Tomorrow,' she said.

'You've uncovered something secret, haven't you, you clever bloody girl, you? What is it?'

'Whatever it is, it has waited eighty years, Julian. It can wait another day.'

He swore again and ended the call. What she should have done, had professionalism dictated her actions, was found a fax machine and faxed him the signed instructions to Coutts to release the strong-box into the charge of the person possessing them. He could have had the deposition in his hands before the bank closed. But she had not even considered doing that. She wanted to see the deposition first. There was no ethical or even logical justification for this. She was there on time Creed paid generously for to discharge her duties to her employer. But when that strong-box was opened and its contents saw the light, she wanted to be there to witness the event in person.

She did not think she had been bloody clever at all. The compliment had not rung true. Creed had meant it sincerely enough. But she felt fate had led her by the nose to the secret harboured by the village priest. She had not needed that helpful guide in the cemetery, with his pewter hair and curious jokes about death. She would have found the grave of Bruno Absalom alone eventually. She would have attended the morning mass too, without his prompting. The old woman who ran the guesthouse could have told her the time of the service. She had not needed to know in advance details about the age and character of Father Berra. He had spoken to her willingly enough. But she had done nothing clever, had she? She had not needed to. The document she carried in her bag had not so much fallen into her lap as been hand-delivered to its rightful recipient.

That was the real reason she had not faxed it to Creed,

she admitted to herself. She had not done so because it had always been meant for her.

She knew that something really unnerving must have happened to make Martin Stride change his mind about the Creed investigation. He had believed in Creed and he was a patient man, by all accounts. He acted with deliberation rather than rashly and was not at all the type of rock star ever to throw his expensive toys out of the pram. In this, he was untypical of the breed generally, but he had taken the even more untypical step of retiring at the height of his fame and commercial popularity with both personal dignity and professional integrity intact. He was measured, intelligent and thoughtful. So something must have happened that had scared him very badly to make him change his mind about using Creed so suddenly.

She had been in Creed's office when the call had come and he had mentioned the escalation and summoned Creed to Wight. Had those hired goons guarding the estate been spooked in his absence by the waiting room? Had their dogs whimpered and strained at the leash in its baleful proximity? Her instinct told her it would have taken more than that to frighten Stride. It would take a direct threat to his family to force his hand so dramatically. He would have to believe that which he most valued was placed under genuine threat. She would not get to meet him now. The thought disappointed her. With her usual awful timing, she realised that a decade after his retirement, she had finally become a fan. Picking intrusively through the minutiae of his life for Creed had made her one. She would not meet him. But she honestly felt more concern than disappointment.

It was something to do with that Owen poem, 'Strange Meeting'. She had read it on the flight out to Italy. It was complex in its ramifications, but straightforward enough as a story. In it, the soldier killer of a soldier enemy met his dead protagonist in hell. It was a very powerful poem. One line of it had stayed with her. It was the poem's penultimate line. The slain soldier had been bayoneted to death. The line was:

*I parried; but my hands were loath and cold.*

It made her shudder to think of it. She looked around. She had found a very comfortable berth for the duration in the VIP lounge to which Creed's upgrade privileges had gained her access. There was a white wine and soda at her elbow and a lavish buffet spread of chilled delicacies should she feel the urge to snack. Music was plangent in here through concealed speakers and the air conditioning squeezed some of the stuffy tedium out of the wait. But the flight information was frozen on the consoles above where she sat and for all the luxury and sophistication of her surroundings, she was aware the place had been rendered helpless by something as old and elemental as a fog.

It would be late by the time she got back to London. It might be after midnight, she thought. There seemed no sign of the fog outside dissipating. Whatever had frightened Stride on Wight, Creed had not been able to placate or reassure him. She hoped the fear had lifted by now and that the family were enjoying wholesome Famous Five adventures on the Island. She was pretty sure that Creed would attempt another visit to the waiting room in their absence. In the army, he had presumably obeyed orders. In civilian life, he only ever gave them. Maybe he would go there tonight. She hoped not. Without learning what the Absalom deposition had to tell them, she felt it was a very dangerous place. She thought of that captured image on the large screen in the edit suite, that reluctant swirl of abstract humanity dragged affronted from a distant time.

*I parried; but my hands were loath and cold.*

Creed reached the Stride domain at dusk. He had come there

cross-country, from the village where Peter and Millie Stride went to school. He did not wear his Van Helsing ensemble on this occasion. He wore the black assault kit he had saved as one of his army souvenirs on leaving the regiment. He had smeared cam cream over his face and hands and a chemical solution over his clothing repellent to a dog. Deterring an attack dog was not a complicated business. You tore the flaps if their jaws got a grip on you and pressed out their eyes with your thumbs. It worked. It was straightforward. But it was messy and cruel and Creed rather liked animals and his mission was not to raise the casualty count among canines only doing what they were trained to. His mission was to find out what was going on in the waiting room and why it was happening now.

Stealing alertly over Stride's land in the gloaming, he considered just how fundamentally wrong his tactics had so far been. He should not have sat in the waiting room like some gormless oaf waiting for a train that would never come. The trains that came and went were not for him. They were no longer of the world to which he was limited. He'd done the right thing on the first visit, because on that occasion he had been properly cynical about the paranormal events allegedly taking place there. But once he had discovered they were for real, he should really have acted differently.

That sly, leering figure which had so enjoyed the grief indulged by the ghost of Lady Ross on his second visit was the key. He was very crafty and elusive. But he was also real. He had seen Peter Stride. He had seen Creed. And both of them had seen him. Whoever he was, he knew more about what was going on at the waiting room than anyone else human. Creed should have staked out the location on his second visit and tackled and confronted the man. He was unnerving to look at, true. But he was slightly built and Creed was confident he could physically subdue most men. Martin Stride might be a handful, he conceded, surprised the thought had occurred to him. But the creep who prowled the platform would be no sort of opponent for a man with his strength and expertise.

And anger, he thought, as darkness spread like crepuscular fingers across the ground he covered. He was indignant now at Stride's disdainful treatment of him. He was insulted by the thought of that pious exhibitionist Degrelle getting a meaty grip on his mystery. He was frustrated with Elena for telling him so little about what she had discovered on her short trip to Italy. He felt like taking it all out on someone and the sly, quick young fellow with the ugly mouth would be the perfect candidate. It wouldn't even be bullying. He was more the trespasser here than Creed was and he knew something about whatever it was that was going on. Was he a psychic freelancer? Was he a trainspotter with a paranormal gift? Whatever he was, Creed intended to stake out the place and confront him and find out.

Peter had seen the fellow in full daylight and said he'd worn a soldier's uniform, the way that those idiots who re-created historic battles did. Creed had been in battles and shared no hunger for their re-creation. You fought battles only out of the grimmest necessity. You did not celebrate them. No battles had been fought on this ground, though, except perhaps in the minds of the shell-shocked soldiers disembarking at Shale Point on the way to Edward Brody's loony bin. Maybe Peter had been mistaken and the bloke was a train nut and the outfit was a train guard's uniform. Now that really would be creepy, he conceded. He hefted the metal flask in his hand. It wore a concealing coat of matt black paint. It was his one concession to luxury and contained coffee for his night vigil. Monica Stride had prepared him coffee for both his previous visits and he was a superstitious man like most soldiers and the coffee here had become a tradition now he would not willingly break with.

He stopped. The gathering darkness was making him aware

of things. He could see the twinkling flashlights of the men guarding the grounds and hear their dogs panting and their call signals as their voices carried sharply through the night. He crouched and counted and waited. And he smiled. They were amateurs, an ill-disciplined lot, completing ragged circuit patrols, half-trained Dobermanns straining at the leash after scenting rabbits and hares. These men would have number-one crops and badly inked forearms and bellies over their belts. Their mission of choice would be a mob-handed tear-up at the local pub. He'd have to put Stride in touch with some security people worthy of his cash should the need in the future ever genuinely arise.

He began to move again. He did not think that there would be a guard on the waiting room itself. These men would be tasked to secure the house. Stride's absence on a school trip would be known about in the village. Times were hard and thieves opportunistic. In employing this firm, Stride had probably given an honest week's work to most of the petty criminals in the region anyway. No, he did not think there would be a guard on the waiting room. Apart from anything else, Stride did not want the haunting to become public knowledge. *Also*, thought Creed somewhat despondently, *he has asked me to stay away and I have agreed and he thinks that I am entirely a man of my word.*

Oh well. He could see the outline of the building. It stood very dark and very still. It had been a terrible pun, but it had been true when he had made it and it remained true: this relic of a place really did seem to be waiting for something. He could smell the fruit from the blackberry bushes that skirted the island platform, overripe in the unseasonal warmth of the days now and starting to corrupt. Its scent in the fresh-ness of the night was cloying and rank. He crept around the platform perimeter. Silence seemed to spread from within the waiting room itself like a dark imposition on the surrounding land. There was no one inside. He would have sensed movement, heard breathing. There was no one outside, either. He did not mount the platform and open the door and enter the place because he did not want to provoke ghostly activity. His quarry tonight was human and he would lie up still and quiet and simply wait the man out.

It was about an hour later that he thought he heard the approach of a train. And he recognised the sound. It was not the troop-carrying iron goliath of his first encounter. It was the small engine suited to a branch line that had delivered the grieving Lady Ross on his last visit here. So far, he had not risked coffee. He was afraid the man he wished to confront might smell it from a distance and take fright. But he was very alert. He suspected the fitful dozing to which the waiting room inclined him was actually imposed by the place. Outside its walls, he felt no inclination to slumber through parts of the night. He was combat-ready, he realised. It was a familiar feeling from his past and as the sound of the approaching train increased, as the forgotten lines began to hum under the burden of phantom iron wheels, he took comfort in it.

The train, unseen, braked and huffed on the far side of the platform from where he lay. He saw steam billow palely around the single building before him. He listened for the approach of curious security personnel. But they did not come. The house was their concern and unaware of the vastness of the grounds, they would not think the carrying sound odd or incongruous. The breeze was a westerly tonight. They probably wouldn't even hear it, he thought, as the waiting room door softly opened and closed again and the engine clanked and wearied away, going nowhere real.

There were blind spots, he knew. His surveillance was incomplete because he could not guard every approach to the platform. He had chosen the spot he had because it was the most dominant piece of ground available with enough bush and scrub to conceal him fully from observing eyes. He was counting on the strange visitor strolling up to the waiting room rather than approaching stealthily, as he had done himself. Most of the approaches he could see. But in the darkness and with the concealing bulk of that building on the platform, it was impossible to monitor all of those possible. That would have taken a vigilant team of three. And there was only one of him.

Light had come on in the waiting room. Its yellow gas lamp had flared into life and he could hear the disconsolate moans of its occupant as the ghost of Lady Ross revisited the anguish of her life. The sound of her grief was faint and the light timid through the arched windows and the waiting room, he knew, could not be seen even from the upper floors of the house. On a bright day, all of it that was visible from there was a patch of umber roof a half a mile away. He tensed anyway, half-expecting summoned shouts and barks and the beams of flashlights. But none came. There was just the crying and pleading of the forlorn and beautiful phantom in her blue coat and remembered madness.

Creed unscrewed his flask and risked pouring a cup of coffee. It was a mild night, not cold at all. But his skin was tingling with goosebumps and he needed the fortification of a hot drink. It scalded his throat and warmed his stomach and filled his mouth with the welcome favour of the real and demonstrable and he was grateful for it. And then the sound in the building out there in Stride's wilderness subtly changed. It was no longer a despairing monologue. It was a conversation. But he could not hear individual words or make out the sense of what was being said, no matter how hard he strained. And he dared not break cover and approach. He did not want to do that until he had the leering stranger firmly in his sights.

He wondered if Mary Ross had summoned the ghost of Edward Brody to comfort and counsel her. He could picture the consumptive psychiatrist in his tweed suit and spectacles, offering words of consolation. And it was this thought, the prospect of this sight that goaded Creed finally into breaking cover. He had no camera with him. There were difficulties anyway in filming here what the eye plainly saw but the lens for some reason failed properly to register. In an ideal word, he would have had Tony Pullen and Mickey Joyce with their Cockney banter and armfuls of reassuring gear flanking him. But even though he did not, the sight of the doctor and his patient, long dead but somehow present and visible together, was too great a temptation to ignore.

He was halfway across the ground when he heard the approach again of the train. It meant the consultation was at an end. Lady Ross was departing. But how had Brody arrived? Creed paused in plain sight, horribly exposed he realised, in no man's land as the engine noise grew louder and the lights in the waiting room began subtly to dim. All he could do was crouch on the ground and wait. He did not dare risk full exposure to the train's arrival. He suspected the psychic shock of that event so colossally close to it might cause him physical harm. It was not meant to be. It affronted the natural order of things, defying physics and chronology. It was enough to smell the steam and see the sparks from the engine's boiler. It was not safe for a thing of flesh and blood to get closer than he had to this snarling assault on normality.

He waited until the train had gone. He saw that the light in the windows of the waiting room had become un-stable and somehow rickety, like the light from an old hurri-cane lamp. It was a dim, uncertain orange glow. He crept closer. He became aware of a sardonic male voice from within, reciting something. It was verse, but though he could make out cadence and rhythm, he could not discern indi-vidual words. Then the voice began to croon a song. It was 'Roses of Picardy'. And the mockery of the tone was in such bitter contrast to the sentiment of the lyrics that it made the performance sound hollow and dispiriting and somehow futile.

Creed's approach was stealthy and silent. You did not

challenge the ground. You colluded with it, damaging nothing underfoot and disturbing nothing either. He progressed around the platform and found the trodden spot Peter and his friends had left with their bike tyres in the thorns. The smell of spoiled fruit reminded him of fleshly decomposition, it was that rich with decay in his nostrils. Then as he gained the platform and neared the waiting room door, it faded. And he became aware of other smells. These were smells from within. The singing had stopped now. All was quiet. And none of these odours should have been there. There was harsh tobacco and heavy cologne; wet wool drying before a coal fire, hair oil and the sour tang of metal polish. Creed had not smelled that since the last time he had polished the bayonet on his rifle and buttons on his dress tunic on the day of his final regimental parade. Bulling kit was not a thing one did in civilian life.

'Major Creed,' said a voice. 'Don't be shy. By all means, come on in and join me. I rather enjoy company. I find it very stimulating.'

Creed had his hand on the doorknob. He began to turn it and at the same time to push. He heard the snick then of calibrated steel and stopped and swallowed. He had recognised the sound. It was the snick of a revolver when you turned the chamber, loading it with bullets.

He could turn and run. But even in the darkness, his back presented a big target. He did not want to be shot in the back. Those old service revolvers punched exit wounds in a man's torso the size of a dinner plate. He thought he knew who it was, now, inviting him into the waiting room. And it was not Brody, the psychiatrist. He thought about the gun and the cold hand cradling it. They had customised their ordnance. They had scored the tips of their bullets so that they opened out on impact like the dum-dum bullets their enemy had used. He took a breath and with his palm greasy with sweat on the brass of the knob, he opened the door.

The waiting room lay cold and empty. There was an open window. Only the odours of recent occupation remained, among them the stagnant smell from the puddles under the blooms that flowered in the presence of Lady Ross's grief. So it had been her. But it had not been Brody with her. He walked over to the window. There was a figure moving elusively and fast over the ground a hundred metres away. He was dressed in dull uniform clothing and Creed thought he caught the leather sliver in starlight of a Sam Browne belt. But the figure was quick and silent and it shrank rapidly to nothing in the night. Creed closed the window. He looked around. There was a glass on the top of the blued iron stove. Next to it, there stood a single bullet. There was half an inch of liquid in the glass and when he raised and sniffed it, it was gin. He put the glass back down. He felt toyed with, mocked. He felt empty. His ill-considered plan had deserved to fail. It had been no plan at all. He had acted out of petulant defiance after being sacked by Martin Stride. There was a line that separated a man of action from a fool acting on impulse and he had crossed it. He had been lucky not to come to actual harm. He needed to know what Elena had discovered. It would be dangerous to come here again before he had. Knowledge was power, after all. He latched the waiting room window, praying she had acquired some.

At first light the following morning, Martin Stride set off on his daily run. He did so after checking his mobile for messages left late the night before, after he and Monica had gone to bed. The one he dreaded getting was the one from Carter, the boss of the security firm guarding the house, saying that they had spotted an intruder on the property. They probably wouldn't catch him. Creed was ex-SAS and no doubt retained all his old fitness and evasive skills. But with Peter frightened and the publicity-hungry priest due after the weekend, a renegade ghost hunter was a complication he just did not need.

Thankfully, there were no messages. Creed was apparently behaving himself.

He set off along the coastal path, towards Steephill Cove. The sea to his left was green and roiling in the early light, dappled and unstill. The air hung heavy with spray and salt and the tough, fibrous grass tugged at his feet as he trailed a dewy path, thinking of the details he had omitted to tell Julian Creed about his decade-long ownership of the land on which the waiting room and its island platform sat.

He had known considerably more about the asylum than he had let on to Creed. He had not told him because he had held just the slightest suspicion that Creed might actually be a fraud. Monica had been the true believer. He had always thought Creed entirely convincing on the television. But there was just the outside possibility that it was all a lucrative act. He had not told Creed everything he knew because he had not wanted to provide the man with material for his illusions if he was a fake. Anyone genuinely in touch with the spirit world would not have need of tips and pointers.

That had been Stride's reasoning, the motive for his reticence. Of course, it didn't matter now. They weren't dealing with troubled spirits, were they? They were confronted by something demonic and it was work not for a ghost hunter but for an exorcist. Degrelle had been emphatic about that after his original visit to the building. But Stride had vacillated, fearing the circus of publicity so often provoked in the press by the occult. He thought of Peter and the poem and hoped as he kept hoping that the delay in allowing Degrelle's ritual had not made things worse and encouraged the malevolent thing threatening them to accelerate and grow. He suspected it had. That had been Degrelle's inference in their uncomfortable telephone conversation of the other night. The longer you left these forces to gather, the stronger they got. The sooner you confronted them, the better. His vacillation had made the exorcist's task vastly more difficult and dangerous.

He ran. The day grew brighter. The sea to his left lightened in colour to a grey so vivid it was almost blue. The country was beautiful here, nowhere lovelier, he didn't think, in the world. But he did not think about the scenery now. His mind was on Barrowclough, the landowner who had sold him the acreage on which the remains of Shale Point station stood at the turn of the millennium when that bellicose old farmer had finally accepted it was one wilderness he would not now live to cultivate.

Barrowclough it was who had told him about the asylum when he first climbed onto the platform and explored the waiting room for himself. Barrowclough had not followed. He was elderly and walked with the aid of a stick. It was a hot day in a blistering July. Heat ripple made the platform under his feet seem insubstantial at its far end amid its angel hair perimeter of thorns. Barrowclough stood and panted, fanning his face with a wide-brimmed hat. There were no trees mature enough to have a stature that would give the old man shade. The ground beneath the farmer's feet was parched, burnished. Stride jumped down.

'Thought rock stars were all drugs and defibrillation.'

'I'm not a rock star any more, Mr Barrowclough.'

'Tom. You move like a fell runner.'

'What was it for, Tom? Why on earth is it here?'

'It served a purpose once. Let's find a spot of shade and I'll tell you a story,' Barrowclough said.

'There's shade up there,' Stride said, nodding towards the waiting room. 'I'll help you onto the platform.'

'I don't care for the shade up there,' Barrowclough said, walking away. Stride followed.

Barrowclough's uncle William had been a conscientious objector to the Great War. He had been called up and refused to go and taken before the court. He was given the choice of serving a prison term or, for the duration of the war, helping with the war effort in a civilian capacity. He had been replacing broken sleepers on the railway line for three months when the Falcon Lodge asylum opened in 1916 and he was told he would work there from then on as a ward assistant.

He thought he would find the work traumatic. He thought that seeing men driven insane by the horrors they faced at the Front would torture his own conscience and make him ashamed of his pacifist refusal to fight. But what he actually found was that helping them back to full health eased the burden of his own guilt. He liked and respected Edward Brody, a man he considered an inspiration to everyone around him. William Barrowclough was not a farmer, as his brother was and his nephew was to become. He was an architect. He had enjoyed a liberal education and he and Brody became firm friends who regarded one another as equals. They walked together. They sat and sipped beer together in the saloon bar of the village pub. They discussed ethics and philosophy and poetry and what the future when the peace was delivered might hold.

When the armistice came, William was allowed to return to his practice. There had been periods of the war when the attitude to 'conchies' was so bitterly contemptuous it led in some instances to actual violence. But the peace brought a sober reappraisal of the war and its motives and consequences and the general feeling was one of futility rather than triumphalism. It had cost much and achieved little if anything. It became fashionable to believe that perhaps if more people had been brave enough to refuse to fight, the conflict would never have achieved its horrific scale and arduous duration. It would have been a smaller war, over quicker. The objectors, in this revisionist perspective, were not cowards. They were brave and principled and had held to the courage of rightful convictions.

In this surprising new climate, William Barrowclough's practice prospered. But he did not forget the asylum or his friend, Edward Brody. He bought a charabanc for the use of the day patients allowed to pick the fruit from apple orchards or enjoy a day of sea bathing in the summer months. And he met the salary of its driver. He received a letter of thanks for this from Sir Robert Paley. When a summer house was proposed for the asylum in the autumn of 1921, he designed the building without charge. He became one of the Friends of Falcon Lodge and sat on its committee of directors, where the insights from his work on the wards were seen as invaluable.

So much was family history. But the interesting part of the story was the part personally related by William to his nephew as he lay on his deathbed in the autumn of 1967, more than forty years after Falcon Lodge had closed down and been rendered to rubble by the sledgehammer and the wrecking ball. This was the tale he related. And Tom Barrowclough never forgot it. And he told it to the man who had just purchased his land in the shade of an oak on a sun-dappled day at the turn of the new century.

In 1924, Brody abruptly announced his decision to resign from his position. William Barrowclough telephoned him on hearing the news. Brody seemed deeply upset. He was distant and uncommunicative, like a man in shock. When the decision became public knowledge, Sir Robert Paley tried to organise a parting dinner for the man who had done so much to make Falcon Lodge such a beacon of hope and focus of healing. William was of course invited. But Brody himself cancelled the dinner, blaming his illness, saying he wasn't up to hosting a formal public occasion of the sort. He planned a trip, he said, to give his ailing lungs some respite from the damp and dirty English air. His departure was imminent. His wellbeing depended upon it. William persisted; a last drink, he said, just a final visit to the pub, for old time's sake.

Brody relented.

William arrived at the hospital at six o'clock on a wet October evening. News of his arrival was relayed from reception to Brody's office. The doctor begs your indulgence and will be with you in fifteen minutes, he was told. He nodded. Brody's workload made it ever thus. To kill the intervening time, he walked back out of the main building and around to the summer-house sited to its right. He had seen lights on in there and heard music playing on his arrival and was curious to see to what use the addition he had designed was now being put.

The music was a recording of the Irish tenor John McCormack. He was singing the sentimental marching song, 'Roses of Picardy'. A nurse in a starched uniform stood in a pool of lamplight next to the gramophone. Before her was a patient in a wheelchair. He was drooling and catatonic, his eyes fixed on some vacant horror and his limbs twisted into the buckled canvas prison of a straitjacket. And William knew him. He was Captain Broad, the infantry hero, the man who had earned a Military Cross at Paschendaele and been committed after stripping off his clothes on the top deck of a bus in Piccadilly a few weeks after the armistice.

William was shocked and deeply saddened to see the Captain in such a state. He had never recovered from his breakdown sufficiently to meet the demands of life outside the asylum. But over recent years, he had been a familiar sight to anyone visiting in the grounds, tending the shrubs, trusted with secateurs, pruning and planting and smiling in his pride at the simple tasks he completed and the rewarding results they brought to his damaged senses. It was awful seeing him like this. This deterioration was the opposite of what Falcon Lodge generally achieved. 'Roses of Picardy' played under the gramophone needle as William approached the drooling wreck of Captain Broad and there was no recognition in his terrified gaze.

Seeing Edward Brody a few minutes later was almost as much of a shock. He appeared shrunken and emaciated. *His disease has finally taken its fatal grip of him*, William thought. *And his hair has turned in weeks entirely grey.*

It was a couple of hours later, in the flush of beer and the warmth of a cheery fire in the snug of the pub when William remembered poor Captain Broad and his catastrophic deterioration. He asked his friend, what could have caused him to revert in such a way?

Brody flinched at the mention of Broad and there was a tremor in his hand when he raised his glass to drink before answering. 'He thought he saw a ghost. He thought he saw the ghost of an old comrade in the garden of the asylum at dusk, grinning at him.'

'Who did he think it was?'

'A young subaltern he'd seen cut to pieces by machine gun fire in France in 1918.'

'Could he not be persuaded that he was mistaken?'

'That he didn't see a ghost, you mean?'

'Yes.'

Brody fished in his pocket for the change for another round. 'He wasn't mistaken.'

'You mean to say he really saw a ghost?'

'No. He didn't. I think it might have been far better for him and for all of us if he had.'

Brody could be persuaded to add nothing more to this enigmatic claim. But William Barrowclough never forgot the plight of Captain Broad or the strange explanation for it. And neither did the nephew to whom he told the story and from whom Martin Stride bought the land on which the station remnants still stood.

Tom Barrowclough had nodded in the direction of the waiting room from under the broad brim of his hat. 'I don't know why it's survived intact so long,' he told Stride. 'That's the truthful answer to your question. I bought the acreage and never did anything with it and I can't really say why. But that's where that poor bugger Broad would have sat with his medal pinned to his chest and waited between his orderlies for the car to take him to Falcon Lodge. His was a one-way ticket. I think that building saw its share of human torment.'

Stride had paid Tom Barrowclough eighty thousand pounds for the land he bought from him. Years later, with Barrowclough dead and buried by then, he learned it was the precise sum the old farmer had subsequently donated to the village church to pay for the new roof it needed.

He had reached St Catherine's Point. It was here that he always stopped and headed back. He had the day's voluntary duties to carry out. But first he would find a quiet spot where no one could spy on him and perform a little ritual. He took a stop watch from where it hung on the ribbon around his neck and in a clearing hung it on a tree branch where it would be at eye level. Then he stripped off his top and shaped his fists into a guard. It was his habit to shadow-box three five-minute rounds, putting everything into his punches. Today was no exception. After a minute, the spent sweat was spraying in droplets from his eyebrows and the tip of his nose as his punches cleaved the air with an audible snap and he grunted out the exhalations, timing them.

He had been eleven when the humiliation of having his schoolmates knock on his door, carrying the hamper they had collected for in class to give to the poor of the parish, finally grew too much for him to bear. His anger overcame him and he vandalised a telephone box, weeping with fury, smashing the tiny panes of glass and wrenching the receiver from its cable. The copper who caught him in the act of doing this was the old-fashioned, unreconstructed sort. He got off his bike and leant it against the phone box and dragged Stride out and hit him so hard on the ear that the lobe tore and the ear began to bleed. Then he took the abused appendage between finger and thumb and dragged his young criminal to the premises a few streets away of the village boxing club.

'This is the place for letting off steam, son,' he said.

The boot up the backside that delivered him into that

soot-stained shack of corrugated tin was his last encounter with the forces of the law. He duly learned to box. He took out his frustration at the injustices of life on the heavy bag. By the age of twelve, he was sparring with the over-sixteens. He was far too much of a handful for anyone younger. He won belts and cups. He won a clutch of junior titles, mostly by knockout. There was heady talk of Olympic gold. But then he discovered music and girls and his anger seemed to dissipate. He retired from the game at sixteen, still unbeaten. It was a long time ago, a part of his secret history, but he had retained the strength and reflexes and he had never forgotten the skills. And so he did his three five-minute rounds, the sweat exploding out of him, the combinations fast and forceful as they cut through space. And he watched the ticking minutes on the stopwatch and thought about the dark threat confronting his family and prayed he was not helpless in the face of it.

Martin Stride thought that there were two sorts of secret. There was the fact you deliberately concealed and there was the thing the world just failed to remember and you failed ever to remind it about. His boxing fell into the latter category. He supposed that the iron-bound chest of stuff he had been willed on Tom Barrowclough's death fell into the former. It resided somewhere in the attic of the house. He had never even opened it. He would have told Julian Creed about its existence eventually. Now though, there was no one worth telling. He dropped to the ground with his shadow-boxing completed and did a hundred thumb-touch press-ups on the sandy earth.

When he got back to the Hambrough, he took a quick shower and changed, ready for the day's activities with Peter's class. Before leaving for the hostel, he checked his phone again. He saw that Carter, the security firm boss, had called, but left no message. He returned the call.

'No real cause for alarm,' Carter said. 'We lost a dog, is all.'

'What do you mean by "lost"?'

'Handler thought he saw someone, a poacher probably, after one of your deer. He let the dog off the leash and that was the last he saw of it until first light.'

'The dog returned then?'

'He found it dead. A Dobermann's a formidable dog, but the breeding makes some of them a bit high strung.'

'What do you mean?'

'It seems to have been spooked, Mr Stride. We think it died of fright.'

Elena was tempted to go straight to Coutts when she woke that morning. She had enjoyed very little sleep. The fog had lifted only late the previous evening. Most of her night had been spent in transit and she had never been comfortable enough with flying to be able to nap at thirty thousand feet. Excitement woke her two hours after her head hit the pillow in her Bermondsey bedroom. She showered and drank a cup of tea and then decided to walk to work. She owed it to Creed to explain to him exactly what had occurred in Italy. She wanted to be at Coutts on the Strand when they opened their doors. That was assuming Creed was going to reach the office early enough. And it was further assuming that he would agree it was her task and not his to fetch the Absalom deposition from the strong-box at the bank. Her decision to walk to work was made simply to kill time she wished already gone.

Creed was at the office when she arrived just after eight thirty and he looked rumpled and unhappy. Actually, she thought, he looked tormented. She remembered then that Martin Stride had put an end to their investigation. The eager anticipation of her Coutts discovery had prevented her from fully considering the consequences of that decision, or even the reason for it. She sat down in Creed's office and took the envelope from her bag and explained what it was and how she had come to possess it. And Creed told her about his brief visit to Ventnor and the Owen poem. And he told her about the previous night and the night occupant of the waiting room.

'Does none of this frighten you?' she said to him when he had concluded his account.

'All of it does,' he said. 'You saw the headstone. What was the year of Bruno Absalom's death?'

'He died in 1927.'

'It seems very ominous that more than eighty years before your visit, he was able to predict it to the point of an accurate physical description. It seems very ominous that the person I tried to confront last night knew not only my name, but my military rank.'

'Most ominous of all is the poem,' Elena said. 'I read it on the flight out.'

'Not an easy read.'

'Poor Peter.'

'He was very shaken and upset, his father said. I don't think he read the verses and I don't think an eleven-year-old would necessarily understand what they were about. But the fact of it was a nasty shock and a violation and I can't see it as anything other than a warning. Stride is right about that.'

Creed looked haggard, she decided. And seeing him, she felt very discouraged. The implications of what had occurred over the last twenty-four hours were becoming plainer to her. 'We're out of our depth,' she said.

That made Creed snort with laughter. 'Who wouldn't be, in this situation? Do you really think Monsignor Degrelle is going to stop all this in its tracks with a little recitation of medieval liturgy and a dab of holy water after the weekend?'

'No. I don't,' she said.

Creed picked up the envelope given her by Father Berra. 'We're out of our depth because anyone would be,' he said. 'Anyone human, I mean. We're dealing with uncommon forces.'

'We're not dealing with them at all,' she said. 'We're being toyed with by them.'

Creed considered this. He had the envelope in his hand. She thought that this experience was changing him. The bluster had gone. The repartee was missing. All the stock phrases on which he relied were inadequate to the situation they were in and he had been forced back verbally into sincerity and spontaneous truth. It was vastly a change for the better and she liked him the better for it.

'I apologise for that terrible pun, Elena.'

'What pun?'

He looked her in the eye. 'Tracks,' he said, 'as in trains.'

Despite herself, she smiled at him. 'Phantom trains,' she said.

He nodded, silent for a moment. 'I should not have gone back to the waiting room last night. I did it motivated by wounded pride. Fraud that I've always been, I'd no right to that pride. And my going there might have placed the Stride family in greater jeopardy after the warning of the poem.'

'Nothing else has happened,' Elena said. 'The Strides are early risers. You would know by now. Martin called you straightaway after finding the poem.'

'Not straightaway. First he comforted his traumatised son.' Creed held out the envelope. 'We can take this where it leads us or we can feed it into the shredder. Reading or not reading the deposition left by Bruno Absalom is entirely a matter of choice. It does not contravene Stride's instructions. Stride has never even heard of Bruno Absalom.'

'You made the connection through Lady Ross,' Elena said. 'You saw her in the waiting room.'

'I did. But that was before Stride fired me. Ethically, I think we've every right to pursue the Absalom enigma as far as it takes us. This is social history, or it's to do with the history of spiritualism or the fashion for spiritualism created by the awful casualty toll of the Great War. Martin Stride has no right to censor history. The Absalom deposition exists outside his ownership and remit.'

Elena nodded. 'Agreed,' she said.

'In the hours and days of your employment, I pay for your time,' Creed said. 'But after last night, I really do not feel comfortable instructing you to probe any further into this particular mystery. I said a minute ago it was our choice. I know what mine is. You need to decide on yours.'

Elena stood and took the envelope from Creed's hand. 'Eighty years is a fair length of time,' she said. 'Do you think they will still have it?'

'I believe they still have correspondence from Byron and Shelley concerning their unauthorised overdrafts,' Creed said. 'This is Coutts, after all. They will have it, all right. It will be safe under lock and key and in the same condition it was in on the day it was deposited.'

She smiled and turned to go. Their choice, he had said. But Elena did not think they had ever really had a choice in this matter at all.

# Chapter Seven

He walked with her to the bank. She thought it an act of old-fashioned chivalry. He was her escort, her chaperone. There was a great deal to like about him, she thought. Men on a construction site recognised him and shouted from their scaffolding and one of them wolf-whistled and he blew them a theatrical kiss.

'I think the whistle was for me.'

'I know,' he said, grinning. 'But they don't know I know.'

A couple of the workmen clambered down and jogged over and he signed their hard hats with the marker pen one of them produced. He wrote a suggestive message across a page from the *Sun* for the wife of a welder it was claimed had a crush on him. It transpired the site foreman had been in the Falklands, at Goose Green and Tumbledown, and there followed the obligatory manly hug and sniff of curtailed emotion beside a skip with traffic cones around it next to the gawping drivers passing along the road at funeral pace.

An elderly woman stopped him as they reached the Strand and asked him to sign his autograph for her grandson. He was all solicitousness as he asked the grandson's name and how old was the lad. He looked better now, refreshed by the open air and the attention and Elena thought, *He lives for this. He does. Fame is the stuff of his life. Recognition vindicates him. Without it, he would wilt like a plant denied the sun.* He still looked rumpled. But it was the look now of a charismatic gambler who'd suffered reckless losses seated at the blackjack table till dawn broke through the casino windows in somewhere like Monte Carlo. It was a cinematic, handsome sort of dishevelment, no longer the look of a man who might have seen a corpse staring back at him that morning from his shaving mirror.

*He scares like anyone else*, she thought, as they entered the grand glass and marble vestibule of the bank. *But he has more than his share of courage and phenomenal resilience.* Liking him like she felt she was starting to do again felt like a betrayal of her principles. But continuing to dislike him required a lot of effort. His remark about the shredder had not been rhetoric or one of his famous double-bluffs. He had meant it. His first concern on hearing about what had happened in Italy had been of the threat it might pose to her wellbeing. Maybe she should try to find it in her heart to forgive him. If she could do that, work would be a lot more fulfilling, she knew. And she would be happier.

After presenting the document, it was taken away for scrutiny while they waited in an ante-room to which they were shown. Elena did not know whether this was standard Coutts procedure or because Julian Creed had been recognised. They sat in a tense silence for about twenty minutes before the door opened and a middle-aged man walked in bearing a deep-sided plastic tray of the sort used at airport security gates for anything that might innocently trigger the metal detector. On, or rather *in* the tray, was an old-fashioned brown briefcase secured by two buckled straps and a brass lock. The man put the briefcase down on the desk at the centre of the room. He dusted his hands together. He took a key from a waistcoat pocket and held it up.

'A moment of history,' he said.

*A moment of theatre*, Elena thought. She looked at Creed, who looked at her and made a gesture of deferral. She was to take the key. She did so and then lifted the briefcase by its handle out of the tray, surprised by the substantial weight of it, aware that whatever it concealed was hard and dense and heavy. She opened the briefcase. It contained only one item. She lifted it out. It was a single volume with a marbled binding and gold leaf gilding the page edges and she put it on the desk and all three people in the room gathered and stared at it. The September sun shone through the high window of the ante-room and Elena was aware that this book was experiencing daylight for the first time after eighty years of darkness. How much darkness, she couldn't help but wonder, did its subject matter contain?

She took a breath and lifted the cover and read the words under the date on the first page. They made her frown. She flicked through further pages. The writing was small and precise and very legible. Bruno Absalom had been in possession of a fine hand and a very good fountain pen.

'It isn't a deposition at all,' Elena said. 'It's a diary.'

'Maybe it's both,' Creed said. 'A diary can be a sort of confession.' He turned to the man from Coutts. 'What would it cost to keep a thing like this secure here for that length of time?'

'I cannot tell you, Mr Creed,' the man said. 'To do so would breach the confidentiality of a valued client.'

'This particular client of yours died in 1927.'

'My father and grandfather worked for this bank. As a young man, my father knew Mr Absalom. Even if it were not for the personal link, his memory would be entitled to the same confidentiality from us he enjoyed in life.'

Creed smiled and reached and tapped the diary with his palm. 'This must run to three hundred pages. It is his personal journal. And it was bequeathed us. I doubt he would mind your betraying a few inconsequential trade secrets.'

The Coutts man cleared his throat and his cheeks coloured slightly. 'Mr Absalom left a very considerable sum deposited with us. I can tell you that the interest alone on that deposit has easily covered the cost of keeping this item secure.'

'What will happen to that money now?' Elena asked.

'All of it will go to charity. That was his instruction, once this item had been rightfully claimed.'

'Can I ask which charity?'

'I cannot see the harm in telling you. It will go to the Commonwealth War Graves Commission.'

'Money for the upkeep of cenotaphs in public squares and church wall plaques,' Creed said. 'Money now destined to pay for the neatly clipped grass on graves on the Somme and for the cleaning of bronze memorials.'

'Indeed,' said the Coutts man.

'It's an odd choice, for an Italian,' Elena said.

'Italy was Britain's ally in the Great War,' Creed said.

'I know that. But it's still an odd choice.'

The man from Coutts said nothing. Elena put the diary back into the briefcase and locked it again. She thanked him for his time and they were escorted with their prize out of the bank.

'That chap knows more than he's letting on,' Creed said, on the walk back to the office.

'Meaning what?'

'Something he heard on his grandfather's lap, perhaps.'

Elena raised the briefcase she was carrying and tapped it with a finger. 'I suspect that when we've read this, we'll know a great deal more than whatever it was his grandfather told him.'

Creed stopped walking. 'Take it home, Elena.'

She stopped too. She was stunned. 'Don't you want me to photocopy it for you?'

'You're a world-class researcher. You're not going to miss anything I'm likely to spot. I've been ignoring my diary ever since this Stride business started and if I don't start attending meetings and responding to calls soon, the media world is going to think there is something seriously amiss with Julian Creed. Today is Thursday. The exorcism is planned for Monday afternoon. The Strides don't return from Wight until

Monday morning. Take the diary home. No distractions. Lock the door and disconnect the phone. Go and read it and when you have read it, précis what you've learned and talk to me.'

Elena thought about the task, about the three hundred pages or so of closely written text in the document she carried. 'It's going to be the weekend.'

'Good. I was hoping you'd say that. I'd very much like it to be before Monday.'

'This investigation is playing havoc with my social life.'

'See? You can even find the time for irony.'

'What a gal,' she said. He smiled. Without knowing she was going to do it until it was done, she reached out and grazed his cheek with her knuckles before turning and making for the Underground.

Millie was with her mummy on the beach at Ventnor. There was a big wooden shed on the promenade that extended out over the beach on stilts and it was painted blue and said 'Blakes' in cream writing on the side. Under the shed, between the stilts, a lady who was one of the Blakes rented out white canvas windbreaks that had sturdy pointed wooden sticks stitched into them at intervals. Some people brought tents to the beach but her daddy said that was cheating. He always rented deckchairs and a windbreak from the friendly Blakes lady with her bag of change on her belt. When it was all four of them, Daddy rented a beach hut from the Blakes too. But it was just Millie and her mummy today and so only the deckchairs and the windbreak.

Mummy did not drive the sticks as deeply into the sand as Daddy did. That was the best bit; the Blakes lady lent you a mallet that looked about a hundred years old with a thick misshapen head and you drove your sticks down through the pebbles and sand of the beach with mallet blows. Well, Millie didn't. She didn't actually do it herself. But she always watched, nervous for the fingers holding the stick steady, while a parent did it. Mummy laughed and shook her head when Daddy did it and said, 'Has someone forecast a hurricane, darling?' and this always made Daddy laugh. Mummy's mallet blows were lighter. But there was no wind at all on the beach today and Millie did not think a hurricane had been forecast and Mummy had secured their windbreak well enough.

It was cosy within. There was no breeze at all. The air was perfectly still. The canvas walls of the windbreak stood behind her and to her right and left and before her she had a view of the sea. The waves tumbled over one another and crashed and hissed through the shingle. The enveloping canvas walls of the windbreak amplified the noise. She reclined on her deckchair in her shorts and flip-flops and cotton sweater and read her Narnia book and tried not to feel grumpy at Peter for taking Daddy away from her and Mummy, but especially from her. It wasn't just Peter, after all. It was Peter and all his smelly, horrible friends. She wouldn't be like them when she was eleven. For one thing, she would be much nicer and friendlier towards eight-year-olds. What was so wrong with being eight? What was so cool about being eleven?

She looked to her left, to the deckchair next to hers, to where her mummy reclined asleep behind her sunglasses in the snug privacy of their windbreak. At least, she thought her mummy was asleep. Now Mummy really was cool. She looked at the sharp cheekbones of her mother's face and the blonde hair pulled elegantly back and thought that if it wasn't for her daddy, her mummy would be the coolest person on the planet. In a bid at emulation, she put her book down. She smoothed back her own hair. She put on her own sunglasses. She reclined and listened to the rhythm of the breaking waves. And in no time at all, just like her mother, Millie had dropped off too.

And she dreamed. She dreamed of the brown room where the man who coughed blood had tried to comfort the lady in the dream she'd had before. He was sharing it now with another visitor. It was a young man, almost a boy. He wore a soldier's uniform and his face was pale and terrible in the light from a desk lamp and when he spoke, his voice was the rasp of a key in a broken lock.

'Remind me of why we went to war, Dr Brody.'

'I believe the original issue was Belgian territorial integrity.'

'Little Belgium, yes,' the boy soldier said. He laughed. And in sleep, Millie's fingers curled to make small fists in agitation at the sound.

'And now little Belgium comes to threaten my own territorial integrity. I find that ironic.'

The doctor groaned. He put his head in his hands. 'I do not know what you are talking about, Patrick.'

'You are right of course, Doctor. It makes no difference. Faith is the issue. What does it matter where this vain priest was born? Faith is the only requirement.' He laughed again. 'He should pray that his is as strong as he thinks it is.'

The doctor spoke through the cradle of his fingers. 'Malicious riddles, Patrick. Your mind is quite broken. I am afraid I can do nothing for you.'

The boy grinned and his tongue lolled between his teeth and he winked back. And on the beach at Ventnor, Millie Stride was overcome by such terror in her sleep that it caused her to wet herself.

Elena thumbed through the diary to give herself an overview. The first entry had been made in 1918 and the last in 1924. It covered six years, but did so intermittently. There were some substantial gaps between some of the entries. Scanning them, she saw that they were linked thematically. And she saw that, though Bruno Absalom had been born and chosen to die in Italy, his English was the idiom of a native speaker. She brewed a pot of coffee, settled into her reading chair and began at the beginning.

**November 1918**

I had dinner tonight with my dear friend, Samuel Ross, and his lovely
wife, Mary. And it was the saddest occasion I can ever remember
having endured. They have lost their only son, Patrick, to the fighting
in France. Even as the war stumbles exhausted to its conclusion, it has
claimed another beautiful and precious life. And tonight was not just
sad but horribly disconcerting. Sam is quite broken by the tragic news.
But Mary's emotions are altogether more complex and fraught than
those of my old friend. She refuses to accept the truth and finality of
the telegram they received. It is mistaken identity, she says. It is a
ghastly clerical error. Patrick will appear at their door with his pack on
his back and his rifle slung over his shoulder and much to tell them
about his adventures with his new pals in the trenches.

Mary was full of that bright, febrile jollity that distinguishes people
who surrender willingly to their delusions. The truth is simply too
painful for her mind to bear. It means that Sam is being obliged to
grieve alone rather than sharing the burden with the wife who has
been his companion and confidante through almost twenty years of the
happiest of marriages. When he showed me to the door at the end of
the evening, he confided in a murmur that he is going to ask the
psychiatrist, Edward Brody, to talk to her. He knows well of Brody's
work through his friend, Sir Robert Paley, and thinks that Brody
possesses the compassion and knowledge to help Mary accept and
accommodate the truth. It is human nature to be hopeful in such
situations. But Mary's delusion, though willing, seemed profound to
me. I do not share Sam's optimistic prognosis. Compelled to accept
that Patrick is never coming back, I think she might simply go mad
with grief.

The strange energy of death was all about their house. Everything
looks the same; every painting and stick of furniture and item of
bric-à-brac and piece of silverware on their dining table looked
identical to how it did before Patrick's recent journey into death's
domain. But I would have known of his departure on walking through
their door even had the news yet to be delivered. His spirit was there,

haunting their home, flitting from room to room in its uncertainty and confusion. I felt it as firmly as I feel the press of this pen in my fingers when I put the nib to the page.

My heart bleeds for poor Mary. The last time I saw her was in Brighton at the trial and the celebratory dinner we had together at the Grand Hotel following my acquittal. She had insisted on volunteering herself as a character witness, though of course my barrister saw to it that she was not called. 'I will not have my son's godfather treated like a common criminal,' she said, with a challenging tilt of that handsome, imperious head. In the event of course, twelve good men and true saw to it that I wasn't. She was so different last night to how she was then. I sometimes think the dead are afflicted by their dying less than anyone. But the dead are a subject I have sworn to leave alone. After the Brighton experience, I am loath to resume my dialogue with those on the far side of the divide.

Patrick was my godson and I loved and mourn him. I console myself with the knowledge that I was dutiful in my titular responsibilities. I tried as best as I could to care for his spiritual welfare. It was not difficult. He was intelligent and delightfully sweet-natured and his character distinguished by a rare grace. He was, in short, a marvellously likeable and promising boy. His is the story of this damned and bloody war in microcosm. They've gone like flower petals in the venting fury of the storm. I walked through the thick fog of the London streets after supper from Sam's address in Westminster to the Savoy and my suite there. The lamps are not lit at night of course and twice I found myself in the shuttered beam of a suspicious policeman's torch. It is my overcoat, Mary used to insist, when her mind was still inclined towards the making of a joke. Only spies and subversives wear astrakhan.

I took off my tie and poured a nightcap brandy and sat and wept for Patrick Ross once I was safely alone behind locked doors in the privacy of my rooms. The appalling irony of how Sam made his fortune will not be lost on my friend when he dwells on the manner of his son's death. I thought back to the time at Cambridge when we were young and hopeful together and wondered honestly if either of us has used his intellectual gifts in a way honourable or really fitting. Sam has conjured weapons that kill and maim on a scale the mind can barely contemplate. I have dabbled at the edge of a godless abyss. These are dark thoughts on which to conclude. But the stopper is back in place on the decanter at my elbow. Sleep beckons. Tomorrow is another day. But I doubt it will dawn any brighter.

## January 1919

Each week, Mary Ross dutifully takes the train to Falcon Lodge to argue for an hour with Edward Brody that her son is alive and sound-bodied somewhere and the victim of a miscount of casualties. She believes he is in Manchester. He was serving in the Second Battalion, the Manchester Regiment, and she believes he has gone to that industrious city in the mistaken belief that it is where his life was lived before the conflict. Amnesia provides her latest reasoning for his having not returned to his home address and the warmth of his welcoming family. No matter that the British Army has demonstrated the logistical capability to return four million men to civilian life. No matter that a captain of the Second Battalion and an MC to boot positively identified Patrick's body where it lay beside the canal they were attempting to cross. I believe that only were she to be confronted with a corpse fresh enough to retain his recognisable features would she accept the fact of her son's death. And almost three months after the fact, that grisly proof is of course impossible to provide.

I met Sam last night at his club and would say his despair at this situation has brought my old friend to the brink of suicide. His wife is become a bustling stranger who busies herself daily with the preparations necessary to welcome home her dead son. She has engaged a private detective to try to discover his whereabouts in Lancashire. She has retained the services of this unscrupulous professional at the cost of twenty guineas a month. The money is nothing to them of course, but the fellow feeds her delusion and gives her hope with fictitious sightings aboard an omnibus or in a theatre box. I told Sam he should use his Whitehall contacts to have the man's licence revoked. But I don't believe my old friend has the energy even to lift the telephone and ask for this to be done.

At the conclusion of our unhappy conversation, he put his hand on my arm and asked me frankly, with his bloodshot eyes on mine, were the rumours true about the research I had carried out into the restitution of the dead. I told him truthfully that I had never attempted to do it and had no intention ever of trying.

'So there is no proof,' he said.

'There is no proof that I know of,' I told him sincerely.

Then, scientist that he's always been, in the absence of a proof, he asked me if I would outline the theory. And I agreed with some reluctance to do so.

'Can you accept the principle that death is a dimension?' I asked him.

He looked at me doubtfully. 'I believe in the immortal soul,' he said.

'Imagine death as a kingdom, or domain,' I suggested. 'For the moment, disregard the soul. Imagine, if you will, that death releases a sort of energy. It exists beyond the confines of the body, but retains its human identity.'

'And roams this separate domain, this dimension?'

'That's it precisely.'

'How do you reconstitute it? How do you bring it back?'

'You lure it,' I told him. 'You remind it of what it was to be human. You assemble what relics you have of that person's life and you distil from them an essence. You can do this in the laboratory.'

Sam nodded in agreement at this. This part of the procedure he could understand, because it lent itself to scientific technique. But I knew that for the rest of it, he would require a leap of faith I imagined entirely beyond him.

'When you have done that,' I said, 'you perform the ritual.'

He looked at me very seriously for a long time. A waiter came over to where we sat to see if we required anything and Sam was so absorbed he remained completely unaware of him. I ordered fresh drinks for both of us. I thought my friend might have need of one and

I certainly did, discussing a subject with such serious ramifications.

'What is the provenance of this ritual?' he asked me.

'It was composed and written by a German alchemist called Gunter Keller in the sixteenth century. I came across it by accident. You know I have always had an interest in the arcane antecedents of modern chemistry. Most of Keller's experimentation was chemically based. I bid for his library, or what remained of it, at auction in Hamburg seven years ago. And I found the ritual examining his accounts of his experiments and formulations.'

'Did he actually try to bring back the dead?'

'It's impossible to say. There are few verifiable details about his life. One can say with certainty that he was burned as a heretic in 1530. Not much else is established fact.'

'But there were rumours?'

'There must have been. It was why he was tried and burned.'

'No smoke without fire,' Sam said. He was a man by then capable only of the grimmest comedy. And of course, where Keller was concerned, he was right. 'Did he just invent this ritual?'

I had my own theory about that. I thought it very old. I thought that the Vikings might have brought it back to Europe on returning from one of their exploratory voyages to some destination lost to history. The Norsemen had no written language of their own, but understood the value of knowledge and believed in a kingdom of the dead. The version Keller had was written in medieval German and I am only an amateur linguist but I thought the phraseology suggestive of a translation from runic script. 'It is ancient,' I told my friend, truthfully. 'It certainly pre-dates Christianity by at least a thousand years.'

'We could distil Patrick's essence,' Sam said, a tiny tremor in the hand holding his whisky glass. 'We have everything of his. Mary has made a shrine of his room. You could have everything from his christening bracelet to the teething ring he used as a toddler to the horsehair in the mattress on which he slept until he volunteered to fight. His bed is barely cold.'

'And if we brought him back,' I said, 'what would it achieve?'

'He would be alive,' Sam said. 'And his mother would no longer be mad. She would find her vindication. She would be right.'

The phone rang then on the table beside her and Elena almost jumped out of her chair with fright. She snatched up the receiver.

'It's me. I thought I told you to unplug this thing?'

'No one ever calls me.'

'Wrong. I'm calling you. What have you learned?'

She slid the volume off her lap and onto the table and stood. It was her habit to pace when she talked on the phone. She looked out of the window, half-expecting to see a spectre in an astrakhan coat, but it was only just after midday and the vista was innocent. 'It's really curious, Julian. I think it is a sort of confession. What I think he's done is copied all the relevant, incriminating diary entries from his original diaries. He's a loquacious writer, a typical diarist, but he's sticking to the point and there are big intervals between some of the entries.'

'Is it relevant to the waiting room?'

'Totally.'

'What's he talking about?'

'I've only just finished the second entry. But he's discussing what seems to be an occult or metaphysical parallel to DNA cloning. He's talking about bringing the dead son of Sir Samuel and Lady Ross back to life.'

'Jesus.'

'Jesus isn't involved. The ritual pre-dates Christianity. And Absalom had a fascination with death bordering on the obsessive. He's hinted at some pretty dark activity. He's talked about the abyss.'

'Unless you're a mountaineer, the abyss means black magic,' Creed said. 'And I don't see Bruno Absalom as the type for crampons and climbing ropes.'

'I'll do you a transcript of the really significant bits and have it ready for you by Sunday,' Elena said.

'You are wonderful,' Creed said. 'You really are, you know. And you're beautiful.' He sounded wistful. He rang off. That earlier parting touch between them had not been lost on him.

She put down the phone and looked at the deposition lying next to it. Absalom seemed a very conflicted man. It was not a term that would have been familiar in his lifetime, not even to the psychiatrist Edward Brody, she did not think. But it was accurate. He strove to be good but was attracted irresistibly to what was dark and macabre. He was a man who took pride in caring for the spiritual welfare of his godson. But he seemed tempted at the same time to want to affront nature in a manner wholly abominable.

## September 1919

I tell myself that I did it mostly for my friend. I really did think Sam Ross close to taking his own life. He was a man alone and the light no longer shone on his existence. Now he has Mary again. He can share her conviction that Patrick is returning because I have made it true. They will need to be patient, of course. This is no easy miracle of Christian resurrection. Christ rose because he was a God. And the miracle of the risen Christ was performed in three days. Patrick Ross was a mortal man and his restitution to that status will take time. Nine months is the term of a mother's pregnancy and when the baby is born it is a helpless, mewling creature incapable of anything but crying and suckling and sleep. Patrick will not be whole when he returns. He will need to learn to be complete. But the boy I remember was strong and intelligent and I did what I have accomplished hopeful for his prospects. His parents are loving and kind and their material resources boundless.

I am confident that nobody has done what I have done in modern times. It is hard not to feel a certain pride at having done it. Reversing nature is more than a mere scientific feat. It confounds religious faith and makes foolish our notions of fate and predestination. The event I have set into chain is very momentous for the physical world. It will make the world, will it not, a subtly but profoundly different place?

Keller's scribblings contain a curious warning. He speaks of a plague of the dead. He warns ominously against it. But he is unspecific about the nature and dangers of this pestilence. And he says nothing about its cause. When Patrick returns, I will watch him very carefully. It remains my duty, after all. I will still be the boy's godfather and flatter myself that his father has no closer or more faithful friend on whom to rely.

Tonight, I strolled along the Embankment. The globes of the ornamental lamps that light it glimmered like strung pearls in the darkness and the river lapped in wavelets beneath me. I heard the great clock behind me boom the hour and a fog-horn mournful from a passing tug, though the night was clear. In the day, you see the amputees and the disfigured more, the hideous human wreckage of four years of mechanised conflict. In the evening, one is more aware of the promenading couples with their silver-topped canes and sable coats and leisurely progress and the light peals of laughter that punctuate conversations once again blessedly carefree. Music issued forth from a party boat. 'Roses of Picardy' was the song, sung in a light tenor voice that carried over the calm black water.

And I had for a moment the curious instinct that I was being watched and followed. It was an uncomfortable sensation. I felt almost stalked, as prey, and awfully vulnerable and exposed and the sensation made me shudder in the snug warmth of my overcoat.

It had quite gone by the time I reached Villiers Street and turned away from the river towards the theatre district. The pubs were full and pianola music and raucous chatter and bright gaslight flooded onto the pavements and honeycombed the cobbles of the streets, and it occurred to me that London is a city of ghosts and how grotesque would be the crush and how hideous the clamour were they all to return like unstrung puppets to some parody of life. And the thought was a very unwelcome one. And I found a café and ordered a large glass of cognac and drank it down at a pavement table with the odours of cheap tobacco and unwashed humanity and fresh horseshit

from the street assailing my nostrils and I thought about the notion of
a plague of the dead and wondered, *What have I done?*

A theatre on the Strand advertised an evening with one of the more
notorious mediums and people queued outside for their encounter with
ectoplasm and impersonation and enigmatic messages claiming to be
from the other side. Testimonials in lurid lettering boasted of his
prowess on sandwich boards paraded by boys. A photograph of this
charlatan wearing a turban and a hypnotic stare had been blown up
to ghastly size and pasted above the foyer where it no doubt entranced
the patient throng waiting to enter beneath. I shook my head in
passing. The toll of the war and the influenza has created a ghoulish
industry. People would rather pay for bogus reassurance than confront
their loss and endure their grief honestly. And who, really, can blame
them? The enormity of the loss has been too great.

Will Patrick Ross remember death? In giving an account of its
mysteries, will he breach some unbreakable rule of the universe? I am
starting to wonder about the repercussions of what I have done. The
truth is that I do not know precisely what I have set in motion by
luring a dead man back to mortal life. There is Keller's warning and it
was portentously phrased but makes no sense, since a plague can only
kill the living. A plague of the dead is a contradiction in terms, an
oxymoron, is it not? I don't know why I lied to Sam about Keller. The
lie was an unimportant one, barely worth the sin of its telling. The
truth is that he was burned not for heresy but for witchcraft. What
honest difference does it make?

The cheap brandy drunk at that dive in Villiers Street has given me
heartburn. An evening stroll that started so promisingly on the river
has left me feeling downcast and filled me with trepidation. I think of
those carefree couples and the bright glitter of their promenading and
know that I will never tread the streets with that lightness of foot or
clarity of conscience again. Everything is different now. I feel like Faust
or Frankenstein. Except that they were fictitious and what I have
accomplished is presently to become real: corporeal, flesh and blood
with a will and a mind and appetites and desires and ambitions.

But will it possess a soul? There is nothing in Keller on this. What would a man be like without a soul? A man devoid of a soul would surely be a fearful creature, craving emptily what it no longer possesses. Is it the soul that makes us human, after all? That is a theological or philosophical question. But it is one to which I suspect I might shortly be able to offer a truthful answer. Patrick will be an experiment. That will have to be his status, though to write it seems very cold and almost cruel. He did not wish, after all, to return. But until we are convinced of his completeness, he will have to be carefully studied and monitored. Sam and Mary have the money to make that practicable. I wonder, have they also the necessary will?

## April 1920

I have been afflicted by a psychic sensitivity since I was a young boy. I first saw a ghost in my father's wine cellar at the age of four. He was cataloguing bottles in racks and I did not know why this industrious servant was so picturesquely dressed. I used to explore the cellar, with its gloomy reaches and catacombs of dusty stock. It was a place of adventure and fantasy for the child I was. Then I described my ghost to my mother and she dropped the embroidery she was engaged in sewing and put her hand to her mouth to stifle a scream and the cellar was made out of bounds to me. Out of bounds: an English phrase from my English education but of course when they sent me to England, exiled from the southern light and gentle hills of Italy, there were far more ghosts for me to encounter than I had been prey to at home.

I have learned something about these visions of the dead. It is how I know that the medium filling the theatre on the Strand that night last autumn was a fraud. Ghosts do not generally communicate with the living. They are, for the most part, unaware of us, as we are unaware of them. Most people never see them. People in their presence might hear music or scent something. They might feel a *frisson* of fright that raises gooseflesh on their arms. But they will see nothing. And even if you are one like me who does occasionally see them, you would be ill-advised to engage them. They are not in the present.

To attempt to communicate with them would be to endeavour to overcome the paradox of time and the consequences would afflict the present rather than the past and therefore be of great potential danger.

It might be different if the ghost engaged the person it confronted. I do not know. I have seen spirits. None has tried to communicate with me and I am glad of it. Times past are often characterised by a nostalgic charm. I would not, though, wish to be lured back into another age, however seductive the notion.

My second encounter took place aboard the boat that brought me to England when I was seven. We endured a dreadful storm on the voyage and I was confined to a small cabin deep in the bowels of the vessel lest a wave caught me and washed me overboard. The sea was furious, broaching the deck with almost every wave. We were battened down and the crew fought the tempest while the passengers filled the wooden world beneath them with the stench of fear and vomit and the cries of those despairing of their prospects of survival.

I turned from where I sat and saw him sitting on my bunk. He was singing softly to himself and carving something elaborate with a dagger out of a piece of driftwood. He was heavily decorated about the arms and neck and bare chest with tattoos etched in blue ink. A thick circle of gold punctured one ear lobe and when he smiled at some secret amusement most of his teeth were rotten or entirely missing. The boat was old. She had experienced more than one life. She was a mixed cargo and passenger vessel in the period of my crossing aboard her. But she had once been a fighting ship and I believe this villainous-looking fellow had served aboard her then. He was altogether too fearsome a spectacle for any occupation in civilian life.

Despite the dagger in his hand, I knew he meant me no harm. But I felt it wise not to draw attention to myself. I had the instinct that it was far safer and more circumspect to stay still than to do anything that might attract his curiosity. He carved deliberately and sang softly until eventually the storm abated and I heard footsteps on the companionway outside my cabin door. Then he faded from sight and a member of the crew knocked and entered to check on me. When I looked, he had left no wood shavings from his carving on the blanket of the bunk. But he had not been dreamt.

One sees them mostly in momentous places. By that, I mean one becomes aware of ghosts in places that have borne witness to great events or dramatic activity or intense human emotion. At Cambridge, I started a sort of occult club I look back on now with embarrassment and shame. And its members discussed magic and alchemy and the possibilities of the spirit world. Almost nothing useful emerged from this period of posturing and dabbling and fancy dress. But I did arrive at the conclusion concerning contact between ghosts and the living in which I still hold trust.

I believe we go back somehow to their time. That is how we see them. The events they were part of have a pull or orbit into which we are dragged as unwilling witnesses. It is as though the intensity of emotion or experience they endured in life cannot be eradicated by the calendar. We are the visitors. And we must observe the protocols of the past or face awful consequences. It would be terrible to be stranded, anomalous, in a time not your own. Yet that is, I believe, the risk if a ghost was to become aware of the person observing it.

It was not much of a risk in my father's cellar, seeing a man from his grandfather's domestic staff inventory wine stock at the age of four. That was only my gentle and mundane introduction to my own psychic gift. It was slightly more of a risk in the storm at sea, sharing a cabin with a sailor I believe died in battle aboard that old craft in the time when Nelson fought his bloody engagements against the French and Spanish Navies. But there are places where the risk is very great and the summoned spirits angry or anguished, and these are locations I have considered it best to avoid.

Patrick Ross is not a ghost and I have not encountered him since his mortal death eighteen months ago. He does not exist as a spirit, in some turbulent recent past. I believe he is alive again and I believe he has made contact with the parents who loved him and wished so ardently for his return. Samuel Ross denies it. Mary Ross is just as adamant. But I know that my oldest friends are lying. I did not expect this. It has come as a dreadful surprise to me. And I do not know the reason why they would lie, though of course I have my fears and suspicions.

The situation makes pious nonsense of my pledge to continue to nurture Patrick's spirit on his return. If his parents continue to deny it, I am unlikely to be able to gain even casual access to the boy. I was always confident they had the material resources to cope with the inevitable difficulties of his rehabilitation. It never occurred to me that they would use their wealth to hide him. But that is what I suspect they are doing. He could be at their house in the country. He could be at the lodge Sam maintains for fishing in Scotland or at their summer place on Wight. He will be at none of those places, of course, if they have bought him a property of his own. Perhaps I should beg the name and address of her private detective from Mary and see what he can discover on my behalf.

Samuel Ross has aged ten years in two months. Mary is as silent and as stone-like as the Sphinx. They are bearing a terrible secret and the toll it is taking on them is obvious for anyone who knows them well to see. Has their son returned disfigured or corrupt? Speculation of this sort is enervating and hopeless but I am prey to it, nevertheless.

My interest in the dead was forced upon me by a psychic sensitivity I never asked for or sought to refine. At Cambridge, I postured stupidly and dabbled with forces a man with greater moral discipline would have left alone. But my sins were those of youth and curiosity rather than real evil or any wish to possess occult powers. I did not seek wealth and influence. I had wealth and therefore enjoyed already the influence it buys. I wish with all my heart I had never heard of Gunter Keller nor bid at that Hamburg auction nor discovered the tract I did among his papers. I wish with all my heart I had not accomplished what I have. I have no proof other than the expressions of masked horror on the faces of my lost friends. But my great and growing fear is that I have summoned a demon from a hero's resting place.

Elena put down the deposition. She looked at her watch. It was two in the afternoon and she had been reading and making notes for just over an hour. She hoped that Julian had been telling the truth about meeting his neglected diary obligations. She knew of his contempt for hired security and thought she understood his priorities where the Stride story was concerned. But she also thought what she had just read vindicated her own feelings about the railway station waiting room on Stride's estate. She thought that it was a very dangerous place for anyone living in the present to visit. And that meant anyone living, didn't it?

She tried to call him. But there was no reply. Perhaps he was in a meeting or at the gym. Maybe he had honoured a long standing lunch engagement. It was one of his idiosyncrasies that he kept his own diary rather than relying on his PA. He had maintained the habit of secrecy from his days of covert operations in the military. He did not always like people to know precisely what he was up to. He said that keeping to a schedule set by someone else made him feel robotic. Nobody as famous and successful as he was could really be free. She supposed the next best thing was being sometimes unpredictable.

Even though his BlackBerry was switched off, she sent him a text. He would get it when he switched it back on. Then she sent him an email saying that he should on no account visit Stride's estate clandestinely before speaking to her. She thought about the grime he had described leaching out of his skin in the sauna and she shivered.

'Like decades of dirt,' he had said, smiling. How right he had been about that, she thought now, and what a lucky escape he had enjoyed. She thought about the image of Lady Ross on the big screen in the edit suite, abstract and distorted because it violated time.

She made herself a cup of tea and sat and sipped it, staring at the open journal on her desk. She looked at the neat and steady characters of Bruno Absalom's handwriting and thought about his grave in the rain on the slope of the hill beyond the wall that bordered sanctified ground at the edge of a small village in Italy. He had been a cultured and intelligent man and fallen victim to hubris, she thought, which he justified to himself as compassion for an old and valued friend. Resurrection was the province of God. He had played God. But in playing God, he seemed to have feared that he had unleashed a devil. The tea was hot but she shivered, nevertheless. Somewhere in these pages, she now expected to find an answer to the mystery of how a man dead for eighty years had been able not just to predict her movements, but to describe her own physical appearance with such accuracy. And she dreaded that discovery. She considered herself a forgiving woman. She thought that she must be, to have recently found it in her heart to forgive Julian Creed. But she found it very difficult to feel a shred of sympathy for Bruno Absalom.

# Chapter Eight

**February 1921**

I write this in the early hours. There is a fog about in London, a blind
mantle of cloud and soot and river filth that coalesced two days ago
and looks and feels as though it might never lift. It is bitter on the
breath when inhaled and obliges the people of the capital to grope
about the streets as helpless as those without sight. Light cannot
penetrate its grimy folds. I am homesick when this metropolitan
phenomenon occurs always for the pure air and gentle sunshine of my
childhood. It dislocates sound, so that car horns bray with sudden
violence and the iron-shod hooves of horses pulling carts ring like a
leper's bell, invisibly. It makes one feel alone and adrift and at the
mercy of the great city's unseen immensity.

Yesterday morning, I received a note from my old friend, Sir
Samuel Ross. It was hand-delivered to the reception desk of the Savoy
and waiting for me after I had taken my bath. It requested that I
meet him most urgently and asked, should I be willing, would I
telephone him at his club to arrange to do so without delay. Concern
as much as remembered fondness for the man prompted me to do so
immediately. The line was clear and he sounded both agitated and
frail. I agreed to meet him at five in the afternoon. I confess I would
have met him sooner, but he had obligations in Harley Street, he said,
that would detain him for the earlier part of the day. I assumed his
health was failing. The Sam I remembered was not a man to consult
doctors without a compelling need.

I doubt I did a very good job of concealing my distress at the sight
of him. He looked shrunken, withered. There were red blotches of high
colour on his cheeks and his limbs were stick-like under the baggy

folds of his suit. His hair has turned white. I have known him since I was eighteen and yet on a clear day, I might have passed him in the street, so little and vaguely did this bony and enfeebled fellow resemble the man I knew.

He thanked me for coming. Then he began to weep. He told me he is to divorce Mary. I had never seen him betrayed by his emotions before. But my shock at his loss of composure was not as great as the shock I felt at hearing of his decision to end his marriage. I did not know what to say. I could think of no fitting comment. I just nodded. After a few moments, he regained himself and said, 'I expect you know that Patrick returned to us.'

'I suspected it.'

'We were obliged at the outset to keep the matter secret. And then matters developed in a way that made secrecy practicable.' He looked at me. There was suffering on his face, the memory of suffering endured. 'Secrecy becomes a habit,' he said, 'in the way that a lie grows in magnitude and significance, the longer it is kept. But I can keep this secret no longer. I wish to unburden myself. You are my oldest friend.'

Again, I simply nodded.

He smiled. 'And of course, you have an interest in the matter.'

'And Mary?'

'Mary is mad,' he said. 'My wife never recovered her sanity after we received that War Office telegram late in the autumn of 1918. She has been a stranger to me since then, a grinning, pantomimic mockery of the woman I loved and cherished for so long.'

'Patrick's return did not restore her reason?'

Sam laughed at that. The sound was hoarse and bitter and it turned heads in the sedate room of which we occupied a secluded corner. 'It did not. When I tell you about the Patrick who returned, you will appreciate why it did not.'

'Then tell,' I said, quietly.

My instincts of a year ago were right. Sam first began to feel a presence in the evening, in his study. It had become his habit to read late into the night. His reading matter comprised petitions on his wealth from needy organisations aware of his intention to dedicate the bulk of his fortune to causes he deemed worthy. He would sit at his desk and sense that the leather armchair over by the window that looked out onto the street was occupied. When he looked, it was not. And he thought it his imagination. The chair had been the one Patrick had sat in as a boy, unobtrusively sharing his father's company when Samuel was obliged to work rather than to play with him.

When first this presence gained physical form, so insubstantial was it that Sam thought he was seeing a phantom. But over time, the figure in the chair achieved substance. Detail clarified. It was there only at night and only for an hour or so at a time. But it began to look like Patrick, pale and staring fixedly, attired in his dress uniform.

'It was more than an apparition at that stage, but much less than a man,' Sam said. 'It seemed to occupy space but had the substance of a ghost. Imagine a projected film observed in three dimensions, if you will. That was how it was. But it grew solid over time the way a child might grow in size and weight and density. It became warm. I could feel the warmth from it in the risen temperature of the room when it appeared and had been there for a while. Then late one evening, it got out of the chair and walked across the room and stared at me. That was its birth, or rebirth, I suppose.'

'Did he speak?'

'Not at that stage, no, it did not. The speech came later.'

'Did Mary know of this?'

'I did not tell her of its presence until the occasion on which it climbed out of the chair. I took that to be the moment of its return to mature human form, to recognisable life. I closed the study door on it and went to fetch her. I had seen a miracle, after all. I hoped for the further miracle of my wife's return to sanity. I thought the sight of Patrick intact and whole once again might deliver that. But she showed no surprise at all at seeing him. The veil of madness did not lift from her face as I had hoped it would. The delusion was too deeply embedded by then in her psyche. She enveloped the creature in an embrace it did not return and began to prattle about the weather in Manchester and scold him for not writing and putting a poor mother's mind at rest. That was the moment at which I realised I had made a terrible mistake in asking you to use the alchemic ritual you did to bring back my son. The wrongness of it was overwhelming. Even then, before anything else occurred, I suspected I had colluded in something so profoundly out of kilter with the natural world that it would be bound to have awful consequences. And, of course, I realised that my principal motive, to return my wife to me, had been both selfish and utterly futile.'

It seemed odd to hear Sam describe Patrick as 'it', rather than 'him'. That detail struck me straightaway, even though the event he described had indeed been a miracle of sorts. It struck me as ominous. He had loved his son every bit as deeply as Patrick's mother had. Yet he referred to the boy returned as a creature. With a sinking heart, I felt sure I would soon discover why this was so.

He told me that, within days, his entire household staff had resigned or simply deserted them. Their story was that their son had been mistakenly identified as a fatal casualty of battle and had actually suffered a serious head-wound in the assault on the canal in which his unit had been engaged. The trauma had cost him his memory. His identity had been confused with that of another soldier, an Irish volunteer. He had spent several months in an Ulster sanatorium before the mistake was revealed. Knowing who he wasn't, but still not who he was, he had found lodgings and a clerical job in one of the Belfast shipyards and gradually his memory had returned to him and with his health restored, he had returned home.

'It sounds reasonably plausible,' I said. 'Mistakes occur in war, do they not? A kitchen-maid would have no cause to question such a tale.'

'Its physical presence, once it was fully established, had some unnerving characteristics,' Sam said. He signalled for the waiter. He ordered a large scotch for himself and then asked me would I like a drink. I told him I would have a gin and water and he scowled and said he could not stomach the aroma of gin. Would I not care for something else? A brandy, I said. He waited until our drinks had been delivered and he had taken a potent swallow from his before mentioning that he drank these days only against his doctor's explicit instructions.

'How is your health?'

'It is as poor as my appearance suggests. I have heart trouble and high blood pressure.'

'You deserve better, after all the good your generosity has done.'

'I colluded in bringing an abomination into the world. I deserve everything I've got.'

Patrick moved silently and was capable of standing as still as something carved from marble. His breathing was inaudible and he did not very often blink. His smile was an expression of such hollow vacancy that it scared and troubled those who saw it. Regardless of how often he bathed or his clothes were laundered, he carried a faint odour. It was like the taint of meat on the point of spoiling. And when he did begin to talk, it soon became apparent that he knew things. He could stare at the cover of a book he had not read and then précis its contents. He could discuss stories printed on the pages of a newspaper he had not read. He did not open conversations or make any effort to sustain them and he ventured only one opinion his father remembered over those first uneasy months of trying to get to know and warm to him. He said that he had served under an officer called Owen who was still obscure now but would one day become more famous than anyone connected with the war.

He encouraged no physical contact. He demonstrated no emotion. He did not seem to need to sleep very often. He drank heavily and against the wishes of his parents. He never showed any sign of intoxication when he drank. Slowly, incrementally and without any specific reason to, his father began to live in fear of him. It was at this point, a few days before the Christmas just past, that he realised he did not think the thing that bore his son's name deserved the dignity of being thought of as a human being.

'I asked it the other night: did nothing impress or delight or move it in any way? It was seated in my study, slumped over the gin decanter. It favours that room. I seldom ever go in there now. It seemed to ponder for a moment and then said Mallory and Irvine's conquest of Everest was a very impressive achievement. To stand on the roof of the world, it said, to have climbed up there to do so.'

This surprised me. I had heard of Mallory, of course. But the fact that Everest had been conquered and that the news had eluded me seemed incredible.

'It hasn't happened yet,' Sam said, wearily. 'It doesn't happen for another three years, Patrick said. And they die descending, apparently. So the world at large remains ignorant of their feat.'

'But Patrick knows,' I said.

'Oh, yes. Patrick knows.'

'He's jesting, making it up, surely?'

'It does not jest. It sometimes laughs. But its laughter is a terrible sound, devoid of humour or human generosity. It is a cruel creature, I am sure. It is very sly and careful, I think, to conceal the cruelty from Mary and me.'

'Then it cares about your feelings.'

'No, Bruno. It just has a stronger instinct for self-preservation than my son ever possessed.'

'What do you intend to do?'

'I plan to send it away. I will send it to one of the dominions. I have mineral interests, as you know, in Canada. I will send it somewhere remote from general humanity where the only men it will encounter are of a tough and uncompromising breed.'

'You think Patrick a danger to people?'

'My son is dead, Bruno. He died a hero serving his country. The soulless thing masquerading as Patrick may well become a danger to people. Earth has been disturbed in our garden. There has been excavation done surreptitiously, I think, while my wife and I sleep. I think he has killed things and buried them there. I will not force an escalation by confronting him with the evidence. He sails for British Columbia next week. I will have the garden dug after his departure.' My friend smiled grimly. 'Knowledge is power,' he said, but he did not look as though he very much believed it.

'How has he reacted to the Canada plan?'

'He is incapable of registering things like enthusiasm or surprise. He reacted to the proposal with equanimity. I think he is capable of anger and even fury. I sense that. But this scheme has not provoked it in him.'

'What will he do there?'

'I have told him he will study geology at the mine. It is a fictitious job. My people there have been briefed. He will be very carefully and discreetly watched. I have the resources to indulge this exercise. Though I never dreamed I would have to use them in such a way.'

'How will Mary react to his departure?'

'I am putting her in the care of Edward Brody at Falcon Lodge.'

'You are having your wife committed?'

'Yes.'

I thought about everything my old friend had just said. I drained the last of my brandy and signalled to the waiter for another. I said, 'Do you really think Patrick has no soul?'

'I'm sure of it,' he said, with a smile that did nothing to lighten the grief expressed in his eyes.

'What will you do with him eventually?'

'I am hoping Canada will provide me with the respite to decide upon that. But eventually is a relative term, my friend, when your health has failed as mine has in these last twelve months.'

I wondered if Patrick himself was not leeching the life out of his father. I wondered if the dead in becoming reanimate required the vitality of the living. Was his existence essentially parasitic? I remembered then Gunter Keller's curious warning about a plague of the dead.

'Would you allow me to see him before his voyage to Canada?'

'There is no point,' he said. 'But if you wish it, I will not prevent it.'

It was dusk when I left him and the fog a dark, yellowing contagion afflicting everything. The air was barely breathable and tasted of ashes and gasoline. I lit a cigar in the way the police and post-mortem practitioners do when the corpse they poke and pick at is decomposed and stinking. I thought of Samuel exiling Patrick to one of the colder and bleaker regions of the world. I did not think he had told me everything. I think decorum and good taste had prevented that. I got the distinct impression he had been diplomatic in discussing the transgressions of his returned son. There was more and it had dismayed him deeply. But I also believed that talking to me had helped a little. The burden of his secret had been lifted. I had lightened the load and he would more easily carry it now. I made the resolution, there in the cloying grip of the mist, to go back and study further what remained of my Gunter Keller archive. There might be more to learn. Despite Sam's ironic joke, I believe that knowledge really is power.

Sam has invited me to see the boy the day after tomorrow. Tomorrow he will take Mary by train to the asylum of Falcon Lodge. She will enter and I fear will never leave. She faces a life sentence of incarceration for her sin of madness. I am glad to have seen so little of her since the armistice. That is a selfish thing to say, I know. But my memories of her remain largely untarnished. I loved her unrequitedly for twenty years. I was not selfish when I watched from afar as she blossomed into womanhood. I took pleasure in her happiness and contentment. There was that moment of romantic intoxication after my Brighton trial, when I hoped we might consummate a passion that was mutual, but it was the champagne thinking on my behalf and I would never have betrayed my oldest friend. Her decline is tragic. 'Sweet Mary, *adieu*,' I said, with no one able to witness my tears through the dark miasma of fog.

Patrick and I were once very close. I loved him. I wonder, will he even know me now? The thought of meeting him is a daunting one. I may be disappointed or even dismayed. But the scientist in me compels me to witness the miracle I enabled. Pride has nothing to do with it. I wish, as any scientist would, simply to see my proof demonstrated.

As Elena Coyle wandered through the fog on his behalf, enduring the dubious company of Bruno Absalom, Julian Creed sat in his car outside the house he had grown up in and tried to summon the courage to get out and knock on the door. He was not a coward. But he thought if his father rejected him now, it would be a blow more crushing than any he had endured in his life. His mother had died when he was a young child. He had no brothers or sisters. He had done something wrong and stupid when drunk to alienate the woman he knew he had fallen for and probably still loved. His dad was all he had. He had seen the looks that passed between Martin and Peter when the Strides strolled off their croquet lawn and remembered what it had been like when he and his father had shared a similar easy intimacy. He was here to try to re-establish that. But he thought that if he failed, he would be emotionally bankrupt. No one in the world would be left genuinely to care about him. And the fear of that was almost enough to undo his resolve.

A premonition had brought him there. It was too strong to be called a hunch. It was the same feeling he had endured on the Isle of Wight by the copse of trees in the hills on the approach to Ventnor. He had told the truth to Elena about addressing the chaos of his abandoned diary and log-jammed schedule. But this was much more urgent business. Both his head and his heart had insisted he come right away.

His father's housekeeper answered the door. If she was surprised to see him, it did not show in her expression.

'Mr Julian,' she said. It was a form of address he disliked. But he smiled warmly at her, thinking that Molly might make an excellent poker player should she ever feel inclined to take up card games.

'How is he?'

'He's ailing, Mr Julian. I'm not sure the shock of seeing you here will be quite what he needs in order to rally. You're intent on it, I suppose?'

'Your employer is my father, Molly,' he said, taking off and handing her his jacket. He thought she was probably thinking about the will. More accurately, she would be thinking he was thinking about the will. She did not watch television and had no real idea, he didn't suppose, of who he'd become over recent years. He wasn't here chasing his father's legacy. It was his affection and approval he craved and his forgiveness he sought now. 'Is he in bed?'

'No. He's on the sofa in the drawing room. He watches the racing on the television in the afternoons.'

'My father doesn't bet.'

'He likes to look at the horses, Mr Julian. Now that he no longer has the strength to ride, it's the only opportunity he gets.'

Creed tried to conceal his shock at his father's gaunt appearance. He wondered how much of the blame for this deterioration in his father's health could be laid at his own door. The drawing room had the aroma of a sick room. The curtains were drawn against low sun interfering with the picture on the television screen. It was dark and stuffy but not very warm. His father looked at him and then looked back stiffly at the television screen. Horses were being paraded around the paddock, saddled but riderless, by trainers in trilbies and tweed. He went across and knelt on the carpet, careful not to allow his body to obscure his father's view of the screen. He lifted his father's hands from the blanket on which his father rested them and was grateful that they did not recoil at his touch.

'I've come to apologise, Dad, for any embarrassment I've caused you. I want to say sorry. And I want to make you a promise. I'm finished with fakery. I will never make another fraudulent claim on camera as long as I live.'

His father smiled, but the smile was thin and he did not meet his son's eyes. 'You're retiring, then?'

'No. I'm not retiring. I'm retiring from embellishment and lies. I intend to continue with my investigations. You may sneer at it, but I've been given recent cause to believe in the paranormal. I don't think it shameful or ridiculous. It was me that was shameful and ridiculous in concocting it and it's that pantomime I'm giving up.'

Now his father did look at him. 'You've not been very honourable in your treatment of ghosts, have you, Julian?'

Creed was incredulous. 'You mean you actually believe in them?'

'Take that ludicrous story you keep trotting out on chat shows. I mean the one about the Alpine mountain rescue mission carried out by that Austrian phantom. Do you really think someone recently dead would have the composure or the inclination for such a task? Do you think the dead are permitted to interfere with fate and save the living? Can you imagine how anarchic the world would be if that were the case?'

'Christ, Dad. You sound as though you've seen a ghost yourself.'

'My own military career wasn't all pomp and parades. I saw active service in the Malayan uprising and later in the Congo. I fought during the Mau-Mau insurrection in Kenya. I've seen some very strange things and heard some very strange stories and they have made me more open-minded than you might think, that's all. I've always been open to the possibility of paranormal activity. But I know a charlatan when I see one, Julian. Sadly, a charlatan is what you have been. Can you imagine what it's like for a father, seeing his progeny earn a lucrative living by lying before a vast audience every week?'

'It takes a certain skill, Dad.'

'So does safe cracking. But that doesn't make it respectable, does it, Julian?'

Creed said nothing to that. His father withdrew his hands. He did not know what more he could sincerely say. At least their conversation had been honest. It was something.

'You enjoy being recognised in the street.'

'Yes. I do. I enjoy being famous. It's shallow and vain and I like it.'

'Notoriety and fame are not the same thing.'

'I've given you my promise.'

'Is this promise of yours one you genuinely intend to keep,

Julian? You aren't saying it to placate me, just because you think I can feel the grave?'

'Can you feel the grave, Dad?'

'Yes. I rather think I can.'

'I mean it. I need to become someone I'm not. I need to be the person I aspire to be. The change is vastly overdue.'

'Then help me to my feet. Get me up. Help a father give the son he loves a proper hug of greeting.'

Monica Stride thought Julian Creed the most attractive man she had ever met as a married woman. Martin was the most attractive she had met when single and she had duly married him and never for a single moment regretted doing so. They had very different qualities. They shared a strong physicality. Both were agile, athletic and powerfully built. But they were a complete contrast as personalities. There was something reckless about Creed. He was charismatic and spontaneous and craved attention. He liked to be at the centre of things. She thought that in a crisis, he would be a courageous individual. There would be no shirking or hiding with him. And in the English phrase, he was someone who wore his heart on his sleeve.

She wished that she could tell him about the dream Millie had recounted to her. Her daughter had awoken on the beach, upset to discover that she had wet herself. Monica had made light of it. But then, when she had been comforted and cleaned up, the detail of the dream had come back to Millie and she had been very distressed. Monica knew from her description that one of the people in the dream had been the occupant of the waiting room who had scared Peter so badly. Millie sat in one of the two chairs on the balcony of their hotel room and recounted the dream with her mother's arm around her. And the words spoken, the verdict delivered on the soldier with the broken mind, chilled Monica to the bone. She did not see what it could have to do with demonic possession or the priestly paraphernalia of exorcism. She knew it had to do with the long-demolished lunatic asylum her husband had told her about. She thought it was in the province far more of the ghost hunter, Julian Creed, than the Belgian priest.

But she did not call Creed. She took Millie to an ice-cream parlour and bought her a peach and apricot sundae and sent a discreet text to Martin asking him to return from his school trip duties as soon as he was able to. He returned at 4pm. Monica did not want Millie to have to endure a third helping of her nightmare by having to recount the story to her father. She hoped that by then the dream was fading from her mind. Children were resilient and she could be relied upon to forget eventually. Instead, she sat Millie in front of a *Little Mermaid* DVD and told Martin herself in the open air beyond the closed balcony door. He listened without taking his eyes off his daughter. When she had finished, he closed his eyes. She saw that his face had grown pale.

'I think this changes things, doesn't it, Martin?'

He took his mobile out of his pocket.

'Who are you calling? Are you calling Julian Creed?'

'No. I may well owe the man an apology. But I'm not calling him now. I'm going to talk to Peter's school head at the hostel and tell him I have to return home on urgent business tonight. It is Friday tomorrow and Saturday and Sunday are water sport days for all the kids with plenty of professional supervision. They can spare me. Or they can spare you, because in my absence you'll have to take care of Millie again tomorrow.'

'Why are you going? Where are you going?'

'I really am going home. There is something there I need to look at. It was left me by Barrowclough, the man from whom I bought the land on which the remains of the railway station stand. It is a box of stuff left to him by his uncle, an architect who knew Edward Brody at the Falcon Lodge asylum. I think that Brody is the other man in Millie's dreams. He coughs blood in the dreams and Brody was consumptive.'

'I don't know that word.'

'He suffered from tuberculosis.'

'The lung disease?' Monica said.

'It was incurable then. It killed him. I think there might be something of Brody's in the chest in our attic.'

'Why would there be?'

'For me to find, that's why. Tom Barrowclough would not go near the waiting room. He gave away the money I paid him for the land. I think he knew something about it he wanted to warn me of. But he waited until after his own death before acting on his conscience.'

'I hate the thought of you going back to the house alone,' Monica said. 'I hate the thought of you leaving me and the children here.' She looked down, out over the pretty bay with its small harbour filled brightly with bobbing craft and the curve of sand and pebbles beyond the breakwater. She looked through the glass balcony door at her daughter smiling at images of mermaids and grumpy lobsters and crabs with her hands linked in her lap.

'I won't be alone,' Stride said. 'The place is crawling with security guards and attack dogs.'

'And you'll send them away. You won't tolerate company not of your choice.'

He looked at her. 'Company not of our choice is what this all seems to be about. I'm not going to cancel Monday's service. The Owen poem "Strange Meeting" is about hell and I think the Belgian monsignor a more fitting adversary for Satan than a ghost hunter, however magnetic and likeable Creed's personality makes him. But you're right. Millie's dream changes things. I need to see what's in that chest Barrowclough left me. Examining that is something I should have done a long time ago.'

'There's probably more than one way of interpreting the

Owen poem, Martin. And if he left it, it is surely ghosts more than devils we're dealing with, is it not?'

He reached out and held her head gently between his hands. 'Owen wrote some very memorable and profound war poems, my darling. Three or four of them, at the very least, are masterpieces. Yet his ghost chose to transcribe that one and none of the others. The choice was deliberate and the warning just can't be ignored.'

'Be careful tonight,' she said. She almost said something about the danger he might face, how unbearable it would be if anything were to happen to him there in the family's absence from home. But she thought the expression on her face probably said it for her. He opened the balcony door and closed it softly on her to say goodbye to his daughter inside.

**February 1921**

Our meeting took place at a neutral location. Samuel is in mourning for his lost wife. She might as well be dead. I think she has been dead in his heart since 1918 and yesterday, when he consigned her to the asylum, signalled for him her burial. After the carefree years of joy and prosperity experienced by the Ross family in that generous Westminster house, I can understand why Sam did not want my encounter with Patrick to take place there.

Patrick enjoys abandoned places. He told me so himself. He is uncomfortable with human tumult, finding crowds of people oppressive and distasteful. He told me he does not like the stink and heat and hubbub of populous locations. He is friendless and contentedly so. He revels in solitude. I can see why the white, high wastes of Everest would appeal to him. He wishes to exist in isolation from humanity. In his mind, I think he lives at some remote, imaginary altitude. He thinks us low and is superior, he supposes, to ordinary men.

His hostility is guarded and discreet, but obvious to anyone who knew him before. The anger his father warned against provoking is very close to the surface in him. I would call it more resentment and contempt, a kind of cold fury at the manner and very nature of the world. He is like an alien species, visiting and bridling at the things he has discovered here. He walks and breathes and, if encouraged, talks. But he is nothing like the generous and spontaneous boy I remember and felt such fondness for. That Patrick inspired pleasure and affection and is entirely gone. The one returned from death is sly and vicious-seeming and provokes only trepidation and uncertain fear.

I met him at the river, beneath the rampart wharves of Wapping, down by the lapping scum of the river's edge at low tide. The fog had entirely cleared. He had been to store supplies at the Pool of London aboard the docked vessel that will transport him to Canada. It was an odd and uncomfortable meeting place and I told him so. There is a pub called the Prospect of Whitby not far from there and I suggested we repair to its saloon to enjoy at least a modicum of comfort. But he refused. He smiled his disconcerting smile and said he preferred to be outside, breathing the clean air of a London afternoon, a sardonic joke, since the air there stank of spilled oil from engine sumps and rotten fish and raw sewage.

An aeroplane flew over us, low in the leaden sky, its struts and canvas skin giving it the appearance of a large, shrill insect. Patrick raised his expressionless eyes at the howl of its engine and showed his teeth in a grin. His teeth seem larger than I remember them in his former life. 'Progress,' he said. 'What an ugly future we face, Uncle.'

He was dressed in a charcoal suit under a black wool overcoat. A dark grey trilby covered his head. I caught the spoiled-meat taint his father had described downwind of him. His attire, conservative in the extreme, should have given him a conventional aspect. But the impression was of a clothed imp, dapper and demonic at the same time; his dancing movements unnaturally lithe as he avoided getting wet his polished shoes when the wake from passing tugs and trains of barges brought the slopping water nearer our feet.

'What do you want?' he asked me.

'I wanted to see you,' I said. I felt abject in his company. He had done nothing really to offend me. But I did not know how my old friend had tolerated this creature living for a year in his home in the guise of his beloved son.

'Well, you've seen me,' he said. 'You have seen what your work has accomplished. You have satisfied your vanity and curiosity. You should go now, Uncle. You are unwise to dawdle, you know. You do not have many years left to live. Why tarry in a dismal place with a person who dismays you? Spend some money on whores and good cigars and decent vintages. Then crawl off to Rome and beg forgiveness for your more significant sins. It won't be given you. You won't earn absolution. But you might achieve some grace in your mortification.'

'What have you buried in your father's garden?'

'It's ironic that you loved my mother. She always thought you queer. She always considered my father your clandestine passion, the unrequited love of your life. Don't you find that funny?'

My eyes started to prick with tears. I have always been a sentimental man. These insults were too much to bear. I had always loved Patrick almost as my own. The cruelty emerging from the mouth of the creature masquerading as my godson was unendurable. It had said at least one truthful thing, in describing that place as dismal. I turned and walked over the pebbles and glass shards and other bits of tidal detritus away from its poisonous orbit, thinking that I had delivered a monster into the world and lower in spirits than I can ever remember feeling in my life. I walked away to the sound of its laughter receding behind me, the mockery of it, the cold glee bringing gooseflesh to my arms and raising the hair against my collar on the back of my neck.

I climbed the steep wooden stairs to the river bank and walked the short distance to the pub. The cobbles clacked against cartwheels and the cries of the stevedores were loud and raucous as they supervised the lifting of bales and sacks and barrels into the warehouses on either side of the narrow street. I smelled tar and tobacco leaf and hemp and fruit and felt indifferent to the ripe assault of life and commerce on my senses. So I had not long to live. Did I have years? Was it merely months? The thing I had made of Patrick had condemned me, as it had condemned Mallory, the mountaineer, with a prophecy. I strode into the Prospect of Whitby and ordered a double cognac and smiled at my reflection in the mirror backing the bar and raised a toast to my own impending death.

Then, God help me, I went back. The Patrick creature was still there at the edge of the water, a vacant look on its face. 'What do you want now, Uncle?'

'Absolution, I suppose,' I said. 'But you've already told me I can't have that. The question is, Patrick, what is it that you want?'

Meeting his gaze, even fortified by the brandy so recently drunk, was an ordeal. It was like looking into an abyss men are spared the sight of because they cannot make sense of its unplumbed depths. He smiled. 'You would call it a plague of the dead,' he said. 'That is my ambition. It will take a long time to realise it. But I have time. And I am patient.'

He crouched suddenly. There was a dead eel at the edge of the water, washed up and swollen with decomposition, its silvery flesh yellowing and bloated. Patrick picked it up in the grip of both fists and bit into it and I heard the crunch of its spine as he chewed and slurped and swallowed. 'I parried, Uncle,' he said; 'but my hands were loath and cold.'

I left him to his corrupt feast. I should not have gone back. But then there are many things I should not have done in my life and will regret for whatever time is left to me.

Elena put the deposition down on the table next to her. She took her pen and wrote the words 'Gunter Keller' in her notebook, underlining them. It was her experience that the age of electronic information had vastly increased the sum and accessibility of human knowledge. Research had become an industry and history had never been a more fashionable subject than it was today. She was sure that more was known about this Hamburg alchemist than had been the case when Bruno Absalom had bid successfully at auction for his papers.

Absalom had been a sort of aesthete fashionable at the Cambridge of his time there as an undergraduate. His interest in alchemy had been wilfully eccentric and necessarily obscure.

He was just posturing, as flamboyant and vain young men were apt to. Nevertheless, his interest had been sustained. He had discovered things of real and terrible significance. And his morbid obsession with death was very obviously genuine and held life-long. But there would surely be much more now in the public domain about Keller than he had been able to discover all those years ago. Elena felt fairly confident that this plague of the dead, its real or metaphorical significance, would have been explored and explained by some scholar, somewhere. It was probably the subject of someone's PhD in theosophy, or heresy, or sixteenth-century German mysticism. She would find out what it was he had alluded to, she was sure.

The phone rang then. It was Julian. She thought of him as Julian all the time now, she realised, and never just as Creed. His rehabilitation in her mind and affections seemed to be almost complete.

'You sound cheerful.'

'I went to see my dad.'

'Bloody hell.'

'It wasn't, actually. It ended up being very pleasant, much better than I thought it would be. I made him a promise, Elena.'

'One you're confident you can keep?'

'No more pantomime, I told him. No more embellishment or lies.'

'That's grim news for Alison Slaney.'

'I'll give her a generous golden goodbye. She won't struggle to make a living, with her talent. She'll get work and she'll get a credit. It's about time her gifts were publicly acknowledged. How are you doing?'

'It isn't a happy story, Julian.'

'I didn't for a moment imagine it was.'

'You need to stay away from the waiting room. At least until you've read my précis of this stuff, you do.'

'I gathered that from your text. And I have to confess I'm in no great hurry to go back there. I'd like to witness Monday's Jesuit cabaret though, I have to admit. Stride's exorcist has a formidable reputation. I'd like to see the substance behind the hype.'

'I've been wondering about that,' Elena said. 'I thought exorcists dealt with possessed people. The waiting room is a place.'

'A place can be possessed,' Creed said. 'At least, in theory, it can. They'll do poltergeists. I wouldn't put it past Degrelle to do weddings and bar mitzvahs, if he thought there might be a camera crew present.'

'Now, now, Julian. Pots and kettles,' Elena said.

'Not any more, love. Anyway, just called to say I got your messages and to reassure you that I'm acting on your advice.' He was silent for a moment. Then he said, 'This stuff is pretty dark, then?'

'On a scale of one to ten?' she said. 'It's as black as obsidian.'

'I don't know what obsidian is, I'm ashamed to say. I didn't pay very much attention at school.'

'Look it up,' she said. 'It's the blackest thing in nature.'

'You're blessed with brains and beauty too, Elena. Have you any notion of how rare that combination is in real life?'

She broke the connection. She actually thought the world into which Bruno Absalom had strayed, the world he had helped conjure, blacker than anything nature was able naturally to create. And immersing herself in its gloomy reality did not sit happily with flirtation over the phone. Besides, it was too soon. She had forgiven Julian. But it had gone no further than that in her mind or intentions.

She should eat. She was hungry. But she did not feel very much like food after reading the account of Patrick Ross's impromptu snack ninety years ago at the edge of the Thames. She decided that she would give herself a break, go down and wander among the stalls of Borough Market, take comfort in the presence and colour of an indifferent crowd of kaleidoscopic people. She thought that it was human instinct to gather together, even for strangers speaking disparate languages brought up in foreign lands. Though it might be different, of course, for those who'd fought in wars as mortal enemies and seen their friends and comrades perish on an industrial scale.

She picked up the deposition again and leafed through it. There was only one more short entry before the date jumped all the way to 1924. She supposed the gap described the length of Patrick's exile in Canada. She would read this entry and then go down to the banter and cheer and bright electric light above of the late afternoon market. Now that really was a place of ghosts, she thought. But they wore brocade waistcoats and mutton-chop whiskers and were out of Dickens rather than Dante.

**March 1921**

Sam had promised to advise me of the results of his garden excavation and he was true, as usual, to his word. The men employed to dig found animal cadavers. There were two dogs, half a dozen cats and a fox among some other, smaller creatures such as wood pigeons and squirrels. Sam did not employ a vet to examine these remains. So great was his gloomy curiosity over the grisly find that he used a Whitehall contact to persuade a Home Office pathologist to carry out a scrupulous post-mortem on the bodies of the larger creatures.

I met him once again at his club. My instinct is that I have set foot for the last time in my old friend's home. The thought saddens me, but in Mary's absence it will not be the same house. And I can quite understand why he would not wish to entertain me as a domestic guest. Our friendship has been undermined in the most gruesome and sinister manner imaginable. Both of us are culpable and both victims. Though I suppose it is fair to say that my guilt is greater than his and his suffering vastly more acute than mine. He looked physically improved, somewhat to my surprise. But he pays expensive doctors who know their trade. And the burden of Mary's insanity is borne now each day by that clever and compassionate man Edward Brody, and not by her husband. And Patrick is gone. The oppression and the stink of him are removed. He is six thousand miles away, learning the study of stones as cold and hard as his own inhuman heart.

The buried creatures were partially eaten, Sam told me, once our pleasantries of greeting had been got out of the way and there was a glass of something strong on the table at my elbow. They had been killed and bled and the meat allowed to begin to decompose before it was consumed. 'They were eaten as carrion, by the thing that calls itself my son, as a vulture might consume a corpse,' he said, 'or as a jackal or some other scavenger might feed. Have you any comment to make on that? Was this something the learned alchemist whose ritual you evoked ever commented upon?'

'I told you, Sam,' I said as gently as I could, 'Keller never admitted to having used the ritual. He discovered and translated it. He did not compose it. He never returned anything from the dead. At least, if he did, he did not confess to it in any of the papers I have seen.'

'I can quite see the reason for his discretion, Bruno. Can't you? If his results resembled yours, it is not an achievement he would wish to boast about. And yet he burned.'

'Yes, he did.'

'For the crime of witchcraft, I have discovered. And not for heresy, as you told me.'

'I was mistaken, Sam.'

'You were misguided, Bruno. We both were, profoundly so.'

'Is there any word from Canada?'

That question made him laugh. 'Do you expect letters from a devoted son to a doting father? I think not. I think that might be an unrealistic expectation, in the circumstances.'

'I asked him what he'd buried, when I spoke to him. I asked outright. He will know about this discovery.'

'It will not care,' Sam said. 'It has a jackal's remorse.'

But despite the pessimism of his words, their bleak tendency towards a sort of desperation, I had the feeling that what he actually felt was relief that Patrick was six thousand miles away and in the charge of tough mining men with little tolerance and less imagination.

In my taxi on the way back to my suite at the Savoy, I thought about Sam's parting words. I said I thought that the experience and environment of Canada might improve Patrick's character a little.

'In manner and demeanour perhaps,' he said, 'but it will be the gloss only. He might wear a more acceptable veneer. Nothing of substance will be achieved. One cannot teach humanity to a creature that has no soul.'

# Chapter Nine

It was eight o'clock and darkness was falling when Martin Stride reached his home. He phoned Carter from aboard the Wight ferry to warn him of his return. He wanted the security men rounded up and ready for departure, if not gone already, by the time he got back. And he wanted any dogs present safely on the leash. He had been bitten by a Dobermann doing his paper round at the age of eleven and had never forgotten the experience. He still had the scar from the bite on his right thigh.

Carter wanted a word in private. Stride wrote him a cheque in his study and thanked him for his vigilance and professionalism, his eyes on the dead hearth and his thoughts on how cold and chilly a place his home seemed even in the temporary absence from it of his family. But Carter stood with the cheque in his hand, making no immediate move to leave.

'Is there something else? I'll compensate you for the dog, just buy a replacement and invoice me.'

'It's not the dog, Mr Stride. Well, it's not specifically the dog.'

'Speak plainly, Mr Carter.'

'It's hard to be specific, sir. My men didn't catch or even sight anyone with what you'd call one hundred per cent conviction. But some of the lads felt they were being watched. I sensed it myself, doing the rounds after it was mentioned during the debrief after the daylight shift on the second night. I think you might have a prowler. He's very shy or very elusive or both. But he's out there, in my opinion.'

'What would you recommend I do?' Stride liked Carter. He was a burly ex-bouncer with deep-set, honest eyes in his bashed-up features. He had made something of himself with his successful business beyond the drink-fuelled tear-ups outside night club doors.

'Given your history, it could be a harmless crank. It could be a stalker. Given your wealth, it could be a Balkan kidnap gang doing their pre-snatch surveillance. All I'm saying is to be on your guard. That's all. Keep your eyes and ears open. Lock your doors tonight.'

'I lock them every night.' He saw Carter through the house to the front door and shook his hand and listened as the last of their vehicles vacated his property. Then he phoned Monica to check on how Millie was doing. They generally ate at the Pond restaurant in Bonchurch village, owned by the hotel and half a mile away. It was a small, intimate place and the food was excellent and nobody had ever bothered him there for his autograph. But they would not be there this evening, he didn't think.

He was right. They were in the room, dining on a room service menu of comfort food after a session in the gaiety amusement arcade on the promenade and a late walk along the coastal path. Millie had been going to Ventnor for these little holidays all her life and the rituals were well-established and reassuring, even if Peter was absent in the hostel at Blackgang Chine with his schoolmates. Stride closed his eyes and thanked God once again that Monica was such a wonderful mother to their children.

'How is she?'

'Missing you-know-who, I would say, though she hasn't said as much.'

Stride nodded to himself. He was back in the study, staring at the cold grate again. Millie and her brother were very close. 'Has she said anything further about the dream?'

'We're pigging our way through a box of Quality Street

and watching *High School Musical*. It's a very low-rent evening, I'm afraid. But exactly what the doctor ordered. Think that's the last thing on her mind.'

'Good.'

'Be careful tonight, Martin.'

'I'm a very cautious man.'

'With no lack of courage, though. I'm concerned that courage more than caution is the thing at the moment guiding you.'

'Don't worry. I'm no competition for Julian Creed. I'll be careful. Love to you and a kiss for my little darling.'

He thought that first he would light the study fire. Then he would go and examine the chest in the attic left him by old Tom Barrowclough. If there was anything in it worth reading, this was where he would bring it. He was not unnerved particularly by the house. But the bigger rooms were more distracting places to be alone in than this one was. And there was a neat symmetry about using this room. This was where he had originally told Monica about the activity centred on the waiting room. This would be the place to discover the reason for it, should the contents of the chest surrender that information.

He climbed the stairs to the attic ladder through the silent house, half-listening for the approach of a steam-driven train or the sentimental lyrics to 'Roses of Picardy' sung by the ghosts of marching soldiers. But there was no sound. It was as though all the recent activity of the security personnel had drained the place. It was still and serene after the crackle of their short-waves and their macho banter and the muscular swagger with which they accomplished everything they did. He could still smell their sweat and cheap aftershave. The odour of their microwaved food still lingered slightly. The dogs had not been in the house, though. He had forbidden that. There was no canine smell. He opened the windows on the landing that led to the trapdoor above. He wanted to air the house and the night outside was fine and clear and mild.

The attic was a repository of his past. There was other stuff up here too, such as Millie's wooden rocking horse and Peter's first pedal cycle. But mostly it was his. There was a trunk of stage costumes and gold discs dusty in gilt frames. The jukebox that had occupied pride of place in his Wapping loft apartment in his bachelor days was up here too. There were stacked guitars in dire need of tuning. And there was the treadmill he had taken with him on the road to stay in shape for the spotlight when meals had mostly comprised gourmet burgers and bottles of beer consumed in the back of a luxury coach. He smiled, thinking that if it all went belly up with his property and investment portfolios, he could make a killing on the memorabilia market by auctioning off all this junk.

The roof of the house was steep and the windows sloped acutely in the attic. But they were large and the view from here was dominant. And when he looked out of one of them, eastward, he could not but notice that a light burned with an oily yellow glimmer half a mile away in the abandoned station's supposedly derelict waiting room. He thought it was like a signal: a summons. It beckoned to him. And in a moment, he thought he might hear the siren song of an old marching tune familiar from Flanders' dusty and forgotten summer roads.

He tried to ignore the intriguing, provocative challenge of the light. He found Barrowclough's chest and blew some of the dust from it. It was secured by a hasp and padlock but, when he had been given it, he had been given the key along with it and had simply Blu-tacked that to the lid of the chest, so it wouldn't get lost. It had never occurred to him that there might be anything of intrinsic value stored in it. Barrowclough was not a generous man and they had never grown close. Following that one revealing afternoon of reminiscence, they had avoided one another generally, neighbours it was true, but private men with little but a single business transaction in common. The truth was that there had been an intimacy to the old farmer's revelation on that hot July afternoon that had prevented their relationship from developing any further. If they could not really go on from that, neither could they go back to the price of peas or the immediate weather prospects. And Barrowclough had died not much more than a year afterwards.

He knelt and put the key in the lock and turned and lifted the chest open, releasing the musty aroma of old paper sewn between leather bindings and photographs turned brittle by time. He took out a heavy volume tied with ribbons and pulled them undone and opened it. It was a photo album and its subject was Falcon Lodge. The building itself was the subject of the first picture. It had been taken before the addition of William Barrowclough's summer-house. A portrait of the senior staff showed young men in civilian attire under white coats and a matron in starched linen. At their centre was a patriarchal figure wearing a broadcloth suit and a white beard. To his right was a pale, thin man, dark-haired and clean-shaven. Stride assumed this was the psychiatrist, Edward Brody.

It was not a particularly interesting album to flick through. There was picture after picture of slender young men in uniform, most of them moustached and carrying canes, some of them wearing dressings over physical wounds, some of them in bath or wheelchairs or on crutches; most of them smiling the same secretive, distant smile worn by those trying to accommodate having endured far too much at far too tender an age. Each would have an individual horror story to tell. All had been patients at the asylum. What they had in common now was that every one of them was long dead.

He put the album down on the attic floor. He stood and went over to the east-facing window. The light burned no brighter half a mile away. But neither had it dimmed. He looked back to where the album lay. He wondered if any of the people pictured there were in the waiting room now, enduring with spectral patience the time until the arrival of the train that would take them back to the Front and their fate. They would be smoking and chatting and their hair would be freshly oiled and their boots buffed to an optimistic lustre. Would the man who had frightened Peter be among them, the man who had caused his daughter to wet herself in her sleep? And was he the same soldierly phantom who had undone the fragile sanity of poor Captain Broad after the war, back in 1924?

He went back to the trunk. There were nine bound volumes lying in it side by side and bundled together by elderly twine. They had the initials E.B. tooled in gold on their spines and each carried a date underneath, ranging from 1916 to 1924. He thought he knew what they were. He prised out the first of them and confirmed that they were Edward Brody's case notes. The significant year was 1924, the year of Brody's resignation, the year of Broad's undoing. Stride was sure of it. Barrowclough had been no sort of raconteur. His story about the Falcon Lodge ghost who had not been a ghost at all had been told to him for a reason. It had been the autumn, hadn't it? It had been the October or November of that year.

He thought he heard a train whistle. It sounded faint and shrill. Then he heard it again, closer. He closed the trunk lid and straightened. He had told Monica he would be careful. He had promised it. But he had to go and investigate the lights and the sound. This was his land and he felt almost exiled from it by events he could not account for or even properly comprehend. Creed had made little evident progress over two night-long vigils in the waiting room. On the other hand, he had come to no harm. He had survived each ordeal intact. Stride knew the land as no one else living did. He could approach in stealth without the need for a light. Surface roots had snagged his feet and caused him to stumble on his first and last approach, it was true. But he had been alarmed and rushing then.

He would be deliberate now. He did not think he would encounter Carter's stalker. Stalkers stood outside your front door and hammered on the knocker, deluded into believing they were welcome in your life and probably entitled to a key. He did not know what he would encounter but it seemed like cowardice not to investigate those lights and noises. The Belgian priest was due to perform his ritual after the weekend. But Stride found himself less and less convinced that exorcism would solve the problem. And he was impatient now with what he saw as his own timidity. The mysterious events on his property had frightened his whole family. He had a responsibility to discover what he could about their cause. It was why he had left his family on Wight and come back here.

He was annoyed with himself. Creed's investigation had been short-lived and inconclusive before the appearance of the poem had obliged him to terminate it. But he should have told Creed everything he knew about the asylum rather than holding information back. The contents of Barrowclough's chest should have been in the hands of Creed's research people at the outset. Stride might now have a clearer idea of what they were dealing with. What had happened to his children on the Island had left him feeling angry as well as fearful. He descended the stairs on his route to the kitchen and the kitchen garden and the path through the orchard that would take him east towards the waiting room, wishing there was some mortal protagonist for him to confront when he got there.

Neglected windfalls bruised and squelched under his feet in the orchard, laying a sharp and acidic smell over the drift of soot and steam and hot engine oil, faint but unmistakeable from the forgotten railway to the east. He progressed beyond the apple trees. He felt more than heard the shudder of steel wheels through the earth as the tender that wasn't there opened its throttle and pulled away. He saw sparks trail a single puffing funnel in the distance. Then silence crept back over the landscape and the air regained its rural, autumnal character, cooling quickly after the warm day, the slight bitterness of bark and turning leaves prominent and subtle at the same time. And Stride looked at the uninvited light brightening in the distance with his progress and thought about how much he had grown to love this place and how sorry he would be to be forced to leave it.

## September 1924

The more I consider it, the more I think Gunter Keller lied about using the ritual to bring somebody back. His warning about the plague of the dead was very specific and solemnly expressed. I think it was something he had experienced first-hand. I suspect it was a pestilence he caused or provoked by doing what I have done myself with Patrick Ross. Curiosity is the compulsion we have to thank for most discoveries about the world. Intelligent men have that above all else in common. Without it, there is no striving for knowledge and therefore no corresponding invention or innovation or even any experimentation. Keller would have been compelled to experiment once the translation of the ritual was his. He was a chemist, so refining the essence of a subject would have been straightforward for him. And the mortality rate among people of all classes in the Europe of the early sixteenth century would have provided him with an abundance of potential subjects.

My guess is that he would have sought a profit from his enterprise. Peasants died easily but owned nothing. He could not have returned a prominent aristocrat to life without the feat attracting attention that would have meant serious consequences for him. But a rich merchant might be a different matter. A rich man not noble could die discreetly. His household might pay handsomely for the restoration of his life, with its trade secrets and revived business acumen. He might reward extravagantly on his own account. A wealthy man would put a generous price on his own life. Keller would score on every count: scientifically, financially and egotistically too. And believe me, ego plays an influential part. I know from personal experience how completely the idea of playing God can intoxicate a man.

Nothing remains of the transcript of Keller's trial, if written testimony was ever even taken. I suspect the court sat *in camera*. I further suspect that this plague of the dead he talked about was what brought him to the attention of the authorities. Germany was a series of city states at the time, secular and temporal authority overlapping, fear determining the outcome of trials more often than the interest of justice. Perhaps he shared his fear with someone and was betrayed. Or perhaps the fear was realised and the pestilence traced back to him because he had warned of it. I believe it was visited upon a village or town and he was hunted down and burned in some ferocious show of civic revenge. I do not know what the plague is, except that it gives the soulless life of Patrick Ross ambition and purpose. I believe it is bad and real and that our time, less arbitrary and decisive in some ways than the past, is less well-equipped to deal with its dire consequences than the hard and unequivocal communities of several centuries ago, when they acted with a cruel and merciless certainty in the austere judgement not of men, but only ever of God.

Until last night, I had not seen Patrick for the better part of three years. I discovered him the same and at the same time much changed. He still stands at a shade under six feet and to the casual eye is slightly built. But he has grown sinewy in the wastes of Canada and has gained formidable physical strength in the period of his absence. I saw him at his own accommodation at his own invitation, sent me at the Savoy where, of course, he knows I keep a suite when in town. He has taken a mews house off Weymouth Street, one of those stable conversions voguish since the motor car and bus have made horse-drawn passenger transportation virtually obsolete.

I tried to ignore his appearance when he opened his door. His clothing was inoffensive enough. He was attired in the trousers and waistcoat of a chalk-stripe suit with a plain white shirt underneath. He now affects eyeglasses with darkened lenses. I suppose this is to conceal the terrible vacancy in his eyes. But the leer of his lips remains undisguised. The lower lip seems to droop as though missing the muscle or nerve to discipline it. This gives his face a permanently disdainful expression. It is both sinister and condescending and, after darkness falls and the shadows increase, it becomes almost fearful. His pale complexion, waxy and somehow granular, adds nothing to his physical charms.

'Uncle,' he said, 'how wonderful it is of you to come.' He lisped slightly saying those words, another effect of what has happened to his mouth.

'How did you know, Patrick? I mean about Irvine and Mallory?' The question was blurted out. A doorstep interrogation had not been my intention but his apparent gift for clairvoyance had haunted my thoughts since the summer.

'Wrong billing, Uncle,' he said. 'History will ever have them the other way around. Mallory was the star, you see. Irvine was chosen to go up there with him only because he was good with the oxygen bottles, poor fellow.'

'How did you know? It only happened in June, for God's sake.'

'It was 6 June, Uncle Bruno. They breakfasted on fried sardines before the final ascent. At the summit, they shared a handshake and a bar of Kendal mint cake.'

'How did you know?'

'Come on in,' he said. His manner was friendly. It was not warm. It seemed like mimicry. But he was not angry and sullen as he'd been at Wapping, during our last encounter. He was much more comfortable and at ease, it seemed, with whatever he was. I took off my coat and hung it on a hook. He poured me a cognac from a Hennessy bottle. It was the seven-star. He refreshed a drink of his own that looked like undiluted gin. He has adopted the new fashion for ice in a drink. Perhaps he has learned the habit in Canada, where ice is very plentiful. I sensed he'd been a quick learner since his awkward reintroduction into the physical world.

'How did you know?' I persisted. He shrugged. We were in his sitting room. We were standing to either side of the hearth. He now wears Vetiver cologne. It failed to conceal a rank bass note. He has not successfully shed, I noticed, the faint odour of spoiled meat his father had first detected about his person.

'How do I know that a pretty flapper will read about me in your diaries one day? I just do. I know things.'

'What in God's name is a flapper?'

'Come on, Uncle. Lady Brett Ashley in *The Sun Also Rises* is a flapper. Louise Brooks is one as Lulu in Pabst's *Pandora's Box*. She might very well be the archetype. Do you neither read nor go to the cinema? Yours will sport a black bob and grey eyes and a seductive mouth and the requisite sexual promiscuity. And she will be English. I'm fairly sure of that.'

What he was saying was nonsense, incomprehensible. I wondered why he had summoned me there but needed to change the subject. 'Your house is very handsome,' I said. 'Conveniently close to the park. Not all that far from the heath.'

He smiled his ghastly smile and slopped gin into his mouth. 'I love all waste and solitary places,' he said. And I recognised the line from Shelley. But I wasn't at all sure that he did. I thought he was less like a personality with a functioning mind than a human Marconi set, random information chattering out of it as you twisted the tuning dial between broadcast frequencies.

His house was opulently furnished in the art nouveau style. His choice of pictures somewhat mirrored my own, when I had been an undergraduate with a fascination with the macabre. He has the Dore etchings of Dante's *Seven Circles of Hell* framed in black ebony and prominently hung on his sitting room wall. He has the El Greco sketches of the atrocities from the peninsular campaign in the Napoleonic wars. There were some portraits of Pre-Raphaelite women and the thought of Patrick with a real woman made me shudder and swallow bile. He has the Dore series also, depicting the Victorian squalor of the London slums and above that, in a neat row, the illustrations to Milton's *Paradise Lost*.

'Look at this, Uncle,' he said. He walked across the room to a large wooden box, reinforced at its corners with an angle iron binding and hooped in iron, somewhat like a barrel would be. He bent and picked it up from the floor and put it on an oak table with a loud, shuddering thump. I understood the impact when he removed the lid and beckoned me across the room to examine the contents of the box. It was full of ore. It must have weighed a colossal amount, several hundred pounds. He had lifted it as a man might lift a hat box onto a luggage rack out of courtesy for a lady, or as one might lift an empty wine case onto a cellar shelf for refilling.

'You have grown strong.'

'No thanks to you,' he said. He was handling the ore, his box of souvenirs, plucking chunks of veined rock and holding them in his palm. 'You let the dead mature, Uncle. You almost destroyed me, bringing me back so fresh. I was barely cold. I barely even knew I was dead.' He grinned, his teeth big and sharp and grown quite yellow. At the sight of them between those drooling lips, I almost recoiled. 'There was only my father for me to gather strength from, and him weak already with angina, Uncle Bruno. He hardly made a suitable host. Canada was better. A blaster at the mine named Kilgore mentored me.'

'And this Kilgore was a vigorous man?'

Patrick cocked his head as if to consider the question and once again I thought the gesture closer to mimicry than any spontaneous response. 'He was vigorous at the outset, certainly. He was dead by the time I left. He'd gone to his grave with the consolation of my gratitude.'

'Why have you asked me here?'

'My spiritual welfare is your concern, is it not, as my godfather?'

'Yes,' I said. I admitted it with a heavy heart, compromised by my guilt.

'I propose to visit my mother at the Falcon Lodge asylum.'

'To what end?'

'It is surely only what should be expected of me, as a dutiful son.'

'You are no kind of son to her, Patrick, as we both know. Desist from this plan. Leave her what consolation she might have found in her seclusion there. Do it if only as a favour to me. Do you enjoy this life, with which I have provided you?'

'More than you can know, Uncle. More than you would wish to know.'

'Then do it as a favour to me.'

He pretended to consider this for a moment, but pretence was all it was. The sneer never departed his lips. 'I wish to see my mother,' he said. 'And I am interested to see her doctor, too. He has some intriguing ideas. I look forward to confounding them.'

'Can you see your own future?'

He ran a hand through his hair. The hand was strong-looking and has become gnarled with physical work and reminded me, with its horny nails, of the talons of a vulture. For an awful moment, I thought he was going to take off his glasses and reveal the abyss of his gaze to me, but he did not. 'Not clearly,' he said. 'It is up to me to make of my future what I can. I must make the very best of myself.' The sneer widened. 'I must honour the memory of my father.'

It was the first mention he had made of Samuel's recent death. I mourned my friend, but it was explicitly requested I did not attend the funeral, so neither of us had been there. I had heard that, apart from a relatively modest sum to cater to Mary's pitiful ongoing needs, the bulk of his vast fortune has been willed entirely to charity. But Sam has unwittingly provided the son he refused to acknowledge with the means to make a fortune of his own. He could do it under the guise of his geological skills. He can see the future. He would know where the next big oil well or gold or diamond mine is going to be discovered. All he needs to do is turn up early. He will drill for his core samples or sink an exploratory well and strike it rich every time and no one will know it is because of his diabolical gift. They will assume it is because of lessons about mineral deposits hard-earned over a three-year apprenticeship in the remoter wastes of Canada.

I tapped my way with my cane through the fog that had descended to afflict Weymouth Street upon my departure. My host had offered me no food during my brief visit but, out of superstition alone, I think I would have refused it. Headlamps were glowing lozenges of yellow light through the mist as cars made slow and serene progress along the road. I tried in vain to hail a cab. I was in Lower Regent Street,

outside the Lanesborough, before I heard and then saw taxis queuing
in a throbbing convoy and thought to ask the doorman there to draw
me one up. Then I changed my mind and went into the hotel instead.
I had no appetite just then for supper. The subtle stench of my godson
was still about me. I went into the Palm Court bar and sat and
presently a waiter came across to me and I ordered a large drink.
Spirits from a bottle no longer raise my own. But I find that resolution
generally comes in a balloon-shaped glass.

It is three years since Patrick boasted of his ambition to me by the
lapping filth of the river edge at Wapping and he made no mention
of it again last night. I sat in that hotel bar and considered it,
nevertheless. He will tell me only what he wishes to and I do not
think a plague of the dead and its specifics the likely subject of any
future conversation between the two of us. I must see what more I can
discover about Gunter Keller. He was necessarily secretive. But men
who strive to achieve things considered impossible are seldom modest
and there may be a record somewhere alluding to the feat that
condemned him to end his life atop the pyre.

Seeing Patrick again reminded me, of course, of his prophesy
concerning my own life, just as reading about the enigmatic fate of
Mallory and Irvine did back in the early part of the summer. I do not
know how long it is I have. I do not know how long is left to me to
investigate or whether there is any point to the investigation beyond
my own curiosity. I would not begin to know how to stop Patrick.
He is sly and strong and very confident of the future he predicts. I
vacillate and in the face of his blithe prediction concerning my own
imminent death, fall prey all the time to ailments that are merely
imaginary. I am no protagonist for him.

Elena frowned after reading this entry. The description of her
was in some ways precisely accurate, though she thought that
calling her promiscuous somewhat extreme. She had slept
with five men in her life. She had never been married or even
engaged. Judged by the standards of 1924, perhaps she was
promiscuous. She did not very much feel it. She searched for

the Hemingway novel on her computer and discovered that *The Sun Also Rises* had not been published until 1926. So there was no human way Patrick could have known about Lady Brett, the flapper prototype of the story. She searched for Pabst's *Lulu* and saw that the film had not been released until 1929. She thought she knew better than he did the real reason why Absalom would be no match for Patrick in any battle of wits. Patrick could see the future. But there was something else. She suspected that by this point in his life, Absalom was drinking heavily. He alluded to the cognac bottle far too often. He had no compunction about drinking alone. Patrick drank heavily too, according to his father's account. But it did not seem to intoxicate him and neither had it sapped his very evident physical strength.

She looked at her watch. It was nine o'clock and outside her window she could hear the raucous din of another Friday night passing her by. She had almost got through the Absalom journal. She would email her précis to Julian tomorrow morning so he could read it before they met on the Sunday. And she would have a whole day between now and then to discover whatever she could about Gunter Keller and why his warning about this plague of the dead he spoke about had been so direly made.

Stride looked back. He had left no lights on in the house. He wished he had. They would have moored him more securely in reality than the blackness all around him. The only illumination was that oily glimmer ahead of him, sly and uncertain and somehow confidential, a secret shared with no one in the world tonight but him. He turned to face it and his heart hitched in his chest.

'I've got the fear,' he said to himself. It was a line from the band's favourite film back in the day and always made him smile and he quoted it because he really did have the fear now and needed to gather his resolution. His respect for Julian Creed was increasing with every step he took. The supernatural was Creed's speciality, of course, it was his chosen profession and he had done very well by it. But the sense of mystery and menace emanating from the derelict building ahead of him was gloomily potent and Creed must have sensed it powerfully. He was psychically gifted. Stride was not, to his knowledge. Yet all the instinct he possessed told him to turn back and put a safe distance between himself and his intended destination. His indignation had drained away. Caution had damped his anger down. He was aware that the temperature had dropped suddenly and by several degrees. It no longer felt like a September evening during an Indian summer; it felt like a chilly late November night. Rain had started to fall, cold and insistent, in drops that whispered through the parched, uncut grass. He could smell soot and iron and coal and the smells were pungently like life and not faint like ghostly memories. The air was sharp with the harsh tang of these industrial odours, delivered on a wintry gust.

Ahead of him, he saw the silvery gleam of parallel rails and the sight stopped him dead. He closed his eyes and put his fingers to his face and rubbed them and then shook his head and opened his eyes again. And they were still there, polished with the heavy grind of iron wheel rims, picked out by the light from the waiting room windows, thinly reflecting it. He was close now, approaching the station remains. The first thing he noticed was that the platform's thorny skirt of surrounding blackberry bushes had gone. He could see the bricks supporting the platform surface, mortar clean and un-pitted between, in a pale, neat lattice that looked much more recent than it should. He climbed onto the platform.

A kiosk faced him. It was made of wood and wore a coat of green gloss paint and newspapers flapped, folded into wire brackets sheltered from the rain by the eaves of its over-hanging roof. A copy of the *Daily Record* had been folded over and clipped behind a hoarding grille with the headline prominent. In the cloudy darkness, in the light leaking from the waiting room, the headline on the front page had been printed in a point-size so huge he could read it clearly. VICTORY, it said: GERMAN SURRENDER. He pulled a paper from the rack and held it close, tilted to the light, and read the date on it. It was the edition from 11 November, 1918. The paper looked yellow in the dim cast of lamplight. But it felt crisp between his fingers and the ink was fresh enough to smudge. He peered into the gloom of the kiosk itself. There was a varnished stool in there and, on a tray, a cloth with a stone to anchor it at the centre of which were piles of the large, old-fashioned pennies it took twelve of to make a shilling. There were neat stacks of cigarette packets on interior shelves and on the narrow counter, trays of liquorice sticks and gobstoppers. There was a smell about the kiosk of newsprint and fresh tobacco and confectionery. *It's real*, Stride thought. *Jesus, it's real and right in front of me. It's as real as I am.*

He was used to the fraudulent nature of props. The band's promo videos had mostly been shot by the one prop-inclined director and he was used to their flimsiness and adhesive smell and the empty way they only had conviction viewed from the angles from which they were being shot. The kiosk on the station platform was no prop. It existed in three solid dimensions. There was a patch of bare wood in the paint on the counter where the passengers dropped their coins to pay and the boy behind it slid them their change. It was the sort of detail you only got authentically, in life. Where was the boy? He would be in breeches and a flat cap with a soot-stained face, and Stride did not at all wish to encounter him. He fingered the bare patch on the counter, smooth with years of wear.

He walked beyond the kiosk, past another structure that was new to him. This one had more permanence. It too was largely constructed of wood, but concrete pillars supported its corners. It was a public lavatory and it reeked with a power to make the eyes and nostrils smart, of chlorine bleach overlaying the acrid stench of stale piss. But piss was organic, wasn't it? The smell of it did not endure for better than ninety years. He walked on and then stopped at an unmistakeable sound. Someone was pissing in the stall. It was roofless and its occupant's bladder hot. He knew that from the steam rising in the cold air above it. He heard a belch. There was a sigh from within of relief. And then whoever was in there started to whistle. The tune was 'Goodbye Dolly Gray'. The door rattled. Stride steeled himself. He would not run away. He had come here not to flee from but to face the danger confronting his family. He could feel the thump of his own heart as the stall door opened inward on its occupant. The hairs were raised and rigid on his forearms. He could barely breathe.

It was a man of about sixty, wearing the uniform of a station guard. He exited the lavatory and sauntered more than walked past Stride, still buttoning his flies. His neck above his collar and tie was livid with the nicks of a hasty shave. His breath smelled strongly of pipe tobacco. And Stride was invisible to him, he knew. His clothes would seem outlandish to this solid ghost, his shoulder-length hair an outrage against convention. The man could not have walked so blandly on had he himself been visible.

'Hey,' he said. And the station guard stopped dead. He turned and looked around, frowning. But there was no focus to the look. He had heard something, but the source and nature of the sound had not been clear to him. He lifted a brass pocket watch from its chain on his waistcoat and sprung the cover and looked at the dial, frowning. Then he put the watch back and turned and walked serenely on.

And Stride allowed him to. The moment that single syllable had left his lips, he had known with a sense of dread it was a terrible mistake. Overwhelming instinct told him he would be in grave danger if he succeeded in communicating with the memory made flesh he'd just encountered. The guard had walked on, past the waiting room. Old because the boys had all been called up to fight, Stride thought, nodding at the realisation. They had taken the fit men first. But the war had devoured them. They accepted volunteers who weren't yet twenty-one and qualified to drink and vote. Then there had been the bantams, the height restriction waived, jockey-sized soldiers no taller than the rifles they carried over the top. And in 1916, the Pals battalions had been sent to the slaughter: sixteen-year-old boys from Macclesfield and Crewe, malnourished factory lads who'd rarely eaten meat and thought their ration packs a feast.

He was there, wasn't he? He was in 1918, Stride knew. He had stumbled through the rainy land he owned into the past. The yellow lamplight from the waiting room faltered and then, nourished by he knew not what, grew brighter as the pant and rumble of an approaching train gained volume and made the rails below him start to thrum expectantly.

Stride felt that he had to go while he still could. He could do nothing here but court danger. He did not precisely understand the danger. But his instinct told him it was real and growing and would become awful if he was still on the platform to witness the arrival of the train. There would be the hiss of brakes and the staccato sound of the slam-doors opening and shutting and the joyous faces of returning troops and the drooling visages of the insane in their buckled restraints between grim orderlies on their way to Brody's madhouse. And there would be the physical casualties: the recently stricken blind and mutilated, the flapping amputees and the gas casualties labouring in vain for a single, satisfying breath. And it all amounted to sights he should not see, to an affront to sense and possibility. *And an affront to time itself,* he thought. *And time will not tolerate the insult and I will be the one to pay the punishment for it.*

The sound of the train grew louder. He leaped from the

platform. He began to jog through the cold and the rain, stumbling over tussocks and roots, away from the trailing sparks and tumult behind him now, away from the solid reality of returning ghosts, tripping and shivering as 'Roses of Picardy' rose forth in ardent chorus from the throats of men long dead, panting and soaked as he ran towards the refuge of the future in which he lived, back to the life he knew and the loved ones he cherished. The song faded. The engine grew distant and silent. He was at the kitchen door before he dared to pause and turn and look back. But when he did so, the lights to the east had been extinguished.

He did not know how he had missed the note from Tom Barrowclough. When he climbed back to the attic and re-opened the chest, the buff envelope containing it was the first thing he saw. He shut the lid and sat on the chest to read it.

Dear Mr Stride,

My conscience has troubled me sorely ever since I sold you the plot on which that damned derelict railway platform stands. I am a pragmatic man. I am a farmer, and the cultivation of the land and the breeding of livestock are labours that preclude anything not practical and immediate and real. But there is something not right with that place. I have known it virtually from the day when I bid for it at auction back in 1964. It did not cost me greatly then. I would say that it has cost me more since in lost sleep and fanciful anxieties.

I told you that story about my uncle William as a sort of preparation for what you are about to discover. Edward Brody left my uncle his papers after his premature death. My uncle left them to me. I did not trouble myself even to open the chest, until the night noises and lights emanating from that blighted place provoked my curiosity to the point where I could no longer resist doing so.

I expect it is the same with you. You did not strike me as a fanciful man, despite your exotic occupation. I expect you have opened up the box and are reading this only because you can no longer ignore the strange goings-on in that place. You will not find answers here as to why it happens, I don't think, unless you are much cleverer than me. But you will discover some grim secrets and I believe the old cliché that forewarned is forearmed to be true, so I hope you benefit from their exposure. Concern yourself with the volume from 1924, Mr Stride. It covers the mystery to which my uncle William referred on his deathbed. I think it explains better than consumption could why poor Brody aged so quickly and so abruptly fled his post at Falcon Lodge.

I would not have sold you the land if you had not been so doggedly persistent in your offers to purchase it from me. I would have steered clear of it and risked no more experience of trains that couldn't run and lights that shouldn't switch on and marching songs sung by soldiers long dead and buried. I heard these things only two or three times in thirty years, but it was enough. And after hearing the sobbing woman on the wind one afternoon, I left the place be entirely until the reluctant tour I gave you.

Has it got worse? I always suspected it would. The station is preparing for something, Mr Stride. Fate hasn't finished with Shale Point yet. That's my intuition, for what it's worth. I hope Brody's case notes are of value to you. I hope they shed some light on something I do not pretend to understand but suspect is very dark. I would not be as optimistic or glib as to ask your forgiveness for my part in whatever ordeal you are enduring. But I would beg you to give that blighted spot the wide berth it requires.

Sincerely,

Tom Barrowclough

Stride read that last paragraph uneasily. He had the strong sense he was not alone up there in his attic. He had the suspicion he was being watched. And something else was curious and disturbing. He thought he could smell a whiff of spoiled meat. He sensed movement and looked up from Barrowclough's letter. And he saw that Millie's old rocking horse was tilting back and forth on its wooden runners, as though playfully tipped. A feeling of dread spread through him so defeating he thought his legs would not possess the strength to get him upright off the chest lid on which he sat. He took a breath and rose. The rotten meat smell had grown richer. He thought he heard, from the reach of the attic shadows, a stifled laugh.

He hadn't switched on all the attic lights, only the one above the spot where he stood. The rest of that large space was shadowy and dim. Now, with his scalp tingling, he went over to the wall and switched all of them on. And he saw that he was quite alone up there. But one of the windows was slightly open. Had he opened it himself? He might have done. He had opened several to air the house, to rid it of the smell of Carter's heavies and their cheap aftershave and grease-laden take away food. Those smells had gone, but the spoiled meat smell up here was stronger and, even in the bright electric light, the air seemed heavy, gravid almost with malevolence.

Stride closed and locked the window. He retrieved the Brody case note volume for 1924. He climbed down from the attic and went into the kitchen and checked the fridge and freezer, but both appliances were working properly and neither anyway was the source of the smell. The bin was empty. There was no smell in the kitchen other than the scent of some floral disinfectant. He sniffed the sink and then forced himself to examine all the bathrooms in the house. But it was not some dead animal decaying in the water tanks or drains. The bathrooms smelled only of the lime-scented detergent used to clean them. He closed down the house and got into his car. When he looked at his watch, he saw that it was ten o'clock. He would drive to Portsmouth and check into a hotel and read what Brody had written there. He would go back to the island in the morning. He would try to enjoy a relaxing weekend with his family. He would not return home until Monday, he decided, and the visit of the priest.

# Chapter Ten

Elena met Julian at one of the bars in the Royal Festival Hall on the South Bank at four o'clock on Sunday afternoon. It was overcast and raining outside the large windows that overlooked the river and the pale row of antique vessels anchored on the far bank. A jazz five-piece played fusion as part of some eclectic concert programme from the ground floor and the sound rose distorted and muted by the challenging acoustics of the large space. She smiled, thinking of how uncharismatic this anonymous band was and what a magnetic performer by contrast had been Martin Stride in his pomp. Apparently, his public past went unlamented, at least by him. He sounded such an intriguing man. After what she had learned about Gunter Keller the previous day, she thought that she might actually get to meet him now. She did not think the Catholic ritual of the Belgian priest the following day was quite going to do the trick.

Julian was on time. She thought that this must be a feature of the new him. He had never really done punctuality except with people from whom he needed something. Perhaps he needed something from her. But she thought it more likely a symptom of his decision to act with honesty. Keeping people waiting was a power ploy and he had given up on playing games. His hair and shoulders were wet. He must have walked there, she thought. His progress was agile through the chairs and tables obstructing his route to the bar and her. He moved with an easy, entirely unconscious grace. She thought, not for the first time, that if he was an animal, he would be a big cat, a panther or a cougar, something like that. And then it occurred to her with a start of surprise that Martin Stride would be, too. They were miles apart in style and temperament. But physically, the two men were actually very similar. The idea of a big cat prowling through the rain was one that made her smile. Down below, the five-piece had lumbered into 'Let's Get Lost'. Cats hated water, didn't they?

'What's so funny?'

'You are.'

'I wouldn't take that from anyone but you.'

'Is that because you respect me so much?'

'No. It's because I love you,' he said.

'Jesus,' she said. She had not anticipated this. She had not expected this at four in the afternoon in a public place on a rainy London day.

'I'm sorry,' he said. He was dripping onto the parquet and his cheeks had coloured. He bit his bottom lip.

'You want to take it back, Julian?'

'No,' he said. 'I'm sorry I said it, that's all. I hadn't planned to. I can't take it back. It's the truth.'

People were looking at them. Eavesdropping tourists occupying nearby chairs sat as rapt as a cinema audience. The girl behind the bar stood wide-eyed.

Elena closed the distance between them and they embraced and kissed.

'You're getting all wet,' Creed said when the kiss broke. And she smiled at him. She did not seem at all to mind getting wet.

'I'll get you a beer,' she said.

'I don't drink during the day. You know I don't.'

'When you hear what I have to say, Julian, you'll need a beer.'

'You're resigning, aren't you? You've decided to build a new life on Australia's Gold Coast with a simple but rugged body-boarder.'

'There's no need to travel to the other side of the world,

Julian. There's someone simple and rugged I can build a new life with here.'

'Less of the simple, please,' he said. He did not think he had ever felt more elated in his life.

They found a table over by the rain-streaked window, away from the cluster of people around the bar. She had sent him her précis of the Absalom deposition the previous morning and he had duly read it. She had spent the rest of Saturday discovering what she could about Gunter Keller and his plague of the dead. They had shared a fairly lengthy phone conversation about the Absalom stuff in the evening. But she had not mentioned her Keller findings then. She had waited to do so until now.

She had done her day's research into Keller with an open mind. But at the back of it had been Bruno Absalom's suspicion that he had used the ritual on someone wealthy, doing so discreetly, for financial gain. In the sixteenth century, alchemists were not offered the status of research fellows. There were no bursaries or grants and there was no government funding. They worked at the very edge of what society would tolerate. They faced official hostility but could not conduct their experiments without finding the money from somewhere to do so. Keller had been the son of a printer, relatively prosperous but still a tradesman. He had certainly not possessed independent wealth and the stuff of alchemy – silver, gold, mercury, even the glass and metal instruments they used and the bellows they needed for the forges they fired – came only at a cost.

She worked back from the date and location of his execution. She looked at census reports and taxes levied and import duties paid and, where she could find them, accounts of the lives and deaths of prominent men. And she looked for signs of pestilence as well. Hamburg had been a port city, a free imperial city of the Hanseatic League, that did a lot of trade with Denmark back in those days. Lutheranism had been officially established there in 1529 and the city divided into four Lutheran parishes. But the religious change had not brought bloodshed. It had done what it was intended to and provided political and administrative stability. Hamburg, relatively speaking, was a prosperous and peaceful and enlightened settlement at the time of Keller's burning.

Eventually, she found her anomaly. A trader named Hans Bader had run a fleet of cargo vessels between a dock on the Elbe and Denmark, carrying mostly fur and fish and wine and candle tallow. He had started out as a boat captain, most of his original crew coming from a quite large extended family. He had lost two brothers and three cousins to a North Sea squall when one of his vessels foundered in the winter of 1511. Neither the boat nor the cargo had been insured. But Bader inventoried the goods stored aboard the sunken craft in a successful attempt to have the loss offset against his city taxes for the following year. In 1515, all record of his trading activity ceased. Then, three years later, it began again. Matters passed uneventfully for a full decade. Then, in 1528, people started to die in Bader's home village, a hamlet of fewer than eighty souls, which could not sustain the loss in population without local government attention and investigation.

'A physician visited those suffering from this mystery affliction,' Elena told Creed. 'He said that they manifested symptoms of malnutrition. There was abundant food, no dire poverty or famine being endured. They could have survived on fish had those circumstances prevailed because the village was near the coast. But they should not have needed to. By the standards of the time, they were relatively prosperous. The fruit and vegetable market, when he visited, was abundant. There was plenty of bread.'

'Did he notice anything else?'

'Yes, he did. He said that a smell of rotten meat pervaded the village. The people lit fires to clean the air as they always did then in time of plague and pestilence. But it did no good.

The village was essentially healthy, he said, but had the character about it of somewhere abject with disease.'

'Good phrase,' Creed said.

'A literal translation,' Elena told him. 'So I did a bit of cross-referencing. I found out where Sir Samuel Ross had owned his mines in British Columbia. I discovered where the dynamite blaster, Kilgore, had worked. You'll remember Patrick Ross said Kilgore mentored him, until his death.'

'Kilgore is a common name in Canada, Elena.'

'But I was looking for someone who died during the three years Patrick was out there, which narrowed it down. And he had to have worked for Sir Samuel, which narrowed it down even further. Peter Kilgore died in April of 1924. He was Patrick's mentor, all right. And the post-mortem established the cause of death as malnutrition.'

'What do you think happened in that village outside Hamburg?'

'It was actually closer to Lübeck.'

'Whatever.'

'First of all, I think that Keller lied. Hans Bader disappeared from administrative records because he stopped trading. I suspect he did so because he was dead. Maybe Keller knew him, had bought imported items from him.'

'Bruno Absalom suspected Keller's copy of the ritual a translation of something originally brought back by Norsemen,' Creed said. 'Bader traded with the Danish ports.'

'I'd forgotten about that,' Elena said. 'And we'll never know for sure. But something linked Keller and Bader, and Bader died and Keller brought him back. And a decade on, lonely for his own kind, Bader brought back his dead brothers and cousins and they each needed a host, just like Patrick Ross did, and people started to die and that's Keller's plague of the dead.'

Creed sipped beer. He looked out of the rain-bleared window. He thought about the disparity between the beautiful woman in front of him and the ghoulish tale she had just related. He had not planned to say anything about his feelings for her. They'd been his hopeless secret. He'd blurted out what he'd felt without thought or preparation. Her response had left him feeling more joyful than he'd thought himself capable of feeling. He really did love her. He could not now imagine a future without her. He wished they were discussing something more to do with themselves, with each other. But he felt he had a duty to the Strides: to Martin and Monica, who had trusted him, to their innocent children in the face of whatever jeopardy threatened them. If he ran away from duty, he was nothing. He certainly wasn't worthy of Elena Coyle.

'I don't buy it,' he said, finally. 'I don't think Keller would risk the stake to bring back Bader's lost crew. He could not return six or eight men from the dead without provoking accusations of witchcraft or black magic. You couldn't exactly do it unnoticed. He was not that stupid, was he?'

'Bader returned them.'

'How would he do that, without the ritual and some means of distilling their essence? Bader was a trader, not an alchemist.'

'He shared their essence,' Elena said. 'He was of the same stuff. He craved his own kind. He didn't require the ritual. He found a way to bring them back, just as Patrick intends to.'

'If he did do it, he only waited a decade.'

'And Patrick has waited almost a hundred years, because the dead grow stronger,' Elena said.

A cold feeling enveloped Creed, an icy second skin. 'It's why he's back in uniform. He wore civilian clothes in the 1920s, according to the Absalom account. But Peter saw him in uniform and I did too and it was the ghost of the soldier, Owen, who delivered a warning. And it's why he's hanging around that waiting room, which has become the place again it was in the Great War. He wants to bring back his dead comrades.'

'And they'll be very strong,' Elena said. 'And they will be very hungry. And their numbers will be of a magnitude we can barely imagine.'

'And they'll be like him, without souls and corrupt,' Creed said.

'Loath and cold,' Elena said, who had remembered the Owen poem.

A man came over to their table. He wore a smile and carried a biro and waved it in front of Julian Creed's face. And the temptation to tell him to eat his pen and then go and fuck himself was almost overwhelming. But the man was middle-aged and Creed thought that the boy hovering nervously behind him was probably his son and he did not want to disillusion a child and spoil a family day out. So he signed a beer mat and beckoned the boy over and managed five minutes of chat and threw in a ghostly anecdote and sent them away happy.

'Sometimes I think your self-control extraordinary,' Elena said, in their aftermath, 'unless you just have an overriding craving to be liked.'

'I don't think I do, any longer. I've learned a lesson in dignity from our Mr Stride. I'm beginning to think fame might have its downside.'

'You like children, don't you, Julian? You're always kind to them.'

'So was Adolf Hitler.'

But she would not be deflected by the joke. 'Why have you never become a father?'

'I had a regular girlfriend back in the regiment. She became pregnant. But our twins were born prematurely and died within an hour of one another.'

'I'm so sorry.'

'When I think of fatherhood, I tend to think of pain and grief.'

'That's awful for you.'

He shrugged. 'I've dealt with it. I've had no choice. The question is, what are we going to do with all this stuff you've discovered?'

But Elena never got the opportunity to answer that question. Creed's BlackBerry began to ring and the number on the display was Martin Stride's. Creed stood and walked over to the window and listened intently, sketching a slow, horizontal line of clarity in the condensation on the glass with his index finger. She watched him. She looked at his broad-shouldered back and watched his head dip in what she thought was an unconscious gesture of sympathy and she thought that he was a good man she could love without regret. He spoke only very sparingly and in a tone so hushed she could not make out what he said. Then he broke the connection and returned to where she sat.

'I hope you don't have any plans for later today.'

'Oh, you know me. Anyway, there isn't much later of today to be had, is there?'

'I'm taking a chopper to Wight. Both of Stride's kids endured terrible dreams last night and he's found out something he wants to share with me. He rightly suspects we've been digging and wants to be brought up to speed on everything we've learned. He's going ahead with the exorcism tomorrow, but more out of desperation than real hope. I told him I'd meet him at a pub in Ventnor at eight o'clock. Since you're the one who knows the most about all this, I took the liberty of telling him I'd bring you along. Are you all right with helicopters?'

'No, I'm not, I bloody hate flying. But this could not really be more serious, I don't think. And I would like to meet Martin Stride.'

'He's an impressive man. That said, just now he might not be at his best.' Creed paused. 'What's up, Ellie? You look as though someone just walked over your grave.'

He had not used his familiar name for her in months.

It sounded good to hear it again. She reached out and took his hand and he squeezed hers gently in the cradle his fingers made. 'He told Bruno Absalom nearly ninety years ago what I would look like when I came searching for his confession. When you almost surprised him in the waiting room, he knew it was you. He knew your name.'

'Maybe he's a fan of the series,' Creed said. But even to his ears, the crack rang pretty hollow. In his mind, he pictured the revolver bullet sitting on its heel on the cold iron of the waiting room stove.

The rain had not reached over the Solent to Wight. The weather was benign and Creed was glad because Elena really was a nervous flyer and he knew from long experience that turbulence was much worse at a few hundred feet aboard a chopper than at thirty thousand in a passenger aircraft designed specifically for the comfort of those aboard. They took a taxi from the airfield booked on their behalf by Stride and waiting for them when they hit the ground. Creed felt pretty nervous himself. The last time he had met Stride at the Spyglass Inn, he had been summarily fired. This time, he was here at Stride's request. But he was going to have to confess to disobeying the man's explicit instructions and visiting the waiting room clandestinely. He had no choice. He had to share the information concerning his most recent experience there. Honesty was more than a commitment in this instance, it was a practical necessity.

'I don't think I like helicopters,' Elena said, somewhat redundantly, when they were on their way to Ventnor in the car.

'They're even less fun when the people on the ground below are shooting at you,' Creed said. She smiled. It was a fair point.

She thought the interior of the pub extraordinary. It was lit by ships' lanterns. There were shelves and display cases everywhere, filled with the burnished brass and tarry wood and rope of nautical implements. They found Stride in a nook all to himself with an antique map framed behind him on the wall, his pint resting on an empty grog barrel doing service as a table. He had chosen the spot well. The pub was busy but this area, which seated three only at a pinch, was an alcove no one had cause to pass on their way to the bar or lavatory or single entrance. They had privacy. It was something they needed now and, she remembered, something the man they had come to see greatly valued anyway in his life.

Creed introduced them. Stride stood. He seemed almost courtly in his manner. He was very handsome, she thought, a glamorous sight with his hair grown down to his shoulders. He was dressed in jeans and a crew-neck sweater the same grey colour as his eyes. He smiled at her. But though he seemed friendly, when he smiled there was a frown that would not lift, creasing his brow. He was clearly troubled. Even without knowing the substance of the dreams recently inflicted on his children, Elena thought that he had every right to be.

He started patting his pockets, obviously trying to remember where he'd put his wallet, and asked them what would they like to drink. But Creed overrode him and headed for the bar. He was never slow to stump up for his round, Elena thought. But she thought he had actually gone because the bar was busy and he would be a couple of minutes getting served and it would give her and Stride an opportunity to say at least a few words to one another.

'He told me about you,' Stride said, sitting back down. 'He said you are a brilliant researcher. I hope to God he was telling the truth.'

'I've found out a few things.'

'He went back to the waiting room, didn't he, after I sacked him?'

'How did you know?'

'He triggered some agitation. A dog was scared to death. Not by him, but by the thing I suspect he agitated.'

'Are you angry he went back?'

Stride pondered this, staring at her. His gaze was very direct. It was attractive too and she did not flinch from it.

'He's a good man, under the bullshit, Elena. I don't suppose I need to tell you that. But it's taken me a while to realise it. He's courageous and he's honourable too, after his peculiar fashion. To tell you the truth, I'm vastly relieved he disobeyed my instructions.' He sipped his beer. 'Were you still working on this matter after I sacked him?'

'I was working on it when you called him this afternoon,' Elena said. 'I'm working on it now. I haven't stopped since I started, except occasionally to sleep.'

Creed returned with their drinks. He sat down. 'I've a confession to make, Martin,' he said.

'Save it, Julian. I know about your surreptitious visit to Shale Point in my absence. I guessed. You angered someone, or you upset something. It took out its anger on a Dobermann dog in a petty act of retribution.'

'Patrick Ross,' Elena said. 'He's the young subaltern with the scary face your son drew and your daughter dreamed of. Julian caught a glimpse of him in the waiting room on the night he shouldn't have been there.'

'He taunted me. He called me by my name.'

Stride looked at Creed. 'You'd better tell me who he is, Julian, or who he was.'

'Elena will tell you all of what we've found out,' Creed said. 'She's the one who's discovered pretty much everything we know. It's her story.'

'Not like you to accept second billing.'

'Less is more,' Creed said, smiling. 'Don't worry. There'll be an eye-catching cameo in it for me somewhere.'

Stride tried to smile but the effort spoiled the result.

'Listen to Elena,' Creed said. He reached out and put a hand on Stride's shoulder with a gentle squeeze of consolation. 'And then tell us everything that's happened to you and your family since that infamous moment outside here when you gave me the sack.'

Elena spoke for an hour. She related the detail fluently. She told him chronologically about everything they had learned about Paley and Brody and Sir Samuel and Lady Ross and their son, Patrick, and Sir Samuel's friend, Bruno Absalom. She interspersed the story with brief accounts of Creed's three vigils in the waiting room. She left nothing out. He smiled wanly when she told him about the concealed camera and his fists clenched where they rested on the grog barrel-top and his eyes switched briefly to Creed. She wound up with what she had lately learned about Gunter Keller and the trader, Hans Bader, and the events at his village near Lübeck. And she concluded with her suspicions about Patrick Ross and the significance of the Owen poem and the real meaning of his ambition to inflict a plague of the dead.

When she had finished, Creed said to Stride, 'I'm sincerely sorry about the camera. I want you to know that going public over all this is now the last thing on my mind.'

'Involving you in the first place was Monica's idea,' Stride said. 'But we both saw the potential risk to our privacy in doing so. You enjoy notoriety. You love fame.'

'Loved,' Creed said. 'I'm a lot more ambivalent about it now than I was ten days ago when all of this began for me.'

'Why?'

Creed blew out a breath. It was a moment before he spoke. 'Fame forces you to be the person people expect you to be. I was reminded of that only this afternoon. It coerces you into becoming something fraudulent. I'd prefer to live what life is left to me honestly and with the minimum of compromise.'

'I believe you,' Stride said. 'And I believe Bruno Absalom. And I think that you had a very narrow escape on your second vigil, Julian. You and your button camera could have found yourselves stranded in the early 1920s. I think your prospects there would have been bleak.'

'Tell us what's been happening with you,' Elena said.

He told them about Tom Barrowclough and his story concerning his uncle William and Edward Brody. He related details of the dream that had caused Millie to wet herself on the beach. He described his ordeal of Friday evening at the house and on the station platform outside the waiting room. And he told them about the contents of the chest. 'I've photocopied all the relevant pages and there's a copy for each of you in rooms I've booked for you at the hotel we're staying at. You're lucky, it's usually fully occupied, but of course weekenders pack up and go on a Sunday. I was able to get you rooms for a single night.'

Creed said, 'Could you describe this dream your children shared last night?'

They had found themselves descended to the hell described by the poet Wilfred Owen in 'Strange Meeting'. All about them were the uniformed dead. The subaltern Stride now knew to be Patrick Ross was there. He still wore the wounds that had killed him in bright blossoms of crimson blood across the face of his tunic. He was honing the blade of a bayonet on a sharpening stone, stopping from time to time to test its edge against the purple protrusion of his tongue. His leer was ugly to look at but his expression was terrible when he widened his lips and opened his mouth. He sheathed the bayonet and grinned at them.

'The children of the troubadour, come to visit me,' he said. 'We shall be neighbours soon. Shall we be friends, do you think?'

Neither of them had answered him. They had not possessed the power of speech in their dream. They had not known how speech was accomplished and, anyway, they would have been too frightened to try, as both of them admitted later to their parents.

A line of soldiers shuffled by, led by an orderly. Each man had placed his hands on the shoulders of the man in front of him for guidance because none of them, but for the orderly, could see. Their heads were bowed and gauze bandage had been thickly wound about their heads, concealing their features. Some of them wore a wet circular bloodstain where their mouths would be under the gauze. They were bleeding from their mouths or lungs when they breathed. Peter knew that they were gas victims. He did not know whether his sister would know and, though he felt pity for the men, thought that she might think them more sinister than sorry. He tried to reach out his hand to her but discovered he could not move in the dream.

'Like you, I had a beautiful mother,' their guide to hell told them. 'We have that, at least, in common. And my father was wealthy, like yours. But we shall not be friends, I do not think. We share no interests, do we? We have very different appetites.'

He grinned. His lower lip reminded Peter of the rubber of a punctured bike tube, pale and distorted when you try to pull it free of the tyre and the rim. But his teeth looked like those of a beast, yellow and long and sharp. Millie was staring at him, at his torso. Peter looked where she was looking to see if doing so could explain the dismayed look on his sister's face. He glimpsed something yellow in one of the florid wounds punched across the soldier's tunic. He thought it might be a piece of intestine.

'I parried, Millie,' the soldier said. 'I parried; but my hands were loath and cold.'

He held out his hands. They looked strong and sinewy and their nails were talons, bony and black with death. And Peter recoiled from their reach and, as he did so, he slipped and his shoe snagged on something and he looked down and saw that it was a belt. The ground below them was made of men, soft and puckering under their tread, in uniforms stained with mud and bleeding. He realised that they stood atop a vast and shifting hill of corpses. And this mountain of the dead was becoming furtive and unstill.

They ate dinner in the hotel restaurant. Monica Stride joined them for their meal. She told them that the children were sleeping peacefully in their suite upstairs. They had decided that after the previous night, Peter should not be obliged to endure another evening at the hostel. He needed to be within physical reach of his parents for the comfort they could provide when he woke as distressed as he'd been. And it was not fair on the other boy, she said, smiling, to have his friend and room-mate wake him with his screaming.

Elena thought Monica Stride one of the most beautiful women she had ever seen. There was a chiselled perfection about her features, softened by the kindness in her eyes. When women looked like she did, it was natural to expect a frosty degree of hauteur from them. But there was none. She was warm and friendly and she smiled readily, though she did seem subtly and understandably preoccupied. She was not a competitive woman, Elena realised. It was a slightly uncharitable thought but, looking like she did, she had probably never needed to be.

The talk over the table at dinner was subdued. They were eating because people needed to. The food in the hotel restaurant was exceptional, Elena thought. Because it was Sunday, they were the only people in the room. She noticed that Creed wasn't singing for his supper in his characteristic way. She did not think this a demonstration of tact on his part. She thought it empathy and relaxation. She had the feeling he was relieved not to have to go through the public performance that generally defined him. He was among friends. She had the intuition that, though he had not known the Strides for very long, he would remain their friend in the future, should they all survive whatever ordeal was to come. He liked them very much and the liking was mutual. He would be loyal to them and they would be loyal to him. She could see very clearly the brave soldier in him now. She wondered what it must have cost his spirit to subsume what was best and most noble about himself for so long.

She noticed that he did not touch his wine. He had restricted himself to a single bottle of ale at the Spyglass. They had their reading to do after the meal. She hoped they would do it in a single room together. She hoped that they would spend the night together. After everything she had discovered and heard, she thought it would be a great comfort to sleep in the arms of someone warm and strong and loving. She had been alone in her heart and habits for too long. And learning the grim things she had about the circumstances surrounding the waiting room on the Stride estate had frightened her. And the fear had heightened her sense of isolation. She had never felt as alone in her life as in those moments at her flat window and in the cloister garden at the church in Italy when she had seen the ghost of Bruno Absalom. She did not want to be alone tonight.

She wouldn't be, she decided. She wouldn't suggest they sleep together. She would bloody well demand it.

'I'd like you both to attend tomorrow's exorcism,' Stride said.

'I'm not sure about that,' Creed said.

'Julian and our Belgian priest have a history,' Monica said, smiling. 'There was an acrimonious spat on *Question Time*, wasn't there? And he's written some high profile pieces claiming you are a fraud.'

'I'm worse than a fraud,' Creed said. 'I'm an affront to his faith. But it isn't that. His spats with me have raised the profile he enjoys so much. It's more that he might feel our presence undermines the gravity of the occasion. It's a very serious ritual.'

'It's actually a sacrament,' Stride said.

'And in the right circumstances, very powerful,' Creed said.

Monica looked at him. 'You obviously don't think these the right circumstances.'

'It's what Martin thinks that matters,' Creed said.

Stride put down his knife and fork. 'I'm like one of those spiritual cynics who gets told their cancer is terminal,' he said. 'And the cynicism evaporates in the face of their desperation. And they resort to crystals and smoke baths and faith healing.' He looked up at the ceiling, to where his children lay asleep. 'I'll do anything.'

'You're not like that at all,' Monica said. 'You are a Catholic and so you are drawn towards a Catholic solution. But this is not a Catholic problem. It is not to do with the Devil at all.'

Creed said, 'Bruno Absalom wrote that he had summoned a demon from a hero's grave. But this is a complex and formidable demon.'

Stride nodded. 'Elena?' he said.

'I agree with Monica. The ritual Absalom evoked was pre-Christian.'

'So is God the Father and we Catholics believe in him.'

'But I don't think the exorcism can do any harm,' Elena said.

'Unless your interloper takes umbrage,' Creed said, 'and frightens the priest to death the way he did the dog.'

'This is not an easy priest to scare,' Stride said. 'Attend tomorrow, both of you, please. The Monsignor is a man who enjoys an audience.'

They lay on the bed together, propped against the pillows and one another, reading side by side. They were on the floor below the Strides and it was quiet in their room. The hotel occupied a commanding spot above the bay but they were too high to hear the sea on such a mild evening as this one was. Brody had typed his case notes. The words had the bluff, blocky character of language stamped out by an old Remington or Royal Upright. They could have been official reports of some kind, Elena thought. That was what they looked like, until you began to read what their writer had written and got the sense of what it was he had said in them.

## 20th September, 1924

One of the strangest things about Lady Ross is the disparity between her mental deterioration and her physical appearance. I have only three female patients, it is true. I am far more familiar with male patients afflicted by maladies of the mind. And since these have, for the most part, been soldiers or former military men, the contrast between their presentable and disciplined selves and their aspect when enduring mental debilitation is physically acute. But even taking this into account, Lady Ross is still an extraordinary exception to the general rule of derangement. Nothing about her suggests madness until she opens her mouth and makes her outlandish claims about her late son, Patrick.

In these, she is entirely consistent. Again today, I tried to introduce some semblance of contradiction into her account. But she adheres rigidly to the terms of her delusion. The details cannot be changed or challenged because, to her damaged mind, they amount to fact. They are irrefutable truths.

Perhaps the depth of the delusion is the reason she looks so serene. She is implacable rather than tormented. She possesses certainty. One day her son will come to visit her and vindicate her beliefs and at a stroke remove the need for her confinement here. He will take her away with him. They will be reunited blissfully. A mother's love and pride will be restored to her. She will enjoy again the deep and resolute affection felt for her by her only child. And she waits patiently for this. Her profound assurance that the moment will come enables her to endure the days and weeks and years of waiting with equanimity. And so blessed by the balm of faith, her beauty endures almost as unfailingly as does her hope. It is quite something to observe, this form of madness. And in three years, I have failed to discover any effective means of treating it. I cannot pierce the dream. I cannot dent the delusion.

It is all about the boy. Some weeks ago, when I was obliged to break to her the news of her former husband's death, she was only concerned for the effect the loss would have on 'poor, dear Patrick'. For herself, she showed no surprise or sorrow or even curiosity concerning the cause of his departure from life. Only her absent son can touch her emotions. Only his return to her can excite them. She lives in a sort of emotional limbo. She is beyond therapeutic reach.

It occurred to me today that I might try hypnotism again. The last time was so unsuccessful that I know only desperation prompts the thought. But I am clinically bankrupt where this patient is concerned and tempted to try again because of it. She did not resist the last time. She succumbed to the trance straightaway and the trance was so deep as to lead me to think she is particularly suggestible. But the regression therapy was hopeless. She remembers nothing before hearing what she insists on calling the mistaken news of Patrick's death. Her memory, her unconscious memory at least, died in the moment she learned that her son had become a fatal casualty of war. And yet she did not believe it. So why did the shock of the news cost her the power of recollection?

I think the patient I treat was born in that moment. I suspect she did believe the news. But when the chasm of grief opened up before her, she chose to step backwards into delusion rather than plunge on into the painful and sane acceptance of fact. The chasm was too deep, not just for her capacity for loss, but for her gift for reason.

I read back these notes with my habitual self-disgust. I am an analyst who shirks methodology. There is no method at all, really, to my treatment of a patient. I know the theory. But the mind is not a physical and quantifiable thing like the brain that enables its life. It is not an organ. It is a flight and a progression, an adventure and sometimes an ordeal. My approach to mental illness would earn the scorn of my learned peers. But my successes have earned me plaudits I have seen as justification and, in my human vanity, enjoyed. Psychoanalysis would not help Lady Ross. I have tried it and it was futile. She has not the will nor the wit in the present to engage.

Her weight was consistent at eight stone, four ounces. Her pulse measured seventy-two beats per minute. Her appetite is good. She is allowed twenty cigarettes a day. She smokes under supervision, to avoid the risk of self-harm. She is not inclined to self-harm. Her general health seems excellent.

'Where are you up to?'

'Halfway down page six,' Elena said.

'Spooky. We read at the same speed.'

'There's a subtext here, Julian.'

'Hopelessness,' Creed said. 'She's the biggest failure of his professional life.'

'And his professional life is everything to Edward Brody. There was no wife and no children. I doubt he even dallied with any of the nurses on his staff.'

'Maybe he was gay.'

'No. He's much too appreciative of Mary Ross's looks. I don't think he'd wax so lyrical about the handsomeness of a male patient. He's exiled himself from personal relationships. Because of the consumption and the infection risk, he's lived his life in a kind of self-imposed quarantine. He's totally dedicated to his work. It's why he feels this failure so very deeply.'

'Do you think he was infatuated with her?'

Elena considered this. 'There's not much to be infatuated with,' she said. 'It would be like falling for a statue, or a painting, wouldn't it?'

'It would be, unless he'd met her before. But he might well have. Falcon Lodge opened in 1916. Paley and Sir Samuel Ross were friends. It's quite possible he'd met her when she was still sane.'

'If he had met and fallen for her in that period, his failure to help her recover her senses would be desperate for him,' Elena said.

# F. G. Cottam

## 27th September, 1924

The most curious thing has occurred. I tried hypnosis with Lady Ross today and it was the total and dispiriting failure I expected it to be. Her mind is not capable of regression. But then a new tactic occurred to me. Without bringing her out of her deep trance, I tried communication with her in the present, in an effort to discover whether her mind in an unconscious state maintains the same delusional logic to which she is otherwise prone. She told me about a letter she has received. All she wished to talk about was this letter. The monotone of her voice in trance could not conceal her excitement concerning it.

In some circumstances, of course, we censor or at least monitor the personal mail our patients receive. But correspondence from former friends has never posed the risk with Lady Ross of causing any deterioration in her condition. She claimed the letter was from her son, Patrick. She told me that she had hidden it for fear that its contents might provoke some change in her treatment. She said that she feared isolation and restraining straps. She confided that the doctor under whose care she is, a good but agnostic man, might react negatively to her son's wish to see her. I asked where she had hidden the letter. She showed me. She had placed it under the window box of flowers on her sill. I brought her out of her trance only after telling her that she would remember nothing of what had been discussed, much as they do in Penny Dreadful stories or the matinée pictures in which hypnotists are all villainous and mysteriously bearded foreigners.

Our consultation took place between four and five. At 6.30 pm, when I knew she would be at table in the dining hall, I entered her room and recovered and read the letter. To my astonishment, it seemed genuine. The hand in which it was written was somewhat spidery, but the sense was perfectly clear and the message emphatically expressed. It was signed Patrick and there was an address, off Weymouth Street in London, a respectable residential area between Regent's Park and Marylebone. The letter was not particularly affectionate in tone. But it expressed the writer's strong desire to visit his mother. The only real peculiarity about it was a slight odour the paper gave off: a whiff of corrupt meat that prompted me to ponder on its contents after replacing it during a walk in the fresh air at twilight around the grounds.

Sir Samuel Ross was a very eminent man. His wealth was only matched by his reputation for philanthropy. He had his wife committed to my care. Afterwards, he divorced her. The proof of her madness, he told me himself, was her refusal to accept that their son had died, valiantly and in the service of his country, in the final days of the war during an assault on a German-held French canal. Many men had died in the engagement. Patrick Ross was one of those fatal casualties.

It has never occurred to me to doubt Sir Samuel's word. He was emphatic, persuasive and grave. And looking into his eyes that sad afternoon, there was no question of his conviction that his son was dead. And I have since had corroboration. One of our patients here, a Captain Broad, earned a Military Cross in the same engagement. He has good reason to recall it vividly. He lost one of his best friends, his comrade-in-arms, the poet Wilfred Owen. And he saw the body of the Ross boy. It was pitiful, he told me, to see a lad of eighteen so brutally cut down. He had been hit by machine gun rounds and then bayoneted to death as he lay wounded and helpless on the ground. The loss was made all the more tragic by occurring only days before the end of the conflict, the Captain commented. The war has left Captain Broad damaged but lucid. He will never recover sufficiently well to leave here, I do not think. But he is not a fantasist about the war in which he served with such distinction.

The letter disconcerted me to such an extent that, half an hour ago, I telephoned Bruno Absalom. I have met him on four or five occasions and never warmed to him. There is something evasive and secretive about his character and he leans rather too heavily on the crutch of alcohol. But Lady Ross speaks fondly of him and he was the boy's godfather. And apparently he discharged his duties in that responsibility with vigilance and generosity. And he was Sir Samuel's best friend until a final and unexplained falling out Sir Robert mentioned to me once.

To my astonishment, Absalom confirmed that the Ross boy is indeed alive. But he cautioned that he is much changed and advised me most strongly against allowing him to visit his mother here.

'I cannot prevent it,' I told him. 'It is their right. She is here under false pretences. I have no justification in further confining her.'

'Is she capable, in your judgement, of taking care of herself?'

'She is not,' I told him truthfully. 'But Patrick is no longer a boy of eighteen. He must be a man by now of twenty-four. Perhaps her son wishes to take care of her.'

Absalom was silent. Then he uttered a groan as abject as any I have ever heard a human being utter. His next words were spoken to himself and, though it was only eight in the evening, I assumed were the consequence of intoxication. 'What have I done?' he said. 'What have I done?' And with that, he severed our connection.

## 5th October, 1924

I am to meet the man claiming to be Patrick Ross tomorrow evening. He is to travel down by train. I have arranged for a car to fetch him here for 6pm from the station at Shale Point. His mystery has only deepened. To the War Office, he remains dead. Sir Samuel died with no living descendants legally recognised. His great fortune was left almost entirely to charity. Their various houses and other properties were sold. There are sufficient funds for Lady Ross to remain under treatment here for however long she should live. But there is to be no glorious Ross dynasty, no trail of dynastic wealth, growing and enriching itself down the decades. War, Sir Samuel's will and his former wife's insanity would seem to have seen to that.

Yet Bruno Absalom is adamant. Patrick is alive and has been living for the past three years in Canada, learning some mining trade. He does not know why in that time he did not once write to his mother. He is at a loss as to why the son allowed the mother to languish in an asylum under false pretences. He cannot explain his own complicity in this long and callous deception. Was he immobilised by apathy? Did he forget the duty of loyalty owed his best friend's former wife, the mother of his godson? He will not say. He is vague and evasive. 'Patrick has changed,' is all he will say, in a tone on the telephone one would use to convey a warning.

## 6th October, 1924

Tonight, I spent an hour with a man who journeyed back from death and left his soul behind as forfeit. Having done so, I am left certain that I cannot entrust his mother to this creature's care. To do so, would be inconceivable. Meeting him made me realise how much of us is cosmetic, mere window dressing. Our morality provides the substance of our humanity. Innate decency is what distinguishes us from beasts. We are restrained and civilised by conscience. When confronted by someone characterised only by an absence of morality, this becomes uncomfortably obvious. If a Savile Row suit was contrived for a jackal, would it make the animal behave like a man? Both the question and the answer to it occurred during my audience with our visitor this evening. And the answer was most emphatic.

His appearance is disturbing. He wears dark glasses and his mouth is as ugly as an unhealed wound. His hands are huge, bony, arachnid things. He is slightly built but there is a coiled tension about him and the sense of ungovernable strength beneath the restraint of his meticulously tailored attire. His voice emerges as if from some deep, lubricious well. It is almost a disembodied sound, a skilled trick of ventriloquism. And there is the stink about him of stale blood; the reek of an unwashed butcher's block in festering heat. I did not wish to leave this freakish apparition alone with Lady Ross. Instinct made me distrust him overwhelmingly. I asked him a series of questions to which only he would have known the answer, about his mother and father both. He answered them all, fully and fluently and without a moment's hesitation. In the pause after I had asked the last of them, he said, 'I would like to see my mother now.'

I showed him in to her.

'Mother,' he said.

She had made herself up. She had brushed and pinned her hair

and wore lipstick and a necklace and diamond earrings descended
from her lobes and at that moment my heart was cleaved in my chest
for her.

She frowned and turned to me. The corner of her mouth twitched
in a nervous half-smile and she blinked. 'This is not my son,' she said.
'There has been a mistake, Dr Brody.' And she turned her back and
stood facing her window as still and resolute as something carved from
marble.

He laughed. The sound was not ironic. It was gleeful. 'Charming,'
he said. Then, 'Come, doctor. Let us not waste the time remaining to
me.' He appraised me, as though seeing me in that instant for the first
time. I could not see his eyes behind their tinted lenses, but his head
moved swiftly up and down as if in study. 'Do not waste the time
remaining to you, doctor,' he said. 'You have ten years before the
disease eats more of your lungs than can reasonably support life.' He
grinned. His teeth were large and yellow and sharp. 'And the time
arrives to gasp a final cheerio.'

It seems absurd as I write it now on the page. But I knew he was
telling me the truth. I don't know how he knows and would not wish
to. But I will die in 1934, I am convinced of it. He can see the future
and was revelling in his prophetic gift.

I took him to my room. We sat down. He folded his arms across his
chest. In doing so, he hid his hands, which I was relieved not to have
to look upon.

'What are you?'

'Hungry,' he said. 'Ambitious.'

'Why did you come here?'

'To see if I could establish a bond with the mother who bore me. I
am alone.'

'What do you believe in?'

'I believe in the future. You live in the bucolic past of country stiles
in sad shires and ale in the gloaming and parish pumps and blue
remembered hills and is there honey still for tea, and I find it dreary
and altogether too cosy and tame.'

'Weren't those some of the things you fought for?'

'I'm not the boy who went to war, Professor. I'm the person who returned. My future will be very different from his past.'

'Was it hard, seeing your mother just now?'

'She is mad. And the part of me that felt for her is dead.'

'All of you died, didn't it, Patrick?'

But he just leered at that remark.

'When we die, something departs us. You have returned without it. How did you achieve this? What enabled the abomination you've become?'

'Religious mysticism from a scientist of the mind,' he said. 'I'd expected more. I'm vastly disappointed, Professor Brody.'

'Does anything frighten you, Patrick?'

'Only ghosts,' he said.

On the floor above where Elena and Creed read Brody's typed case notes, Martin and Monica Stride stood looking at their sleeping children, peacefully oblivious, side by side in single beds pushed together for the comfort delivered by proximity. They both slept on their backs and their faces looked untroubled by the dream that had so disturbed them. Children were resilient. But it was a parent's instinct to protect and Monica was very concerned to spare them further fright.

'I'm thinking of taking them away, Martin,' she said.

'Where would you take them to?'

'To Denmark. We'll stay with my parents, just until this whole thing settles down. I don't want to be away from you.'

'You never have been before.'

'No. And I don't want to leave you in any danger, either. But I suppose you have to confront this thing.'

Stride smiled. 'Yes. I have to confront it, with my valiant ally at my side.'

'He is valiant,' Monica said. 'And his girlfriend is clever and beautiful.'

'She's his researcher.'

'And you are sometimes hopeless, darling. Did you not see the looks that passed between them? They are like newly-weds.'

'I don't think we can run away from this,' Stride said, turning to look at his wife. 'I think that was the message of the dream the children had. We cannot just flee from it. We are a part of it and it has become a part of us.'

'I know. I know that. But I still think the children would be better with their grandparents in Aalborg, at least until after the exorcism and the demolition. I don't want Peter and Millie smelling the incense and the candle wax and seeing the ground sown with salt. I want them spared that ghastly Catholic cabaret. I'm sorry.'

'No, you're right. Take them tomorrow. You're absolutely right.'

'I'm sorry I called it a cabaret. And you are very brave, Martin. You have courage equal to your valiant friend.'

'I hope I do,' Stride said. He reached for his wife and held her. 'I think I might yet have need of it.'

# Chapter Eleven

Creed woke early the following morning. There was something he felt he needed to look at again and ponder on. It was the final part of the Absalom deposition. Elena had précised the document for him but left the final entry unedited. He had read the whole account as soon as he had got it. But he believed very strongly in the old dictum about knowing your enemy.

He climbed out of bed, careful not to wake her. He studied her. He regarded her as a sort of miracle. She was not the miracle, but her presence in his room was, lying there asleep for him to look upon. He had not imagined that he would get this second chance with her. He had not dared to hope for it. He touched his fingers to his lips and traced the kiss gently across her cheek and she sighed and stirred slightly but did not wake. He listened to her breathe for a while and inhaled her warm scent and, as his eyes adjusted to the absence of light, took a moment just to look at her lovely face and her hair framing it, black and glossy against the white purity of the pillow her head rested upon. He did not think there was a more fortunate man in the world.

He went and sat by the balcony doors. He parted the curtains slightly. All was not silent. He could hear the stirring of the morning sea in the bay below. Dawn was an hour away, but the luminescent coastal sky and the diffuse glow of a streetlamp outside gave him enough light to read by without switching on a lamp and disturbing Elena. He opened his briefcase and took the Absalom papers from it. Elena had transcribed and printed them off for him and he was looking not at the author's precise penmanship but at a bland, modern

F. G. Cottam

typeface chosen from a list of fonts on a laptop. The contents, though, were no less sinister for that.

## December 1924

I read in the newspaper this morning about a young prospector who has struck gold in a remote part of California thought long exhausted of any mineral wealth. This fortunate fellow is insisting on maintaining anonymity. But the report gave his age as twenty-five and said he is a skilled geologist, someone who learned his craft in Canada. I cannot be certain it is him. But if it is, the deaths shall follow. And then I will know.

After reading the report, I took a taxi through the persistent freezing rain to his mews off Weymouth Street. The traffic moved at a weary trudge. The London air was heavy with soot and sulphur: industrious, grey and unclean. When I got there, the house had a cold and abandoned look. There was moss on the cobbles and I slithered across them, my shoes struggling to find purchase in the wet. I pushed at his bell and when this failed to summon a response, hammered on the door with the flat of my hand. But he was not there. A chink in one of the closed curtains over his windows revealed a gloomy room occupied only by emptiness and dust.

It was the animal cadavers recovered from Sir Samuel's garden that prompted my investigation. The cadavers and the grisly fate the pathologist concluded they had met. I did not think that this version of Patrick returned to us would lose his appetite for dead flesh. I feared that, as he grew stronger and more mature, it would very likely increase. I had a private detective comb the newspapers published in that part of British Columbia for the duration of his secondment there. He was not the hopeless fraud poor Mary Ross employed to find her son in Manchester. He was a respectable American, Pinkerton-trained, the head of a thriving firm of investigators based at smart premises off Oxford Street.

What he discovered was worse than I could have imagined. He gave me the usual provisos about shifting populations and accelerated mortality rates among pioneer communities working in arduous conditions. He talked about itinerant drift and nomadic mining trends. But he agreed that the anomaly was too great and consistent for coincidence. Over the three years Patrick worked at his mine, close to forty young men and women in the surrounding settlements and shanties simply vanished out of existence. There was nothing to compare to it before his arrival. And the disappearances stopped, as abruptly as they had begun, after his departure. I think he killed them. And then when their meat had matured to his taste, I think he ate of them.

All the evidence of course is circumstantial. And it does not really amount to very much. The garden burials had been naïve and the discovery embarrassing for him. But he had not repeated the mistake. Either he had changed his tastes and nature, or he was a quick learner. I do not believe he is capable of improvement, quite the opposite. But his cunning is as acute as his hunger is strong.

I think I may have seen the last of Patrick Ross. The thought offers no shred of comfort. I lured a monster back into the world. I have said it before, but it bears repeating. I have summoned a demon from a hero's resting place. He will be nomadic himself now, finding a fortune in the ground everywhere he settles for a while, shiftless because the cost of satisfying his appetite cannot be concealed for long, even in the most remote and volatile communities. In America, they have police forces. Some officers are corrupt and some are stupid. But there are clever and honest ones too, vigilant to the patterns of serious crime. If it is him in California, he will not be there for long.

'I love all waste and solitary places,' he once said to me, at his mews house off Weymouth Street. I don't think he knew that the lines were borrowed from Shelley. He thought they were his and he was being truthful. He will live in the waste and solitary places of the world because his habits compel him to. He will not age as men do, I do not think. And he will not change. He has no soul and so possesses no human desire to improve himself. Salvation is unavailable to him. He will inhabit the waste and solitary places and then one day, when he is ready, he will attempt to fulfil his dream of inflicting on the world his plague of the dead.

I am responsible. The affront to God and nature that is Patrick Ross is as much my fault as if it were my creation. I will write no more on the subject, I do not think. He has said I will not find absolution and his gift of prophesy seems real enough. But that will not prevent me from seeking it. I will spend the remainder of the life left to me begging forgiveness from God for this terrible sin. I will give all I have to good causes and live in poverty and humility. I shall go back to Italy, to the place of my birth, to pay my penance. I will be buried there. And this document will be recovered there, as the abomination has itself predicted. It is my confession to the world and I was obliged by conscience to write it. I hope that it may be of practical value in preventing further wrongs.

Bruno Absalom

Creed yawned, finishing reading this for the second time in forty-eight hours. He did not think he had ever come across anyone as vain, pompous and irresolute as Bruno Absalom had been. He sensed movement outside and fingered the edge of the curtain, focusing on below. It was the tall figure of Martin Stride, wearing a tracksuit, embarking just before daybreak on what was probably his daily run. He watched Stride descend the hairpin turns of the route down to the promenade. He moved easily, his muscles already warm, his rhythm loping and powerful. He had ample time for the run. It was a more pleasant ritual than the one they faced later in the day back at the derelict railway station on his land that had once been called Shale Point. He had time because they were giving him a lift aboard the helicopter. Creed did not know what travel plans were being made for Monica and the kids. The children would not make it back in time for school. He did not think they should be present for the exorcism. But they would not really want to stay on the island, he didn't think, without their dad.

He thought about that quote from Shelley. He liked poetry and not just the Wilfred Owen war sonnet variety. It was a private enthusiasm. He did not think his audience would appreciate or understand his passion for something they would regard as fey and questionable. But that was the price paid for television fame. It was all about the lowest common denominator. You could not deliver the really huge ratings figures without thoroughly debasing yourself. He had become a back-slapping, muscled, garrulous self-caricature, typified by wise-cracks and machismo. You confused the fans at your peril. They watched in colour and high definition. But their values tended to be black and white. So he kept his love of poetry and much other stuff to himself.

He knew the poem. It was 'Julian and Maddalo' and its two debating protagonists were believed to have been based on Shelley and his friend, Lord Byron. These picturesque chums had travelled together in Italy for a while and that was the setting for the poem. It referred to a barren stretch of the Adriatic coast. The lines ran:

> . . . *I love all waste*
> *And solitary places; where we taste*
> *The pleasure of believing what we see*
> *Is boundless, as we wish our souls to be.*

Shelley was an atheist. He drowned not far from the spot where he set the poem. Patrick Ross had not possessed a soul on his return to mortal life. The poetic reference was probably his mordant joke, made at the expense of the man to whom he quoted it. But Bruno Absalom had not picked up on this. He had not really had a sense of humour and wouldn't have thought it funny even if he had. He finished his deposition in the conviction that he was damned. He later went to his grave that way.

In the bed, Elena moaned softly in her sleep. Creed put back his gathered pages into his case. He had not put on any clothes to do his reading. He was still in his underwear. He had endured during his life far colder places and times than he was in now. He stood and walked back to the bed and slipped beneath the covers. Elena would wake in a moment, he knew, and when she did so, he wanted to hold the warmth and weight of her in his arms to give him resolution for what he feared the day might bring for both of them.

The Belgian cleric arrived at the gates of the Stride estate in a metallic purple people carrier on the stroke of 2 p.m. He did not come alone. There were three priests in the car. They wore black cassocks under their overcoats and smelled strongly of cigarette smoke when the doors opened and they got out and Stride greeted them on his drive. Elena saw their stuff through the glass of the rear door: their bright silk stoles and polished brass incense burners and their ornate brass candle holders and the thick cylinders of wax that would support their hopeful flames.

Degrelle was obviously in charge. Elena recognised him from the television and newspaper features. They had cuttings in the office. In life, he had a swarthy, strutting charisma. He did not much look to her like a man of the cloth. He was well over six feet tall and had the burly physical character of a prize-fighter gone slightly to seed. There was a belligerence about him, she thought, there in the vapid sunshine of a late September afternoon. He wandered onto the croquet lawn, stretching his legs after the drive, absurd amid the painted hoops on the manicured grass in his Crombie overcoat and heavily polished leather shoes. And she thought, *Of course he looks belligerent; he is a man who regularly fights the Devil with the cudgelling fists of his faith.*

He frowned when he saw Julian Creed. Or more accurately, his existing frown deepened. He looked from Creed to Elena and back to Stride. 'What is the meaning of this?' His accent was thick and his voice a chain-smoker's guttural rasp.

'These people are my friends,' Stride said.

'Julian Creed is your friend?'

'Yes.'

'He cannot observe what we do. This is not a spectator sport, Mr Stride.'

'I know what you do,' Creed said. 'Half the world has seen Max von Sydow perform an exorcism on the cinema screen. And the other half owns it on DVD.'

To Elena's amazement, Degrelle smiled at that. 'Wonderful casting,' he said. 'But though he did so with distinction, he was acting. He was not dealing with a real case of possession.'

'Damn,' Creed said. 'And there's me thinking it was a documentary.'

But Degrelle had tired already of Creed's repartee. He turned back to Stride. 'Where can we change and prepare?'

'In the conservatory,' Stride said. 'Come, I'll show you.'

With his slender musculature and flowing, shoulder-length hair, Stride looked a different species from the priests as he led them away.

Elena walked on the lawn with Creed. It smelled of the previous night's rain in the wan warmth of the afternoon sun.

'He's quite something,' Elena said.

'He looks like the sort of priest who would have taken Al Capone's confession,' Creed said. 'He's old school. I'll bet he prays in Latin. I wouldn't be surprised if there's a hair shirt under all that bristling vanity.'

'Do they still wear them?'

'His sort does. Church fashions come and go. But the beliefs and traditions to which that man adheres have remained the same for centuries.'

'You sound as though you respect him.'

'In a way, I do. He knows no fear. And it's faith, rather than ignorance, that fuels his courage.'

'So if he had been Al Capone's confessor, he'd have given his supplicant a whole rosary of Hail Marys to say.'

Creed looked at her. 'He'd have done more than that, Ellie. He'd have taken the gun out of his shoulder holster. He'd have confiscated his baseball bat.'

'You seem cheerful,' she said. 'Are you sneakily optimistic that this ceremony might succeed?'

'I'm cheerful because I'm with you,' he said. 'I've got no hope whatsoever that this liturgical pantomime will do anything other than increase the danger already existing.' He turned. A rumble of sound was coming from the drive. Diesel fumes rose from a convoy of vehicles hidden by a bank of trees. Then they came into sight: a crane armed with a wrecking ball on the back of a flatbed truck and two bull-dozers and a whole fleet of wagons bearing skips.

'The cavalry,' Creed said.

'Our host means business,' Elena said. She had met the Stride children briefly at breakfast. She had witnessed their father saying goodbye to them. Having done so, she did not blame Stride in the slightest for what he planned to do today. She thought that perhaps if he had done it sooner, the ordeal endured by his family might have been shorter. Like Creed, she had no great faith in the ritual of exorcism. But she thought eradicating all physical trace of the station platform and the waiting room that stood on it both sensible and overdue.

'I'd like to see it before it's destroyed,' she said to Creed. 'Do you think there's time?'

He looked at his watch. 'Yes, if Martin has no objection. The priests will be at least half an hour, praying and doing general preparation. And they will walk there in procession to perform their sacrament. So there's time. I'll ask him.'

Stride was with the priests in the conservatory as they went through their preparations. He did not object to Elena's brief bit of sightseeing. The three priests assisting decanted holy water from a plastic gallon container into the ceremonial silver and gold scrolled buckets from which their brushes would flick the stuff about. Degrelle sat and smoked, heavy-featured and dark-skinned above the waxy whiteness of his clerical collar. He looked from Stride to Creed and back again and the look was shrewd and seemed somehow secretly knowing. But Creed could draw no conclusions from it.

He walked with Elena to the abandoned station. He thought that it was too late to start calling their destination Shale Point. Soon it would be dust and memories; a scar in the earth that, by next spring, would have faded and overgrown with wild grass and the product of whatever late pollen was still abroad now. How it would bewilder the grief-stricken ghost of Lady Ross, no longer to be able to step off the train onto its platform. Is that how it would work? Would the train just rattle on, careering through another time without a destination? He did not know. None of them did, neither he, nor Elena nor Stride and certainly not his three performing priests. They would have to wait until the demolition was complete to learn fully its consequences.

The platform and the building on it came into view and Elena gasped. Nothing had prepared her for the sheer surreal strangeness of it. There was a stillness about the waiting room entirely alien to its purpose. It should have been picturesque. It possessed architectural characteristics that generally combined to create a sleepy, rural cosiness. Its roof of umber tiles was a charming period detail. The Gothic windows were perfectly proportioned. Their panes fractured the late afternoon light pleasingly in their leaded panels. The whole structure had a vernacular rightness. And she thought it all disturbingly wrong. It wore its Edwardian features like some sly mask. It was not restful, she did not think. It did not repose, sagging and forgotten. It waited. It was a terrible pun, but it did. It waited; it bided its time. But its patience, she sensed, was almost exhausted now.

The smell of rotten fruit from the blackberry bushes skirting the platform hit her nostrils in a bouquet of corruption so cloying that Elena almost gagged on it. She reached for the grip of Creed's fingers. 'I don't know how you stayed the night here, Julian. The threat of this place is almost palpable.'

'It's benign enough in the day,' he said. He squeezed her hand.

'Martin said Millie heard the singing in the day.'

'So it's Martin, now, is it?' Creed said. 'Next, you'll be asking for his autograph. You're on the star-struck path to seduction. I should have known.'

She looked at him. He was grinning at her. She did not know how he could joke in the proximity of this baleful place, after the things he had witnessed there. But he had spent the first half of his adult life governing fear, she supposed. He had fought on battlefields.

'Do you want to go in?'

She nodded. She did not want to go in. It was the last thing she wanted. But she thought that she would be a coward if she did not and she felt curiosity as well as dread as they approached the obstacle of blackberry thorns.

'This way,' he said. He hauled her onto the platform. *Mind the gap*, she thought giddily. Peter and his friends had made the gap on the day of their puncture, on the day that Peter had seen Patrick Ross leer out at him in his subaltern's uniform from a waiting room window. She thought then that she heard a sound from within. She dismissed it as heightened imagination. It had not been the low croon of female grief it had briefly sounded like. It had been some nearby bird, the call of a species she didn't know. The Stride domain was full of birds. She looked at Creed. He was frowning.

'Come on,' he said.

He turned the brass handle and pushed open the door for her, ever the gallant gentleman. And she shook her head. 'You first,' she said, in a whisper. She had the strong intuition that they were breaching some protocol. Entering the place seemed almost an act of blasphemy or desecration. She had not felt so guilty or fearful in her life. The air had thickened in front of her with impending dread. The hairs bristled on her arms and neck and her heartbeat was fluttery and uncontrollable. Her sense that they were not alone, that they were being sardonically watched, was so strong it was almost a certainty.

'Do you feel it?' she whispered.

'I do,' he said.

'What do you think?'

'I think the Monsignor is going to have his work cut out today.'

The door closed with a sigh behind them. Elena looked around. She saw posters on the walls she recognised from her research into the Great War: propaganda and recruitment posters and posters intended to alarm those looking upon them with the urgent need for discretion. They had a curled and faded look. Kitchener was missing one demented eye to damp or just to time. There was a stove at the centre of the room. It was chopped at and broken, its pipe curtailed on its upward path to the ventilation aperture in the ceiling; half the length of it sheered away and taken by some scavenger for scrap. Bench seats lined the walls. They were scored with graffiti and scorched by occasional acts of vandalism and tarnished altogether by the passage of neglectful years.

'Strange,' Creed said. 'I've seen the place look better.'

'I don't want to see it look any better,' Elena said. 'I don't want rolling stock and a grieving mother. I'm happy to be spared Stride's veteran porter, or guard or whatever he was. I wanted to see it and I have. I've seen enough. I want to leave now.'

She went out onto the platform. He followed her. The smell from the rotting blackberry bushes skirting the platform was a heavy, sticky miasma of decay. Cloud was spreading from the west and concealing the clarity of the sky. It was vast enough to rob the day of light. It was the colour of a bruise.

'It's going to rain,' Creed said. Elena shivered and held herself. There was a clatter of abrupt noise from inside the waiting room. And then it stopped. Creed turned to go back in and see what had caused it. Elena pulled at his jacket, restraining him. He looked at her. She shrugged, biting her lip, and followed him.

It was the stretcher with the straps. It had fallen out of its narrow cupboard in the wall onto the floor and unfolded itself. It lay there: wood and worn canvas and tarnished brass buckles on leather restraining straps that Elena saw were rimmed with old bloodstains. Someone had struggled, strapped into it, and the struggle had chafed their wrists and ankles and broken the skin. They would have arched and screamed and strained against their confinement. And who could blame them? She thought of the public spectacle they would have made on the stretcher, threaded through the throng on the platform, carried by a pair of grim warders en route to spending life in the padded cell and straitjacket of a madhouse. She heard the steady drip, drip of something. 'Look,' she said to Creed. But he was looking already.

Flowers in wire baskets decorated the four corners of the waiting room. Looking around, Elena thought that its character had brightened, spruced up subtly in their momentary absence from it. The flowers smelled pungent and fresh. They were dwarf orchids and lilies; the florid floral choice of an earlier time. She could hear human voices over the dripping of the hanging baskets onto the waiting room floor. That sound was coming through the window. It was the approaching priests. They sounded still some distance away. They were reciting some sung prayer in Latin. She went to the window closest to the source of the sound. She saw a puff of incense rise a hundred and fifty metres away into the darkening air.

'Come on,' Creed said, taking her hand. 'We'll follow the scenic route back, through the woods. We might get rained on, but I don't want to confront and interrupt them. They've started already. You up to a country walk?'

Elena looked at the stretcher on the floor. 'I'm up to anything that gets me out of here,' she said.

It was close to six before the priests returned, soaked in

the deluge in their vestments, the brass and precious metal of their crosses and candlesticks and holy-water buckets rain-dribbled and dull in the damp light. Their faces were pale as they entered the conservatory. Elena and Creed sat with Stride and looked at them as the rain drummed ceaselessly on the panes above. Stride rose from his chair. 'Is it done?'

Degrelle raised his head and coughed and swallowed and then vomited copiously into one of the flowerpots flanking the conservatory door. 'It's done,' he said. 'Please fetch me some tea, a mugful. I take it strong and sweet.'

He sat ashen with his tea in the grip of meaty fingers. Then he pulled a hip flask from his pocket and poured something potent into the brew. Then he blew on it and slurped alternately until he had drunk it to the dregs. Only then was some colour restored to his face. He lit a cigarette. He looked tired and very preoccupied.

Stride had gone to oversee the demolition. The priests changed and packed their instruments of salvation into their bags and put those into their people carrier. Creed stood watching them in the rain. Elena remained in the conservatory, where the air was starting to sour slightly with the odour of vomit. Creed went across as they got into their vehicle and shook Degrelle by the hand. The priest smiled at him, a pugnacious smile under his dark eyes and thickly oiled hair. 'Have we converted you to our witchcraft from Rome?'

'No, you haven't,' Creed said. 'But I recognise courage. And I respect it.'

'Not courage,' Degrelle said, 'but faith. I am fortunate to have faith.'

Stride had returned to express his gratitude and say his good-byes. He was wearing a rain-slicker but was bare-headed and his hair hung in wet ropes to his shoulders. Creed studied his features as he bent to the window and thanked Degrelle and his acolytes. He was a very handsome man. But he had a slight thickening of the skin over the bones above his eye sockets and

Creed thought this curious. His eyebrows almost concealed it. It was very slight. But it was a feature he had only ever known boxers to possess. It was a consequence of taking educated blows. Stride rose from the car window and an interior button sealed the vehicle from the rain and the priests were gone.

'How's the demolition?'

'Progressing,' Stride said.

'Did you ever box?'

Stride laughed. 'What an odd question. Yes, a lifetime ago.'

Creed looked at the sky. 'They'll have to finish soon. It will be dark.'

Stride shook his head. 'They've brought floodlights,' he said. 'They'll work through the night. They're being paid enough. I want that place gone from my property. Want to take a look?'

'Sure,' Creed said. 'I'll fetch Elena.'

'Do,' Stride said. 'I'm sure she'll appreciate a stroll through the gloaming in the deluge. There are waterproofs on hooks by the kitchen door. Help yourselves.'

The demolition vehicles had churned the earth. Black topsoil turning to mud and smashed saplings and trampled down bushes formed a damaged, messy path. Darkness had not yet fallen. But they had switched the floodlights on already. They formed a bright dome of illumination ahead of them, where the throb of generators and the grind of engines in low gear rumbled and growled. They could hear the wrecking ball pulverising masonry and pneumatic drills puncturing the old paving on the station platform.

Nobody spoke on the walk. It all seemed wrong to Elena, this loud and lurid act of destruction. But it seemed wrong in a curious and subtle way. There was something not quite sacrilegious about it; the waiting room was not after all a consecrated building. It was not a place of worship. But it seemed an offence of that character, a sort of crime against tradition, or history or custom. She remembered the contempt expressed by Patrick Ross in Brody's account for the little England of sad shires and blue remembered hills. But that's what Stride's domain was, wasn't it? It was the smudged, gentle landscape of Woolf and Housman and Brooke. It was tranquil and sedate.

The waiting room had been a relic upon it of a time of turmoil and deep-felt national pain and sacrifice. Instinct told her that the land should have been left here in its ancient peace. And the relic of war upon it should have been allowed to stand for what it represented. She could justify in her mind the visit of the priests. She could not justify the razing of the one surviving building. She thought of the bronze stoicism of Jagger's sentinel, guarding the entry to the War Museum's Great War exhibits. She remembered that Bruno Absalom had left a generous legacy to the War Graves Commission. She thought that in a place with the memories of the land on which she trod, you ignored or disrespected the legacy of that epic conflict at your own peril.

These thoughts confused her. They were at odds with the fear she had felt in the proximity of the waiting room in the afternoon. Then, she had thought it a deeply uncertain and dispiriting place. Then, she would have happily watched it dismembered brick by sinister brick. Now, she felt uneasy presentiments, picking a path through the damaged, violated land. And the demolition site came into clear view and Elena felt only a sick clutch at her stomach of dismay.

The roof had gone. Only one wall of the waiting room remained. The wrecking ball had bashed and shuddered the plaster from it and the lattice of supporting beams stood naked and pitiful in the white glare of the lights like exposed bones. Fragments of glass and roof tiles lay heaped like spoil. Periodically, a bulldozer bit into this hill of ruin and raised its bucket and carried rubble off to one of the waiting trucks.

'You did not save the glass,' Elena said to Stride. 'Martin,

I cannot believe you allowed those beautiful windows to be destroyed.'

He turned to her. His face was dripping in the rain and his eyes were very bright in the stark illumination of the lights. She thought that he looked exultant. And then she realised that it wasn't exultation, it was anger. He was furious. 'I told my son he would be coming home, Elena. I told Peter, when he found the Owen poem and I comforted him, that he would be coming home. And he's had to flee with his mother to another country and I've broken my promise to him. How many promises to my son do you think I've broken?'

'One,' she said.

He nodded. 'One is enough. I never want to have to break another.'

She understood. But intuition still insisted that there was something profoundly wrong about the destruction being done there under the white glare of the wreckers' halogen lamps.

On the way back to the house, Creed tried to lighten the mood. He did not know what was wrong with Elena, but she was very pale and quiet and Stride was sombre and silent and more marching than walking through the darkness over the ruined land.

'When was the last time you boxed, Martin?'

'I was a kid. Don't make a mountain out of a molehill.'

'When was the last time you hit someone?'

'For fuck's sake, Julian, I can't remember. If I'd been violent by nature, I'd have done what you did and joined the SAS so I could kill people without being gaoled.'

'So you're saying you're a pacifist?'

Stride stopped. 'You don't give up, do you?'

Elena had to smile. They were standing in the persistent rain. They were cold and, if the other two felt like she did, they were hungry too. But Julian could do this. He could get a reaction from people. Stride too was smiling now, he couldn't help himself.

'Go on. You weren't a member of the peace and love generation. You were too young. You never wore flowers in your hair. Probably never even wore flowers on your shirt. When did you last give someone a proper dig?'

Stride started walking, but his pace was less severe. He wasn't marching now. The dark temper had left him. 'We were supporting a heavy metal band. I won't mention names. But they were one of those outfits that like to think it's tough by association. We were doing a gig in Rotterdam and they used a local biker gang as security. Neanderthals, total thugs. You know what biker security really is?'

'A chance to get heavy without facing any legal consequences,' Elena said.

'So I'm on stage and this girl gets up and all she wants is a cuddle or a kiss on the cheek or something and this biker comes out of nowhere and literally kicks her into the crowd. He was wearing engineer boots. She must have weighed all of five stone.'

'What did you do?'

'I lost it completely, since you're so anxious to know. I decked him. I broke his jaw.'

'With a single punch?'

'Yes. I must have got lucky.'

'Yeah,' Creed said. 'You must have.'

They were there. They walked through the apple orchard towards the kitchen door. It was completely dark now. It was almost eight o'clock. It was still raining hard. 'Can either of you cook?' Stride said.

Creed and Elena looked at one another. 'Both of us can, I think,' Creed said. Elena nodded.

'Would one of you put something on? Something quick, I'm famished. You must be too. And help yourselves to drinks. There's everything.'

'Where are you going?' Elena said.

'For cloths and hot water and disinfectant,' Stride said. 'I've still got an ornamental pot full of clerical puke to clean up.'

They ate a dinner of pasta washed down with beer and red wine. Stride invited Creed and Elena to stay and they accepted. The helicopter had departed for home immediately after dropping them. The day had been long and eventful and they had no car to take them back to London. It would be easier to arrange that in the morning than to summon a minicab to drive them back at night on wet roads through the rain. At ten o'clock, Stride left them to call Monica and, at eleven, the foreman of the demolition team knocked on the door to say that the job was pretty much complete. The ground had become so wet that they had been obliged to leave half a dozen loads and the heavy vehicles with caterpillar tracks on site. They would return for those when the ground firmed up. But nothing intact or upright remained of the structures they had been sent there to eradicate. Stride pulled a roll of bills from his pocket and gave the man a generous tip for his team. He walked back into the sitting room, to where Creed and Elena sat and he sat down too and closed his eyes.

'You've never been away from them before, have you?' Elena said.

He shook his head. 'Not for a single night.' He looked from Elena to Creed. 'How many appointments did you have to scratch today?'

Creed just laughed. 'I've lost count, to tell you the truth,' he said. 'I think my PA would probably have me committed, the number of complaining calls she's had to field.'

'Tomorrow is another day,' Stride said. 'Let's all hope it passes uneventfully.'

Elena was thinking as he said this about how comfortable she felt in the house. It was very grand in scale and finished to a very high specification. It really was luxurious. But it was a family home. There was warmth and an authentic feel of domesticity about it. And the threat she had felt in the proximity of the waiting room, the sense of restless, impatient malevolence, did not seem to impinge at all upon this place. She hoped that the ceremony carried out by the priests had done its work. But she could still not help thinking of the demolition as an insult and as provocation too. She thought of Patrick Ross in his interview with Brody and she could almost see the spite oozing from his waxy, granular skin. She shuddered.

Creed said, 'When will you allow your family to come home?'

Stride got to his feet and poked the logs into brighter, fiercer life in the grate in front of where they sat. He had seen Elena shiver. He replaced the poker in its stand and sat back down. 'It's Monica's decision as much as it's mine,' he said. 'The kids don't see enough of their grandparents and they've only got the one set, so they'll be there at least a few days, I would have thought. By then, we should know whether it's safe for them to return.'

*What if it isn't safe for them to return?* Elena thought. She knew that Creed would be thinking that too. But neither of them would pose the question. Stride had endured a good deal over recent days and to do so would be gratuitous and cruel. They would know soon enough whether the action he had sanctioned had been effective or not. She looked around the room, imagining the house abandoned, the family fled, in residence a new tenant with arachnid hands and the conscience of a jackal and an appetite for dead flesh and pestilent company.

Creed gave Elena the following day off. It was Tuesday and she had worked the weekend and he did not think there were any pressing research projects for her to embark upon. He looked at his long list of cancelled and postponed appointments and regretted missing none of them. The events of the past fortnight or so had been terrible for the Stride family and sometimes an ordeal for him too. They had recently unsettled Elena. But he was better for them, he knew. They had reverberated into his private life and professional aspirations in a way that was wholly positive. He would never have predicted it. But he was very glad that it had happened. He decided he would call his father. It seemed more a priority at that moment than anything else.

He was still on the phone to his dad twenty minutes later when there was a discreet knock on his office door and someone came in and a note was slid onto his desk. The message had been handwritten in red biro and torn from a pad. It said, 'Call Father Degrelle.' It was finished with three exclamation marks, which Creed thought excessively theatrical. He could not imagine what insult the priest wished to impart now that he could not have voiced in person at the Stride house the day before.

'Come and talk to me,' the priest said. 'Allow me to talk to you.'

Creed opened his diary. 'When do you have a window, Monsignor?'

'Fuck your windows,' he said. His voice was as harsh as iron on the phone. 'Ours is not the subject matter for lunch at some restaurant in Kensington or cocktails at your private members' club. Take down the address. Get over here as soon as you can.'

It was a seminary. It was located in Highgate and Creed took a cab. The tube would have been much quicker, but he did not want to have to endure conversation with strangers in the carriage of an underground train. He was not in the mood for vacant chit chat and smiling and signing autographs. The priest's tone had worried him. So he spent ninety minutes instead crawling on choked roads through the rain to north London while a cabbie treated him to a long monologue about the haunted hotel on the coast of Crete where he and his wife had spent their spooky honeymoon.

The seminary was Victorian Gothic. It had been built back from the road on a generous plot. Christ writhed in agony nailed to a large wooden cross to the left of the gate from which he entered the grounds. Rain dripped from the cross-piece and the nail heads jutting from his hands and feet. The Redeemer in this instance was rendered from bronze. He was life-sized. *He would be worth a lot as scrap, melted down*, Creed thought. But he was safe enough from that fate in his death throes here. The traveller communities mostly responsible for the theft of scrap metal in this part of London were all devoutly Catholic.

The main door was also made of metal. Reliefs had been engraved into it, Latin inscriptions and pictures from scripture Creed had either never read or long forgotten. He thought the ritual and atmosphere of organised religion leaden and oppressive. It was anachronistic too. And the priest he was here to call on personified this impression of belonging to another time. That was why Creed had made the joke the day before about Al Capone. Monsignor Degrelle would have been much more at home, he thought, in the 1920s, in the time of Benito Mussolini and for that matter, Bruno Absalom.

He rang the bell. The door opened on the smells of floor polish and candle wax and the stale water of flower vases, all mingled. A nun in spectacles blinked at him. Evidently she knew why he was there. Before he had the chance to explain his business, she turned and led him along the marble vestibule to a corridor lined with identical doors. She stopped outside one of them. She smiled slightly and retreated and Creed knocked and the voice of the Monsignor, muffled but still unmistakeable, bade him enter.

He did so upon a cell. There was a single bed resembling an army cot to his left with a shelf of books above it. The bed was tautly covered by a coarse blanket. To his right was a small desk and on the wall above that, a wooden crucifix. The air was sour with the tang of tobacco smoke. The Monsignor was stripped to the waist and facing the window at the far end of the room. There was a sink on the other side of him. He was shaving and Creed could hear the plop and swirl of him rinsing his safety razor in the water there after each measured stroke. There was an ashtray to his left on the edge of which a cigarette smouldered. His back was broad and hirsute and from this angle he looked more than ever like an old prize-fighter, risen wearily here from the stool for one last bout.

He rinsed his face and turned. He patted his cheeks dry with a small towel and retrieved his shirt and clerical collar from a hook by the mirror above the sink and put them on.

'This is where you live?'

'Yes.'

'I'd have expected something grander.'

'We try to live in a state of grace. Poverty is considered helpful in achieving that.'

Creed nodded. He felt chastened. He hadn't honestly expected anything grander. He'd half-expected the hair shirt he'd mentioned to Ellie. It dawned on him that the press publicity courted by Degrelle down the years had been much more to promote the power of Catholic belief than to pander to his own ego. He wondered why he was there.

'We have a quite lovely garden,' Degrelle said. 'Contemplation of beautiful things is also helpful in achieving the state in which we seek to live our lives and serve God. We shall walk and talk in it together.'

'It's raining,' Creed said.

Degrelle smiled at him. He held out his arms expansively, his blunt, pugilistic fingers almost touching the walls to either side. 'I think the rain might stop for us,' he said.

When they got outside, it had stopped raining. The garden dripped and gurgled from its branches and in its gutters pleasantly. Degrelle had put on his black suit coat, but was bare-headed. Even so soon after his shave, he still looked swarthy. There was an air of physical vulgarity about him Creed thought quite at odds with his piety and intellect. He was a belligerent opponent of the Devil, but he was not at all the uncouth man he looked. The spines of the books on the shelf above his bed had been cracked with use. And books in several languages had been present in the row.

'I owe you an apology, Mr Creed,' he said. 'I always thought you a fraud. Yesterday I realised that you are not. You are quite the opposite, aren't you?'

'What do you mean?'

'I mean your psychic gift.'

'You don't believe in all that stuff.'

'I do not share the conviction some people have concerning its general significance, Mr Creed. But it commits no heresy to believe in ghosts. I do believe in them. Furthermore, I believe you personally can see them and quite possibly communicate with them also.'

Creed stopped walking. 'I'll level with you, Monsignor,' he said. 'This isn't the confessional. I'm not even a Catholic. But my whole professional life as a chaser after phantoms was a lie right up to the point when I first spent the night in Stride's waiting room. I was a total fraud until two weeks ago. Before then, I'd never been in the presence of a ghost.'

'But now you have.'

'Yes. Now I have.'

Degrelle had stopped because Creed had. Now he started walking on again. The path was gravel, narrow and puddled. His heavy shoes crunched and splashed on it. 'We wasted our time yesterday, my colleagues and I, Mr Creed. What's going on at that troubled location is nothing to do with demonic possession.'

'Then why did you bother?'

'I only reached my conclusion after we had performed the ritual. It was only later, when I saw you and Stride and the woman you employ, together, that it became obvious to me.'

Creed remembered the unreadable look Degrelle had given him in the Stride conservatory.

'I can sense the Devil, Mr Creed. Satan was not present yesterday. But something evil was there, something utterly corrupt. Some ancient magic delivered it, I suspect. And something else: three people who share a gift so rare it struck me like three outlandish lightning strikes of improbability.'

Creed laughed. He couldn't help it. 'You're saying that Elena and Martin Stride are psychically gifted too?'

'I'm saying more than that. I'm saying there's a reason for the three of you being there in that one place together.'

Creed shrugged. Degrelle looked at him and the look was serious. 'Half the world chooses to believe in ghosts,' he said. 'How many people can honestly claim to have seen one? Yet Stride has seen a ghost. And I'm confident so has Elena Coyle.'

'Why isn't belief in them heretical? Where precisely do phantoms fit into your scheme of heaven and hell?'

'They don't. I believe that when you see them, you are seeing the past. They are not the past come to the present. They are there instead because you have journeyed back.'

'The same theory held by Bruno Absalom.'

Degrelle did not react to this remark.

'Elena's ghost was Bruno Absalom.'

Degrelle went pale. He crossed himself.

'I see the name means something to you.'

'I am not permitted to discuss Absalom or his sins,' Degrelle said.

'I'll bet you're pretty high up, in Vatican circles, despite your vow of poverty. I'd reckon you'd have to be close to the summit of the hierarchy, right there at the top table, to know about Absalom and what he did.'

'I cannot discuss that matter. It is forbidden for me to do so. I brought you here to tell you that the exorcism was unsuccessful and to caution care. Your gift is a very dangerous one. Be careful, Mr Creed, for God's sake and your own.'

# Chapter Twelve

Elena saw the man in the astrakhan coat at his usual spot under the streetlamp on the other side of Borough High Street when she went to close her curtains just after dusk. Until that point, her day had been very pleasantly spent. She had not concerned herself unduly about whether or not the exorcism had been a success. She considered both Martin Stride and Julian Creed formidable men in their contrasting ways and thought they would think of other strategies if the priestly one had failed. They were the stronger for being so together in all this. Their growing friendship made them formidable. They were a team, sort of. They were more than the sum of their parts. Not that their parts were exactly lacking.

She had spent most of the day smiling to herself. She felt that a burden had been lifted from her. She was no different from any other modern woman, she supposed. Fulfilment was an expectation. Unhappiness was a personal failure. Loneliness was a crime. She knew objectively, in her brain, that it was pathetic to reduce your thinking to these notions. But almost everyone did it. Women put themselves under pressure to succeed according to a set of values no less insidious for being universally applied. She had been miserable for a long time. In partnership with Julian Creed, she could imagine being happy. And she was confident that he would be happy too. The want was mutual and so were the benefits. It would be an equal partnership. She wouldn't, in all honesty, have settled for anything less. She was looking forward to the future. She felt excited about it.

He was a strong and confident man and he wanted her intact.

She would not be pressured to change to accommodate any insecurities he harboured. He didn't harbour insecurities. He had no intention of inhibiting or competing with her. What he liked about her was the finished article. With him, she would never come under any pressure to pretend to be anyone other than who she was.

She skipped over to the curtains to close them and there was that portly figure in astrakhan, puffing at his cigar and peering up at her window. If she had only ever seen him in the one place, she would have done nothing about it. There was a stout lock on her door and he did not really look fit enough to labour up the three flights of stairs it was necessary to climb to get to her flat. But it was the same person she had glimpsed in the cloister garden at the church in Italy. She was sure of it. And she wanted to know what it was that he wanted with her. She put on her shoes and grabbed her coat and went out to confront him.

The road was always busy. Crossing it was always a trial. Darkness was descending and most of the cars and lorries and buses had their headlamps on. Jaywalking was tricky because of the motorbikes and the cyclists and their reckless disregard for lane discipline. Couriers paid by the job took no prisoners where pedestrians were concerned. They gave no quarter. He was still there when she reached the traffic island in the middle of the road. But as she made for his side of it, she thought that he saw her and he turned and made for the entrance twenty yards from where he stood to London Bridge Underground station.

She followed him. She descended the steps, dodging around commuters and late season tourist groups just out of the London Dungeon or on their way back from the *Belfast* moored close by on the Thames. She caught sight of his back, or thought she did, labouring up the long tunnel that would take her to the ticket barrier for the Northern Line. The coils of astrakhan on his coat glittered like black serpents when she saw his back through the bodies under the yellow flush of tunnel light.

Elena followed. The tunnel seemed to grow dimmer and more restricted. She could hear the clack of leather-shod feet on the stone floor. It bounced and echoed around the walls. She could hear a legion of feet. It was odd, because tourists generally wore trainers and moved in ponderous silence. As she pursued, she became aware of something else: smells she was unfamiliar with. She thought that she could smell pungent perfume and hair oil and strong tobacco which was impossible, because nobody had been allowed to smoke on the Underground for more than twenty years. She passed people in hats. Everyone seemed to be wearing a hat. And they weren't beanie hats and baseball caps; they were cloche hats and pillbox hats and trilbies and bowlers. And the light was wrong. It was yellow in refraction against the tiny white tiles with which the tunnel was walled as she followed Bruno Absalom along its narrow length.

It was a buttoned boot that stopped her. She looked down, trying to dodge past some human obstacle, and saw a buttoned boot too big for a woman to wear. It was on a man's foot, under a leg of narrow pinstripe trouser with a pressed and precise half-inch of turn-up. Men did not wear shoes like that any longer. Her eyes focused on another pair of feet and this pair filled her with something like dread because men certainly no longer wore canvas spats. She looked up. The lamps illuminating the tunnel were yellow orbs of glass placed at intervals along its spine. Their light was uncertain because flames provided it. She could smell the toxic gas that fuelled them.

She turned around. She closed her eyes. People from a dead time stirred and shuffled, hurrying by. She felt that if she looked any of these lost commuters in the face, her soul might be snatched from her and she would be stranded here. With her hand on one slick wall, with a paper seller's urchin cry echoing in her ears, Elena stole blindly back the way she had come, imploring providence with every step to allow her back into her present from the hectic, forgotten limbo of Bruno Absalom's London past.

Monica Stride left it late into the evening before making the decision to call Martin. She thought he had probably invested a lot of hope in Degrelle, the belligerent priest. She thought that he would be relaxed and relieved at home and she did not want to be the one to undo the reassurance he felt and put an end so swiftly to his new contentment. But the exorcism had failed, hadn't it? She was certain of it. She knew because the night before, the children had dreamed the same dream as one another. And Patrick Ross had come in the dream to visit them again.

She loved her husband very much. Before the events for which she held the waiting room responsible, she would have said their lives were perfect. The children were healthy and beautiful. They had no anxieties over money. They were happy in their lovely home on their idyllic wilderness of English land. It had endured for better than a decade, this blessed existence. She thought now that perhaps that was all they had been entitled to. Maybe happiness was a finite thing. Martin was a good and generous man who gave a lot of money to deserving causes. She involved herself as much as she could in community and voluntary work. But it hadn't mattered. Everything had perished. All of it had gone. In the house where she had grown up, where her elderly parents now slept peacefully and she hoped her children did too, she picked up the phone. She could not imagine feeling happy again, she thought. She could not conceive of ever again feeling safe.

They had been on the beach at Ventnor. It had been night-time. They never played on the beach in the darkness and that was how they had each known they were dreaming. They could hear the water breaking not far from where they played. It sounded sluggish and smelled more sweet to them than salt.

There was no freshness to the sea and the air on the beach was very still. They were each buried in the sand. Sand weighed heavy on their prone bodies and there was a smattering of shingle on them too. The shingle was shaped as buttons and belts and cuffs. It decorated them. It was a mystery how they had both managed to bury themselves. Usually they took turns to bury one another. But dreams had their own logic and both Peter and Millie knew they were dreaming.

It was very dark on the beach and they could not see the promenade at all. It was as though Ventnor Beach existed at the beginning or the end of the world. There was the sea wall and beyond it nothing, a still and absolute void of blackness. But the beach huts beneath the sea wall were there. And an uncertain light burned in one of them, like that of a candle flame, or the wick of an old-fashioned lamp.

Patrick Ross came out of the beach hut. He was wearing his uniform, of course. He left the hut door ajar and light was cast in a yellow trickle down the beach to the sea. He crunched through the shingle in his roan leather boots. The children saw that there was a big leather revolver case fastened to his Sam Browne belt. He squatted down beside them. He looked very smart in his uniform: immaculate, their mother would have said. But there was a smell about him that was foul. And when he breathed, there was a wet noise, they thought a consequence of the thing his mouth had become.

'The burial game,' he said. 'Are you having fun, children?'

'Yes,' they both said. But they knew it was no longer true. He had come and, though he sounded friendly, he troubled and frightened them. Millie had recently learned the word. Peter had known it a while. He sounded sarcastic, didn't he? Their soldier visitor sounded sarcastic. And the look in his eyes was hungry.

'I'll have some playmates of my own soon,' he said. 'It's only a matter of days now, less than a week. I've been very patient and terribly lonely, if you want to know the truth. But soon I'll revel in the company of some former comrades.'

'Will you talk about old times?' Peter asked him. He did not care about the answer. But he thought it safer in the dream to be friendly.

Patrick Ross grinned and reached out a hand and tousled Peter's hair. His touch was coarse and cold. Peter tried to look away from the grin but was buried to his neck and couldn't. 'There'll be no time for sentimental reminiscing, Peter,' he said. 'There'll be no time for that at all.' He stood. He pointed down the incline of the beach, along the yellow trickle of his beach hut lamplight. 'Look, children,' he said. 'Observe the blood-dimmed tide.'

Confined as they were, the children struggled to look. In the yellow cast of the soldier's light, they saw that the sea was crimson.

Creed answered his phone early on Wednesday morning and was not at all surprised to hear Martin Stride on the other end of the line. 'You need to get down here, please,' he said. 'Something has happened, Julian. I've never needed help in my life like I need yours now.'

'Jesus, mate. Nothing has happened to the kids, has it?'

'Yes. No. Just get down here as soon as you can.'

He drove the Jag. The day seemed decades ago when he had calculated the effect of his appearance on Martin and his family, driving to the Stride domain in that stupid fucking suit, at the wheel of the Morgan for the sake of a sort of modesty, all quirky and picturesque. The pretence had gone and with it the calculation. That at least was a relief. He tried not to speculate as he drove on what might have occurred to bring this urgent summons. After his conversation at the seminary, he was naturally concerned. But Stride was still in one piece and sounded sane. He would build on that. The Jag was equipped with a hands-free phone and en route he called Elena and she told him about her odd and unnerving episode of the previous evening.

'I thought I was going to be stranded there,' she said. 'In the London of Bruno Absalom with his smog and gloom and brandy habit back in 1924.'

'Well,' Creed said, 'you've got the haircut for it.'

She laughed, but reluctantly.

'How did it feel, Ellie?'

'Claustrophobic,' she said. 'Sinister. It was bloody terrifying. Should I go in today?'

'I wouldn't mind you down here,' he said.

'You mean to research something for you?'

'I mean just to hold my hand.'

She did not laugh at that at all. But he had not really meant it as a joke.

Stride was waiting for him at the gate. He did not have his characteristic air of detachment, his usual, enviable poise. His hair was dishevelled. His eyes had a slightly wild look. He seemed tense and shaken and distracted. 'Thanks for coming,' he said, into the open driver's window. His hands were white-knuckled on the sill. 'I appreciate it more than you will ever know.'

Creed got out of the car and held out his arms and embraced him. Martin Stride had become his friend and he sensed the contact was what he most needed at that moment. He was tormented and alone and he needed some humanity and warmth. Stride returned the embrace. They held each other hard. When he let go of him, Creed saw that there were tears spilling out of his eyes and down his cheeks.

'The kids had another dream,' he said. 'Monica called and told me about it last night. It meant the exorcism hadn't worked. I went to look at the site where the remains of the station had been. I shouldn't have done. It was a mistake. I should have left it till this morning.' He sniffed and rubbed the tears from his face with the back of his hand.

'You've been up all night?'

'I'm so worried about Monica and the children, Julian. I just don't know what else to do.'

'Come on. Show me the site. Show me what you found.'

They walked there directly from the gate. There was a wood obstructing their route from that direction and their view of the site almost until they were upon it. It revealed itself suddenly and Creed stopped dead in his tracks and gasped.

The island platform stood unblemished. The building upon it rose solitary and intact. It was the same, but subtly different, as though it had sneaked back into reality, brick by renegade brick. The roof looked shabbier. There were gaps between the umber tiles. One of the windows had been smashed in a way that suggested the hurled missile of deliberate vandalism. Another had a sheet of corrugated tin hammered over it. The door was canted at an odd angle, as though one of its hinges had given way and was no longer anchored securely by screws to the wall. As they got closer, Creed saw that there were small patches of graffiti on the exterior walls. They had not been done in the lavish spray of an aerosol can. They had been done with felt pen or crayon. They were scruffy and peevish-looking. The two men mounted the platform. Creed got close enough to read one of the scrawls. *Dell loves Maggie*, it said. *True. 1961.*

He went inside. Stride did not go in with him. He looked around. The bench seating was still there but had been removed entirely from one wall, at the centre of which a gas fire had been installed. The fire still stood on its mountings and still possessed a tap. But the copper pipe it must have been attached to had been torn out and, Creed assumed, taken away for scrap. He lifted his eyes and looked at the walls. There were posters. One showed a pilot and a flight attendant grinning in sky-blue uniforms as they descended a set of aluminium steps from the body of an aircraft. *Fly BOAC*, said the legend above their heads. Another poster pictured a cigarette packet superimposed over a waterfall. A good-looking man was leading a woman on a horse through the water at the brink of the drop. She had long hair, Lady Godiva-like. *Consulate*, the wording said. *The cooler smoke*.

The floor felt different under Creed's feet. He looked down. It was linoleum. It was worn in places and faded but had once been red and patterned like the tiles that might have floored a Roman villa in the times of the Caesars. The theme was continued in the gas fire surround, which boasted a lino mosaic of faux-marble chips. He shook his head. There were things he felt he needed to work out. He very much wished that clever, beautiful Ellie Coyle was there with him and not just to hold his hand. He saw an empty bottle on a window sill. The brand name of the drink was raised in relief on the glass. *Vimto*, it said. He thought that he had seen enough. He inhaled the dereliction in the dusty air and sighed and walked back out onto the platform.

'What do you think?'

'I think that the early 1960s was probably a low point in the design and decoration of public amenities.'

'Do you think it will regress further?'

'Not without help, no.' He was thinking about what Degrelle had said, about lightning strikes and improbability. 'This is its true state. This is what was abandoned when the branch line was closed.'

'But I had it pulled down.'

'No. You didn't. What you had pulled down was an illusion, a lie, a conceit.' He gestured. 'This is real.'

'What I had demolished was real,' Stride said.

'If it was,' Creed said, 'it was only because we made it so.'

'I lived here in peace for a decade, Julian. For ten blissful years, this place was benign. The kids played in that building, for Christ's sake.'

'When this began, you asked me why it was happening only now. And I promised you I would discover the answer to that question and I have to say the promise seems a rash one in retrospect. But I do think I know. Patrick Ross has come back here. He has stirred up some old ghosts, memories of this place in its pomp. He was an imposter to his mother, an abomination to Dr Brody and the walking, grinning nightmare that robbed Captain Broad of what remained of his sanity at Falcon Lodge. I'd bet a pound to a penny Broad spent time strapped to that stretcher you showed me on my first visit to this place.'

'You haven't answered the question.'

'You did it, Martin. The psychic power in you that priest picked up on did it. Ross was the catalyst.'

Stride kicked some loose bit of masonry. It skittered along the platform and then stopped. 'What do we do now, Julian?'

'First, we shift the lorry and earth-movers the demo squad left here to the other side of the house. They can pick them up at their leisure from where we leave them in the middle of your drive. The ground is solid enough, that bit of rain has soaked in and the surface will be hard again after all the dry weather we've been having. You can't let those blokes see this. If you do, they'll talk about it and in days you'll have the world's press plus every freak on the planet camped outside your door. And you're a man who likes your privacy.

'When we've done that, I call Elena Coyle. We need reinforcements. Then you tell me about the dream your children had two nights ago. Then I make us both a bite to eat. And then, mate, you try to get a couple of hours of sleep.'

Stride was asleep in bed by the time Elena arrived. She did so in some style, at the wheel of Creed's borrowed Morgan. She did not own a car. And, of course, there were no trains she could take to anywhere convenient for the Stride property. There had been Shale Point. But Shale Point had finally closed in the days when aircraft still flew with the BOAC logo and it was still permissible to advertise menthol cigarettes on the walls of railway station waiting rooms. Creed watched her pull up. At the wheel of his roadster, she really did look like a flapper, with that strong jaw and sensuous mouth and the black bob always restored to glossy perfection with a simple shake of her head. She had brought an overnight bag, as he had suggested she should. He could borrow clothes from Stride. They were of a similar size and shape. At a push, Ellie could borrow clothes from Monica. But that was assuming Monica could be persuaded to return. And it was further assuming that Ellie, advised of what was going on, could be persuaded to stay.

He left a note in the kitchen for Stride and walked her to the waiting room. They followed the churned tracks left by the demolition men. The ground was dry now and forlornly scarred by all their pointless industry. On the route, he told her about his meeting at the seminary with Degrelle and the claims about them all the priest had made. Then he told her about the dream the Stride children had endured in their Aalborg beds. She remained silent until he had finished.

'After my encounter with Bruno Absalom last night, I wouldn't take serious issue with the claim that I have at least some psychic sensitivity,' she said. 'I was there, however briefly and reluctantly. It was his time. It was his moment.'

Creed nodded.

'How does Martin feel about the most recent dream?'

'He says he'd like five minutes with Patrick Ross in a jammed lift. He admits ten might be even better.'

'That's not going to happen.'

'You can't blame him. They're his children, enduring nightmares deliberately conjured.'

'Conjured for what purpose?'

'Amusement, I think.'

'Did he understand the significance of the blood-dimmed tide?'

'He didn't. He does now. He wasn't familiar with the Yeats poem. Somewhat reluctantly, I told him what it was about.'

'Poetry has had rather unfortunate connotations for him lately.'

Creed did not respond to this.

'Jesus,' she said. The waiting room had come into sight.

They walked around it and then went inside. There was nothing subtly different about the interior from what Creed had earlier seen. It was firmly moored in the present. The moment of the past to which it most closely related was, naturally enough, the one that had abandoned it. It was Edwardian in origin but a relic of the 1960s now.

Creed thought back to his first night vigil there. And he thought about the sense of exhilaration and overdue vindication he had felt the following morning when he left it after an experience that had been truly revelatory. He had hummed that Van Morrison song, hadn't he, the one from *Astral Weeks* the first track of the album with the repeated phrase, almost a mantra, about being born again. The Yeats poem was about that too, wasn't it? The poem Patrick Ross had referenced in the Stride children's dream was about a man being reborn. And he knew now, Creed thought. He finally understood. He looked down at the floor, at the worn red flush of linoleum, at the illusion of terracotta tiles. And he understood.

'They will come through here,' he said to Elena. 'This is where his plague of the dead will begin, in a location familiar to them. They will have come through here on their way to die and so they know it. This is the gateway, or the portal. Or this is just their strange and familiar meeting place. But this is where they will be born again, Elena. And Patrick Ross, after all this time, will not be one to miss what he has accomplished.'

'What can we do?'

'Run away? Emigrate?'

'I mean, to stop it happening,' she said.

He closed his eyes. He was reminded with relief and gratitude why it was he loved her. 'There is only one way,' he said. 'And it will require all of us to do it. And I don't even know whether it will work. There isn't a great deal of time.

Ross told the children only a few days. And that was two nights ago.'

'We'd better get on with it then,' Elena said. She dusted her hands together. She smiled. She crossed the distance between them and held his head in her hands and kissed him. 'Come on, soldier boy,' she said. 'Come and tell us all about your plan.'

Creed had come to believe what Absalom had believed about ghosts and what Elena had so strongly suspected after seeing the image of Lady Ross taken with the hidden camera and blown up in their Soho edit suite. The image had looked dragged from another time because it was. It had been an affront to history, to chronology and nature. People who saw ghosts saw them because they possessed a psychic gift. But that gift did not drag the spirits they saw into a reluctant present. It delivered those who saw them into their past. He had not really been convinced of it after his own experience. He had not even been totally convinced after Stride's vivid account of seeing the porter and smelling the acrid stench of fresh piss in the platform stall. The priest had finally persuaded him. He had thought the explanation of ghosts he had heard in the seminary more reasonable than any other.

A fortnight ago, after a night vigil in the waiting room, he had cleaned the accumulated grime of decades from his own skin under the shower heads of a designer gym in Soho. The previous night, Elena had almost been trapped in the weary catacombs of the London Underground in the early 1920s. Stride had experienced the station closest to its pomp, seen a veteran employee pressed back into service during the Great War by the toll on manpower at the Front. He had come close to being heard and seen on the station platform, there and then, during a night that had unfolded over ninety years ago.

It was true. Degrelle's lightning strike of improbability was three-fold. They all of them shared a psychic sensitivity so strong it could deliver the past back into the present in this powerfully haunted place. Absalom had warned ominously about the danger faced in confronting ghosts. And after Elena's recent experience, Creed thought the warning well made. But he also thought that their hand had been forced. They really had no choice. The only way to stop Patrick Ross and destroy his pestilent ambition was to bring back the waiting room's past. They had to try to return the place to the time before his death. He could not be what he was if he had not perished in those last weeks of the war. If he had lived instead of died in the way he had in the past, he would not now threaten their present so terribly.

Martin Stride listened patiently as Creed outlined all this. He knew that his own recent experience half a mile to the east of where he now sat had been real. It made sense that the three of them together could affect the waiting room more potently than one of them alone. One small detail impressed him, and it was the way the dripping hanging baskets had appeared again, provoked by Elena's first visit there. They did, all three of them, seem to possess the power to influence the place, to lure it back into its heyday, somehow. He did not doubt the logic of what Julian said. He just did not see how engaging with ghosts could hinder Patrick Ross. Surely it would simply endanger them?

'Brody asked Patrick was there anything he feared,' Elena said. 'Do you remember? He asked him the question in their one interview together. Do you remember what Patrick said, how he replied?'

'He said, "Only ghosts,"' Stride said.

There was a silence between them.

'So what do we do, Julian?' Stride said. 'Do we sit cross-legged in a circle on the waiting room floor, holding hands and singing "Roses of Picardy" with our eyes tight shut until we hear steam trains chuffing and smell gaslight?'

'You wouldn't suggest a song if you had heard my singing

voice,' Creed said. 'But that scenario's not a million miles removed. We go there and we wait. It's a waiting room, after all. We wait and see if our being there can provoke the present into the past.'

'Or the past into the present,' Stride said.

'No,' Elena said. 'I've been there.' Her voice sounded bleak. 'It's the past, all right.'

'We've each done it individually,' Creed said. 'Together, we could be exponentially stronger.'

'Please don't tell me I have to involve my family in this,' Stride said.

Creed had already thought about that. And he had recently changed his mind about it too. He did not know whether Monica Stride had any psychic sensitivity. He wasn't really sure about the children either. Peter had seen the grinning spectre of Patrick Ross through the waiting room window. But Ross was not a ghost, was he? And the ghost of Wilfred Owen had written out his warning verses in the boy's exercise book. Millie had heard long-dead soldiers singing one of their sentimental marching songs, but that was a modest accomplishment compared to what her father had evoked out there on the night he returned to recover Brody's papers.

Creed had weighed coldly in the balance the pluses and minuses of having all the Stride family intact and at home. They were a strong unit. They had never been apart before. Having them here would be a compelling reminder every second to Martin Stride of what he stood to lose should they fail in their task. On the other hand, the family would be a distraction. He and Elena would need Martin focused and alert and totally dedicated to the fight. It would be better if they stayed away. Better and safer, too. He did not really expect himself or his companions to survive the ordeal unscathed. The risk to the children and their mother vastly outweighed any possible benefit in having them there.

'Your family stays in Aalborg until we've finished,' he said.

*Or until we're finished*, he thought, *in which case they will probably never come back*. An image came to him then of the attic above them as Stride had described it, Millie's rocking horse cantering back and forth on its wooden runners under dust, in darkness.

Elena thought it natural that Julian had taken command. He'd been used to the habit of command in the regiment and been his own boss in civilian life. Stride too had been his own boss and the rock star lifestyle, with its retinues and court flatterers and extravagant tours, sometimes reminded her of the way that medieval kings had lived. There was also the fact that this was his land, his domain, and their own status there, strictly, was the humble status of guests. But Creed had been summoned here originally to help. And now he really was helping. It was the only objective of his mission. There was no contradiction or conflict in him. She suspected he would succeed or die trying. He would give of his best. She thought that Stride knew this deep down too. It was the condition of leadership and he accepted it. And he trusted Julian Creed completely.

There was not really anything more to be said. Stride called Monica while Creed and Elena gathered clothing and provisions. He told her what it was they were going to attempt to do. She was privy to the content of the children's dreams. She had heard everything on Wight that Creed and Elena had travelled there to tell them. She had read the Brody papers. And her husband had never lied to her and was not about to start to do so on the eve of something he did not confidently expect to live through.

'I love you,' he said in conclusion. It was everything.

'I love you,' she said.

'A kiss, please, for both of my children.'

The connection broke. He closed his eyes. He replaced the receiver. Then he opened his eyes again and gathered his formidable will.

They settled down with about two hours of daylight left to them. They had brought a sleeping bag each and a couple of changes of clothes. They had been careful to bring with them nothing anachronistic in the past they would strive to achieve. Elena was very conscious still of the image of Lady Ross, the deformed figure in cornflower blue projected onto their edit room screen with such unsettling reluctance. Creed's button-hole camera had been an affront. It had offended nature. They had with them a Primus stove to heat their food and drinks and hurricane lamps to illuminate their nights. They had not brought a cellular phone and none of them wore a digital wristwatch. Creed had his BlackBerry in his pocket. It had become, over the years of his recent success, almost a good luck charm and like almost all soldiers, of course he was superstitious. But he had switched it off and would not risk switching it on again.

'Do you think we'll sleep?' Stride said.

'Like babies, if my previous experience is anything to go by,' Creed said.

'Not me. I'll be too frightened to sleep,' Elena said.

'I was terrified,' Creed said. 'You'd have to be a moron not to be. I still slept. It's like there's a spell about the place, as though it is in some way charmed.'

Elena laughed, despite herself. Her eyes were on the gas fire, on its faux-marble mosaic surround, the Caesars' heads in profile you could pick out of the lino pattern if you squinted at it. 'It doesn't appear to have a lot of charm at the moment.'

'I didn't mean that kind of charm,' Creed said, 'idiot.'

'Now, now, children,' Stride said. 'Let's not squabble on our first night in camp together. I'll make some tea. Then we can draw lots to decide who tells the first story.'

They did sleep. Almost as soon as it went dark, the three of them slept. Outside the waiting room, across the wilderness of the Stride estate, through its grassland and woods, through its gentle, undulant English fields, all was quiet. Instinct kept the animals still and silent at bay in their warrens and burrows and nests. The wind did not seem to possess the will to shift a single turning leaf. Nothing moved, other than in the attic of the Stride house, where the old rocking horse belonging to Millie shifted very slightly on its runners and the odour of meat gone rotten strengthened through the dark hours of implacable waiting.

Stride was the first of them to awaken the following morning. The first thing he realised was that the lino had gone from the floor. There were boards and they were varnished. As the light began to slant in through the windows, he saw the countless scarred depressions under the varnish caused by pacing stiletto heels. And there were scorch marks from cigarettes ground hastily out by the heavy leather shoes of men surprised by early trains. He rubbed his eyes. The bench on which he lay in his sleeping bag ran the whole perimeter of the room. *Elena will be relieved*, he thought. She had hated that gas fire's hideous surround. Looking up, he saw that there was a ceiling fan. It was somewhat optimistic for the climate but had been a very fashionable item of equipment once.

'Where are we?' Elena said. She had woken and sat up and sighed.

'When, might be a better question,' Stride said. 'I think the line might be back in private hands.'

'Christ,' she said. 'Julian was right. It's changed again. It's us. It really is.'

'Oh ye of little faith,' Creed said, yawning. He turned to Stride. 'When are we then, since you seem to know?'

'A nationalised railway doesn't pay for a ceiling fan in a temperate climate,' he said. 'It would be seen as a folly, frowned upon as an extravagance. Then there's the style of it.'

'It looks like an old-fashioned aeroplane propeller,' Elena said. 'We're in the 1930s, I'd say.'

'If we are,' Creed said, 'at this rate, we won't be there for very long.'

Stride stood. He stretched and walked over to one of the windows. They were not the originals, with their stained-glass engine depictions in the upper arch panels. But they were intact and they were clean. The smashed panes and patch of corrugated tin were gone decades ago. Or more accurately, he thought, they were still to be inflicted, decades into the waiting room's future. 'The blades of the fan are Bakelite,' he said. 'Anyone like to hazard a guess at a year?'

Creed looked around. The sun was coming up and the new windows let in a lot of light. The one poster on the wall depicted a grinning family in a Morris touring car. There seemed enough wood embellishing the bodywork to build a garden shed from. The dad was handsome and the mother beautiful and blonde and the grinning kids cute and they reminded him of the Strides and he hoped the picture would not have the same effect on Martin. 'Hitler's in power,' he said. 'But the world is still at peace. I'm guessing about 1935.'

'It's fucking incredible,' Elena said. 'I mean, sorry for the language and all, but it really is a miracle.'

Creed did not think it a miracle at all. He thought there was a strong aspect of inevitability about it. And he thought, the more he considered it, that this conflict, the conflict to come, was one that would have come as no surprise to a Belgian priest of his acquaintance. Degrelle had known that this was how it was going to turn out. He had known since his failed exorcism. There was something fated, or predestined about it, wasn't there? He did not know where Degrelle stood on predestination. He thought his theology surprisingly shaky all round for a Catholic priest. How many of them would admit to a belief in ghosts? But Monsignor Degrelle had known it would happen like this, just as surely as he had been informed of the secret nature of Bruno Absalom's original sin.

Stride was staring at the poster on the wall. It was not necessary to be very intuitive to imagine what he was thinking.

'Come on, Martin,' Creed said, giving his shoulder a squeeze. 'I'll make us some breakfast. You're in charge of beverages and the mood I'm in, your coffee had better be good.'

The changes came more slowly and more subtly in the day. Elena thought that it was a bit like when you watched the minute hand on an old-fashioned clock. If the face and hands were big enough, you could see the hand move, almost imperceptibly, as the wound tension of the mainspring worked against its regulating cogs and levers and shifted it. But if you looked away and then looked back again, the shift was much more obvious. So it was with the décor and general character of the waiting room. It was mid-afternoon before any of them noticed that the poster on the wall had been replaced by one advertising the attractions of Brighton Pier. And it was almost dusk before Stride remarked that there were metal ashtrays on each of the windowsills and Creed spotted a naked row of coat hooks screwed into the wall next to the door.

The really significant shifts occurred at night. At eight o'clock on their second night, blackly aware that she was losing consciousness and that the other two were already fast asleep, Elena's drowsy reasoning insisted to her that it worked like this to spare them. Their minds could only process so much. They could not govern their psychic gift. Sensation had to be rationed or it would overcome them and make them mad. Perhaps they were mad already, she thought, seeing the first of the figures that would join them for the pestilent future planned by Patrick Ross.

He was still there in the morning. He was exactly as Sir Samuel Ross had described. He was like a three-dimensional projection, less solid-seeming than a hologram, dull rather than vibrant, grey-complexioned in an army greatcoat on a portion of bench to the left side of the waiting room door. He sat entirely still. His forearms rested on his splayed knees and his head sunk between his shoulders and bowed towards the floor, concealing his expression. A smell came off him.

This odour was cold and earthy and rank. He had gained in solidity in the night. And by morning, he had been joined by another wraith. Elena thought their posture deliberate. She thought they looked at the floor like that to hide the hunger on their faces.

There were other changes on the second morning. These were more encouraging. The original waiting room windows had returned. The hanging baskets dripped from the corners. Kitchener stared sternly from his recruitment poster on the wall. The blued iron stove rose from the centre of the floor, its chimney intact. Bunting flapped against the exterior walls. They heard frequent trains and marshalling whistles and cries of luggage porters and a paper seller hawking the latest edition in the piercing cry of a voice not yet broken by puberty. Creed began to think that one more night might do it; one more night might deliver them. They were stronger together, more potent, regressing fast. He thought that by dusk on the second day, they were probably in the early 1920s. He half-expected to see the portly, self-important figure of Bruno Absalom stroll through the door, wafting brandy fumes and waving a plump cigar, affluently downcast at the enormity of his recent sin.

But no one came in. And the three silent, monochromatic figures on the bench beside the door were joined as darkness fell by the wraith of a fourth. The stench was becoming overwhelming. The three mortal people in the waiting room barely dared move or speak. The first of Patrick Ross's pestilent dead was almost wholly solid now. Creed thought that under the greatcoat he possessed a statue's still, colossal strength. When movement occurred in him and it would not be long, he would rise with the power to crush a man. Creed glanced quickly and caught the expression on the dead soldier's face. His eyes had opened and were fixed on Elena and the look in them was ravenous.

Stride was seated on the cold metal of the stove with his

head in his hands. Creed went to where Elena sat and put his arms around her and held her.

'We're running out of time,' she said.

'We just need one more night, Ellie. Just one,' he said.

'We don't have another night,' Stride said.

Creed was about to reply when he heard an approaching train and recognised the sound made by the engine that had in the past, in his past in this place, delivered Lady Ross to the waiting room.

'Sweet Lady Mary,' Stride said, guessing. He smiled, but the smile was bitter and Creed thought, *He has all but given up*. He looked to where the first of their grey companions sat and saw the dead soldier contract his earth-grimed fingers slyly into fists.

The train approached. It slowed with a familiar hiss of brakes. Creed closed his eyes and he prayed, holding on to Elena for strength. The thought of what he was about to do delivered such fear and dread at the possible consequences that it brought him close to helplessness. What year was it? It was somewhere during the years before her committal, when she had come here freely at the suggestion of the man who was still her husband, to attend pointless sessions with Edward Brody while she employed a detective to search in Manchester for the son she insisted was only missing.

The problem was that he was dead by then. The time wasn't yet early enough. The date needed to be before the armistice and the assault on the canal. It wasn't yet a moment to be of any help to them, there amid the pestilent dead assembling in the waiting room. But Creed knew, as the door opened, that he had to try despite this. He looked into Elena's eyes. He stroked her hair and face and kissed her tenderly on the mouth. He lingered over the kiss, knowing it would be the last they would share. Then he stood.

'Stay silent,' he said, 'both of you. Don't engage her. If either of you do, if she becomes aware of you, we're finished.'

She came through the door. In whatever season she had left, it was raining. She shook out her umbrella and leaned it against a portion of bench. She could not see her dead son's grey, seated sentinels, that much at least was plain. She was as oblivious to them as they were to her.

'Good day, Lady Ross,' Creed said.

She turned sharply around. Elena studied her from where she sat, resplendent in the cornflower-blue wool of her coat in the gas lamps now burning brightly in the gathering darkness, chiselled and haughty, beautiful but for the hint of delusion in the hard set of her sculpted mouth and her eyes. There was a pause while it appeared as though it might not happen. But then her focus fixed, quite firmly, on Julian Creed.

'You are not Dr Brody.'

Creed swallowed. 'No, madam, I am not.'

'Dr Brody always comes to fetch me himself. He is very considerate.'

'He sends his sincere apologies.'

'There is a vile man lurking on the platform outside. He leered at me. He is an insult to the uniform he wears. Such people are intolerable.'

She had not finished speaking these words before Martin Stride was out of the waiting room door and onto the platform. Patrick Ross stood under a spread of light from one of a row of lamps hanging from the platform roof. He was indeed dressed in uniform, though he was bare-headed. He saw Stride and started to undo the flap that held his revolver secure in its leather case on his belt. Stride had time to see that he cast no shadow before the distance between them was closed and the piston of his right fist buried itself in Patrick's face. Patrick stumbled back a step and dropped the weapon and it skittered off the platform onto the line.

Stride hit him again. He had never met a man he believed could have stayed on his feet under the impact of the first punch, but it did not matter. Patrick staggered, trying to raise his hands and Stride simply walked forward, smashing pulverising rights and lefts into his face and head until his knuckles were raw and his arms were almost too heavy to lift and Patrick grinned at him through a mask of stinking gore. He licked blood from his upper lip and swallowed it and winked and whispered, 'My turn now, troubadour.'

She was very suggestible, that's what Brody had said. She wasn't sane, but Lady Ross was perfectly reasonable just so long as you did not insist on the unacceptable fact of the loss in the war of her son. He would not make that mistake with her. The Lady Ross known to Brody had been born in the moment the news about her son was broken to her. The psychiatrist had been convinced of it. Creed was just as certain she could be born again, there in the waiting room, into the time when she had been whole. Very suggestible, Brody had said. Creed hoped that she would react positively to what he was about to suggest to her now.

He sat her down. Elena watched. The plague of death gathered potency in the soulless, growing ranks, seated by the door. Creed smiled at Lady Ross and Elena could not believe his composure in the chaos they were amid. She watched him summon and then unleash the full force of his seductive charm on the distracted ghost he engaged. She could hear the blows from the platform outside as the thing that had once been Patrick Ross spent some of the strength Absalom had spoken of beating the life out of brave Martin Stride. She could see another disinterred figure start to swirl into abject existence as the first and second of them swapped a complicit nod, almost ready to indulge their appetites.

'Come, Lady Ross,' Creed said. 'Sir Robert and your husband are waiting. Falcon Lodge opens today, with much fanfare and hope. You are among the guests of honour. We cannot be late for the ceremony and there is no time to lose. The motor of your car is already running.'

'I am confused,' Lady Ross said. She looked doubtful. 'Are you quite sure about the year? My son—'

'Your son is at school, Lady Ross,' Creed said. 'He leads the batting averages for the first eleven at cricket. Soon he will join you at home for the holidays. Patrick is so looking forward to that. Come, we must not tarry.'

Elena saw it quite clearly, despite everything. And she heard it, quite distinctly. Creed's voice was not really his, but it was familiar to her. He had spoken to Lady Ross in that velvet, voiceover croon that had won him so much conviction with his weekly television audience. On the platform outside, Stride's countering punches were brave but feeble as Patrick Ross broke and maimed him with unearthly strength. In the corner, the bearers of plague were grinning in dark comradeship. In the waiting room, at the speed they had regressed, the war to end wars had probably not long stumbled to its weary conclusion. But Lady Ross wanted to believe. She so ardently wanted to believe. She wanted it to be a spring afternoon in 1916 with the sun shining and her precious boy at school and her husband faithfully loving her. Elena could see it plainly in the conflict on her face.

And she blinked and nodded and smiled and it was so. There was no strain to the smile. The fraught look had gone from her eyes. Her expression was serene, animated only by a slight hint of excitement at the occasion for which she now was certain she had travelled there. Creed opened the door for her. He took her gloved hand in his to lead her through it. And Elena saw it widen on a splash of spring brightness as he eased himself and Lady Ross both back into a past that could unmake the present. Her last cogent thought was that Julian Creed had willingly sacrificed himself. It had been his unspoken intention all along, the part of the plan he had not revealed to them, the only possible conclusion if they were going to succeed. A sob caught in her throat and she raised a helpless hand. The door closed. And she no longer had the vaguest idea where she was.

There was a marching band on the Shale Point platform. Creed recognised some of the people there from pictures he had seen. Sir Robert Paley was there and pale, thin Edward Brody and Sir Samuel and a corpulent man he knew to be Bruno Absalom. The bandstand was swathed in gayly coloured bunting. The brass of the band's instruments was burnished by the sun. The players were red with beer and effort; they were English and bucolic and they had never seen a cellular phone or a laptop computer and none of them ever would. They were middle-aged. The young men were all at war. It was 1916. The men on the bandstand in front of him would never hear a Beatles song played on the radio. They would not live to see the first motorway built.

He would make himself scarce. The paranoia so deeply and generally felt after the crushing losses on the Somme would not start to become widespread for a few weeks yet. But his appearance was outlandish. His hair was far too long and his clothing alien. He slipped away from Lady Ross as he saw her wave eagerly towards her waiting husband. Sir Samuel saw her and he beamed. There was love and optimism in his expression and perhaps a measure too of justified pride. Creed slipped down from the platform and away from the station and the crowd, using the cover of a goods train and a row of second and third-class passenger coaches. Occupying parallel lines, the two stalled convoys of rolling stock offered a tunnel of seclusion along which he could progress away from the celebratory scene unobserved.

He stopped to gather himself. Loss and victory were battling in him. And it was an unequal contest, because he had lost Elena Coyle. Grief threatened to unman him as he squatted in the shadow of the trains and he felt a moment of loneliness and self-pity so strong he almost cried out at how wounding and overwhelming it was. He could not think this way. He could not permit such self-indulgence. If he did, he would fail and his sacrifice would end up being worthless.

None of it had happened yet. Patrick's death, his poor mother's madness, Bruno Absalom's tinkering, pagan sin: none it had happened. Martin Stride might yet lead the untroubled life that noble soul of his surely deserved. But Elena would never know or love him. That was the reality he was obliged to confront. He would delight no more in her company. He would never again lie next to her. He could not now make her happy. The fulfilment he had so recently come to have such genuine hope for was gone for ever. He had seen her for the last time. He could still smell the scent she wore on the fingers that had stroked her neck as they shared their final kiss. He had lost her and he knelt on the gravel between the sets of iron rails and bowed his head and the loss cleaved him.

It was a while before he found the fortitude to compose himself. When he did, he considered only the task confronting him. He had a tragedy and its awful repercussions to try to prevent. To achieve that, he had a war to fight and to try to survive. Would he be able, at his age, to enlist? He tried to think analytically about his prospects where this was concerned. He had never smoked and only ever drunk moderately. He had kept scrupulously fit through exercise all his adult life. He had eaten with fastidious regard for nutrition. He had topped up his tan safely on salon beds and always worn sun block. His teeth were good and there was no grey yet in his hair. How old did he look, by the standards of 1916? The toil of farm and factory life aged men prematurely. The horrors of trench life aged them even faster. He would probably be able to claim thirty-five, he thought, without being laughed at incredulously.

He speculated on the expression on the recruiting sergeant's face. He reckoned that he would be accepted straightaway. Even if he wasn't, he would be after the infantry losses July would deliver with Haig's Western Front master-plan. When the casualty figures were tolled after that catastrophe, they would not be choosy, would they? He knew his history well enough to know what the future would hold. They would welcome him with open arms and few if any questions.

He would need a birth certificate and some other forged papers to enlist, but the originals were unsophisticated and there was no such thing as a database to check forgeries against. He would need a place to lay his head and some walking-around money in the meantime, but they could be obtained easily enough. There could not be many men better qualified than he was to cope with such a situation. He could thrive in challenging circumstances. He might even enjoy himself. If it was not for Ellie, he thought. If it was not for the abject loss of the woman he so desperately loved.

He got to his feet. Somewhere in the background he could hear the marching band. He could smell coal from the freight wagon in the lee of which he stood. He could smell apple blossom too on the breeze and fancied it might come from the orchard on the land that would one day belong to a friend he had made and lost in a matter of weeks.

He reached into his pocket and pulled his BlackBerry out. Already it looked outlandish, anachronistic and utterly redundant in the grip of his hand. He smiled, nostalgic for a moment for that remote time in the future in which he had so enjoyed his colourful past. He tossed it up into the coal wagon, where it clattered down through the load and settled in darkness amid the soft, black slack of a truck bed. He could not imagine any implement more useless. He needed food, he was hungry. But first, he had to find a clothes line and something inconspicuous to wear. *To be born again*, he thought. The lyric came from that favourite Van Morrison song insinuating itself once more into his mind. It seemed appropriate. And so he walked away from Shale Point, softly humming a melody composed by a musician who had not yet been born to write it.

# Epilogue

She only just caught the train. She had to sprint along the platform with her overnight bag in one hand and her laptop case in the other and she only just got aboard as it pulled out of the station. Had it been the new type, the type with automatic doors, she wouldn't have made it. She would have had another hour and a half to wait on a platform in rural Cornwall with the batteries flat on everything and nothing in her bag to read and nothing even resembling a newspaper kiosk to buy a book or a magazine from to pass the time with.

She hadn't thought the old slam-doors still in use. She thought they had been banned or completely superseded. Perhaps that was only the case on some of the busier and more profitable lines. It was quite nostalgic, to see a train corridor and compartments where groups of disparate travellers faced each other from opposing seats. A train with this much wood and glass in it rattled in a way she had almost forgotten they used to do. It reminded her a bit of adventures in childhood. She could smell the smells absorbed over decades by the quilted plush of the seat upholstery.

Sure enough, the luggage rack was made of netting, shaped like a baggy hammock strung between metal supports. And there was a dinky little curtain next to the window when she sat down. She put her stuff on the seat beside her, took off her coat because the sprint for the train had made her hot and went to put the bag and laptop on the rack. The compartment had only one other occupant. He was in uniform. She became aware he was getting to his feet behind her.

'May I help you with those?'

'I'm quite capable, thank you.'

'Of course you are,' he said. He sat back down.

She hadn't meant to sound grumpy. She didn't want to get hit on by some military type embarking on a short period of lust-fuelled leave. That was all. She had a change at Penzance and faced a long journey back to London from there. The trip had been a waste of time. She was researching freelance for a toad called Alex Dupree. He was the sort of psychic investigator who would have sold snake oil from the back of a horse-drawn wagon in the Wild West. He was completely bogus and totally unprincipled and she could not believe the gullibility of the television-viewing public in having made him so successful and rich. He was obese and had halitosis but his fans could only see the piercing blue eyes and extravagant halo of blond hair. And he did possess that gravelly, hypnotic voice that was sort of his trademark.

The irony was that her own vague belief in the paranormal had been one of the factors in her taking the job in the first place. She had undergone a couple of experiences in her life that, looked back upon, could not easily be explained or rationalised. One of these had occurred in a maze at a country house. On another occasion, it had been an abandoned aircraft hangar from the pioneering days of aviation.

The locations did not need to be intrinsically creepy. It had happened to her once when she had been asked for directions to a particular, isolated pub in the Lake District as dusk descended by a rock climber strolling alone down the path she was hiking along. She had been familiar with the pub, had stayed in one of the rooms upstairs there, and had been able to tell him the way precisely. He nodded and smiled and thanked her. There was a notable poise about him, a pale intensity to the gaze of his eyes. These characteristics made her curious enough to watch him walk away and observe that he moved over the uneven ground as smoothly and as lightly as a cat.

Only later had it occurred to her that the man had been anachronistically dressed. There had been a hemp rope slung bandolier fashion over his shoulder and he'd worn leather boots and woollen breeches. She put it down to a fashion for retro clothing among the rock climbing fraternity. But his face had been somehow familiar and if the experience did not haunt her, it would not easily slip from her mind. And then two years later, researching something about the Himalayas, she carried out a quick study of the attempts to climb Everest and learned that George Mallory had died near the peak in 1924. And when she looked at his picture, she was staring into the face of the man who had asked her as darkness fell for directions to a Cumbrian pub.

She had made the mistake of mentioning this story to Dupree, before she knew much about the true nature of his character or the soulless depth of his cynicism concerning matters paranormal. It had been on a bonding trip in Bournemouth funded by the production company responsible for the show. She had been thrilled, as a lowly freelance, that they had been generous enough to invite her along. But she had drunk too much and related her Mallory story to Dupree and he had choked on his vodka and tonic and then laughed in her face.

She had been hurt and insisted that the experience had been real and he had sneeringly contradicted her, saying that if the encounter had taken place, she would have had a picture to prove it. That was his simplistic thinking and also characteristic of his mentality. Everything the audience saw on his show was an illusion. It was all concocted by a clever special effects girl from Ireland called Alison Slaney. She had been obliged to sign a confidentiality form at the outset of her employment, promising never to reveal the truth behind Alison Slaney's skilful tricks.

Half a dozen times in the last year, she had been on the brink of resigning. Maybe she would actually do it this time. The haunted lighthouse she had just checked out had been a stubby pebbledash construction ripe for conversion into an artist's studio or a holiday home for a young couple. It had been about as sinister as the surf shops and bars that had sprung up in its vicinity. It totally lacked the scale, remoteness and history for her to be able to make anything of it at all. It would defeat even Alison Slaney and her bag of computer-generated effects. It was hopeless. And Dupree's remuneration scheme was strictly airtime-dependent. So she would be out of pocket on this job. When she got back, she should see if the money she had saved was enough to enable her to pack it in and look for something else. She felt that she was paying a high price in integrity for continuing to work for her boss. At some level, Elena Coyle nursed an uneasy belief in karma.

The soldier was actually very good-looking, when she sneaked a glance at him. She thought 'dashing' probably the right word. There was a bullet scar or shrapnel graze on his right cheekbone, so he must have seen active service. But he was high-ranking and fairly mature, she guessed in his early to mid-forties. She had researched the Angels of Mons story once for Dupree. She knew a bit about army insignia. This fellow was an infantry colonel. He was wearing his dress uniform. And he wore a ribbon awarded for gallantry prominent among the campaign ribbons stitched above the left breast pocket on his tunic.

She coughed and he looked at her and smiled.

'Do you mind if I ask you a question?'

'Not at all,' he said.

'How did you earn your Military Cross?'

'I was involved in an assault on a canal. The enemy were dug in, entrenched. They were defending their position with heavy machine guns. We were outgunned, suffering casualties. A young subaltern in my section was hit in the shoulder and hip. He fell and could not get up again. The enemy were bayoneting our wounded. I rallied a counter attack and was able to rescue him.'

'He lived?'

'Indeed he did. He will always walk with a slight limp, but he lived. He is a fine young man. I believe he has made his parents very proud.'

'I wasn't aware the bayonet was still used. That's utterly barbaric.'

'War is barbaric.'

'Should a soldier really be saying that?'

'I can say it now my war has been fought and won. And I can tell you that being awarded a medal for saving life is far more satisfying than getting one for taking it.'

She nodded. He had just told her, in a roundabout way, that he had done both. She thought him a more interesting man with every word he said. She was so comfortable in his company it was as though she had met him before. But she couldn't have. She would have recalled meeting someone as physically attractive as he was. She would not have been able to forget in the first place. 'Where are you going?'

'I'm going home,' he said.

'And what's at home?'

'A stream, a cottage,' he laughed, she thought to himself. 'Blue remembered hills.'

'It sounds idyllic.'

'I think it is. Perhaps one day I might get the opportunity to show it to you.'

The train whistle hooted and the brakes began to screech. She thought that they must be coming in to Penzance station. She smiled at the soldier. 'I suppose it is possible we'll meet again,' she said.

'It's possible, of course,' he said.

But disembarking, climbing down onto the colour and bustle and noise of the platform, she had the strong feeling that it wasn't a possibility at all. Elena suspected it was a certainty. A surfer type decorated with Maori tattoos brushed past her, laughing into his mobile. She looked up, blinking.

The sky was blue but for a criss-cross pattern of vapour trails from aircraft cruising, six miles high. It was odd, she thought. Had she stepped onto a platform decorated with Woodbine and Brylcreem hoardings, had a bi-plane roared through the air a few hundred feet above her head, it would have seemed somehow more fitting to the train from which she had just alighted.

In his compartment on the train, as it slipped out of the station, Colonel Creed took his newspaper from the satchel on the seat beside him and shook it out and began to read from where he had been obliged to stop. He had hidden it on seeing Elena in the corridor. He knew how observant she was and he thought that, if she'd spotted it, the date might have confused or alarmed her. A carriage with its original fittings was a novelty. A man seated in it reading a copy of *The Times* printed in June of 1919 was not.

He was very happy to have seen her. But he was not really very surprised. His last three years had been eventful and significant. But he had truly loved her and pondered often, as a man would in his predicament, on the nature of fate. And he had asked himself often if a psychic sensitivity such as theirs was simply a random endowment, or if there was some point or purpose to it. He did not know the answer to that question. But he smiled, over his paper. He thought that he would get an opportunity to show Elena Coyle his stream and his cottage and his blue remembered hills. He had reason for hope. He was faithful to his memories. He was patient. And he felt in his heart that time was on his side.